BARREN
ISLAND

a novel

Carol Zoref

New Issues Poetry & Prose

Western Michigan University
Kalamazoo, Michigan 49008

First American Edition, 2017.

ISBN-13: 978-1-936970-44-5

Library of Congress Cataloging-in-Publication Data:
Zoref, Carol.
Barren Island/Carol Zoref
Library of Congress Control Number: 2016930279

Editor: William Olsen
Managing Editor: Kimberly Kolbe
Layout Editor: Sarah Kidd
Copy Editor: Sarah Kidd
Art Direction: Nick Kuder
Cover Design: Kelsi Miller
Production Manager: Paul Sizer
The Design Center, Gwen Frostic School of Art
College of Fine Arts
Western Michigan University

This book is the winner of the Association of Writers & Writing Programs (AWP) Award for the Novel. AWP is a national, nonprofit organization dedicated to serving American letters, writers, and programs of writing.

Go to www.awpwriter.org for more information.

BARREN

ISLAND

a novel

Carol Zoref

NEW ISSUES

 WESTERN MICHIGAN UNIVERSITY

Acknowledgments

Spend seven years writing a novel and you will have many people to thank, whether they know of their helpfulness or not. Among them:

For comments on the manuscript: Melvin Jules Bukiet and Mary La Chapelle. For homes away from home in which to write: Scott Browning (Hall Farm, Vermont), and Spyroula Konstantopoulos & Charles Goldie (Exeter, UK). For challenges as well as assurances, current and former members of the Sarah Lawrence College community, in particular Barbara Kaplan, Micheal Rengers, and Ilja Wachs. For all manner of the ineffable: Lola Konstantopoulos, Sue Schwimmer, Phyllis Arnold & Deidre Leipziger, Alison Kuller, MC Gee & Judy Myers, Susan Thames, and Marion Hart. And for my sister, Joan Zoref.

Gratitude as well to: The Association of Writers & Writing Programs (AWP) and author Paul Harding (*Tinkers*, *Enon*), who selected *Barren Island* for the 2015 AWP Award for The Novel; the staff at New Issues Press/Western Michigan University; and Mira Singer, assiduous proofreader.

For my parents
Selma Spielman Zoref & Leonard Zoref

For my wife
Pamela Walter

CHAPTER 0

Ask about the smell. That is what everyone asks no matter who or why or where they might be. It is the detail they want most when they hear about the horses and dogs and pigs that filled the barges; about the wake of stench when the meat markets closed for the day and the surgeries closed for the morning and the rest of New York paused in coffee shops and automats, in lunchrooms and kitchens and union halls, on curbsides and at cleared-away corners of the cutting tables in the garment factories on 39th Street to eat sandwiches made from animal parts, the ones that would not be burned that day on Barren Shoal.

Cow bone, pig bone, sheep bone, horse bone. Chicken bone, turkey bone, dog bone, cat bone. Maggot-covered cow skins, postulated hog snouts, ulcerated sheep hides, abscessed horse heads, festering dog tails, cat jaws. Wet smells settled in the creases of human skin, rose like cruel heat across the harbor, lingered on the silent curls of factory smoke. They were smells one could touch, a gummy scrim over every breathing hour. Fleas, flies, snakes, worms, beetles, lice, mites, ticks, mold, mildew, and fungus gorged on the smells that not even the furnaces on Barren Shoal burned away.

My family lived on Barren Shoal for twenty-five years, my father glad to have work to keep us clothed in something better than the rags that the pickers scavenged and stitched and salvaged and wore and sold and traded and wore down into rags again. Bones became glue, thread became cloth, and in the end everyone was different and everyone was unchanged.

About things such as these, an 80-year-old woman like me, Marta Eisenstein Lane, of sound mind and in full possession of her senses, should know.

My parents came to Barren Shoal in 1914 after who knows how many days at Ellis Island and six weeks of exhausted, listless sleep on the benevolent floor of Aunt Sara and Uncle David's one bedroom apartment in Borough Park. My cousin, Flat Sammy, born eight months earlier, wailed every hour of every one of those weeks, a protest against the mean circumstances of his life. Sara, my father's sister and only living relative, had been kicked in the stomach by a coal-cart horse gone crazy three weeks before her delivery date. She was carried upstairs just in time for Sammy to arrive through a confusion of spasms, his soft, fetal head irreparably misshapen. The horse, still hitched to the coal cart and having spasms of its own, dropped dead on the cobblestone, saliva rolling from its jaw like the blistering scum on a pot of boiling soup.

The coal horse, like every dead horse in New York City, was carried that night by barge to either Barren Island or Barren Shoal, where it was butchered and boiled down for glue and grease. Flat Sammy—that is what we called him on account of the horseshoe-shaped dent on the back of his head and so as not to confuse him with Uncle David's brother who lived in Philadelphia, also named Sam—Flat Sammy did not die. Flat Sammy survived for no reason except that most of us die in pieces, not all at once. Even the horse that kicked Aunt Sara.

I have examined the history books and public documents, have read how the first garbage barge arrived at Barren Island, the bigger and nearest neighbor to Barren Shoal, in 1852. I have learned how before the word was anglicized, the Dutch called it Beeren Island for the bears they believed lived there feeding off fish and clams and crabs, though there is no record, official or anecdotal, of any Dutch settler ever sighting a bear among the pine stands and sage and white sand beaches of the islands in Jamaica Bay.

For who-knows-how-long prior to the Dutch and their imaginary bears, the Native Americans called this place by their own word, Equindito, meaning Broken Lands. It was a name that was custom fit to the small islands it contained. One of the smallest, sandiest pieces was our own small island, the flat and forsaken Barren Shoal, separated from the better known Barren Island by the merest of shallows at low tide and a few feet of water when the tide was high. Most of the natives who lived on Equindito were massacred by Dutch settlers, who chased away the survivors who did not die. This does not change the fact that Equindito was their home for a time that mattered, meaning any amount of time at all.

The last public garbage incinerator on Barren Island, according to the city records, was closed in 1918; the last glue factory, in 1933. But that was Barren Island, not Barren Shoal, about which there are no records. Not even my grandson Eric, the anthropologist, has had any luck with finding out more than I, and he knows how to find things better than anyone.

Today, on this very day, if someone searches for Barren Shoal on a map, they will come up empty-handed. If their interest outweighs this disappointment, they might search an atlas dating back a century or so. If they are anything like Eric, our homegrown scholar, they might sift through the New York Municipal Archives, laying their hands on once-important documents that no one has touched in years. If they are thorough—or lucky—they will come upon the name "Barren Island" in the disintegrating tax records, land grants, and minutes of the meetings of the old Common Council or the City Committee on Planning and Survey. But they will not find a single word about Barren Shoal. They can nose around the Port Authority of New York & New Jersey and will have no more luck finding Barren Shoal than they would finding the places where the government buries its unwanted uranium, hoping that we will forget.

Believe what you will. Everyone does. The fact that every trace of Barren Shoal is gone does not mean it was never there.

CHAPTER 1

In the very beginning of his very first days in America, my ever-hopeful father accompanied Uncle David to Manhattan, where David had a job cutting fabric for men's shirts. My father was waiting for someone to lead him somewhere, looking for a place where a man with no English could earn a wage. My father kept close by Uncle David, his center of gravity still rocking from the journey across the Atlantic.

The wooden floor of the factory hummed and droned, my father would later recall, with vibrations from row after row of sewing machines. There were scores of them—a choir of foot-pedaled Singers. A voice rose above the chorus: "You!" That is how it all began, my father would say when he told this story. "You!" flying bullet-like from a thin man in a white shirt with a blue tie and darker blue trousers. "*You*," my father would boom, exaggerating the thin man's trembling baritone. He told the story in English for the sake of my siblings and me, even though everyone at the factory spoke in Yiddish.

"Sort these," ordered Mr. Gretzky, Uncle David's boss, as

he rolled a laundry hopper across the cutting room. My father threw out his arms to stop the hopper from crashing into him and Uncle David, who was hovering at his cutting table over a bolt of white pima cotton, persuading it to yield gracefully to his scissors. *Fabrics are living things*, Uncle David liked to tell us youngsters, *because they're the way I make a living.*

"What's he telling me?" my father asked Uncle David, whisper-shouting over the noise of the factory floor. The palms of his hands stung where the wood frame of the bin had smacked into them. He wondered if Mr. Gretzky had mistaken him for someone who worked there.

Inside the hopper were scraps of fabric discarded by the cutters, who were scissoring out arms and backs and pockets and collars for men's shirts or ladies' blouses. Why one is called one thing and the other called another is one of those mysteries, like the difference between slacks and pants and trousers. I know: I digress. But the mind must be allowed to wander so it can remember. Forgive me.

"Pull out the pieces big enough for rags," instructed Uncle David, looking up from the sleeve he was cutting. "Gretzky pays by the pound. He sells them to a ragman. The more efficient I am as a cutter, the less you make, so forget about me and go pick up after the others." My uncle rotated the fabric he was working and waved his scissors in the direction of the other cutters. "A lot of these schmucks know nothing about making the most of a bolt of cloth, never mind making a pie out of shit, which is, no kidding, what a picker does. Never mind that, Sol. Get to it before Gretzky —who some union goon should fuck up good—splits the pile with some other poor bastard."

My father, who was a shoemaker, knew nothing about clothing. He had been trained by his own father in Zyrmuny, in the room on the side of their house that was a repair shop. Factories were the stuff that cities like Babruysk and Minsk were made of, not muddy *shtetls* like Zyrmuny. The Industrial Revolution went right by Zyrmuny until the Germans built a death camp at Maly Trostinec, if you do not mind my saying so. Plenty of people say I should stop already. Enough already. Soon. Soon enough I will stop forever.

On 39th Street, however, The International Ladies Garment Workers Union, the I.L.G.W.U., had already organized two factories in the same building.

"Are they communists?" asked my father.

"Sentimentalists," said David. "Socialists gone mainstream." He looked to see who might be listening. "Later, when you and Rachel get settled, we'll go to a meeting. See for yourself."

"If later ever comes," said my father, still exhausted from the ordeal of getting from Zyrmuny to Borough Park. "The *Kabbalists*: they're the ones who know better about 'later.' Not men sorting rags on 39th Street."

Uncle David smoothed the white cotton sleeve he was trimming while my father sorted. "I'm talking about the 'later' on this earth, not some later they can't know if they'll ever know it or not," said David, who did not become religious until much later, when he read in *Das Kapital* that religion was the "opiate of the masses." David got hot on religion out of spite, angered by what he described as the "oppression of ideologies."

"Crazy guys anyway," said my father, referring to the *Kabbalah*-reading mystics. "Like a bunch of Tibetan monks squirreled away with their prayers and..."

"Since when did you become an expert about Tibet?" teased Uncle David while he smoothed out the sleeve he had just finished.

Out of the waistband of his pants my father pulled a battered *National Geographic*. On the cover was a yellow-framed image of a toothless man smiling. He was, according to the caption, standing at the palace-capital of Lhasa.

"There's stacks of magazines on the street," explained my father. "With the garbage."

David laughed at him. "Between the garbage and here you're reading English?"

My father tucked the magazine back in his waistband. "I read Russian, I read Yiddish, I read pictures." English was not just his third language; it was his third alphabet.

When the shift ended at 6:00 p.m., my father had this many bagfuls of cloth and that many pounds of scrap and had sifted more rags than anyone ever remembered a man sorting in a single day. Precisely how many bags he filled grew larger in the telling every year, until he was the exact age I am on this very day and his storytelling days, which is to say all of his days, came to an end and no one was left to tell the stories but my brother Noah and me.

"I can stay longer," my father told Mr. Gretzky when the shift bell rang, signaling everyone to go home. There were loose pieces of fabric in the corners and on the floor and dust from the trimmings everywhere. When the light was just right, even the air was threaded with cotton fibers.

"You've cleaned us out," said an amused Mr. Gretzky. Or maybe the word my father used was "impressed." I am working hard to remember.

The tables were clearing out, the cutters setting down the backs and arms and collars of shirts they would return to tomorrow. The overhead lights were covered by lint that the heat glued to the metal and glass. The night watchman followed Mr. Gretzky down the rows, dimming the bulbs with a half-rotation of the rag in his hand so that only one lamp would be left burning through the night.

Mr. Gretzky's fingertips traveled the piles of finished work, roughly counting the completed pieces by pressing down the stacks. More pieces equaled more pay. "Come back tomorrow in the afternoon," he repeated.

"Morning," insisted my father. The afternoon could be too late. Some other man, more eager or younger, or maybe some friend of a cousin of Mr. Gretzky's wife, or who-knows-who could snap up his place as if he had never been there. Gretzky did not even know my father's name.

"Give the cutters time to get things going, fella," said Mr. Gretzky.

"It's Eisenstein," said my father. "Don't forget."

"Who the hell are you that I should remember?"

My father's eyes were bloodshot, unaccustomed to the lint drifting about the cutting room. His fingertips were red and chafed from hours of sorting. How much longer could they stay at David and Sara's, what with Flat Sammy wailing and the older girl, my cousin Ruthie, sleeping on the floor? The situation was impossible but for the fact that there they were, in Borough Park, living the impossible. My father trailed Mr. Gretzky, who was two steps ahead of the night watchman. Mr. Gretzky continued his inventory-taking as the room grew darker.

"For God's sake," Mr. Gretzky called out when my father finally walked away, "get some rest."

Maybe this was my father embellishing again, like when he embellished the numbers of hoppers he sorted. Maybe he was making Mr. Gretzky kinder in the telling than he really was, making the story of his own life more bearable to himself and all of us.

My father returned to the factory early the next day with Uncle David, not ready yet to find his own way there through the heart of the golem that is New York. He stood by Uncle David's side that entire morning, watching David scissor the parts of a shirt from a handsome bolt of cotton. To become a cutter in

America, thought my father: that would be something.

Halfway through the shift, Mr. Gretzky appeared with a half-filled hopper. "Hey early bird," he called to my father, "here comes the worms." Mr. Gretzky sent the scrap-filled bin clattering across the uneven wood floorboards, the way he had done the day before. Each of the nearby cutters dipped protectively over their work as they heard the hopper approaching down the narrow aisle.

My father sorted scraps again the following day and the day after and on Saturday morning, even though it was the Sabbath. He would have rather worked by himself on Sunday for half wages than break his own father's far away heart by working on Shabbat, but that was no more up to my father than it was to Uncle David or anyone else.

My father might have been sorting scraps forever, might have even worked his way up to becoming one of Mr. Gretzky's cutters, had he not one day said a few words to the driver of the rag cart about needing a room that he and my mother could rent, things being so crowded with my aunt and uncle and cousins. The driver said something about there being better sorting jobs somewhere else in New York, a place where they gave a man a job and a house and the people walked to work. And how, if my father slipped him a bin of rags that also contained an unspoiled, uncut bolt of cloth, the driver would be certain to get my father an introduction.

My father punched the ragman across the jaw. "You think I'm an animal that would steal for you? Maybe get arrested? Get deported?"

"Are you crazy, Sol?" cried Uncle David, who had been waiting for my father so they could begin the subway trip home. He pulled my father away from the ragman, but my father struggled out of his grip. My uncle locked his arms around my father's chest. My father always vowed in a pious way, though not without a touch of pride, that this was the one and only time he ever punched another grown man.

The startled ragman, still stunned, crawled out of the scummy puddle he had fallen into. He wiped his bloodied lower lip with a rag that he then buried back in his cart. To their astonishment, the ragman introduced my father and uncle to a man at the reins of the next cart over. "You deserve it, you filthy, greenhorn, sons-of-a-bitches Yids," the ragman yelled as he rode off.

"You'll never get out of there," cried Aunt Sara that evening when she heard the news about the job on Barren Shoal. She was shaking her head and weeping and soon Flat Sammy was wailing in unison. My father tried distracting Sammy with a hand puppet he fashioned from a sock, hoping that Sara would get distracted too. "The stench there is poison," cried my aunt, who was my father's oldest sister. "The smell of it will kill you, living out there like an Italian, sorting through garbage."

"It's a factory job, Sara. And a place to live."

"We smell that place in the summer when the wind blows. *Fheh*! The cows in the Queens, they stop giving milk. The rich people complain up on Carnegie Hill. I know this; one of the ladies in our building, Mrs. Aryeh, does sewing there."

"On Barren Island?" asked my uncle.

"*Carnegie Hill*," my aunt replied.

"This isn't Barren Island," said Uncle David. "It's another place: Barren Shoal."

"Did you wake up today stupid? It's called Barren because nothing grows there," she went on.

"It will be better for us all if..." my father began.

"Don't tell me things you don't know," she stammered.

"Now you're some kind of authority? What do you know from better?"

She was addressing not just my father, but my uncle as well, who she was holding equally responsible for the idea. Knowing my aunt, she was speaking to anyone who would listen, including Mrs. Aryeh, from downstairs, who was also part of my aunt's sewing circle, and who came up in the middle of the commotion to drop off some cloth. "Tell them, Frieda," my aunt said to Mrs. Aryeh. "Tell them about your ladies up on Carnegie Hill."

"There's probably more fresh air on Barren Shoal, by the ocean, than in all of Brooklyn," said my uncle. "And smells don't kill you, for heaven's sake."

"What's heaven got to do with it?" she said, louder.

"Let it go, Sara," shouted Uncle David, who was now cradling Flat Sammy like an oversized doll too large to tuck completely into his lap.

"There's no going back and forth so easy," she shouted in return, "no subway to the incinerators. You go, you're gone."

"Enough, Sara," said my father. "You'll see us plenty." He took Flat Sammy from my uncle's arms, kissed the flat of his head, and stroked the back of his neck with the hand puppet. The only sound left was the whistle of Sammy's troubled breathing.

According to my father, it was Mrs. Aryeh who broke the silence. "Stanley," she yelled out the window to her husband's little ground floor studio, where he took pictures on weekends because what he was paid making pictures for the newspapers was not enough. "Come up to the roof and bring the camera. This family needs a picture!" I do not know why she suggested the roof, where Mr. Aryeh's pigeon flock cooped. Maybe his little studio was impossibly small for a whole family.

There is a family portrait from that day, a copy of which is now tucked in the frame of my bedroom mirror. My mother is slender, her thick auburn hair pulled back into a handsome French braid. My beautiful father, still a boy really, has one arm around my mother's waist and the other around a stony-faced Sara. My aunt is cradling Flat Sammy in her arms, the flat back of his skull resting against her breast. Uncle David, a head taller than my father, is standing behind the three of them, his long, slender arms wrapped around their shoulders. Standing before them, leaning against her father's knees, is my cousin Ruthie.

Five days later my parents went to live among the twenty other families on Barren Shoal.

CHAPTER 2

My father could have been a butcher. The animals he dismembered on Barren Shoal were just a different kind of dead. Hundreds of carcasses arrived every day: work horses that collapsed from illness or exhaustion; dogs found roaming in packs and shot for sport by policemen; pigs, goats, and cows too diseased to be disguised and dressed as meat. The Barren Shoal cutters beheaded and quartered them, gutted them, severed their limbs, spilling new blood on top of the old blood that clotted the cutting room floor. The loaders—less skilled and fewer in numbers—shoveled the usable pieces into vats where they were rendered into commercial grease and glue. The unusable body parts went into ovens where they were burned down to ash and smoke.

"You must know a little about chopping animals from making shoes," said Mr. Boyle, the plant foreman, on my father's first day. "Heh, heh, heh." His laughter was deep and low, and no one ever knew if he was talking the sound or really laughing because his teeth were clenching the cigar he always had lit to camouflage the smell in the air. My father, who had only a dozen words of English at his disposal, laughed with him.

My brother Noah was born in 1914, seven months after my parents arrived on Barren Shoal. On the morning that my mother was in their cabin in labor, gasping and pushing and moaning my father's name, my father was butchering a draft horse that had died of the colic. A midwife, a Jewish lady who lived on Barren Island, came over on the high tide by rowboat to help my mother; she sent her son to fetch my father when Noah finally arrived. Mr. Boyle told the boy to wait while my father finished slitting the dead horse's belly in order that its knotted intestines could be pulled away.

Noah was named in memory of my father's great uncle, Noach Eisenstein, but I like to think it was in honor of my brother being conceived on a ship crossing the Atlantic. I was born five years later and named Marta in honor of my mother's mother Magda, though she told me it was in memory of some great uncle whose name was Moishe. My mother made up her own rules regarding the traditions about giving names, certain that once she left for America she would never lay eyes on her mother again and that the prohibition against naming a newborn for someone living would not matter. About that she was right.

My mother never saw the baby blanket that my grandmother knitted after the letter arrived back in Zyrmuny announcing the birth of Noah. My grandmother slept with it every night, she explained in a letter to my mother, the only way she had of swaddling her first grandchild. The blanket was made of sheep wool dyed with turmeric, which turned it amber. I would like to have seen it. My younger sister Helen arrived three years later, also in July, and Grandma knitted another blanket, this one dyed burgundy with beetroot. I am surprised that I do not remember the color of the blanket she knit for me, but I cannot. Such a silly thing to forget. The Olympic Games took place in Paris the summer

Helen was born and my mother said that this baby kicking so hard in the final weeks of her pregnancy must be an Olympian. She named her Helen, from the ancient Greek story that was even told by people in Zyrmuny, which was not really all that far from ancient Troy. In 1926, Sofia Paradissis and her parents, brother Yorgos, and grandmother moved next door. A family from a place even closer to Troy. Sofia was as dark-haired as I was blonde, straight haired to my curls, with brown eyes to my hazel and a round face just like mine. Sofia was 18 months older than me, the girl on the Barren Shoal closest to my age.

The Paradissis family had traveled from their village in Greece to Ellis Island to Brooklyn. From there, Mr. Paradissis' childhood friend from the village, Mr. Kostas, brought them to Barren Shoal to take the place of Mr. DeWitt, who Mr. Boyle moved from the cutting room into the gatehouse on account of the arthritis in his hands. Between the worsening arthritis and the years of contact with enzymes in the dead animal meat, Mr. DeWitt's thumbs had curled into fat utility hooks. At night we would see him sitting at his post clenching a horsehide pouch filled with smoldering coals. Mr. Boyle had fired Mr. Morgan, one of the old Negro coal stokers who had become the gatekeeper when his back gave out, so that Mr. DeWitt could have his job. The company took back Mr. DeWitt's house for the Paradissises to live in. Mr. DeWitt, who lived alone, moved into a new gatehouse some of the men built for him so that he did not have to live in a black man's room. It was shameful, people being shuffled around from one house to another and Mr. Morgan being sent away from Barren Shoal. But no one talked about it. From then on Mr. DeWitt sat at his post clenching the horsehide pouch filled with the smoldering coals, the heat a medication for the pain in his joints. Soon enough the gatehouse became a place where the men would gather.

Mr. Morgan watched the demolition of his gatehouse from the stern of the garbage barge on which he made the crossing to Sheepshead Bay, where, I imagine, he took a streetcar to the apartment where his wife lived after he lost his job as a stoker and their Barren Shoal house was given to the stoker that followed, also a black man. The stokers were always black. It was the most dangerous job on account of being closest to the fires. The worst paying job, too, I later found out when the union troubles began and Mr. Boyle posted the men's salaries in order to turn them against each other. The old gatehouse was in pieces before the barge with Mr. Morgan cleared the harbor.

Within weeks of her family's arrival, Sofia and I were rambling back and forth all day from her house to mine and to hers again. Mr. Paradissis, a carpenter in Greece, got assigned to the cutting room with my father. Sofia's mother, like all the mothers, raised chickens that kept the family in eggs until the coldest days of winter, when the hens refused to lay. The Paradissises, like everyone, planted a vegetable garden on every inch of the sandy patch behind their little house. My mother raised lettuces and cucumbers, pole beans and squashes, cabbages, garlic, beets, tomatoes, radishes, dill, bay leaf, and parsley; Mrs. Paradissis introduced her to dandelion greens and escarole, eggplant and zucchini, rosemary and oregano. Mr. Paradissis set up hives. Soon we had real honey. He built a little arbor for growing grapes. We fed the plants a muck of garden scraps, eggshells, and disintegrated fish.

Noah and Yorgos, close in age, were more cautious about friendship than Sofia and I. Noah never spoke with anyone, even me, unless he had to. Though he was around plenty, the door to his room was always closed. One day, a couple of months after the Paradissises moved to Barren Shoal, my mother said I could go fishing with Noah if Sofia came along to stop me from pestering him. Mrs. Paradissis said yes but only if Yorgos went along to watch over Sofia. Mrs. Paradissis was very old world, even if she had nothing to worry about with Noah.

My father rigged poles for each of us, and after that we never returned home empty-handed. Most days we got flounder and blowfish. When the current was cold there were plenty of blues. Our mothers split the catch evenly no matter which one of us had pulled in what or how many. There were lots of blue crabs and chowder clams for the taking, gorged on what the garbage scows lost to the sea. These we carried home in a burlap sack for the Paradissises. It was impossible to keep kosher on Barren Shoal, but my mother said it was easy enough not to eat *traif*. My mother sometimes sent Helen along with us so she could run herself tired in the sand. She was only three years old then, but Yorgos made a toy pole for her from a driftwood stick and some string. She would carry it proudly until she got tired and then she would cry for someone to carry her. Sometimes we made her walk home anyway to stop her from becoming spoiled, we told ourselves. The fact was I did not want her bothering me any more than Noah wanted me pestering him.

By the time the Paradissis family celebrated their first year on Barren Shoal, Sofia and I were inseparable, and our parents had given us permission to wander the entire island, together, on our own.

On a foul-smelling September day, after a successful afternoon of crabbing near the saltwater marsh, Sofia and I triumphantly returned with a dozen blue crabs struggling in the burlap catch bag. Our first stop was to return Helen to my mother; next we went to surprise Mrs. Paradissis with our bounty. We had stopped at twelve crabs because thirteen was an unlucky number, according to Mrs. Paradissis, who was a believer in things that were no harder to imagine believing in than the things my own parents still believed in, like an intervening God, you should pardon me.

Sofia set the bag on the kitchen table like a trophy. Mrs. Paradissis did not look up from the thin, fragile sheets of phyllo pastry she was brushing with oil using one of the duck feathers we collected for her from the beach. Sofia and I helped ourselves to the plate of special-occasion-only *kourabiedes* cookies airing on a sideboard.

"Lucky I don't feed you to the crabs," said Mrs. Paradissis, whose attention turned to us from wherever it had been.

We stood there with half-eaten cookies in our hands and telltale confectioner's sugar dusting our lips and noses.

Mrs. Paradissis removed the plate of cookies from the sideboard, relocating them closer to where she was working the phyllo. "Look how people feeding themselves," she said. "Poor people eat the barge. And you stealing cookies and not ask." We knew she meant the people who scavenged the barges on the trip over from Brooklyn and Manhattan, picking through the dead animals for anything they could eat.

Sofia lifted the catch bag with the crabs from the table and signaled for me to follow. She quietly placed the bag on the floor. One more step and we could both be out the door.

"You live like them, those barge people, and need steal food?" Mrs. Paradissis continued, her voice rising in the broken English she was speaking for my benefit. Sofia and I shook our heads. "You some goat you can't speak?"

"No," said Sofia. Her cheeks puffed up the way they did when she got upset, like a small blowfish.

"Every day something bad, these girls," said Mrs. Paradissis, like she was talking to someone else. Grandma Paradissis hardly counted since she was stone deaf and spoke no English. "And you,

Marta, such a pretty girl. Your mommy and daddy say to take and not asking?" She shook her head in a scolding way and said we were old enough to know better. I was seven; Sofia was eight and a half.

"I told Marta it was okay," said Sofia. She treasured occasions, even bad ones, that allowed her to remind me that she was the boss.

"Marta knows better. You too. You girls want, first you ask."

It could have ended there, but Sofia would not let it go.

"Why the kourabiedes, Mommy? There's no holiday."

"Your brother asked," said Mrs. Paradissis. She lifted the burlap catch bag and dumped the crabs into the sink. They were quiet for a moment, stunned by the light and air. Then they scratched and crawled over one another, like they could fight their way back to the beach. Mrs. Paradissis did not thank us for the crabs; she never thanked us for things that were expected.

Sofia's cheeks got puffy again. "It's not Yorgos' birthday."

Yorgos was six years older than Sofia. Mrs. Paradissis treated him like Zeus, a god trapped among us simple, mortal human beings. Sofia said this was the way all Greek mothers treated their boys.

"If he gets them, I want..."

"*Signomi!*" Mrs. Paradissis shouted, though she was smiling. She cautiously extracted a crab from the sink and held it up for inspection. The crab flailed about furiously, pinching the kitchen air with its pincers.

"What?" I asked Sofia.

"'Sorry,'" Sofia translated.

"I accept," said Mrs. Paradissis triumphantly, though it was obvious that Sofia was interpreting, not apologizing. "Now go," she said, pleased with herself for tricking Sofia. She pressed another kourabiedes into my hand and pushed me out the door.

After waiting a lifetime we entered grade school in September. The center of our universes shifted overnight from our little houses and yards to the schoolhouse, where it stayed until I had a universe large enough to keep me busy for a lifetime.

A whitewashed wood and tar cabin identical to our houses, the schoolhouse was little more than a frail box with a thin roof and walls. Our parents were grateful for those boxes even though they were poorly insulated—even though the toilets were outside in tiny huts and the indoor tap ran cold. They did not yet know that Mr. Boyle's monthly "occupancy charge" went straight into his pocket, a fact revealed when there were union troubles. We knew nothing, either, of how in other parts of New York the schools had desks with inkwells, instead of discarded tables with legs sawed short for the smaller children and planks of wood balanced on saw horses for the big ones. The one black child in the school said that in the Negro schools in Brooklyn the pupils sat on church pews and used their laps as desks. Our teacher, Miss Finn, made do with a 30-year-old globe commemorating the dawning of the 20th century. On its base were the words: **Human Progress Through Technology.**

Every day on our walk to school Sofia and I saw the barge scavengers Mrs. Paradissis compared us to when we swiped her cookies. The factory owners did not care about the scavengers. Glue was made from bones, not from the rotting meat and sinew that the scavengers picked until the carcasses barely resembled the animals they had been. So long as the factory got the bones, no one bothered the scavengers coming and going. The men on Barren Shoal did not talk about them, as if that kind of poverty was contagious. Every day Sofia and I saw children foraging with adults. Some of the adult scavengers would wave a child over to work a rich find; others pushed them away. They ate while they worked, stuffing extra little pieces into their pockets and spitting into the water the unchewable. It was enough to make anyone sick, which it surely did, but it was better than starving. As for our mothers, they went on feeding us as much as they could.

On one of those early weeks of school, a small girl, her fingers swollen and copper-colored from animal flesh, looked in our direction. Surrounding her was a score of screaming seagulls, as busy as she was picking at the dead animals. I did not remember seeing this particular girl before, though I recognized the others scrounging around her, including Joey Pessara, a boy from Barren Shoal close in age to Noah and Yorgos. He was wearing a blue rag tied around his brow to keep the sweat from his eyes, and was working his knife into the ribcage of a horse. I was surprised to see someone we knew so feverously groping for something to eat.

"Look," said Sofia, pointing. "A girl."

"She's got a knife," I said.

The barge was shifting on the swell of the tide and a breeze was rushing the skirt of the girl's brown dress between her legs. The girl raised one arm. The seagulls scattered. I raised my hand and waved. There was a look of surprise on her face as she grabbed at the air with both hands, which I now saw was her intention all along. I lifted my other hand too, as if doing this would keep the girl from falling. A moment later the girl regained her balance and turned her short knife back to the draft horse she was working on. I felt silly. The girl was trying not to fall into that hell, you should pardon me, and I thought she was waving. The seagulls settled back around her. Whatever remained of the horse—imagine how much was there to begin with if so much was left after so much had been taken—would be carted onto the greasy, bloodstained cutting floor where Mr. Paradissis and my father and the rest of the cutters would trim it down to smaller pieces still.

Sofia and I corkscrewed our nostrils as we walked but did not dare pinch our noses closed. The girl in the brown dress might think our disgust was meant for her. And maybe Mrs. Paradissis did possess the power to appear out of nowhere, like she said she could, and would be angry. Maybe the girl would tell. What were we so afraid of? That we would be punished for being impolite? To a scavenger? I am ashamed to say that no one would have cared.

We were anxious to get far past the factory, the stinking flotilla of waste at the dock, and the new girl in the brown dress. We walked slowly at first, not wanting the girl to think we were afraid of her, assuming she noticed us. The morning stench was mixing with the ash from the furnace, soaking in through our ears and mouths and the tiniest porous openings of our skin. I pressed my hand to my nose and mouth and I ran.

"You girls have no business being late," Miss Finn scolded when Sofia and I rushed into the single, drafty classroom that was our school. "Young girls work spindles in textile mills and boys are sorters in coal mines," Miss Finn continued as we settled into our chairs. "Sharecropper children and tenant farmer children and migrant farmer children plant and pick, as do the children of families who own their own land. Federal child labor laws mean little without the mechanisms for enforcing them." Miss Finn turned everything into a lesson, including our being late.

She set Sofia and me and the other small children to work copying alphabet letters. She turned the attention of the older students to current events. *The Young Plan*, she wrote on the board. She raised a newspaper and read aloud that the "Young Plan Meets New Opposition." Miss Finn brought newspapers that her sister in Brooklyn saved up to the island every Monday: *The New York Times, The New York Post, The Herald-Tribune*. The week-old newspapers took on second lives at Barren Shoal as our textbooks. Come the third week they were cut into toilet paper for the outhouses, except for the ones that Sofia and I took for our Odyssey Project. We were keeping a scrapbook of articles about all the places in the world we wanted to visit. We collected countries the way that older girls clipped out photos of Clark Gable and Greta Garbo.

"'The Young Committee on Reparations is meeting resistance from conservative Germans and their right-wing leadership,'" Miss Finn read.

It was hard to concentrate on penmanship while Miss Finn was speaking. My strokes became confused with the Aleph-Bet-Gimmels that my father had taught me, which looked nothing like the Roman letters we were learning. Sofia confused her letters with the mysterious Alpha-Beta-Gammas of Modern Greek.

"Look," I whispered to Sofia. "This U is a horse's foot; this A is a house."

"Sofia, Marta!" Miss Finn hushed us from the other side of the room. Sofia kicked my foot beneath the desk. I dropped my head lower and lower to keep from laughing until my nose touched my sheet of paper.

"Yorgos," said Miss Finn to Sofia's brother, "can you tell us about The Young Plan?"

Yorgos Paradissis was handsome at fourteen, already mannish with a five o'clock shadow.

"The Young Plan..." Yorgos stumbled, "is... is..."

I perked up. "It has something to do with..."

"No one's asking you," said Yorgos.

I wanted to redeem myself with Miss Finn. Children yearn for the clean slate. Mind you, if I had a clean slate now there would be nothing to remember. We make mistakes, we apologize, we take corrective action, and we remember. This is what it means to be a person. You forget, you are nothing.

But I knew as little about the Young Plan as Yorgos, who elbowed Noah, who was sitting next to him.

"Tell Miss Finn about the Young Plan, Noah," said Yorgos to my brother. Better to be bested by Noah than by a little girl.

Miss Finn ignored the exchange between the boys. "The Young Plan will be a blueprint for German reparations for The Great War. Who will please define 'reparations'?"

More silence.

Yorgos had been rescued from Miss Finn's questioning, but not the rest of the class. I forgive us for not knowing about the Young Plan; we were children, even the older ones. You would think that if I could forgive us, I could forgive others for their silences too. But I cannot.

The smell from the furnaces thickened like it always did as the sun rose higher. Miss Finn was still waiting for an answer. The only sound now was the thin whistle of Marie Dowd's breath, the remnants of a childhood bout of rheumatic fever. Marie was already fifteen.

"A definition for reparations?" Miss Finn repeated.

Her voice settled into the background while she explained.

At seven years old I had already heard endless talk about the war. It was one of the reasons my parents left Poland or Russia, or wherever it was they had lived, the borders forever shifting. The new rulers had changed the names of the old towns again and again to their liking. My parents left a place that was no longer the place they had fled.

The world of the classroom was restored by the sound of Joey Pessara, who belched loudly as he wandered in late. "For heaven's sake, Giuseppe, take your seat," declared Miss Finn, sparing him a lecture like she had given to Sofia and me.

Seeing Joey reminded me of the girl in the brown dress, her muck-caked hands keeping her steady as she cut for food. I turned back to my copying.

Miss Finn tolerated Joey more than she did the rest of us because Joey was orphaned in 1919, when Barren Shoal got clobbered by the influenza. Joey was six when his parents died; he never matured much beyond that. The three older Pessara boys —Massimo, Niccolo, and Vincenzo—left school to take factory jobs that were opened up by the epidemic. They did nothing for Joey other than let him sleep by the stove. When it was warm they made him sleep outside. Massimo, Nick, and Vince wolfed down most of what grew in their garden or was laid by their chickens. Joey ate hard bread for breakfast and spaghetti for lunch and dinner. Joey went hungry. Maybe there was not enough food to go around; maybe they did not notice; maybe they hated him; maybe Joey was lazy. Maybe, maybe, maybe. Who knows why people do what they do?

The breeze finally turned, as it did any number of times during the day, and for a while blew the factory smell off-island. Daylight filled the classroom as the sun started its slow descent on the other side of the schoolhouse. The barges were gone from the factory dock when school let out. All of the scavengers, including the girl in the brown dress, were gone too. It was warm outside when Sofia and I wandered toward home. We decided to see if any good, hand-sized clam shells had been beached by the incoming tide. Mrs. Paradissis used these shells as ramekins until they cracked, which they always did. Then we would break them into smaller pieces that we spread outside our houses to hold down the sand.

On our way we passed the small gatekeeper's allotment on the far side of Barren Shoal. The Negro gatekeeper, Mr. Morgan, had grown vegetables where Mr. DeWitt now kept chickens and a couple of roosters that crowed morning and night, fooled by the glow of the big furnace. Mr. DeWitt had assembled a chicken coop using wood planks from the old gatehouse, leaving attached the newspapers and other paper that Mr. Morgan had tacked up for insulation. The chickens pretty much pecked most of that away, making nests from ads for Baptist churches and race music. There were still a couple of weatherworn photos on the outside, their edges curled by the damp sea air. Mr. Morgan was in one of them. Seated in front of him was a woman with grey hair, his wife I suppose, who moved off the island when I was too young to remember. Next to her sat a youngish woman with processed hair, who was seated in front of a young man who was two heads taller than his father. Standing to the right and left of the woman were two little girls, one with the most serious face I ever saw on a child.

Sofia and I pulled off our school shoes and walked barefoot once we passed the coop, our toes curling in the heat buried in the sand. The clear, briny smell of the sea was intoxicating. The next best thing to being in school was not having to be anywhere at all. Sofia found two driftwood sticks in the shallows and we practiced drawing the alphabet in the sand. We wrote our names over and over until we grew bored with the pointless repetition. Then we traded names and her version of mine looked as lovely, as elegant as I was already wishing I could be. I was still working on her name when we heard screeches coming from the reeds on the small dune behind us.

"Seagulls," I said to Sofia.

"Not seagulls, stupid."

"You're the stupid one."

"You're the baby." If Helen had been with us we could have both turned on her, but Helen was home with my mother.

We heard the screech again. "Let's go see," I dared her.

"You won't want to," she said in a superior tone.

I tugged at her. We crawled through the dune grasses. The sounds disappeared as we came closer. Then they grew louder again.

Maybe a cat, or something worse from one of the barges, was nesting. Maybe a rat had delivered a litter. A sand dune shifted; a shadow ran down the middle. It had a once-white T-shirt and short, dark hair. The dune was, in fact, Joey Pessara's rear end. The sounds belonged to Marie Dowd, into whom he was pushing.

Sofia and I were still kneeling on the sand.

A voice moaned a question and an answer rolled into one.

Sofia and I jumped to our feet.

"Hey!" we heard Joey call after us.

"What?" cried Marie.

"What the hell!" shouted Joey.

We ran as fast as we could back to the water, where the tide had already washed our calligraphy away. I reached for our shoes, giggling. Sofia was giggling too. I covered my mouth. "Shsssh!" I warned through a space I made between my fingers. Sofia picked up our writing sticks and hurled them into the bay. No one would know we had been there. She led our race across the sand, back out of the marshes, and finally home.

CHAPTER 3

The image of Joey heaving himself into Marie drifted for years in my schoolgirl mind like the sea plants that rooted in the Jamaica Bay shallows. It was my whole idea of sex until I was grown and had experiences of my own. Sofia and I never told anyone what we were running from that day. There was plenty enough taking place in the world to keep everyone busy, what with the stock market crash and the Depression and things growing worse by the day in Europe.

The world of Barren Shoal was unchanged in those first, early days after the Crash. The Wall Street types got hit hard and fast, but everyone was touched by it sooner or later. Everyone except people who could lose a fortune and still had loads to lose. I bet they cried anyway, those greedy sons-of-guns who lived plenty well while others starved. They cried for themselves and they let it happen, just like the English let the Irish starve 100 years earlier. Does it ever end?

The dead animals kept arriving. Carthorses were now worked until they collapsed instead of being put down when they got old. We could see their ribs through their hides. When the scavenging men pulled off their shirts in the heat we could see their ribs too. My parents talked endlessly about the Depression and Europe and being grateful for my father's steady job and Europe and the unions and Europe and the smell. Every day they talked about the smell. Every day they talked about the family back in Zyrmuny and about getting them visas. And they argued about Uncle David getting roughed up again by company goons after he spoke up at a meeting of the I.L.G.W.U.

The first time Uncle David was attacked, my father begged a ride on an empty garbage scow to Brooklyn. Aunt Sara had sent word by mail, which arrived on Mondays and Fridays on the same boat that carried Miss Finn back and forth from Brooklyn. A canvas sack went first to the little store on Barren Island, the so-called post office where it was sorted and sent on to Barren Shoal by rowboat. My father read Aunt Sara's note aloud at dinner that night after reading it first to himself: *Talk to him, Sol. Next time they'll kill him. And for what? Why does he still believe the answer is UNION? Your loving sister, Sara.*

My father returned the next morning on a loaded scow in time for his shift in the cutting room. When he came home that evening, he described a bruise on Uncle David's face that left him with what my father called his "parrot eye."

"There's this big splotch of red..."

"Blood?" asked Noah.

"Blue-red like raspberries."

Wild raspberries grew on Barren Shoal on vines tangled in with marsh brush and poison ivy. The berries ripened in July and August, the beach plums in September, and whatever we picked and did not eat right that very minute our mothers put up in jars for the winter.

"Raspberries are magenta," Noah corrected him.

"On top of the magenta a blotch of purple—okay Mr.-Know-The-Word-of-Everything?—halfway down his face. More black & bluesers up and down his left arm, and a deep cut over his parrot eye, all swollen out to here." He held his finger an inch away from Noah's brow. "He coulda lost that eye."

The following night my father came home late from work. Instead of smelling the factory when I hugged him, I smelled liquor. Mr. Stavros, the loader who had brought Sofia's family to Barren Shoal, had been crushed to death that afternoon. The bosses refused to blow the emergency horn, which would have brought the entire plant to a halt. The details were not clear.

"Boyle gave us some nonsense about the back half of a horse tied by a rope to its front end, and how only the head and legs had been completely removed. How could this be? The horses get cut in pieces before it gets to the loaders. It's supposed to go by Dowd or Paradissis or me. Where did this horse come from? How did it get to the chute?"

My mother led him to the table. "Your hands are shaking. I'll make some tea."

Mr. Stavros evidently threw the legs and head into the cauldron. Two larger parts of the torso came sliding down the loading chute, knocking him over and crushing him. Just like that. The plant foreman said Mr. Stavros never knew what hit him. What else would he say? That Mr. Stavros suffered? That he was terrified and in agony? The higher the power, the greater the silence.

When I asked my father to explain, he muttered something to my mother in Yiddish and told me to find something better to think about. I never considered the obvious until much later. Someone deliberately tied the pieces of that horse together. Someone wanted Mr. Stavros to die in a bad way.

After the accident at the loading shoot, Mr. Boyle gave Mrs. Stavros and the six children two weeks to vacate their house. Mr. Paradissis took up a collection among the Greeks on Barren Shoal and Barren Island. My father passed the collection among the Jews, then gave it to Mr. Baldwin, a stoker and a Baptist, who sent it to the other black families. Mr. Baldwin handed it over to Mr. Dowd, Marie's father, also a cutter. He saw to it that the Catholic priest who came to hear confession every third Sunday got it to Mrs. Stavros via the Greek Orthodox priest, who made a special trip over from Brooklyn to beg for the family to stay in their house until the end of their forty days of mourning. Rumor had it that the two priests had loud words with Mr. Boyle about that, but this all took place in Boyle's office behind closed doors and was hearsay. I do not know where Mr. Stavros was buried or how the family went to the grave every day that first year like Greeks are supposed to, there being no cemetery on Barren Island. The Greek Orthodox priest arranged for the police boat to take the Stavros family to Sheepshead Bay. Otherwise they would have made this trip in the usual way, on an empty garbage scow heading back to Manhattan. From Sheepshead Bay they went to the rooms that the priest found for them in Astoria, near his church, one of the first Greek families to move there. Seven people in two sad rooms, the toilet down the hallway. My grandson Eric lives in a room that he calls a studio. He can call it whatever he likes; it is still a room.

Two years would pass without hearing another word about Uncle David being mixed up with the unions and without running across Joey Pessara alone with a girl, which just as likely means it was all going on without my knowing. After all, when Miss Finn announced the discovery of Pluto after we had worked hard to master the names of the eight known planets it turned out that Pluto had been there all along without anyone knowing. I wondered if there were even more planets. I worried, the way children do, if there were things about me that no one knew, including me. It did not help that Miss Finn pulled Sofia and me aside at the start of the school year and announced, "On Monday, girls, you'll stay after with me, yes? For a lesson in hygiene." Sofia was eleven and a half years old and I was ten.

"What did *we* do?" Sofia asked.

Just then, Joey swiped my lunch out of my hands.

"Hey!" I cried, reaching to grab it back, but Joey swallowed my sandwich in a couple of sticky bites that he chewed with his mouth open.

I did not tell Miss Finn about Joey. He stole my lunch that day; the next day it would be someone else's or who knows, maybe mine again. Joey's thieving was partly from necessity and partly for sport. We knew that he was hungry—why else would a boy pick through corpses on a barge?—but Joey also stole because he liked getting away with it. He had delight in his eyes when he snatched the sandwich out of my hands.

Joey's parents came to Barren Shoal from villages near Sulmona, a valley town in Abruzzi near Mount Morrone in Italy. Sulmona had a Renaissance fountain, churches built by the town's *padrones*, cobblestone streets in the fashionable sections, and market days filled with buyers and sellers from the surrounding villages. Sofia knew about it from Yorgos, who was Joey's friend. Joey's father, Ezio, came from Antonni, a village partway up the mountain and so poor that nobody there but the priest had enough to eat except in late spring, when wild greens pushed up through the limestone. A lot of the people there starved to death, especially children. A lot of women on the verge of starvation died in childbirth, after which their newborn babies died too.

Ezio's own father—Joey's grandfather and also the father of five other children—instructed Ezio to go to Sulmona on the first market day after his fifteenth birthday, some six weeks after his mother died giving birth to the last of his brothers. He was to wait until he spotted a policeman, then steal something off the cart of the closest farmer and make a half-hearted attempt to run away. The plan was for Ezio to get arrested, hopefully without being too badly beaten. He was young and had all his teeth—if he survived the beating, the police would hand him over to the army. Forget about starving to death in Antonni like the others, his father told him; Ezio would become a soldier. With a full belly, a clever boy like Ezio might get a promotion.

Ezio was not convinced that the army was going to fatten up a half-starved boy from Mount Morrone just to fill another spot in the barracks; he was not so sure that he was cut out to be a soldier. Partway down the mountain, Ezio stopped to get some water from a spring. He spotted a donkey pulling a cart up the road from Sulmona. At the reins was a man who was sleeping, no doubt confident that the donkey knew his way home.

Ezio ripped the sleeves off his shirt.

As the donkey came to a halt to drink from the spring, Ezio jumped onto the cart and tied a sleeve around the farmer's mouth. Then he tied the farmer's hands behind his back, lifted him off his seat, and set him down behind some rocks so someone could find him but not too soon. It would take the farmer a long time to shimmy down to the road, tied up the way he was. The farmer, fully awake now and struggling, kicked at Ezio, knocking him off his feet. Ezio threw a fistful of dirt in the farmer's face to blind him, and landed two kicks to the small of his back before making off with the cart. In the cart were baskets of string beans, a wheel of white cheese, and the farmer's jacket. At least that is how Joey told it.

Ezio rode past Sulmona and onto Rome, eating cheese and trading baskets of string beans for bread and wine. When he arrived at the port at Civitavecchia, he sold the donkey and cart to a Gypsy family—Romany, you should excuse me—and with that money plus a job cleaning the ship's latrines, bought a steerage ticket to America. His only possessions were the last basket of string beans, a half wheel of cheese, and the farmer's blue jacket, which he never removed for the eight days it took to cross the Atlantic. On the ship he met a girl two years younger, also from a village near Sulmona, who was being sent by her family to be a maid in the house of the cousin who paid for her ticket. Ezio decided that this coincidence of her coming from Abruzzi was a sign from above absolving him of the sin of stealing the cart. By the time they docked in New York, the girl was on her way to becoming the mother of Joey's oldest brother.

The cousin who paid her way looked for her all along the pier. After finding her name on the ship's manifest, he reported her missing to the harbormaster and returned home empty-handed to the equally angry disappointment of his wife. A year after Joey's parents died of the influenza, Joey's oldest brother—the same boy conceived on the ship—tried to give Joey away to this cousin as a servant in order to "settle the debt." The cousin laughed at the sight of Joey, six years old then with legs bowed from rickets, and took Joey's ten year old brother instead.

This story did not change the fact that Joey wolfed down my sandwich that day in school. Sofia gave me half of hers, a cold piece of leftover bluefish with grilled eggplant. There was also a ripe tomato that we shared, plus a very small piece of pound cake that my mother gave me for a snack. When Miss Finn gave us arithmetic problems after lunch, we knew from being hungry that one half a sandwich plus one half a sandwich equals only one sandwich, even when it has to equal two lunches.

The older students were reading aloud from *Julius Caesar* and we could hear Marie Dowd saying, "'If I could pray to move,

prayers would move me; But I am constant as the northern star...'"
The older students read *Julius Caesar* aloud every year, and every
one of those times, that northern star made me think of Pluto, and
how only one year, then two years, then three years before, no one
even knew it existed. I was getting old enough to wonder about
everything I did not know about the world, never mind not know
about myself.

We were hungry after school and walked to the dunes in
search of late summer beach plums and a place where we would
not be bothered. We cut a wide circle past where Noah, Yorgos,
and Joey were fishing. We did not want to be forced to do errands
for them, like running their catch home to be cleaned. Just the
week before, Yorgos threw seaweed at Sofia to chase us away
from one of their outings. The boys were always together now,
although only one year ago they had ignored each other. Noah was
an introvert, Yorgos was arrogant, and Joey was...well, Joey was
Joey, a guy who ate trash and stole sandwiches from little kids.
They did not seem to have much in common, but on a small island
there is not much choice.

"I could hear your parents fighting last night," I said.

Our little houses were so close that we could hear the
clinking of knives and forks when the windows were open, never
mind the loud clashes between people. "That was my grandmother
going crazy," Sofia explained. "My father told Mommy last night
that Mr. Kostas got a job in the Bronx and it was suddenly like
Grandma got all her hearing back." Mr. Kostas was from the one
other Greek family that lived on Barren Shoal. It meant the world
to Grandma Paradissis—who everyone said was stone deaf and
very lonely though we all knew she could hear some—to have
someone outside the family to complain to in Greek. "Grandma
called Daddy a liar and threw a pot of dandelion weeds in his
face."

"From the stove?"

"It was cooled," she assured me, "but there were weeds all over and my mother was yelling at my father that he was stupid and should clean them up and Grandma was crying and Yorgos told them all to shut up and knocked the table over. Ba yelled at me to clean up the mess and I said, 'Why me?' and he said, 'Because I said so.'" Ba was what she called him instead of Dad or Daddy. It was like calling him "Pa."

Then she said something in Greek I did not understand but which I knew was a curse. Not a profanity, but like the evil eye.

"Your family fights a lot," I observed.

"They weren't fighting," she insisted, though I knew the constant tumult embarrassed her. Families on Barren Shoal tried to argue quietly, yelling and shouting in whispers so that their neighbors, who lived right on top of them, a breath away in houses that were barely better than shacks, could not hear. "They're just loud," she said, which was also true.

"Your grandma threw food in your father's face! That's not fighting?"

"She's his mother." Sofia shrugged as if this made sense.

Commotion was the electricity that turned all the wheels in the Paradissis house. What turned the wheels in the Eisenstein house? I want to say worry, but even that is not quite it. It was more of a perpetual, low-grade fear, an existential fever that never broke.

"What kind of job?" I asked. Fortune on Barren Shoal was measured by a job somewhere else that did not smell. *My father should only be so lucky* was what I thought.

"What?" she asked. She had kneeled down by a vine that was full of beach plums.

"Mr. Kostas. His new job."

"How should I know?" she said, concentrating on pulling

the plums from the stems without bursting them.

"You were right there. I could hear them all the way next door. I couldn't fall asleep and..."

"You should've tried counting sheep instead of poking your nose into someone else's business. Am I the only one working here?"

I kneeled down. "They could've been quieter." My mother had said the same exact thing about sheep when I went downstairs to complain. "Which sheep?" I asked Sofia, as I had asked my mother the night before. "Dead or alive sheep? The sheep on the garbage barge or the ones in the meadow?"

The newspapers had reported that the city was thinking of moving the sheep out of Central Park's Sheep Meadow. There was concern that people from the shantytown there would steal them and eat them. They would ship sheep to the country rather than feed them to hungry people. But there were lots of reports in the newspapers about things the city said it would do but never did. Like turn all of Jamaica Bay into a shipping port. There was an article about that in the paper too, but Mr. Boyle told the men that the city said the same thing twenty years earlier. He reminded them that nothing came of that either.

"You're disgusting," Sofia said.

"Says who?" I answered. I continued picking.

"Says me," she said.

"And who are you?" I emptied a handful of plums into the bucket.

We got quiet and stayed quiet while we searched the dunes for more ripe plums, which we ate on the walk back home.

My mother was polishing Helen's school shoes, the way she did every night, when I returned. Helen was at the table shelling peas, an easy enough chore for a little girl. She would count a few, get distracted by a pod that was hard to open, lose count, and start all over again from One. She did not become frustrated. Helen was the lucky youngest child of our trio. She thought that everyone in the house but her was an adult, including Noah and me, who she sometimes called Daddy or Momma by mistake. It must have been something to feel so well protected.

"More beach plums," I announced, setting down the fluted piece of newspaper in which I carried home my share of what was left. September was the time for putting up preserves and my mother was also filling jars with tomatoes and string beans, pickling eggplants and beets and cucumbers to last the winter.

Helen reached for the beach plums.

"Not for you," I snapped. I shook her hand to open her fingers.

"Let me go," Helen complained.

I pried her fingers apart and took away all but the two with split skins. Sticky juice leaked all over Helen's little palms and onto mine.

"Where's Noah?" my mother asked.

"With Yorgos and Joey." I pulled Helen to the sink, washed our hands, and returned her to the peas.

"Where?" she asked, holding up Helen's shoe to examine her handiwork.

"Fishing."

"The more time they spend fishing, the less they bring home." She smiled a little, but her voice was full of resignation.

"They said it's none of my business. They threw seaweed at us."

"Who?"

"The other day. All of them."

"Don't bother those boys."

"Momma!"

"You can stand there complaining or you can bring in the washtub before it rains," she said, turning her attention back to Helen's shoes.

The laundry tub was large and was kept outside. We only brought it in when my mother washed our laundry, which she did in the kitchen where she boiled the water.

"And remember your shoes." She made us polish our own shoes every night as soon as we were old enough. Every single school night. As if our shoes were not covered again in dust by the time we reached the schoolhouse. As if the shoes she was shining that day for Helen and later for my father would protect us from the sorry state of affairs in Europe and the hundred-and-one diseases and infections that could have struck any of us without warning or from the Depression. Half the country was now out of work and still my mother polished.

At dinner that night my father described how an unused, rotting pier was being replaced before it collapsed. He said that one of the carpenters told Mr. Boyle that all the tools supplied by the plant were falling apart. My father overheard this and told Boyle that the knives in the cutting room were falling apart too.

"I told him we can keep sharpening the blades, but that won't stop the handles from wearing down."

"Be careful of him, Sol," she said. "Boyle is not your friend. Don't forget that."

"I can talk to the man," said my father. He was twirling a clean teaspoon between his fingers like a baton. "There's a way things work at the factory that you can't understand unless..."

I drifted away. I wondered what Sofia and I had done to make Miss Finn think we needed hygiene instruction. Sofia and I did not spit; we did not eat from the barge like Joey, that filthy pig; we arrived at school with our hands and faces clean. We were unworldly girls with limited possibilities; we were girls who lived with the inescapable stench of Barren Shoal, but that did not make us dirty.

After I washed the dishes I went to find Sofia. Crossing the broken clamshell path between the houses, I could hear Mr. Paradissis shouting in Greek and the *thwunk* of him pounding his fist on the table.

"What's going on?" I asked through the open door.

"Something about a broken hatchet," Sofia translated.

"My father talked about it at dinner!" I said, as if it were something greater than coincidence.

She slipped through the doorway and we went out back to the bench that Yorgos had built out of driftwood.

"Ba was splitting the back of a draft horse this afternoon. The blade stuck in the horse but the handle stayed in Ba's hand. He spent an extra hour after his shift mending it together, but didn't get an extra hour's pay. Mr. Boyle said it's Ba's fault the hatchet was broken and maybe he should even be docked for breaking it."

We sat facing each other as if the bench was a seesaw.

"My father said the men asked for new tools."

"My father said your father is wasting his time with Mr. Boyle."

"I don't wanna stay tomorrow," I said.

"What?"

"Miss Finn."

"It's because my father was listening to Gus Hall on the radio." She was swinging her legs so that her shoes dragged on the dirt.

"I meant Miss Finn and her hygiene business."

"I'm saying: it's on account of Ba and Gus Hall. The newspaper said Gus Hall is a dirty communist."

I laughed. "Not *that* kind of dirty—not like he needs a bath. That's not why she said hygiene. They mean he's evil."

"Don't make fun of my English, little girl." *Swing, swing, swing.*

"What does Miss Finn know about your father, anyway?"

"She came to the house."

"TO DO WHAT?" I slammed one of my hands on each of her knees to keep her still. The way Sofia took her time explaining was driving me crazy. Well, that is one thing that never changed.

"About Mr. Stavros," she said.

"Mr. Stavros has been dead forever." By then it had been two years.

"To bring my parents news about his family. Things Mrs. Stavros won't ask anyone to write for her in a letter."

The episode was still the subject of widespread speculation.

"What's Mrs. Stavros got to do with us?" I asked. I wondered if this had something to do with Mr. Kostas leaving Barren Shoal, but I could not put the pieces together.

"Miss Finn says Mrs. Stavros still cries all day; she yells at the priest when he comes to see her. Miss Finn says she worries for the children. She says her being in mourning for so long, the way Mrs. Stavros is, is unhealthy. That it's contagious. That she's making the children sick."

"Not *that* kind of contagious. Not like measles or influenza."

"I told you, little girl..." she said, wagging a finger at me as a reminder not to tease her. "The children cry all day, too."

"What did Miss Finn say about Gus Hall?" I asked.

"What...are...you...talking...about?" she asked, pausing after each word. I was not the only one who could sound condescending.

"That's where you started. Your father listening to the radio." The sun was setting now; with the dusk came more dampness and biting bugs. It was time to go in.

"Better than what your father listens to, Kimosabe." In

addition to the communists, Mr. Paradissis also tuned into the Lone Ranger. Not my father, who listened to the Yiddish radio shows on WLTH and WEVD. Sometimes he would have us children sit with him, even though we barely understood a word of Yiddish. It hardly mattered when they were playing music and he would take turns dancing with each of us, including Noah. Later on we would listen with him to Roosevelt's Fireside Chats. And in the darkest hours he would sometimes have us listen to Father Coughlin broadcasting live from his radio pulpit in Detroit about...*the international conspiracy of greedy Jewish bankers... filthy, bloodsucking, Christ-killing vermin who eat the feces of swine*...Sometimes my father would have Noah or me sit with him. I understand his point now, that it is important to know what people who hate us are thinking, but we were just children. Did we have to know so soon? Did it change anything to know how much people hated us? Did it make us any safer? Was there some purpose in our being defined by someone else's hate? Is it any surprise that we would define ourselves that way too? What does it mean to be a Jew? Aha! A complicated question with a complicated answer but for this: a Jew is a person who an anti-Semite hates. So I repeat: is there *any* purpose in this at all?

My father rewarded us with the Eddie Cantor Hour on Sunday nights. On Saturday afternoons we listened with him to the broadcast from the Metropolitan Opera when he came home from work. But never the Lone Ranger—not when my father was home—and never, ever Gus Hall. It was one thing to be a socialist, which my father was, but another thing altogether to be a communist. Especially a Stalinist. My father did not go for that whole "dictatorship of the masses" business which, to him, was just another form of fascism masquerading as fairness.

On Monday, Sofia and I pulled our chairs to either side of

Miss Finn after school. Miss Finn told us how the author of the book she was holding was her sister, Dr. Finn.

We nodded, though I cannot imagine what we were agreeing to.

The title was *Human Reproduction* by Marion Finn, M.D.

Miss Finn propped the book up on a desk so we could see the pictures. We had both seen naked bodies before in Miss Finn's books of paintings from the Renaissance and in old *National Geographics*. She had even taken some older students to the Brooklyn Museum on her day off, riding them over on a just-emptied scow on Saturday morning and sending them home on a newly-loaded one Saturday night.

Miss Finn read aloud:

> Men have glands called testes that make sperm cells,
> whereas female glands make eggs. Testes make sperm
> all the time. Women go through a four-week cycle
> beginning in puberty, during which eggs develop.
> If the fully developed egg does not become fertilized
> at this time, it dies and is released from the body
> with menstrual blood. Sexual intercourse can introduce
> the sperm into an egg to start a new life. During
> intercourse, the man ejaculates sperm into the vagina.

She explained all about eggs and ovaries and ovulation, ejaculation, semen, insemination, gestation, birthing, and lactation. I already had the first few strands of underarm hair, which the book said was a sign. I was even certain, with a new nervousness, that my underarm perspiration smelled.

"Your mothers," Miss Finn assured us, "are modern women. They want you to understand the reasons for your monthly periods."

Our mothers? When Miss Finn offered, they were probably afraid to say no to her.

"This way you'll be well prepared instead of being caught off guard alone in those outhouses looking for a rag."

My mother had a bag of small rags that she kept in their bedroom. They were little mysteries that I now realized I never saw her wash or hang to dry. She must have done so when Noah and I were out of the house, and Helen, being so young still, would have no need to understand why.

The world is always full of people on missions: Miss Finn with her lessons on reproduction; Father Coughlin spewing venom; Franklin Delano Roosevelt preaching the virtues of personal strength and the welfare state all in one breath.

"Abstinence is the form of birth control you'll practice until you marry," Miss Finn explained. "Not knowing things gets young girls in trouble. You're not living in some Garden of Eden over here."

Garden of Eden. I remember her saying those exact words. Barren Shoal was such a cheap joke that even people with good intentions had trouble resisting.

"She's telling the truth?" I asked Sofia after Miss Finn finished and set us free.

"It was in the book," said Sofia.

"Plenty of things in books are make-believe. 'Hansel and Gretel,' 'Peter and the Wolf,' 'Cinderella.'"

An image of my mother and father together that way surfaced in my mind's eye. Just as suddenly, they turned into Joey and Marie Dowd on the beach.

"You know what Yorgos calls it?" said Sofia. Yorgos, now sixteen, had taken to smacking Sofia around if she did not make him the sandwich he wanted, or took too long to clear the table after dinner, or did not make his bed before leaving for school.

She did not even complain to anyone. *He's violent*, I would tell her. *He's just a man*, she would reply. He had decided to apply to City College, at Miss Finn's urging, after which his parents became afraid of him too.

I did not want to know, but there was no stopping Sofia.

"Yorgos calls it '*fucking*,'" said Sofia, giggling.

"*Fucker, fuckface, fuckhead*," I said, giggling as well, because, after all, it was the first time any of those words came out of my mouth, you should pardon me. "That's what the men on the pier call each other. That means they fuck each other too?"

"That's stupid," said Sofia. "They're just being disgusting."

"If it's so disgusting then why should we do it?" Was this disgusting thing inevitable? Or was it the other way around?

"You're such a baby," she said, needling me. "Remember that time when we saw Joey Pessara in the dunes with Marie Dowd?"

I nodded. We had not spoken of it since it happened.

"That's what they were doing. On the beach. Fucking. All that noise? Because they were fucking."

"Miss Finn didn't mention noise," I said.

"Well I heard Yorgos telling Joey that Marie is still a good fuck, so he must know."

"What makes a good fuck not a bad fuck?" I asked. "And how can Yorgos tell?" I could feel something stirring inside me as we spoke, a feeling I tried to push away.

Not until I was in bed that night did I think about what I did in my room when I was sure Helen was sleeping, having graduated from my pillow to my fingers, you should pardon me. Except what I did never hurt; it always felt good, if you do not mind my saying so.

Miss Finn, we later found out from Marie Dowd, had this

sit-down talk with every girl. The boys were supposed to learn all about it from their fathers. Noah, even later, confirmed this, though our father provided him with seriously limited information.

"What little I knew about girls I mostly learned from Yorgos and Joey," he told me after the war, by which time we both knew plenty. "A lot of good that did me."

"Can you imagine anything worse?" I said. "Me learning from that saint, you learning from a couple of slobs. No wonder it didn't sound appealing."

"We were kids, Marta, who fell for everything they told us."

"Until we didn't," I reminded him.

"Right," he said, and laughed. "Until we didn't."

CHAPTER 4

Sofia turned twelve a year later and her period came just like Miss Finn said it would, and the consequences of boys became different to her, like Miss Finn also promised. Sofia decided that the safest strategy was to bring her stained rags over to our house Sunday nights to dry in the little room upstairs in the eaves that I shared with Helen. Our room had a peaked ceiling, which held heat in the summer and cold in the winter. It is what nowadays they would call "rustic." It is what I would call crummy. Those cabins were no good to begin with. The steps up were so steep that when my mother's arthritis got the best of her she could not come to our room for days. Helen never noticed the rags; Noah barely acknowledged Helen or me, never mind come upstairs anyway.

My mother, though she had left all these matters for Miss Finn to explain, understood the private needs of girls. One evening she kept Helen with her after dinner when Sofia brought over her rags to hang. My father was at the gatehouse, the site of the nightly poker games that Mr. DeWitt had formerly hosted in his cabin. Cutters played on Monday nights, skinners played on Tuesday, and the stokers, all of them Negro men, played on Wednesdays. Friday night was Catholic night, Saturday night was Protestant night—all denominations welcomed—and Sunday night was for Jews. The men sat on empty coal oil drums, playing for cigarettes, smoking their reserve funds and profits.

Every man was welcomed to play on Thursdays, payday, the only night of the week that the men played for cash, even the ones without an extra dime to lose. The mothers would send the children to retrieve the men, even if the youngest girls had no business walking to the factory at night when it was so dark and damp. All it took to close out a game was one tough skinned, foul-mouthed man shamed into folding his hand by a sleepy-eyed little girl.

I do not know if my father lost more cigarettes than he won or what the outcome was of all those Thursdays. There must have been some consenting to these outings on the part of my mother, because she always waited a couple of hours before sending Helen and me to bring him home. Poker, my father insisted, was as American as playing baseball, and the players bet on that game too, didn't they? Harmless, he insisted, not like the Black Sox throwing a World Series game. Or Pete Rose, that fool, who my father lived long enough to see get kicked out of baseball for betting on the game. My father, just into his nineties by then, was thrilled: *Imagine that crook comparing himself to Joe DiMaggio,* he said. *Throwing a tantrum when he didn't break DiMaggio's hitting streak. What chutzpah.*

The small window in our bedroom was wide open when Sofia found me struggling with arithmetic problems. The salt air was blowing off the ocean, a sweet and cooling breeze that, when the wind was coming from the south, did not stink. The only stench was coming from Joey, who was in the yard with Yorgos and Noah. Joey, like Mr. Boyle, used chain smoking as a deodorant. Sofia hung her wet things from a length of rope that we hung from stubby nails across a corner. She settled into replicating the drawings from Miss Doctor Finn's Sex Manual, as we now called the hygiene book, by cutting out paper dolls. I was clipping newspaper articles on China for our Odyssey Project. China and Japan were having little outbursts here and there of warfare, which was why there were so many articles. Even so, we dreamed of seeing the Forbidden City and the Great Wall some day. Sofia's dolls performed acts on one another that went far beyond the illustrations in Miss Doctor Finn's book. At one point The Man's face was between The Woman's legs. I never asked Sofia where she got this idea, one that took me a very long time to appreciate, if you do not mind my saying so.

"How am I supposed to concentrate," I asked her, "when Clark and Claudette are creating such a racket?" Sofia named her cutouts for celebrities. She knew plenty from listening to the radio and reading Walter Winchell's column.

"It doesn't bother *them*," she answered, pointing Clark's head in the direction of the back window. Her cutouts were blessed with the energy of newlyweds.

"I'm being serious here while you're fooling around with paper dolls."

Sofia lifted the cutouts high above her head and dropped them, letting them drift to the floor like parachute jumpers. She walked over to the window and leaned her elbows on the frame.

"Come here," she said, waving me over.

"What?"

"*Here*," she whispered emphatically.

I slipped in beside her. I could see the boys below, sitting at the edge of the garden. Beyond that, some moonlight was reflecting brightly on Barren Shoal as if the sand and water were as clear as the upper reaches of the sky and beyond, all the way to the newly discovered Pluto. Even Barren Shoal, at moments, was beautiful.

"No shit," Joey was saying. His language, of course, not mine. "We don't get hospital stuff. That goes into incinerators at the hospitals, *whoosh*, right down the chute into the fire. No fucking around."

"That crap you eat is going to your fucking head," said Yorgos. "Why you so sure the hospitals play by the stinking rules? They might slip a couple of bodies onto a barge here and there, maybe an amputated leg..."

Joey lit a cigarette off the one he had just finished. Embers rose off the butt, which he flicked live into the garden. My mother hated it when he did that. "Will you listen? It was a whole set of little foot bones: little thumb toe, little pinkie, little..."

"What are you?" asked Noah, "an anatomist?"

"I'm no antichrist. That would be you, Jew-boy."

"Maybe it was baby back ribs you saw."

"Maybe they've got some of those starving Ukrainians," chimed in Yorgos, "direct from the famine. They're eating people over there!" The Soviets kept the grain exports going out even as people starved, just like the Brits did in Ireland 100 years earlier. Am I repeating myself?

"Fuck you," said Joey. "I told you they were a little person's toe bones."

"Just one foot? What'd it do, hop onto the barge?" Yorgos hopped around on one leg. "Please, sir, can you tell me the way to Barren Shoal?" he squeaked in a baby girl's voice.

"I sure as hell didn't go digging for the other one."

"You missed a free meal!?"

I pulled Sofia from the window. I was going to say something, who knows what; I was disgusted, horrorstruck, mortified. She pressed a hand over my mouth and whispered, "Don't say a word. Promise."

I nodded, wanting nothing more than Joey's discovery of those little toes to disappear. I gestured to the opposite side of the room. We crawled on our hands and knees.

"It's not like they..." I said quietly.

She glared. I stopped speaking. "*Sssshhhh*!" Sofia repeated.

"Shouldn't Joey tell someone?" I whispered into her ear.

"Don't be so serious," she whispered back. "He's being disgusting on purpose."

"Then why are we whispering?"

"Just never mind him, okay?"

I returned to my China clippings. Sofia retrieved the paper dolls off the floor, crumpled them into a ball, and tossed them out the open window. She ducked low so the boys could not see her.

"Hey, they'll know we're up here!"

She rested her hands on her hips. "Grow up already, *please*!"

"I'm going to Mr. Dewitt's to get my father."

"You're going nowhere."

"I want him to come home."

Mr. Dowd opened the gatehouse door. My father sat at a table with Mr. DeWitt, Mr. Paradissis, and a couple of others. Sofia stood to the side of me, in the shadows, where her father could not see her. The new gatehouse, which was what everyone still called it, was barely large enough for a cot and the table, which was made from the old gatehouse door and two sawhorses. There was also a swivel chair that must have had a previous life when the sheen was worn off the curvatures for the buttocks and the wooden arms stained dark from hand oils. There was a small black stove against the wall opposite the door, and a small window on each of the other two walls. For light Mr. DeWitt used tallow candles made from the rendered animal fat from the factory. With the exception of Mrs. Weems, the Negro woman who did his laundry, no woman regularly went inside. Some said Mrs. Weems was a relation to one of the Scottsboro Boys, but I never heard that confirmed. The only thing I knew from the newspapers was that one of them was also named Weems.

All those years when he lived on the other side of the Paradissises, he paid another black woman, Mr. Morgan's wife, to straighten up. He had more personal contact with blacks on Barren Shoal than anyone I can think of. I am not making excuses for how we did things. I am just describing how it was.

"What is it, honey?" asked my father.

"Time to come home," I said.

"Your mother sent you so early." The worry lines showed on his forehead.

I shook my head. "She's busy with Helen."

"What, then?" he asked.

I shrugged. "I don't know."

"Go on now," he said.

The boys were gone from the yard when we got back to the house. Sofia said she would come for her things after school on Monday, if that was okay. Helen was already sleeping when I went upstairs.

It was sometime around then that a letter came from my mother's brother back in Zyrmuny. She read it quietly to herself— it was a couple of pages at least—while Helen played with shells she had collected on the beach and I ironed our dresses.

"What?" asked my father.

"It's so hot today," she said. "You girls should be outside. Marta, take Helen."

"But my school dress," I said.

"It can wait. Go." She slipped the letter into the pocket of her apron.

"What about Noah?"

"Go."

"Come on," I said, tugging Helen's hand.

"I don't want to," she whined. Who wants to go somewhere with someone who does not want to go in the first place?

"And take water," said my mother. She filled a mason jar and handed it to me so that we would not run back inside for drinks.

We walked in the direction of the bay. It was warm out, though not like my mother said it was. Helen was carrying the can in which she collected shells and rocks from the beach. Helen's prized possessions were a sand dollar, which she had found perfectly intact, and two starfish. When she brought home a third, my mother told her enough with the starfish, which smelled rotten as they dried. As they died. Like that.

She walked along the shoreline, picking up shells and stones, examining them, and dropping most of them back onto the sand. I tried skipping stones the way Noah did, but they plunked into the surf. Helen found a piece of a horseshoe crab and I drew a picture around it in the sand to show her what it would look like had she found it whole. I had talent as a forensic sand comber.

"Let's play," said Helen.

Play? "We *are* playing."

"Let's build." She dropped to her knees and scooped sand into piles. Then she started digging without a word about what she was digging for.

"How about a town?" I suggested.

I scooped out gullies between Helen's piles of sand and circled them with a trench. "Look," I said, pointing. "This is Barren Shoal; that's Barren Island. Over here, that's Brooklyn." In my rendering, Barren Shoal was equal in size to Barren Island, which in truth it was not; Brooklyn was out of scale too, smaller and farther away. It did not matter. We made room for some extra little islands to represent the ones in Jamaica Bay that had no names. Helen shaped these by packing sand into a large clamshell. I dug the trenches deeper until I hit wet sand.

"Now you fill the trenches and make a real Jamaica Bay."

Helen was proud of this assignment, running back and forth with her can, half the water splashing out before she could pour it in.

"Go slow," I instructed.

"Let's make it bigger," she said.

"Tomorrow," I told her. I did not even want to do this today, never mind make a promise about doing it again.

The sand sucked up a lot of the water, but even so, the water level kept rising. It was a good thing that 5-year-olds can run forever.

"That's enough," I finally said.

She kept going.

All it took was one can too many for the entire scene to collapse. The little islands disappeared; the trench around Barren Island filled with sand; Barren Shoal was completely under water. Helen began crying. "Fix them!" she wailed. "Put them up again!"

"Tomorrow," I said, just to stop her crying.

"Promise," she said, wiping her nose on her arm.

A couple of weeks after discovering the little set of toes on the barge, Joey announced he was leaving school for a job on the pier. I do not know how his brothers arranged for him to get this job while others were begging and the pictures in the newspapers showed the breadlines still growing. Some said the Pessara brothers had a grip on things, especially Massimo. People were always saying things like that about other people. Other people said it was something about the mysterious circumstances under which their father died.

"Mr. Pessara died in the influenza epidemic," I reminded Sofia, who was restoring order to the broken clamshells between our houses.

She rolled her eyes. "You believe everything you're told."

"So maybe I shouldn't believe about the baby bones." I was half helping her by spreading the shells around with my foot.

"Don't be stupid. You'd need a reason to think Joey lied."

Sofia was right. Joey was so primitive, so downright dumb, that while he might mistake one thing for another, he was not clever enough to make this story up.

Joey was now officially a receiving raker, directing the larger carcasses to the butchering room and the smaller pieces to a trolley that went straight to the chutes. The crew began its 12-hour shift at 6:00 a.m. Every morning Joey greeted the filthiest, most corrupted, stinking garbage that ever traveled New York. He also greeted the scavengers, the poorest of the poor, who took for themselves all the tails, hooves, blood, skin, and head meat they could manage. They even sucked marrow from the maggot-infested bones. Like I have said.

If Joey's brothers—not including the one four years older who was handed off to the cousin as a servant and never heard from again—if Joey's brothers ever cared that Joey might be starving too were it not for what he scavenged from the barges, I never heard it. Maybe, like Sofia and me and who knows how many others, the only thought the brothers ever said about Joey was that he had Hollywood looks and that he was disgusting. Who knows. Maybe the brothers simply did not care, their parents dead and no one else willing to make them bother.

On our way to school, Sofia and I saw Joey scavenging beside the girl in the brown dress, who had become a regular. We knew neither her name, nor where she slept, nor anything else. I cannot even say that she still wore that same brown dress. She was like those seagulls she scavenged with, who also disappeared at night. Whatever dress she had on was hidden by a grease-stained coat that was too long and which she cinched at the waist with rope.

When we got right up near Joey, we could see him excavating what was left of a blackened banana, extracting the last little piece from the place where the peels meet just above the nubby stem. I know that there is a name for that, but who can remember? A banana was a rare find among the animal cadavers. Joey tossed the peel into the transport cart and returned to shoveling.

"Disgusting," said Sofia, who was watching him carefully.

"Double disgusting," I agreed. I was not as fascinated as Sofia by this episode, but it seemed the thing to say. This was the boy who used to steal our sandwiches, who cursed at us. Had we ever observed anyone else taking pity on him or any pity on the other people who picked their meals off the scows? I am rationalizing, of course. I wish I could say instead how we were more virtuous than we were.

Joey and his discovery of the foot popped back into my mind later that day when Miss Finn read current events aloud from the newspapers. There was more about the famine in the Ukraine. Thousands of people starving to death. I have no idea how Sofia already knew about it, but she did.

"Who will locate The Ukraine for us?" asked Miss Finn.

Sofia's hand shot up even quicker than Marie Dowd's, who was the smartest one in the class and who was applying to Hunter College. Marie settled back into her wooden seat, a smirk on her face like she was waiting for Sofia to trip up.

"The Ukraine," Sofia announced on her way to the globe, "is the breadbasket of the Soviet Union."

Sofia rotated the globe a couple of times. "Where's Greece," she said aloud to herself. Once she had established her bearings on the world, Sofia ran her little finger from Athens north to Thessalonica, near the village where her mother was born, then across to Istanbul, which on Miss Finn's old globe was still Constantinople. Having found Constantinople on the globe, Sofia ran her finger due north across the Black Sea, where it finally hit land at Odessa.

"The Ukraine's capital city is Kiev," said Miss Finn, "an important trading partner for Soviet goods through what is now called Istanbul, not Constantinople."

Sofia's hand was resting on the globe, one finger on Kiev and another on what Miss Finn called *Istanbul-not-Constantinople*.

"Where did you learn so much about The Ukraine?" asked Miss Finn.

Sofia shrugged. "Just do."

"From your father," I said. A guess.

Sofia glared. She was right: sometimes I was so childish.

"What about your father?" asked Miss Finn.

"He showed me a map in the newspapers." She did not mention that the newspaper was *The Daily Worker*. She did not mention that after Mr. Stavros' gruesome death in the loading chute Mr. Paradissis began getting *The Daily Worker* from Parson Otis, one of the men who piloted a garbage barge. Everyone knew Captain Otis, a sallow little man with a handlebar moustache, because he was always drunk and always talking about himself to himself: *Captain Otis got a stinkin' load; Captain Otis got this goddamned low tide; Captain Otis is dockin'*. Sofia would read *The Daily Worker* aloud for her father after dinner. Mr. Paradissis, who could read just fine in Greek, was never at home in the English alphabet. I mean the Roman alphabet. Or the fact that Constantinople was now called Istanbul. He was no fan of the Turks, and who can blame him?

Mr. Paradissis would burn the newspaper in the stove when they finished because Mrs. Paradissis got frantic about it sitting out where someone could see it. I did not need to speak Greek to understand that she was afraid. Everyone on Barren Shoal, except the blacks who were descended from slaves, was afraid of being shipped back to the country where they came from. As if Immigration & Naturalization could still find those places, what with borders and names changing all the time. The black people would not have even known where to go to if they could have gotten the money to leave, what with the way the traders sold their ancestors here and there without records of where they came from. I think now that some of those black people on Barren Shoal remembered grandparents or great-grandparents who were born as slaves. Oh yes: there have been enough atrocities all around. I am not digressing. I am keeping track; I am enraged.

Sofia returned to her seat. Miss Finn finished reading the article on the starving Ukrainians. "We should celebrate our good fortune about living in a place where few, if any, people starve."

Even I knew that this was not true. *The Daily Worker* said plenty of Americans were starving. I got a bad taste in my mouth, like sucking on a penny. I raised my hand. "If The Ukraine is the Soviet Union's breadbasket, how come those people have no food?"

"Oh, Marta," said Miss Finn, her voice sounding very, very tired. "It's complicated."

The color rose in my cheeks. *It's complicated.* More complicated than what? Just like "fuck," this was a phrase that did not always say what it meant. In fact, Marie Dowd had used the same exact words when I interrupted her class report to ask why, if there were plenty of other crops being shipped over to England, so many Irish starved during the Potato Famine. She also said "it's complicated." What was there to it I could not understand? The

Irish starved 100 years ago; the Ukrainians were starving now. Even a child could see the inevitability of more people starving soon.

"We don't have enough information," said Miss Finn. "Some say there's a drought. Others say that it's because of new Soviet policies for collectivizing farms. And others—the officials in Moscow—say that there's no such famine. There are even newspaper reports of huge harvests. But the same newspapers run eyewitness reports of starving villagers and warnings of cannibalism."

I pictured Joey's fingers and their telltale stains. Everything was connecting; I understood how people will do anything, eat anything, so as not to starve. I pictured the Paradissis family, including the already-withered, widowed Grandma Paradissis in steerage on the ship from Piraeus to New York with a sack of salted cod, a sack of fresh lemons, and a string of dried figs hanging like pearls around each of their necks. I pictured my own parents arriving at Ellis Island. What did my parents eat on their crossing? Cans of smoked sprats is all I remember, but what else? I never asked. I asked instead where our family came from. "Belarus," said my father, "which is either in Poland or Russia depending on who's just won what war."

"Am I Polish or a Russian?"

My father frowned. "You're a Jew," he said. "You're a beautiful Jewish girl."

"That's not a place, Dad."

"You were born in my heart, in your mother's soul."

My father loved speaking in sentimental terms. I knew better than to correct him with scientific details that I learned from Miss Doctor Finn's book.

Could people be citizens of an idea instead of a place? I might have become a believer if some kind of voice had said

Yes, this can be. But I heard nothing. And what about nomadic people, the Gypsies, the Inuit and Bedouins, Mongols, Laps, and Travelers? I mean the Romany? The questions sent the globe inside my head spinning. Everyone, including 10-year-olds, wants certainties. Every single person wants guarantees.

"Come here," Yorgos called to Sofia after school that day. We were outside the schoolhouse, debating whether or not we had time to go to the salt marsh before our mothers expected us home.

"What?" Sofia asked him.

"This," said Yorgos. He slapped her on the back of her head.

"What's that for?" cried Sofia.

"For showing off." Yorgos slapped her again. "And opening your fat mouth about Ba."

"But I read about The Ukraine in the paper and I didn't say it was Daddy's anyway and..."

"Shut up," Yorgos shouted. "And keep it shut."

"But I never..."

"That's right," said Yorgos. "Never open that fat little trap of yours again."

My mother was frying eggplants with tomato and garlic when I got home. The garden was bulging with purple skins now that the days were shorter and the harvest season was at its peak. More tomatoes were simmering in another pot, these destined for the mason jars and a shelf in a shallow cupboard against the back wall of the house.

"Momma," I began. I had planned to ask her about the foot that Joey found, how it could be that a little baby foot got mixed in with hooves and ropes of horse intestines and why Mr. Paradissis was reading *The Daily Worker* and why my own father did not.

"Momma, can Sofia sleep over?" I asked instead.

"On a school night?" *Stir, stir, stir.*

"We have a lot of work. It will go faster," I reasoned.

"That teacher should be more careful about you girls, all that homework she gives."

"It's our Odyssey project, Momma, not Miss Finn. It takes so much time."

"What does Mrs. Paradissis say?"

Had my mother come to me, had she poured quiet cups of tea for us instead of standing with her back to me working at the stove, spooning bits of garlic in the sizzling oil, I would have told her about Yorgos hitting Sofia; I would have cried about what Joey found on the barge. I could have asked her about a lot of things.

"She says fine."

"You promise to be serious up there?"

I was afraid that if Sofia slept at home that Yorgos would hit her again. I was just as afraid of the thing that had already happened, the slaps across her face when I said nothing.

"Cross my heart, hope to die."

"Heaven forbid!"

CHAPTER 5

The next morning, like all of our mornings, was announced by the usual mad chirping of the sparrows and plovers and other small birds that flocked to Jamaica Bay. They could have nested someplace more beautiful than Barren Shoal, but the birds returned every year to the dune grasses and weeds, to the reedy thistles that in summer choked the salt marsh. I do not know if all birds have a sense of smell or what it means to them, but it is plain enough to see how the birds' reactions were different than our own. On Barren Shoal, their busy chirping threaded with the wailing of the gulls, which lived there by the hundreds, their endless feeding frenzy made possible by all the garbage. The ever-busy gulls were our sentries, warning us of any new barge crossing the bay.

Neither the birds nor the gulls were able to camouflage the sounds of human screaming.

I heard Helen screaming, my mother screaming, Helen screaming faster, my mother screaming louder, the pitch of Helen's screams rising higher. Then nothing. Then my mother screaming *Helen, Helen, Helen.*

I do not remember kicking down my blankets or jumping out of bed or trampling the schoolwork that I had worked on the night before or Sofia's paper cutout sex dolls. I do not remember if Sofia was awake or sleeping. I do not remember racing down the stairs nor getting the wood splinter in my foot, where I still have a scar 70 years later. I do not remember my mother plunging her bare hands into the washtub or her pulling Helen's body from the scalding water. I did not know if Helen was already dead or if she was in the process of dying right there in my mother's arms. How can these be memories when I still live them again and again? I hear both of them screaming and the cries that were Helen's last sounds. I see my mother clutching Helen's burning body against her own.

"My father!" I cried to Sofia. How long had she been standing there?

My mother folded herself over Helen, hiding Helen's face against her breast. The pitch of the moan coming out of her was a sound I never heard before and I have never heard again since. The cry of pain so deep always sounds new.

"We've got to find my father," I cried. "Now! Now!"

My mother was clutching Helen. Noah, as usual, was nowhere to be seen.

My mother must have heard me cry that I was going for my father. I grabbed Sofia's wrist and pulled her out the door. I do not know why I did not ask her to wait with my mother, or why I did not send her for my father alone. It does not matter. Nothing would have changed the agonizing, unbearable facts, the unbearable horror of what had happened.

We ran barefoot over clamshells and cigarette stubs, across the weeds that grew as fast as we pulled them. We trampled the last of the tomato vines and the first new winter squashes that were just beginning to show, tight green globes as hard as bocce balls. Between my toes I could feel the dew that the just-ended night left on all things, hard or soft. Dirt packed the cut on my foot and slowed the bleeding. The air was soaked with the stench of drying seaweed and the stench of the garbage scows and the stench from the factory. And the sweet smell, too, of the sea, like the taste of salt on my lips. I could hear the birds in the little gardens we flattened and the gulls even louder as the piers came into view; I could feel the new sun rising against my neck.

A girl could run from the cabins where the families lived down to the docks in less than ten minutes by taking these shortcuts through dunes instead of the more formal, more circuitous route on the island's cleared path. Though the factory's stern, tapered smokestack was in view the whole time we were running, the more it filled my frame of vision, the farther away it became. I even believed that if I found my father right away, he would run home and save Helen. This was me reaching for anything that might change things. If it meant making things up, so be it. Was it any different than being taught to believe in the unbelievable?

People were pointing and laughing as Sofia and I ran past them because we were still in our nightclothes. Some people looked curious and others looked surprised, but no one came after us or helped us or got in our way. Joey was on a barge when we got to the dock, where he was maneuvering a small horse that had been flayed except for the coat on its head. It was illegal to sell those hides—some said that they carried anthrax—but the scavengers had to cut through them to get to the meat. I bet that they took whatever hides they could and sold them anyway. But what business was it of mine if they took the hides? Why am I so bothered by this now?

"My father!" I yelled on I don't know what breath, panting so hard. Something in my cry made Joey turn. Perhaps there is a pitch of terror that everyone can recognize. Joey jumped onto the pier.

He was in front of us now, charging like a gladiator through the factory gates, his shovel rising up and down in his hand like a piston, Sofia and me following behind him, me bellowing, "Dad, Dad, Dad." Bigger, stronger men jumped out of his way. Others did double-takes. Someone recognized me because soon I heard deeper voices calling *Eisenstein. Eeeeyyyyesenstein.*

We raced past wooden barrels that were lined up in soldierly rows. To the side of them were stacks of burlap bags. At the very upper reaches of the walls were some greasy windows where a little light was filtering through an overlay of grime. Below the windows were chutes and shafts and pipes poking out in every direction imaginable. They all funneled into or out of the furnace that was everything's final destination. It did not matter.

I had never been inside the factory before, but all those years of imaginings and expectations collapsed in the face of my purpose. All that I cared about was finding my father. Useless drafts of air pushed through the open windows, all hot and damp and hopeless. The floor was thick with something slimy that seeped between my bare toes. The stench, which I had always imagined as something gaseous, became liquid inside my mouth, coating my throat and tongue.

Joey, still swinging his arms, charged into the cutting room. It was damp and hazy there too, but I found my father anyway, spotted his dark eyes and the dark wave of his hair. The sight of him made me stop. This was what I wanted. I wanted my father to make everything stop. He was hovering over a table with a butcher's saw in one hand and the leg of an animal in the other. He was clutching it just above the hoof. Surrounding him, I could see, were more horses. They were stacked next to barrels, between more piles of burlap bags: whole ones and pieces of ones and legs in a pile here and heads in a pile there.

Some of them were still moving.

No. That was impossible. It was my own legs that were moving; it was my own legs giving way. I reached for my father, who was still holding the butcher's saw and horse leg. I landed first on my knees; then my arms and legs splayed out into that filthy slime.

"Dad!" I wailed. My father dropped his butcher's saw; the horse leg slid to the floor. I plowed my head into his legs, howling as wildly as my mother over Helen.

"Helen fell into the washtub," said Sofia, sobbing. I had forgotten that she was running right behind me.

My father wiped his hands on the rough rag tucked around his waist. He pulled me up. What took him so long? He wiped my hands with his rag. "Come now!" cried Sofia.

My father pulled me away from him so he could see my face. His lips were trembling, the top one rolling over his teeth to cover his bite.

He did not ask if Helen was okay or if my mother was okay or anything about Noah. "Get them out of here!" he shouted at Joey.

My father ran ahead, stepping on horse heads and hindquarters when he had to and any other animal part that got in his way. These were no longer pathetic mounds of flesh to be transformed into fertilizer, or bones rendered into grease and glue. They had become cruel obstacles over which my father vaulted.

Joey hurried us out of the factory. We stumbled past everything my father had already raced over, grasping at one another, afraid of what our hands might land on as we struggled to keep our balance. The men we passed were silent now; I felt important. We were in the middle of a family tragedy and the lives that mattered most for that rare moment were ours, was mine.

My father was still calling my mother's name when Sofia

and I got back to the house. He ran upstairs, as if Helen might be there alive and unharmed, resting in our attic bedroom. Noah surfaced out of nowhere. "Down at the beach," he said, his voice full of impatience, as if this was obvious.

My father followed Noah through the dune grass and the marshes. Yorgos jumped into the chase with Sofia, Joey, and me, no one waiting for anyone else to keep up even when I had to stop to pull the splinter out of my foot. The pain, no longer camouflaged by the rush of adrenaline, was climbing up the back of my leg. From the skin stuck a toothpick-length sliver of wood. The moment it was out, the pain disappeared to almost nothing. If I had taken it out sooner, the cut would have never gotten infected. Everything I thought of that day I thought of too late.

We found my mother in the cold water, up to her chest in it, Helen in her arms.

My father plunged in beside them, his arms lifted high to keep him steady. "What are you doing?" he cried.

"She's so hot, Abe. Feel..." My mother raised Helen's body. She did not notice the rest of us.

"Oh Rachel," said my father, wrapping his arms around her and Helen, pressing his face into my mother's hair. "It's no good, no good."

We stood in silence on the sand, watching them huddle. The tide lapped indifferently against our legs. Soon there were other people standing with us. First the women came down from the houses, startled away from their work by the commotion. Then the men arrived from the factory. Even Mr. Boyle had walked out, just like that.

Other than Mrs. Paradissis, who stood beside us, I could not bear the anguished faces of these grown men and women. Mrs. Paradissis, in a hushed tone, said something to Noah that I could not hear. My brother, my know-it-all brother, let his head fall against her thick shoulder. Yorgos cupped his hands around a match and lit a cigarette. He passed the cigarette to Joey, whose shirt was soaked with sweat. Sofia had hold of my hand. She was rubbing the tip of my thumb over and over, squeezing the nail. It did not feel good, but I would not have stopped her for anything.

I cannot say how long this went on or what my father said to my mother that convinced her to come out of the water. Neither Sofia nor Noah knows either. I can see my father rocking her in his arms until she was ready, then lifting Helen from my mother and carrying her body back to shore. Helen's face was twisted, her lips blistered in a silent howl. Her skin was scorched and puckered. My mother's arms were burned and blistering, too.

My father carried Helen that whole horrible journey back to our house with his lips touching her head. My mother walked beside him, one arm around her own waist and the other curled around Helen's legs. She was sobbing as they walked, but if she was in pain from the burns on her arms it did not show. The rest of us followed behind, a funeral cortége for the service that had not yet taken place.

There were no doctors on Barren Shoal. It would have changed nothing. Helen was already dead from shock. You hardly hear of it these days, but children died from scalding all the time. Or often enough that it was not uncommon. But what did that matter? Helen's body was laid out in my parents' bedroom. Mrs. Paradissis sent Sofia next door to break off a piece of her aloe plant, the juice of which she was now squeezing onto my mother's blistering arms. Yorgos and Joey returned to the house with Miss Finn, who was hugging one of those white, metal First Aid kits to her chest. Sweat had turned her blouse opaline grey.

Mr. Boyle sent the men back to work, including Joey and Mr.

Paradissis. He brought Noah to the dock to speak to the bosses so someone would get word to shore. A message was carried by the next barge captain, who would hand it over to a boy in Brooklyn, who would deliver it to Uncle David and Aunt Sara, who did not have a telephone. A funeral would take place the next day.

When Miss Finn noticed me, she kissed my forehead. I could smell the lavender water she was wearing.

She touched my shoulder and I followed her into the room. We approached the bed where Helen was lying. I could not look.

"Steady," said Miss Finn.

I opened my eyes and kissed Helen's forehead the way Miss Finn had just kissed mine. When I kissed Helen I smelled seawater. When I straightened up I could smell the factory again.

Miss Finn wrapped surgical gauze around my mother's burning arms and blistering fingers and soon my mother looked like she was wearing mittens. No: mittens are too benign. Boxing gloves. White ones.

My mother never complained about the pain itself, though the fact was she cried the whole time without ever once drawing her gaze from Helen. My mother was weeping for Helen and for the hollow inside herself that once held Helen, not for her own scorched skin. She never said, but I know this as well as I know anything.

My father held a small glass of brandy to my mother's lips and, to my surprise, she drank it. Then he poured one for himself, though it was not yet nine o'clock in the morning. Experience tells me it is unlikely that the alcohol did a thing to them or for them, but I understand his trying to dull their pain.

My mother's weeping, muffled by the alcohol and who knows what else, became a low and constant moan. Anyone who has ever heard a foghorn would recognize the sound. My father's face, usually red from the heat of the cutting room, was pale; his eyes, always full of expression, were cloudy. The whites had turned pink. "Go help them," he said, motioning in the direction of the kitchen.

Sofia was chopping the ice block from our icebox into something resembling crushed ice, like Miss Finn told her to. Chips were flying everywhere, melting on contact with whatever they landed on. Mrs. Dowd was rolling the best of Sofia's efforts into clean kitchen towels, which she handed to me to bring into the bedroom. Miss Finn swaddled these towels around my mother's scalded arms.

"Take Sofia and find more ice," said Mrs. Dowd.

Grandma Paradissis looked up from her needlework when we walked in. "Aya, aya, aya," she said. Grandma Paradissis nodded rhythmically. "Aya, aya, aya," she kept saying, even when she returned her attention to her sewing. "Aya, aya, aya."

We returned with enough towels to shroud a mummy. This sounds childish, but it was true. Miss Finn was sitting with Mrs. Dowd at the kitchen table, charting the order in which families would donate their ice.

"They have to ice her until it doesn't hurt," Miss Finn was explaining.

"A couple of hours?" asked Mrs. Dowd.

"Days," said Miss Finn.

Miss Finn left it to Mrs. Dowd to figure out a schedule, deciding who would provide food, who would give up their ice, who would store food for the people with no ice left, and so on. She juggled and adjusted. She could have cleared Napoleon's way to Moscow, given the chance. Imagine what that would have done to the history.

"The Pessaras are not on the list," Miss Finn pointed out.

"If they're near food they'll eat it," said Mrs. Dowd.

"What about ice?"

"They'd eat that too."

All day women were coming and going, bringing food and ice and their own muted fears to the house. Mr. DeWitt slaughtered a couple of his older chickens kosher style and made potted chicken on his stove in the guardhouse, probably the only man on Barren Shoal who could cook. Come evening, the men from the processing plant joined the rest of the people assembled in the yard, talking in low tones, smoking cigarettes, eating dinners standing up from plates carried over by their wives.

Sofia never left my side. When I stepped out into the yard she stepped with me; when I went to the outhouse she stood beside the door. She found two forks so we could share the lamb stew her mother brought for dinner. I could not eat, but I remember the sharp, clean smell of cinnamon and cloves.

Noah walked back and forth, checking on my father, checking on me. Sometimes he huddled outside with Joey and Yorgos, the three of them sharing a cigarette, but he was always watchful. They were discussing something I could not hear, going at it with all the seriousness that looked right for the day.

A handful of Jewish men and boys, including people called over from Barren Island, assembled in the kitchen come sundown to say *Kaddish* with my father. There were not the ten Jewish men needed to form a *minyan*, but they said the prayer anyway. Noah, to my surprise, knew the words.

"Doing okay?" asked my father when the prayers were done. He placed a hand on my shoulder, then the back of my neck, then my head, like he was checking to make sure that all the parts of me were there.

No one went home after they ate, not even women nursing infants, and the place was filled by the din of people murmuring.

Mrs. Paradissis said I should get some sleep at their house.

"My babies stay in *my* house," cried my mother. "*Helen... Helen...*"

She wailed Helen's name as if our sister was as alive as Noah and me.

"Shhsssh, shhssh," said Mrs. Paradissis. She combed her fingers through my hair in a sweet and comforting way, as if I was the one wailing.

The offer to stay at their house was impossible anyway, what with Sofia sleeping on the living room floor and Grandma Paradissis on the couch. Only Yorgos had his own room. If the Paradissis men were the kings, Yorgos had become emperor when he announced his plans for college.

"Can Sofia stay with me instead?" I asked Mrs. Paradissis.

She gazed at me, thinking, thinking, thinking, I am sure, about what bad luck it could bring if Sofia slept in Helen's bed, the bed of a dead girl.

"Please?" I said. My sister was dead; I wanted what I wanted.

Mrs. Paradissis, however she came to it, must have decided that no curse would befall her if Sofia stayed.

"Okay, girls. Be sweet, girls. *Kalinihta.*"

" 'Night, Mommy."

"Goodnight, Mrs. Paradissis."

"Wait a second, girls," she said.

Maybe she was going to change her mind. Instead, she stood arranging a plate of kourabiedes, the same special-occasion cookies that had once gotten us into so much trouble. She wrapped a napkin around the plate, which she handed to me. She then poured two small cups of milk, which she passed to Sofia.

We climbed up the narrow stairs, sat on the floor, and leaned our backs against my bed. We could hear adult voices rising from the kitchen, directly below us.

"My father says tomorrow you go to Brooklyn," said Sofia. She might as well have said we were flying to Pluto, which was a real planet then, never mind this new hullabaloo over Pluto being a planet or something else. It is still Pluto, yes? It does not matter what the scientists call it; it is still there, circling the sun. Now, indeed, I digress.

I had not left Barren Shoal since Noah's bar mitzvah three years earlier. Sofia, since arriving from Greece, had never traveled any further than across the shallows to Barren Island.

"For the funeral," she explained.

I could not put the idea of Helen and a funeral together. And why should I have? Why expect me to understand?

"You're coming?" I asked.

"Just your family," she said. She got up to look out the window. We both heard voices below, but she cared more than I did. Or maybe all this grief was making her restless.

"What?" I asked.

"Some men," she said, "with wood. A coffin."

She sat down again and we ate all the kourabiedes, drank the milk, and agreed not to go downstairs to brush our teeth. The idea of saying goodnight again was unbearable, but I found myself hoping that Noah might come upstairs to check on us. He had never come up to our room in all the years Helen or I had slept there. Not once.

"I'm sleeping in your bed," announced Sofia.

I crossed to Helen's side of the room. I did not blame Sofia for not wanting to sleep there.

"I'm sleeping with you."

We had shared my bed any number of times, Helen usually staying upstairs with us in her own bed instead of crawling in with my folks like we wished she would.

I turned away when I got under the covers instead of turning toward Sofia into the better position for girls trading secrets in the dark.

Sofia turned on her side too, settling us like spoons. It was the first time anyone had done that with me. She pulled her arm tight around me. I buried my face against my arm and I cried.

CHAPTER 6

My parents' door was closed in the morning, Noah's room was empty, and there was no sign of the coffin other than the wrinkled pinewood shavings in the yard. The kitchen was still and in order, and on the table sat a cut glass vase—I did not recognize it, it must have come from someone else—filled with marigolds. Beside it were: a fresh-baked walnut coffee cake that still smelled warm; a bowl of purple-skinned plums, the size and shape of pullet eggs; Irish soda bread with raisins; and a shimmering dish of hand-cut marmalade. Knives, forks, and teaspoons had been set out too, positioned as if someone meant to assemble one of those beautiful old Dutch still-life paintings.

The better of my two dresses, freshly ironed, was hanging from the doorframe to Noah's room, as were trousers and a shirt for Noah. Our shoes had been polished and placed in a row, including Sofia's. The floor was immaculate; the broom was tucked between the icebox and the stove instead of in its usual place by the back door. It would be difficult to retrieve except for someone with longer arms than mine.

Sofia reached for a knife.

I placed my fingertips on the warm coffee cake. "Not for us."

"Why no..." She stopped herself. "Come." She led us across the narrow clamshell path between our houses. It was long past dawn; the sunlight reflecting off the water surrounding Barren Shoal was brighter than the rising sun itself. Mr. Paradissis was in the yard tending his beehives before going to the plant; Grandma Paradissis was curled over her needlework, a never-empty basket of socks and napkins and shirts that needed mending. Yorgos was who-knows-where, much to my relief.

Mrs. Paradissis was preparing cheese and tomato sandwiches. She had to be using a loaf of yesterday's bread because the kitchen did not smell of baking. This meant it was Wednesday, washday. A box of Ivory soap flakes was sitting on the table and a washtub was propped against a wall. Getting it ready for her mother was Sofia's chore, just the same as I did for mine.

"You girls sleep?" asked Mrs. Paradissis, her eyes never straying from her cutting board and knife.

"Yes, Mommy."

"Marta?" asked Mrs. Paradissis. She did not make eye contact with me either.

"Uh-huh," I said.

I had fallen off fast, Sofia's arm tucked around me and the arrhythmic banging of hammers drowning out the men's voices. Later in the night, when they had finished and it grew quiet, I woke again and again, afraid that if I moved, Sofia's arm would move too.

"Not enough sleep," said Mrs. Paradissis. That woman kept to herself, but she was something else I never gave her enough credit for. Maybe all the powers she believed in were true. "You eat?"

Now, of course, I realize that Mrs. Paradissis was conjugating the usual concerns about the simplest elements of survival. Sleep. Food. The only thing she did not ask about was the outhouse.

She buttered pieces of bread for us cut from the same, dwindling loaf that she was using for sandwiches. She served this with black tea and Mr. Paradissis' honey. What a glorious feeling that morning to have someone paying attention. Not that it changed anything; what was done was done. But still.

I cannot know how I would have felt had Sofia begun filling the washtub with boiling water and soap flakes when we finished the bread and tea. Maybe I would have found comfort in seeing the wooden scrub rack in the tub, Sofia or Mrs. Paradissis kneeling before it on a worn remnant of burgundy carpet, their backs rising and falling as they pumped their arms. Maybe there would have been solace in an indispensable routine. If I was the type, though I was not, I might have become hysterical. It is hard to describe: I felt everything and felt nothing, as if I could *see* what I was feeling without fully feeling it. There was no clear path for that first full day without Helen. There was only a new sense of how grief could be specific, of how my heart could be broken by an event that only bruised the hearts of others.

"I have seven brothers and sisters in Greece," said Mrs. Paradissis. She was packing up the tomato sandwiches in a cloth for Mr. Paradissis. "Athena, Demetria, Sofia, Christopher, Peter, Nikolas, and Yorgos." She pulled a cookie tin from a shelf over the sink. "My husband, he have seven too." She lined the tin with a sheet of wax paper and lay down on it a row of her *melomakarona*, the cinnamon sweet cakes even more special than her special-occasion-only kourabiedes. "In America, I have only Nikolas. My husband have two brothers in the Florida. Tarpon Springs." She drizzled honey onto the spoon-shaped cakes before giving them a final sprinkling of finely chopped nuts. "I never see others again. No more Greek allowed to America. America say no. I pray for them."

"Ma!" said Sofia.

"I see again in Heaven. You see Helen. You see again, too."

This was cold comfort. Mrs. Paradissis did not know that Jews did not put much stock in an afterlife. This did not mean that there was no heaven. It meant that what matters most is our life here on earth. And Helen was not in it.

"For your Brooklyn aunt," said Mrs. Paradissis, passing the now-full cookie tin to me. She was pretty formal about the way she handed it over. "Hold it careful and the cookies not break. And no tasting!"

It felt good being told what to do.

I held the tin carefully like Mrs. Paradissis said, as if a collision of cookies might bring more bad luck. Mrs. Paradissis' superstitions made no sense to me, but perhaps all explanations are equal when it comes to the inexplicable. Helen's death was all I needed in order to believe in the power of randomness.

Mrs. Paradissis padded back to the counter, her house slippers *shush-shushing* across the floor. She lifted the towel from her yellow ceramic mixing bowl and began punching down the bread dough that must have been rising since last night.

"Now go," she instructed. *Punch, punch.* Pause. *Punch.* Her eyes filled. Perhaps I was wrong. Perhaps Helen's death had broken Mrs. Paradissis' heart too. "Don't make them be looking for you," she said, her tear-filled gaze locked on the dough.

Barren Shoal took up a collection so Helen's coffin—and our family—would not have to cross to Brooklyn on a lousy garbage barge. Dimes and quarters, a couple of silver dollars too, went into a coffee tin just like the one that Helen had used for her shells. These coffee cans were the vaults of our local economy. No one had extra money. No one had bank accounts, which was not such a bad thing after all: the banks had crashed two years earlier and people with small savings had been wiped out, not that we knew anyone who had enough for a bank account to begin with.

People on Barren Shoal were well-versed in taking up collections: when Mr. Stavros was killed in that accident, the family moved to Astoria with the help of a coffee tin; when Mrs. Dowd came down with the influenza after giving birth to one of their eight, a collection paid for a wet nurse, a woman sent to the island by Miss Doctor Finn. And so on. People did not need to go looking for trouble when it had no trouble finding Barren Shoal.

Even so, not everyone contributed. Later on, Sofia would sometimes say something about someone who *should fend for themselves*.

"It's okay," I would say, "people had nothing. Not a dime to spare."

"But they had a nickel," she would say.

"Not even."

But, you know, I lied. People can always do something. If not a nickel then a bowl of plums. Even a small one. They can sweep a floor, iron a blouse, wash a dish. They can stay up all night building a coffin.

Some gave out of sympathy, but some gave in fear that one day they too would need that coffee tin. They were buying moral insurance, as if acts of generosity could erase prior or future transgressions. The day of Helen's funeral was not a time to ask if they helped for the right reasons, but even so I judge.

My father was helping my mother get ready when Sofia and I came home. He had somehow gotten her into her blue gabardine dress, which she had made elegant with the lace collar she had sewn for it, held in place by a snap in the back. Instead of sitting square on her shoulders like it was designed to, the collar was favoring one side. It made her look like she was falling over. My father's tie, which he always knotted precisely on the rare occasions he wore one, was bulging where it should have lain smooth. Seeing them like that...it was terrible. I lost hold of the cookie tin and everyone jumped.

"I ate next door," I explained as I picked it up. It was something to say.

"Bread and honey and tea," added Sofia. Her voice trembled.

Anyone would have been uncomfortable. The kitchen, the center of activity and the source of the good smells of my mother's cooking, was gloomy, as if the room was grieving too. The light was switched off and the chairs pushed flush against the table. A large wedge was gone from the coffee cake and a knife was resting in the empty triangle of space. None of the settings had been used.

"Where's Noah?" I asked. His outfit was no longer hanging from his door.

One of my mother's bandaged arms sprang outward, as if my question announced another tragedy. Her hand landed against her collarbone, taking with it the lace collar of her dress, which folded onto itself. But she did not speak.

"Out back with the boys," said my father, addressing my mother's new anguish more than my question. I knew this because he did not look at me. It was just like Mrs. Paradissis. No one could bear looking anyone else in the eye. If the eyes are truly the windows to the soul, then can we see the place where anguish is born? I think people are embarrassed when grief is doggedly naked.

My father lifted my mother's hand and led it back to her chest; he smoothed her collar.

"Please give the house key to your mother," he told Sofia.

I did not even know there was one.

"And thank her from us. Thank her for everything."

Sofia and Mrs. Paradissis were to remove food from the icebox that would spoil while we were gone. There were bowls and plates the neighbors brought the night before, enough food for a couple of days had we not been leaving for Brooklyn. Not a bit would go to waste if Sofia brought Joey, but the thought of Joey's filthy hands in our icebox made my stomach sting, the thought of him eating and leaving shells and skins behind. I know: on Barren Shoal death equaled opportunity. Dead horses, dead mules, dead husbands: every death meant that someone was guaranteed a job, that people would not starve. But not the death of child? No. Nothing. Not from Helen.

"Don't let Joey into the house," I begged Sofia.

"Why would I?" she asked.

"Just promise."

"It's time, girls," said my father, unaware of the gravity of the moment, of these promises between girls. "Quick," he said. "And get Noah."

Our things were in sad little carpetbags, the ones my mother used for socks and shirts and sheets that needed darning, stitching, new buttons. It sounds mawkish but bears repeating: everything about that house meant my mother's time.

Noah reached for the bags.

"Noah...?" I said. I did not even know what I wanted to ask.

"Hi, kid," he answered. These were quite possibly the first kind words he had ever said to me in my entire life.

My mother shuffled down the sandy road to the dock, the collar of her dress twisted again. Her bandaged hands lay folded across her dress, just like I imagined Helen's hands in her coffin. The sky was clear and the sun was rising easy. No mournful clouds. No shattering rain.

Noah followed behind my parents, flanked by Yorgos and Joey. Each had taken one of the carpetbags from him, carrying them on the outside so as not to bump him. Noah's hands were jammed into his pockets. Sofia and I brought up the rear, her fingers knitted with mine.

People stopped as we marched by, some of them stepping away from their chores to offer more condolences. Others stared at the ground. In their silence I saw a mix of compassion, fear, and pity. I could not make room for the possibility of anyone's indifference.

I locked my eyes on Noah's back as we walked by. He moved stiffly but with a rhythm that I recognized as the throbbing of our family tragedy. I wanted to bury my face in him. I paused for a moment to consider this, that Noah could actually be a source of comfort. Sofia, still holding my hand, pulled me forward.

Mr. Boyle was standing at the pier when we arrived. He was poking his finger at a boat captain's chest and the boatman was nodding his head at whatever Mr. Boyle was saying. Miss Finn was there too, wearing a black pleated skirt and black sweater. I drifted towards her, my steps turned about so that Sofia was now the one in tow.

"Marta," she said, holding out her hands as if to embrace me.

My father called me back. "Wait by your mother," he said, and stepped off to speak to Mr. Boyle, who kept checking his pocket watch, and the boatman, who was puffing busily at his cigarette and pinching his nostrils. He probably thought better of saying something about the smell.

Miss Finn followed us to my mother's side. She whispered something, her lips nearly touching my mother's ear, their heads nodding together, Miss Finn's hand massaging a circle on my mother's back. There is no need to imagine what she was saying.

Miss Finn rested the same hand on the crown of my head just before leading Sofia away. There was no time for a real good-bye. I raised my hand in a weak salute. I wanted to follow them to the schoolhouse. I wanted someone's hand gently rubbing my back, someone whispering in my ear. I wanted to also be the center of someone's concern.

I have compassion—and patience—for the girl who was me 69 years ago, for the girl who thought that Barren Shoal was the world, a whole big important world drowning in anguish. I want to pull that girl in my arms now and console her, this girl who did not know that the world would survive our family's suffering.

"This goes towards the arrangements, Eisenstein," said Mr. Boyle. He pressed some money on my father, a roll of dollars as tight as the boatman's cigarette, and shook my father's free hand.

My mother gasped, wheezing like someone who is tubercular. "Arrangements?" she cried. "What the hell do you mean by 'arrangements'?" These were the first words she had spoken since yesterday.

I swiveled on the balls of my feet. Noah was buffered between Yorgos and Joey, their heads bobbing up and down in serious agreement about something, like buoys on a windy day.

"Rachel!" my father gasped. My mother never used words like "hell," never mind speaking that way to my father's boss.

Imagine the deepening lines perpendicular to my father's mouth, his greying pallor, the way the living can appear less present than the dead. I have searched for the words to describe his shock and embarrassment at my mother's profanity. I have failed. I offer in their place the way my face turned red and my eyes filled. I am sorry that once again the history cites me, but that is what I have.

Mr. Boyle removed his hat and waved it in the direction of

the boat, as if he did not hear her, as if he was shooing away flies. His head was bald and unblemished except for some dull brown hair trimmed in a horseshoe around the crown. I had never before seen him without his hat, not that I had seen him that many times.

An incoming barge was blowing its horn for the small boat to pull out of its way.

"Get going," Mr. Boyle told my father and the boatman. He shoved his hands into his pockets. No more handshakes. No more nothing.

The small pine box holding Helen was set aboard by Mr. Paradissis and Yorgos. The captain covered it with a large, grey cloth. Mr. Paradissis knelt down to straighten the cloth over a bare corner.

My father guided my mother aboard. Joey and Yorgos handed our bags down to Noah, after which Noah did a second extraordinary thing that day: he lifted me so gracefully that we became dancers in a mourners' *pas de deux*.

My father stood by my mother's side in the aft of the boat. Noah approached the captain, who revved the engine. Joey released the clove hitch, coiled the rope, and tossed it into the bow. Nobody sat. I do not know why.

Seagulls were hovering and swooping, searching for a boat's usual promise of garbage and debris. The captain raised the throttle; the engine knocked. The gulls swept closer, their cries growing louder with disappointment. The engine knocked again as we picked up speed. The boat broke through the small waves created by the garbage barge as it passed. I did not see the swells coming. Noah grabbed my shoulders to stop me from falling.

"Hold on," he said. I grabbed his arms.

The boat was now far enough from the shallows for the captain to fully throttle up the engine. The fumes blasted away the stench of garbage; the spray off the bow was a thin shower of dirty needles. Barren Shoal should have looked smaller as we moved away, but at first it appeared larger. When I was on the island, I could only see one thing at a time: the factory, or the school, or our house, or the edge of the salt marsh. There was no way to see all of Barren Shoal as a whole. Now I could make out the dock and the smoke stack and the schoolhouse all at once; then our houses came into sight too and finally the beach at the eastern shore. At last I saw Barren Shoal in its entirety. At this very moment—when it reached this wholeness—the island ceased growing. It became smaller as the boat pulled further away, until, finally, it disappeared.

Uncle David met us at the Sheepshead Bay pier with a rabbi and a man from the cemetery. All three were dressed in dark jackets and dark ties, though it was still early in the day. After kissing my parents on both cheeks, Uncle David kissed my forehead like he was blessing me or checking for a fever. The other men shook hands, including Noah, who rocked a little in his shoes, as if he was still keeping steady on the boat. Aunt Sara, explained Uncle David, was making things ready at their apartment. We would go there to rest before it was time for the cemetery.

The captain called to a couple of men, who lifted Helen's coffin off the boat. It was so small that one of them could have done it, but I never saw anyone carry it alone. The rabbi stepped forward and raised the lid. Lid. It is too dull a word for something so singularly sad. My mother's face turned opaline grey, like Miss Finn's blouse. And then.

"Rachel," cried my father, bracing her face in his hands.

"Make him stop," I pleaded with Noah, meaning the rabbi. But how could I say that? What I wanted, of course, was for my mother to stop screaming.

People passing by stopped to see why. The boat captain

waved at them to move on.

"The rabbi wants to view the body before signing the certificate," explained the man from the cemetery. He turned to Noah and me. "If you want you can look."

I had not seen Helen since my father carried her from the water's edge and set her on my parents' bed. I understood how there was nothing left of Helen to be afraid of. This, I am certain, was what frightened me most.

"The city needs documents," added Noah, "to verify it's her."

"Who else could it be!"

"Do you want to see her?" he asked.

Noah approached the coffin alone. The rabbi said something to him. "Of course," said Noah. His voice was filled with new certainty. The rabbi made a gesture towards my parents. Noah nodded and returned to my side. He took my hand the way my parents would tell him to when we were little.

The rabbi raised the lid just enough to see inside.

My mother's wailing grew louder. Noah squeezed my hand harder; I squeezed back.

"Rachel," pleaded my father, "for God's sake, please..."

"For God's sake?" she wailed. "What more does God need?"

She started in the direction of the coffin, her bandaged hands raised above her head. My uncle and father rushed to either side of her, each grabbing a shoulder and cupping one of her elbows as her legs gave way. Her body was dropping, dropping, dropping, as if the power of muscles and bones was leaking out of her. My father and uncle raised her back up just before she hit the ground. She was sobbing the way people do when no one is watching, convulsing with absolute abandon. They carried her to the waiting car. Noah's collar was soaked with sweat. I leaned into him and he squeezed my hand harder.

Uncle David directed Noah and me into the front of the car with the cemetery man, Noah next to the window and me in the middle. Mrs. Paradissis' tin of melomakarona appeared on my lap.

The cemetery man steered the hearse past passenger cars, horse-drawn carts, and flatbed trucks from which men were cutting ice, bagging fruits, and shoveling coal. Women were pushing carriages down sidewalks, beating rugs with broomsticks, airing blankets over fire escapes, sweeping the stoops in front of storefronts and narrow, brick houses. There were shops selling plates and glasses, pots and pans. Next to these were shops selling sheets and towels, their overflow stock on tables outside on the sidewalk. Everywhere were men squatting on stoops, men crowding outside corner grocery stores, men leaning against every kind of building. There was a queue of men snaking around a church and other men were leaving the church eating sandwiches and green apples. There were men not working everywhere.

The building where my relatives lived was busy with children playing on the stoop and in the lobby, in the stairwells and in the hallways, making games out of wood boxes and jump ropes out of knotted cord. Despite all those children, the building had an old-people smell to it, the walls and floors and doors, I now know, releasing the scent of remembering.

The rabbi and the man from the funeral home announced they would come back for us in two hours. My father guided my mother up the steps to the second floor landing; my uncle and Noah carried up our carpetbags. I was clutching Mrs. Paradissis' cookie tin so tightly that the rim grooved lines in my skin. And Helen? No one said a word about the little coffin, or where it had been taken.

I expected my cousins would be waiting when we arrived,

but my Aunt Sara had sent cousin Ruthie to take Flat Sammy for a walk. My aunt led my mother into the bedroom to lie down; my uncle led the rest of us into the kitchen. A pound cake, still warm from the oven, was cooling on the table. Did this woman ever stop cooking? My uncle cut slices for Noah and me, served glasses of milk. He did not ask if we had eaten. I set Mrs. Paradissis' melomakarona next to my plate. For himself and my father, my uncle poured shots of Canadian whiskey. I looked at the clock; it was 10:00 a.m. "You kids eat in here," said my uncle. "Your father and I need to talk. Make the plans."

My mouth was already full of pound cake, but Noah did not touch his. An angry blush was rising up his neck.

"What?" I asked. Little bits of half-chewed cake flew from my mouth; I wiped my lips with the back of my hand. My uncle had not thought to give us napkins like my aunt certainly would have. It was a small omission but noticed.

"*You kids?*" he whisper-shouted.

"What's the matter with you?" I asked impatiently.

Helen was dead and Mom's arms were burned and Dad was drinking whiskey in the morning and now Noah was looking to pick a fight.

"I should be there too. Out there with them. Making plans."

My cousins, it turned out, were not coming back to the apartment before the funeral, which was to be held graveside. A friend of my aunt and uncle's, Mrs. Aryeh from the building—the same one whose husband took the family photo before my parents moved to Barren Shoal—was riding with them to the cemetery on the streetcar. Mr. Aryeh would be at the cemetery as well. There was only room in the funeral car—and barely that—for my parents and aunt and uncle and the rabbi. Noah and I sat on jump seats.

I was relieved to see cousin Ruthie and even Flat Sammy,

who greeted Noah and me with happy, sloppy hugs. Ruthie, almost eighteen, had grown so tall in the year since we had seen them. She had bobbed her long hair. She was beautiful. Sammy was still short and flat-topped. He seemed to be growing out instead of up; he had an ample, spreading center. He was holding hands with Uncle David's brother Sam, his namesake, who had come up by train from Philadelphia.

"Where is everyone?" I asked Ruth. I had assembled a whole congregation of people in my mind.

"There is no everyone," said Noah. "Last night on Barren Shoal: that's as much of a funeral as Helen's getting. All that's left is the burial."

Last night, all those people, all that food had been last night. Sofia sleeping over was only last night. And Helen: Helen was yesterday.

I stepped between my cousins so they could bookend me. Noah pulled me back.

I gave him one of those *Why?* looks.

"Later," he whispered.

Maybe Sammy and his faraway grin made him nervous. Maybe he was over-awed by Ruth's new beauty. Maybe the only reason he pulled back was because he wanted to. All I can do is guess.

The rabbi started the reading from his prayer book. My father and uncle read with him in what I thought, at the time, was Hebrew; the old prayers, it turned out, were said in Aramaic. My mother's face was still grey, like the headstones on either side of the newly dug up grave. She was no longer crying, nor was she was sedated like the men with their shots of whiskey. I do not know what she was.

The men continued saying Kaddish, even though there were not enough adults to form a minyan. Again.

"We include the Lord, Adonai, our God, in our number today," assured the rabbi. "And Sammy."

"Can he do that? Don't we always count God," I asked Noah, "if God's always here, if God's everywhere?" That was how it was supposed to work: we believed in God, and God was everywhere. What kind of everywhere? Here is what my dear Walker, rest his soul, used to say: if God exists, he is a war criminal. So tell me: was he wrong in thinking that?

"Not now, Marta," said Noah.

My father, my uncle, my uncle's brother, my brother, the rabbi, the funeral director, Mr. Aryeh, and the two gravediggers. If they included God, they got what they needed.

Then, as I now know always happens, professional mourners appeared from the broken paths between the gravestones. This is a job? Apparently so.

The mourners' prayer contains not a single word about death. No wonder the rabbi went ahead and counted God, since that is what the prayer is all about:

> Magnified and sanctified be His great name in the world
>> which He created according to His will.
> And may He establish His kingdom
> During your life and during your days, and during the life
>> of all the
> House of Israel, speedily and in the near future, and say
>> Amen.
> May there be abundant peace from heaven and life for us
>> and for all
> Israel, and say Amen.
> May he who makes peace in the heavens, make peace for
>> us and for
> All Israel, and say Amen.

It is a tricky business, this prayer and this translation, this business about what God makes in the heavens, versus what he *may* make on earth. Was the moment of Helen's death in that scalding tub of water God's choosing too? But the divine should bear no resemblance to the impulses of human will. After setting a world in motion, why would you make such a mess of your creation?

The rabbi filled the back side of shovel with dirt, emptied it into the grave, and handed the shovel to my father. My father shoveled and passed it to Noah, who shoveled and passed it to my uncle, who passed it to his brother Sam, who passed it to Mr. Aryeh, who must have come directly from the newspaper because he had his camera box with him. Mr. Aryeh then firmly handed it to Sammy, who grinned and swayed. The coffin was not yet fully buried.

My mother dropped to her knees. Fistful by fistful she filled the grave. She refused the shovel that Mr. Aryeh offered.

"Let the men finish," my father offered.

She ignored him, remaining on her knees. She was swaying and moaning, her body lonesomely trembling.

Everyone was crying now, including Sammy, who could barely know what he was crying for. Not that it made any difference, this being a loss that no one else understood any better than he did. What was there to understand? Some things do not deserve our understanding. Helen dying that awful way, in such agony, such a betrayal by life: that deserved nothing but outrage.

My mother threw endless, exhausted handfuls of dirt into the grave. It took forever; it took no time at all. We had all the time in the world; we had none. Sammy was soon rocking like my mother and humming like the men did in prayer and now my father was kneeling beside my mother, folding his arms around her waist, pressing his face into her back, his own back throbbing against the rhythm of their swaying. When the whole gaping hole had been filled, my mother pulled away from my father's grip, crawled over what she had done and lay down, pressing her mouth into the soil the way my father's face had been pressed into her back.

Some neighbors were already gathered in my aunt and uncle's apartment to prepare for our return. Mrs. Aryeh handed a pitcher to my aunt and she poured water over my parents' hands, still stained with dirt from the cemetery. My mother stared off into the somewhere of anywhere while my aunt used a muslin towel to whisk the dirt off her bandages. I can only imagine that my mother's burns were throbbing, yet she did not wince or say a word.

On a side table near the door was my aunt's prized possession, a small Limoges porcelain bowl. In it were hardboiled eggs. The bowl had scalloped edges, a gold rim, and a decorative spray of orchids on a bone-white background. My aunt had carried this bowl with her from Europe, much in the way that I had vigilantly carried the tin of melomakarona cookies all the way from Barren Shoal.

My father ate a hardboiled egg, according to custom. My mother refused.

"I can't, I won't," she moaned. She slid into an empty chair.

"Rachel," my father pleaded.

My father spoke my mother's name more times in those 36 hours than I ever heard him say it before or after all added up, as if repeating her name would call her back to him.

"Noooo," my mother moaned. She refused to eat the egg and the challah or take part in any of the other rituals of loss and symbols of ongoingness. She wanted nothing to do with any of it or any of us.

"Let me," offered my aunt. She guided my mother to the bedroom and closed the door. My mother's renewed wailing was soon penetrating through the walls. Everyone could hear her crying Helen's name.

I started for the bedroom, unable to stand the sound of my mother crying even a little, which always set me off too, not that she cried often. I would not be surprised if I had been crying along with her all morning without knowing it. I was just that way.

"You don't want to go in there, honey." The voice behind me belonged to my uncle, who might have been absolutely right from his perspective on things. From mine, of which he knew nothing, he was completely wrong. He won.

My uncle herded me back into the kitchen.

"There's bread, eggs, cheese, sprats if you want, in one of those cabinets are some cans. Milk's in the icebox and more pound cake. Mrs. Mendelssohn brought a noodle pudding, under that towel there, still warm. Mrs. Aryeh roasted chicken, you should have some. Ruthie, please take care of things. Sammy, keep away from those knives."

Ruthie, evidently, was to be stage manager of some after-tragedy eating frenzy, much in the way that Noah imagined himself running our lives when we returned to Barren Shoal. As if someone stepping in that way could change things.

I could not eat, would not eat, did not want to eat. I could not stand the crowded kitchen, the endless food, the closed doors. Noah ate some noodle pudding, picking the apricots out; Sammy wanted to set his aside too. "Like Noah," he said, because Noah was a 'regular' boy who was nice to him when other boys were not. Someone had put up a pot of coffee, which perked so long that it burned. I climbed out onto the fire escape for air. Like a terrace. There was no such thing as window guards, child guards, whatever they call them.

"No!" cried Sammy. "No, no, noooo!" I turned around and there was Sammy, leaning out the window, stabbing the air with his fork.

"Sammy!" yelled Noah. He grabbed Sammy from behind, bear-hugging him until he stopped writhing. Sammy dropped the fork, which fell the two flights to the street. Seconds later, Sammy was cuddling in Noah's arms, safe and newly contented.

"We'll all go to the roof when we're done eating," Ruthie told Sammy, which pacified him even further.

The roof looked exactly like it did in the family picture from the day my parents announced that they were moving to Barren Shoal. That was so many years earlier, but the view was unchanged. In the distant background of that old photo is the Brooklyn skyline, a scattering of wooden water tanks, and the upper floors of the Williamsburg Savings Bank downtown. Anyone seeing the picture—especially back in Europe—could be persuaded that this was the brilliant, insistent skyline of Manhattan.

Mr. Aryeh was there too, changed out of his work clothes and cleaning his pigeon coop. He was sweeping the coop with a straw broom, the bristles of which had worn unevenly, so that the lip of it cut to a slope, sort of like Mr. Paradissis' moustache. The temporarily emancipated pigeons were dipping and swooping over the nearby rooftops.

It took Mr. Aryeh time to work up to what he wanted to say. "Your sister died," he finally said matter-of-factly, addressing Noah.

"Me and her," my brother answered, pointing in my direction. "Her sister too."

"It'll be rough," said Mr. Aryeh, like he was giving an instruction and making a prediction all in one.

"One of my boys died." *Brush. Brush.* "Influenza."

Ruth took a seat at the furthest possible point on the

parapet wall. She had obviously heard this story before. Flat Sammy, meanwhile, busied himself with a toy truck someone had fashioned out of tin cans. The wheels, made from wine bottle corks, were loosely screwed into position and defiantly turned.

"A friend of ours, Joey, he lost his parents to the influenza..." said Noah to show he understood.

Sammy, still wheeling the tin can truck, sang the rhyme that children were singing all over:

> I had a little bird
> Its name was Enza
> Opened the window
> And in-fluenza.

"Cut it out," said Noah.

"*Awwww*," Sammy whimpered.

"Your friend's parents died last year?" asked Mr. Aryeh.

"When he was seven," explained Noah.

"Six," I corrected.

Noah shot me a cross look. He hated being corrected.

"After the war, over 600,000 people died in the U.S. from the Spanish Influenza," said Mr. Aryeh. "An epidemic. That's what they called it here. They say 20,000,000 people died all over the world. Maybe 40,000,000 by 1918, 1919. And that's just in the places they were counting. But die of influenza like our boy did? When the epidemic was long over? Ha! That was something special."

"My father's whole family died except Aunt Sara," said Noah.

"The world'll never get crazier than that," said Mr. Aryeh.

He stuck his arm out of the coop and offered Noah a cigarette.

"We thought our boy had a cold. Then he got the fever, the delirium. We're wiping him down with towels, wrapping him in ice. This goes on for a couple of days."

Mr. Aryeh stepped out of the coop, mopping his face with a handkerchief.

"We're up with him all night. He finally sleeps. We sleep. He never wakes up. And so, just like that, he's gone." He was leaning on the broomstick now and the pole was swaying beneath his weight. "I'm the lucky one: I go to work every day, I take my pictures, I talk to the people. My wife? All day in the house except when she takes in the sewing up on Carnegie Hill. 'Let's move, May,' I say to her. 'Let's go to The Bronx. The kids will make new friends. Better for the new baby when it's born. We can move near Mosholu Parkway, it's beautiful with all those trees. Do we have to stay in Boro Park forever?' Ahhh," he said in disgust, whipping his hand through the air.

He must have told this story a hundred times. I was embarrassed by this, for him needing to tell it so much that he was telling it to children.

Mr. Aryeh stepped back into the coop. He swept up the pile of bird droppings into a mop bucket and disappeared down the staircase into the building.

That night, when everyone was asleep, I was woken by what I was certain were pigeons cooing. Then Mr. Aryeh's voice, which I could also hear through the open windows. "Are you hungry? Do you want some water? Oh, I see: you want to go out on the town?" He was talking to them like they were people. It was the middle of the night. He sounded crazy.

I slid from my spot on the living room floor and padded past Noah and my cousins. Mrs. Paradissis' cookie tin was on the kitchen table and inside remained eight or nine melomakarona. I smelled the sticky honey from Mr. Paradissis' hives. I could smell their house and Mrs. Paradissis baking bread. I longed to be back on Barren Shoal with Sofia. And for Helen to be in our room. I ate a second cookie, then a third. I went on eating melomakarona until there were none.

CHAPTER 7

"Marta, wake up." My mother was on her knees, her elbows balanced on the floor next to my head. Her bandaged forearms were raised at an angle to her chest, her bandaged hands raised to her temples. Her breathing hummed across my skin. The smell of the disinfectant that Miss Finn had coated over her scalded arms sent stingers of information up my nostrils and the taste of something rotten down my throat.

"Mom?" I said. "Mom, I'm sleeping."

I licked my lips to moisten them and tasted the cookies that I had eaten in the middle of the night. The flavor of honey came alive when I circled my teeth with my tongue.

"Wake up," urged my mother. Her breath had a sourdough smell from hours and hours of crying. She had wept herself to sleep in my aunt and uncle's bedroom, by which point my aunt had fallen asleep as well. From my bed on the living room floor, I could hear my uncle telling my father to let the women stay that way for the night. It was my aunt, I imagine, who helped my mother out of her blue dress and into the nightgown she was now wearing, something ivory-colored, sleeveless, and unfamiliar.

I wiped my eyes with the heels of my hands, uncertain if the light through the living room windows was from a gas streetlight or from the new morning. Nights on Barren Shoal were so dark, but days were bright even when it rained. Every kind of light reflected more light off the water, even in the long winter hours of dusk.

"Come," she whispered. A conspiratorial tone threaded her voice and I sat up, ready to be included again. I would have done anything she asked to regain her attention, to restore our world, the one that in a single morning changed into an ancient, obsolete globe like the one in Miss Finn's classroom.

My mother rose quietly, her bandaged arms dangling at her sides. I tiptoed past my father, uncle, Noah, and Flat Sammy, all of whom were also sleeping on the floor. Ruth was on the couch, where she always slept; there had been no room to open Sammy's cot. The warmth of so many bodies filled the room with a smoky heat. Sammy, curled on his side, stirred as I passed. There was only a thin sheet over him, through which I could see the outline of his knees pulled to his chest and his hands balled into fists beneath his chin. Ruth had her face turned to the back of the couch, but my father, uncle, and Noah were all sleeping on their backs and snoring. I could also see through the sheet that Noah had an erection. I do not know if my mother saw this too or if she cared. I followed her to the kitchen.

"Get a pencil," she said. She pointed to the shelf where my aunt stored the small distractions she kept at hand for Sammy. "And a paper. I want you to write." The back glow from yet another streetlamp draped a corona around her face.

"I'm not very..."

"I'll go slow."

Why not wake Noah, who could certainly write faster than

me?

"Dear Momma and Daddy," she began. She exhaled, her breath full of ocean sounds, her windpipe filled with mucous from hours of crying.

My mother wrote letters to her parents in Zyrmuny every week describing the dailyness of our lives. *That's something to tell Grandma and Grandpa*, she said when Helen took her first steps. Or when Noah, reading *Hamlet* for the first time with Miss Finn, recited the Dane's soliloquy at dinner one night. Or when Sofia and I found a brown bottle on the sand with a piece of paper in it, just enough water having leaked through the wax corking to wash the inky message off the page. She would put all of those things in her letters.

Now, she looked at her useless hands, at the blank piece of paper, cleared her throat, and began again:

Dear Momma and Daddy,

Nothing in the world you ever told me or taught me or promised would happen prepared me for this moment when I have to write that our girl Helen died yesterday. What kind of world did God make that I have to tell you it couldn't have been more my fault if I had killed her with my own hands, the washtub sitting in the kitchen and my darling girl running and falling into the scalding water. If it wasn't a sin I would spare the others the shame of living with me, a murderer now, though I don't understand why that shame is worse than any other. Nor do I understand why Helen is dead and Sammy, this sad and pathetic drooling boy, is alive. Is that what this is about? God didn't manage to take all of Sammy when he wanted him, so he can't leave our Helen alone? How many lives does God need?

"That's all," said my mother. Some hair fell across her face when she looked up again. She brushed it aside by wiping her cheek against her shoulder, but the hair drifted down again, like strands of corn silk. I gathered it, looping it around her ear the way she would do for me. It was a strange feeling, touching her that way, taking care of her. But that is what it was.

"How should I sign it?" I asked.

"There's nothing to sign," she said.

"But *who*...?"

"It's not from anyone."

"Momma, who..."

"Tear it," she said.

"What about Grandma and Grandpa? What you wrote?"

"They can't read it," she sighed. "They don't know English."

My parents, after they immigrated to New York, never heard their own parents' voices again, just the way I never heard their voices again after they died. This will not happen to my children, who have so many versions of their father's voice on film and video. Mine, too. I think it is comforting to them, much in the way that I have spent these last two years sleeping in Walker's T-shirts because the scent of him lingers in the fibers.

"You write to them every week!"

"In Yiddish. Which you can't write. Now tear."

Noah would have refused. I just know.

"But the envelopes you send: I can read them."

She brought her elbow down hard on the kitchen table. "Enough questions. American mailmen don't read Yiddish. Tear."

I held out the pieces for her to see.

"Smaller," she said. "Again."

I shredded until the pile on the table was confetti.

"Take it downstairs to the trash barrel. Quick."

"Dad says I can't leave the apartment alone."

"And *I'm* telling you: go."

I do not begrudge the girl I was for having a grand sense of importance as I ran down those steps. I thought our tragedy made us exceptional. How could a child know that history is the world's story of human suffering? This is what Walker was referring to when he would say, please understand, that God is a war criminal.

There was an orderly row of garbage pails on the street, each one with the building number, 121, painted in black on the top and side. Somewhere a horse was clopping up another cobblestone street. My heart was thumping. I struggled to pull a lid from a pail. Something grey scratched up and over the rim. I jumped. How was it that for the second time in two days I was outdoors in my pajamas without shoes? Two days. If I did not sleep through the night, would it always be only two days? It is an equation I have tried again since to halt the progress of pain, even if I come up with the same, hopeless results. But why not try? Why set out a welcome mat for misery?

The smell of rotting trash in the barrel was dull compared to the stench of Barren Shoal. There was no smell of raw flesh. There was no smell of raw flesh burning. I dropped the shredded letter and dropped the lid.

The sound of the horse came closer, as did the *ping ping ping* of glass bottles. Then the horse itself came into sight, drawing a Sheffield Farms milk wagon. It was a simple draft horse, her shoulders wide from years of pulling. She had a chestnut-colored coat and blonde tail.

"Girl," the driver called to me. "What are you doing there?"

The draft horse came to a dead halt when the milkman spoke.

"Your folks know you're out here in your pajamas?"

I raced back inside without answering.

The door was open, the hallway light was on, but my mother was gone. I checked the kitchen. Empty. The door to my aunt and uncle's bedroom was closed. It was hard to believe that my mother had gone back to bed and left me.

My mother, it turned out, never went back to bed. Who can blame Aunt Sara for not noticing? No one even knew until Mr. Aryeh knocked on the door to say that my mother apparently spent the night on the roof with his pigeons. She was still up there. Uncle David woke my aunt; my aunt came to the living room to get my father.

"I could hear my pigeons through the open window, some big commotion upstairs," said Mr. Aryeh. "When I get up there, the door to the coop is wide open. Mrs. Eisenstein is sitting on the parapet wall, pigeons roosting on her head and her arms like she's one of those marble Italian statues. How she got their attention, I don't know. I didn't know what to do. I say I'll come down and get you. She says no; it's the middle of the night and you should sleep. So I offer her a cigarette to get her away from the ledge."

"She doesn't smoke," said my father. "She dis—"

"She does now," said Mr. Aryeh. "Or at least she did last night. But forget about the cigarettes. They're nothing. You got to keep her off the roof."

"Come on, Aryeh, did she bother your lousy pigeons?" asked Uncle David.

"It's not about pigeons, damn it. You people should keep an eye on her. There are things she said last night you don't tell people. You don't even think them."

"The woman just lost her baby, for God's sake. You don't think you'd say crazy things? You go nuts when one of your Homers doesn't come back!"

"Are you forgetting my boy?"

"Damn it, Aryeh. I didn't mean..."

"The children," cautioned Mr. Aryeh. I was the only one standing there. Ruthie had slipped out with Sammy for a walk. Noah had taken her place on the couch and was reading Uncle David's union paper.

"They don't need to hear..." said my father.

"What they need is a mother alive and in one piece," said Mr. Aryeh.

It was Mr. Aryeh's cigarettes that kept my mother from jumping off the roof that night. She and Mr. Aryeh evidently burned through the better part of the pack of Lucky Strikes while he told her all about the habits of English Trumpeters, Fantails, Jacobins, Pointers, and Tumblers. He recounted for her the heroic adventures of the Homers that had perched on her arms. When I say it was cigarettes that saved her, I mean Mr. Aryeh and his smoking habit. What one person calls coincidence another calls destiny, except it only looks like destiny after it happens. All that matters is that he was kind.

My father went upstairs to get her.

"I want to go home," my mother announced when they came back down. They were standing in the little entrance vestibule at the door, but we could hear them in the living room.

"Yom Kippur starts tomorrow night," said my father. "We should stay, be with the family."

I have no doubt she would have gotten up and gone had she been able to travel alone to Barren Shoal.

"You think I need to atone for killing Helen," she argued.

"There was an accident," he said. "A tragic accident. God knows the difference between misfortune and malice."

"What makes you so certain that God knows anything about this? About anything at all?"

"Let's take a walk," Uncle David said to Noah. "I need

some papers from the union hall."

"Me too?" I begged. I did not want to be alone with this. Things were already so awful. I did not want to be around if my parents were going to fight.

"You can help me," said my aunt.

"Why can't I go with them?"

"Because I asked you," she said.

My aunt motioned for me to follow her into the bedroom. She pointed for me to sit on the bed while she packed my parents' things in their carpetbag, starting with the blue dress that my mother wore yesterday, which was hanging in the closet.

"How are you holding up, my darling?" she asked me. My aunt called everyone darling.

"I'm all right," I said. I was sitting on my hands the way I had during Miss Finn's lesson on hygiene. I had been doing that a lot lately, at a loss for what else to do with them.

"Your mother is going to need you even more until her hands heal."

"Will it take long?"

"A couple of weeks, at least. Probably more." She folded my father's shirt, undershirt, and good trousers. She laid his tie neatly on top.

A couple of weeks is not an impossible amount of time in the overall scheme of things, but what could I have known about that?

"Then things will be okay?" I asked.

"*Okay*? *Okay*? What's 'okay,' Marta? No one knows what's going to be other than how it is right now. You'll go to school, Noah will go to school, your father will go back to work. That's the beginning of 'okay.' Your mother's hands will heal a little better every day. Then they'll be as 'okay' as they're going to get and that, my darling, is a life."

She did not say anything about Helen's role in this equation.

"Maybe we should stay with you until she's better."

She sat on the bed. "How many nights can you sleep on the floor, Marta?" she asked.

"Sofia does every night," I said.

"That was a rhetorical question. Do you know what this is? 'Rhetorical'?"

I shook my head.

"It's a question when you don't expect an answer."

"So why ask?"

"To make a point."

"Why not just make it?"

She pulled me close and kissed the top of my head. "You ask too many questions."

"I don't think so."

"You're trouble," she said, and kissed my head some more.

My aunt packed up every bit of food that could safely travel with us, from the rest of Mrs. Mendelssohn's noodle pudding to a whole chicken that she had roasted and which she expertly cut away from the bone. She filled Mrs. Paradissis' cookie tin with home made *mandelbrodt* for the holiday. "Wash out the tin good before you return it," she reminded me.

My uncle came back with Noah, both of them loaded down with packages they had stopped for on the way home. Noah was all worked up because my uncle had introduced him to a man who, it turned out, was waiting to tell my uncle about a meeting with Carlo Tresca, the labor leader, but who did not want to "talk with the boy around." Plans were underway to organize the factory where David worked.

My uncle took Noah and me aside. "Sara, please join us. You kids, you're good children. You need to be better than good until things settle down. It won't be so hard. I promise."

It was not clear what he was promising.

To Noah he handed a box around which a cord was tied into a handle. Noah himself had carried it upstairs.

"Go on, my darling," said my aunt.

Noah pulled aside one of the flaps. Beneath it was a radio, used, of course, but beautiful.

"You polish it up. It plays good. Real mahogany," said Uncle David.

"And you, young lady, are the beneficiary of my good fortune. Look at this: a genuine Kodak won in the New York Post contest. I played our house number, 121. Never won anything before in my whole darn life."

What did I know about cameras?

"Mr. Aryeh will give you some pointers," he added, reading my mind.

"They're not staying tonight," said my aunt. "Rachel's worn out. She needs to be home. Let them go easy, David."

My father still wanted to stay through Yom Kippur, anxious, no doubt, about being with my mother without my aunt or my uncle to help. Noah would have been glad to stay in Brooklyn forever, maybe become a regular at the union hall. He had been soaking up every word of Mr. Paradissis' *Daily Workers*. He was hungry for a piece of the action, as they call it.

And me? I wanted Helen to be alive instead of the tragic figure who would haunt us all of our lives the way Joey's dead parents haunted him. I wanted to get home to Barren Shoal as much as I never wanted to see Barren Shoal, or that washtub, or Helen's empty bed ever again.

CHAPTER 8

Joey was shoveling green, stringy matter into a transfer cart when our boat docked at Barren Shoal. The usual blue rag knotted around his brow kept the sweat from his eyes. He was clenching a cigarette in the corner of his mouth, as always, to camouflage the smell. A bunch of horses arrived along with smaller animals jumbled into who-knows-what-size lots. There could have been one dog; there could have been twenty. Scummy residue floated scrim-like on the surface of the oily water. Sofia was sitting on the mooring, still dressed for school. She was laughing.

The wind was low; the sickly burnt-caramel stench from the factory was startling. I tell people to think of a dead mouse beneath a radiator the first time the heat comes up for the winter. Surround by raw, unrefrigerated chicken that has been left out overnight. Multiply by a thousand, a million. Whatever it takes until it is the only smell that you smell. You will know.

"Hey!" I cried. My voice cracked. It was an unfamiliar, plaintive sound that caught me by surprise. Helen was dead; my mother was crazy with grief; the architecture of our family was collapsing. I was afraid that things would get worse because new troubles amplify the old, the same way that new joy intensifies the happiness that preceded it. I had already felt this as a child. Now, at 80 years, it is still true.

The captain put in at the moor and Mr. DeWitt emerged from the guardhouse. I stepped on the ledge of the boat and jumped. Sofia rose to steady me even though it was not much of a stretch and I made a solid landing. Noah leaped past us with the radio box in his hands. Mr. DeWitt lashed the boat to the mooring and the captain dropped our carpetbags onto the dock. He then helped my father, who half guided/half carried my mother to shore.

"We're almost home now," said my father.

My mother shrugged.

"Are you sure you can manage?"

She shrugged again and started off in the direction of home. She had not said a single word the entire trip over. The last thing she said to me was the night before, when she told me to shred her letter.

"I missed you," I told Sophia. I missed everyone. A new feeling. I missed how our lives had been only two days before.

Noah called Joey over to see his new radio. Joey kept shoveling, though he slowed down. Mr. Boyle approached them both.

"Save it for later, boys," he muttered through a big puff of cigar smoke. There was nothing harsh about the way he said this. He was just doing his job, which was to make sure that Joey did his. And so on. It was just that way.

Sofia smoothed the lines of her navy blue dress matter-of-factly. "I'll walk you," she offered.

"Help me with these," I asked.

We each lifted a carpetbag while my parents moved slowly through a gauntlet of men offering fresh words of condolence. Mr.

Boyle told them to get out of my parents' way. It was one thing for Joey to slow his shoveling. It was another thing for the plant to come to a halt, which is what Mr. Boyle told them.

Sofia and I were soon far ahead of my parents. The carpetbags were bumping against our legs. A seagull took a couple of passes to see if the carpetbags were something to eat. It flew so close I could hear its wings.

"I hate it," I said.

Sofia changed hands so that the carpetbag she was carrying was on the outside.

"It's a stupid seagull."

"Not that," I said.

"We'll be sad for a long time," she replied.

My father returned to the cutting room two days later. There was no such thing as personal leave from the factory. The only policy was No Work, No Pay. My mother had been holed up in their room since we returned, but I did not mind so much. I was afraid to see her. She did not emerge until the morning my father went back to work. When he asked if she wanted some bread and butter, she shrugged. When he asked if she was hungry for something else, she shook her head.

"Do you have a sore throat?" I chimed in. "Do you want some tea and honey?"

She dropped her gaze. She was looking at the floor. I looked at my father. He signaled for me to follow him outside.

"Give her time," said my father. "She'll come around."

"Why isn't she talking?" I whispered, as if my speaking in a normal voice would further upend things.

"Be patient. You'll see."

Noah right away rejoined the huddle with Yorgos and Joey.

The three of them now convened every night in his room to listen to his radio and read the *Daily Worker*, which Yorgos now carried around freely. The Spanish monarchy had fallen. People in Europe were choosing sides, what with the monarchists and the fascists, and the communists, and so on. All of their highfalutin ideas, crumbled into useless dogmas, were little more than excuses for another war.

When Noah was alone, he would let me listen with him. *That's Gus Hall speaking to the Wobblies at Union Square*, he would explain. *That's Walter Reuther addressing the autoworkers*, he would say. He played that thing for hours on end until my father finally complained about the price of electricity.

We learned about Hoovervilles, about German-American Bund meetings, about the Nazis strolling freely through the Yorkville section of Manhattan. Come the end of July we heard the speeches by the Bonus Marchers in Washington, who were trying to collect the cash they needed *now*, they said, *not in 1945 when the Great War pensions are due*. Who knew what life would look like in 1945, except more of the same?

"These are veterans," my brother said, "guys who saved Europe from the Kaiser. They're out of work. The farms are dry. They're starving."

I told him to save his speeches for Union Square.

"Shut up," he said.

"You shut up." Do all brothers and sisters have this same exact conversation? It might be one of the few things in the world that people can count on. "Roosevelt won't let them starve. He's the *president*."

I was not the first person, nor the oldest, to confuse Franklin D. Roosevelt with God, you should pardon me. Everyone, whole nations, were looking for saviors. People were pouring their faith into the hands of anyone who swore to deliver, whether it was

Franco, Stalin, Mussolini, Roosevelt, Hitler, Churchill, or that Emperor of Japan.

"Then why *are* people starving?" he said, disgusted.

"Mom says Mr. Roosevelt's keeping us alive."

"She sure didn't say that anytime recently."

I repeat: Our mother had spoken her final words when she asked me to throw away the letter to her parents. This is no exaggeration. *I'm telling you: go.* Those were her last words—to me, at least—for years. If Noah's radio was a voice without a body, my mother became a body without a voice. For four years she spoke through her scarred hands, inventing a sign language that the rest of us had to learn. I never stopped missing her voice the whole time. I missed Helen; I dreamt of my dead sister. Our mother was so consumed by grief that I do not think she saw that Noah and I were grieving too. May I repeat this as well: I missed everyone.

Noah tried filling the emptiness with other sounds. He memorized Abraham Lincoln's speeches while pacing the rows in the garden, reciting them aloud; he taught himself French from a book he got from Miss Finn and was soon calling everything by its French name, speaking sentences with a lot of English thrown in because no one could correct him. *Everything français, mon la soeur.* My privacy-loving brother would leave his French notebook out on the table, a reminder of how he was setting himself aside in a world that no one was invited to penetrate. *Quelle est l'heure de la marée haute?* he now asked, instead of asking in English about the tides. My father refused to respond when Noah spoke French, not that he understood what Noah was saying. Refusing to speak in our house was contagious. Who knows what my mother heard or did not hear or what she thought? I picked up phrases here and there from the ones he used over and over. *Laissez-moi tranquille Casse-toi! Ce n'est malheureusement pas possible. Ca ne me plait pas.* I never realized there are so many ways to say no.

French was easier than figuring out the unions, about which Yorgos and Noah were all gung-ho. They spent oh-so-many evenings debating the Trotskyites versus the Bolsheviks and the Socialists, the ones that elected women to their governing boards versus the ones that refused, or if the Anarchists were covertly supporting some group while threatening them in public. Noah made a chart of all the locals. He wrote his personal commentary in French on the facing page.

I began reading his union leaflets when he would go out, sneaking into his room uninvited. I confess, as well, to looking through his notebook, the one in French, though I barely understood what I was reading. Soon enough my mother caught me coming and going from Noah's room. She did not break her silence even for this.

Months passed. Noah tracked the shifting alliances of the unions and locals and devoutly revised his charts. In time, he swore, he would choose which union was best for Barren Shoal, as if all this was his decision to make.

I threw myself into my schoolwork until that year came to a close and then another, and when I finally pulled my head out of the sand that I was stuck in after Helen died, I was twelve, almost thirteen. Two years had passed, two years in which my mother only spoke through gestures. Her hands would quiver through the air, the purple burn marks and crocodile skin a prelude to whatever else she was trying to convey. Sometimes I dreamt of her speaking, the night-sound of her voice changing as the months passed. Then I would wake up in my attic room and it became harder to remember how she sounded at all. When I woke up one morning in pajamas soaked in blood I ran to Sofia, not my mother.

Sofia was asleep in her usual spot on the living room floor

between a couch and a low table. "I'm hemorrhaging!" I said, shaking her. Grandma Paradissis, who slept on the couch, poked out from her blankets, nodding and smiling her toothless grin, wagging her bony fingers at something only she could see.

"Come on," Sofia said. "Let's get you some rags."

It was my turn and Sofia, being Sofia, had made it easier for me by having gone first. We did not have to acknowledge what we both knew.

When we got me cleaned up, she made me drink some ouzo straight from the bottle to help my cramps, which, unlike Sofia's, hurt like the dickens. After, we slipped outside to get away from her grandmother's disapproving gaze.

"Typhoid, typhus, diphtheria, cholera…" Noah was outside with the boys reading aloud from a pamphlet he got from Uncle David's union. It was called "Diseases of the Working Poor."

Sofia and I plopped ourselves down to crush clamshells, though I missed as many as I hit.

"…yellow fever, malaria…"

"There's no malaria on Barren Shoal," said Yorgos.

"There are a zillion in the mud flats," said Noah.

"Not all mosquitoes are malaria," said Yorgos, correcting him.

"I'll be damned: it's Albert Schweitzer," said Noah.

"What did you call me?" said Yorgos.

"Water plus heat makes mosquitoes," chimed in Joey.

"Another genius," said Noah. "Humidity *hatches* mosquitoes. The larvae have to be there to…"

"Asshole," said Joey. He flicked his cigarette butt at Noah's feet, but it landed on Noah's shoe.

Noah cuffed Joey on the shoulder and they wrestled each other to the ground, rolling through Mrs. Paradissis' pole beans and tomatoes.

"Cut it out!" hollered Sofia.

Yorgos trampled a row of tomato stakes when he tried pulling them apart. "My mother'll go nuts if you mess up her garden. One crazy mother around here is enough for—"

"Shut up, Yorgos." Sofia was now standing in the vegetable patch, too.

Noah and Joey quit tumbling.

"Shut up yourself," said Yorgos, giving her a shove. I waited for him to smack her.

Noah and Joey brushed the dirt from their trousers.

"The point is this," said Noah, as if he and Joey had never laid a hand on one another. "The bosses know the science. They know the stink here won't kill you. But the stuff growing in the garbage will make you sick; the gasses that form in the trash become poison."

"If you eat that crap you can die," added Yorgos, his eyes now on Joey.

Sofia was still standing between the three of them.

"That's why you gotta know what you're doing," said Joey, as if Noah was confirming what Joey knew all along. "Those fucking scavengers eat anything."

"You eat any crap you get your hands on," said Yorgos.

"Go to hell," said Joey.

"That mystery stuff from the hospital and..."

"Quit saying that," said Joey. "There's no hospital stuff."

"You think they burn it all in the city?" asked Yorgos. "In their own incinerators? Burn all those arms and legs that got gangrene? You think the Rockefellers and Astors would put up with that stink?"

"What are you saying?" Joey barked. He grabbed Yorgos' wrist.

"I'm not saying anything," said Yorgos. He twisted Joey's

arm to hold him back. "I'm just making a point."

"And doing what the Rockefellers and Astors and all those others want, us fighting us instead of them."

"More *Daily Worker* crap," said Yorgos.

"Your father knows," said Noah. "Ask him how he likes the new fence."

Mr. Boyle had a gate built around the factory after Walter Reuther and his union started that job action in Detroit. There had been grumbling, too, about Robert Moses and who got hired to work on the Triborough Bridge construction site, never mind all those roads and parks he was building. There had even been a Negro riot in Harlem, more of them out of work than anyone and none of them getting what little was handed out.

Some of the Barren Shoal men, including Mr. Paradissis, went to Mr. Boyle to complain about the fence. *What if there is an accident, an explosion? What if we have to get out fast?* they had asked. *We put it in to protect you guys,* replied Mr. Boyle. *You get agitators in here and someone's gonna get hurt. They don't care about you. They just care about making a buck off a' union dues.*

Mr. Paradissis got drunk that night at the cutters' poker game and threw up on my father, who washed him down with a bucket of cold water and walked him home.

"Is your father in this too?" asked Joey. He had a feeling for my father, probably because my father was not the kind of guy who bullied losers. Or bullied anyone, for that matter.

There was no negotiating with Boyle over the gate. Someone had recently cut a cable at Ford's River Rouge plant in Dearborn and a chassis broke loose, crushing a worker who was attaching an axle. There was talk among blacks everywhere that it was the union that timed the accident so that a black man just up from North Carolina was the one killed. They said the union would not sacrifice a white man like that for the cause. At least that was the talk at the Wednesday night poker game for the Negro stokers, which Mr. DeWitt then reported to all the others on the nights that followed.

"My father has enough troubles keeping our family organized, never mind organizing a labor union," said Noah, obviously disappointed. "Plus, on top of that, he's still afraid of getting deported, you know—all that crap about Communism and Jews. You'd think Immigration agents were pounding down doors on Barren Shoal."

"The unions aren't all Communists," said Joey.

"Another astonishing observation from our resident genius!" cried Yorgos.

"You think we only talk about garbage at the plant?" said Joey. "Get a real job, you schoolboy, and you'll see."

That happened faster than anyone could have foreseen. Within weeks of them being installed, Mr. DeWitt wrecked his already arthritic wrist wrapping the chain around the new gates. The chain was made of 6-gage steel with a lock that was heavy as hell, though heaven knows a thinner chain and a lighter lock would have been strong enough. If Mr. Boyle found out about Mr. DeWitt's wrist, he might fire him and give the job to someone else. Mr. DeWitt—and his poker game—would be sent into exile.

Noah, to our surprise, volunteered to cover for Mr. DeWitt until his broken wrist healed. He had to slip into the factory before the gates closed for the evening and stay out of sight. He was there to do anything Mr. DeWitt could not. Before that he had just been angry—now he was alive.

"My uncle says he's gonna introduce me to Stanley Morrow, the union guy trying to organize the shirt factory," he told Yorgos and Joey.

Uncle David had stayed away from the unions when he first

started in the shirt factory. He had said it was no business of his to risk his job to fight over how things were done in America. Then the floor manager, the same Mr. Greene who paid my father to separate scraps when he arrived in New York, announced that on account of business being bad and getting worse, the men would work the usual six days but for five and a half days' pay. If they did not like it, Mr. Greene said, someone else would. As it turned out, my uncle did not like it one bit and started going to meetings. I do not know how Noah knew this; I never asked. But there were plenty of things about Noah I did not know.

"So we've got to figure out when we can get off-island to meet up with your uncle," said Yorgos.

"What's this 'we' business?" said Noah.

"What do you think? You're doing this alone? *We're* going to Brooklyn."

"And what am I supposed to tell my father? And DeWitt?"

"You're not telling anyone anything. Your uncle will keep quiet, for sure. He wants this, right? And your father: I'll let him know that it's time for his nice Jewish boy to go to New York and get a girl. He'll help DeWitt lock up for the night."

"Are you fucking crazy?" said Noah, laughing. "No way I'm telling my father about a whore."

Noah finessed permission from my father to leave Barren Shoal with a promise of staying the night at Joey's relatives' in Bensonhurst, not that Joey even knew where they lived. I can only imagine that, having his hands full with my mother, it was easier for my father to say yes. Yes. All of a sudden leaving Barren Shoal became easy, as if they had been going back and forth like that for years.

In return for getting to meet Stanley Morrow, Yorgos did in fact arrange for Noah to have sex with a woman in New York. The description of it in Noah's notebook, written in French, was remarkably brief. It took time for me to figure out, not so much because of the words he used, but because among other facts it contained a description of eating lemons. I knew the word *citron* and thought that Noah was describing a sexual technique not included in Miss Dr. Finn's book. Years later he explained that he sucked on lemons to get the taste of the prostitute out of his mouth. Not that it helped.

The boys came back from Brooklyn with the name Stanley Morrow on their tongues in every conversation. Uncle David knew Mr. Morrow from the union hall and Morrow said sure, he would come to Barren Shoal, to the horse heaps, if the boys could guarantee a safe place to meet and at least ten men at the meeting. A union minyan. Noah also brought back a stack of reading material that Uncle David collected from the IWW and CIO and AF of L and YCL and YSPL and the Amalgamated this and the International that. Some had the word "union" printed in English, Italian, Yiddish, Russian, German, Greek, and Chinese. All those languages on one. These must have been from the Wobblies, since "international" in the name did not always mean "integrated." The unions were full of bigots like everywhere else.

"Look at this," Noah said in amazement to no one in particular, which only meant my father or me since my mother was in their bedroom with the door closed, as always. She had not uttered a word yet in public. Not a single word. Before he had to leave that night to help Mr. DeWitt, Noah read aloud a leaflet from the ILGWU about a retreat in Ulster County sponsored by Local 22. "'*Swimming. Dancing. Lectures by David Dubinsky, Charles Zimmerman, Arturo Giovannitti. Separate housing for single men, families, and young ladies.*' Sounds swell."

"A bunch of Jews and an Italian," said my father with a mix of pride and fear. "Is that what you want from union dues? Foolish lectures and ridiculous parties?"

"Nothing wrong with clean air for a couple of days," said Noah, who knew so many ways to hurt my father. "Why is that hard to understand?"

"Lots of things are hard to understand, Noah. You going to Brooklyn and not showing up at Uncle David's when you promised. You and Joey fighting behind the house like a couple of palookas. You and Yorgos yelling and swearing at each other in front of the girls. Talking French. And that notebook you leave sitting around: *that's* hard to understand."

Noah folded the leaflet in half, in half again, and shoved it into his pocket. "It's no big deal between me and Joey. Or me and Yorgos. My only beef is with Barren Shoal."

"Maybe it is," said my father, "but it may turn out it's not. Maybe it's not your place at all."

"Do you have to make this so hard?" said Noah. He slammed outside; my father slipped into the bedroom.

Noah approached Miss Finn the next day after class, his face soft and his doe-brown eyes sincere. I went over to erase the blackboard so I could hear what he was saying. On the board were the remnants of that day's lessons, including the usual spelling exercise for the little kids and a civics lesson for us older ones, both based on the letters "WPA."

"...on a Saturday night, or maybe a Sunday, it won't interfere with school. You won't even be on the island so no one can hold you responsible."

"And if you get caught?" asked Miss Finn.

"We'll say we jimmied the lock."

"You've got to work smarter, Noah, so you don't have to lie," said Miss Finn. "The thing to do is put up a notice on the school door in advance announcing a lecture. You need to come up with a topic that is broad."

"Such as?"

"Such as you're going to have to figure that one out for yourself. But don't put up the announcement until Friday night, when the factory is closed."

"And you're gone," Noah pointed out.

"If you get caught and they know I helped you, I'll get fired. Which means I won't be here to help after, which is when you'll need me."

"You'll help?" said Noah, hoping, I'm sure, that she was ready to jump on the union bandwagon.

"It's best to keep me in reserve. When you make your sign, be certain to write the words *Everyone Welcome*. That way it won't look like you're meeting in secret. You tell them you thought this fellow Morrow worked for the Farm Administration or something like that. Better yet, ask this Mr. Morrow. He'll know what to do."

Getting ten men to attend a meeting was not so simple, but somehow Joey persuaded Massimo, Nick, and Vince to come, even if their mistreatment of Joey made the factory managers' pale by comparison. Joey and his brothers and Mr. Paradissis made five right there; Mr. Dowd made six plus Mr. Baldwin made seven, Mr. DeWitt made eight, Yorgos made nine, and one by one the list in Noah's notebook grew to twenty. My father said he would not go, what with my mother and all. No one held it against him. Tragedy had a way of drawing a protective circle around him. He gave Noah some coins anyway to buy a bottle for the men to share.

"You're not getting them drunk, Noah. Just a shot for each, a little blood warmer to set the tone. Ask your uncle about the brotherhood. It's a family."

"You'll reconsider coming tonight?" pressed Noah.

"You go for us all," said my father.

After, Noah made a point of telling me that I was not to come anywhere near the schoolhouse during the meeting. He told me I was not even to leave our house for a walk. If anyone came looking for him or Yorgos or Joey, I was to say they were learning how to plant better vegetable gardens.

"I'll have to tell them where you are."

"And you'll have to lie about the rest," he said.

I made a show of going to his room and switching on his radio. He followed me in.

"I'm telling you: stay home," he said again, and gathered his things, including the bottle of whiskey.

When he was gone for long enough to have walked all the way to the schoolhouse, I opened the French notebook that he always left out. A loose piece of paper fell out on which he had scribbled this in English:

DeWitt kisses my mouth before he sticks his prick in me. He rubs me down good after he pulls out. He says he would take me up his own ass but he can't. Not even if he gets all greased up. Too old. He works his mouth around my dick instead. He gets down on his knees while I sit back in his swivel chair. Sometimes I hold back. Make him work harder. When I'm done, he starts again.

After, he wipes down his chair with a rag. Wipes me off. Then he gives me something to eat, maybe potatoes from the coal fire. We talk about the plant, about school. Maybe people think it's wrong, but thinking is different than feeling. We talk about the unions. He talks about his wife and he gets all choked up. He says he can go to Brooklyn for a woman when he wants to. He says that has nothing to do with what's between him and me.

That is where Noah stopped and returned to the carefully written French that could be anyone speaking anywhere.

C'est la vie! Fantastique!

He should have thrown that piece of paper in the trash if he did not know enough French to write what he wanted to say.

I had heard the boys refer to their dicks more times than I care to remember, you should pardon me. It never mattered if Sofia and I were listening. I knew what kissing was and I knew about human reproduction because of Miss Finn's so-called hygiene lesson. The combination of sex and love and desire, however, was a mystery. Growing up is hard enough without other people making it hell, especially for people like Noah.

I slipped the piece of paper back into the notebook, returned the notebook to its spot on the floor, and went upstairs to my own room.

CHAPTER 9

Noah returned home from that first Barren Shoal organizing meeting so wound up and speaking so fast that the spit pooled in the corners of his mouth, giving him a mad-dog look. It was 10:00 p.m. and quiet the way it could get at night on Barren Shoal, when the sound of the tide reaching shore could be heard from anywhere. "Shssshh," I warned him, "you'll wake them." I still missed my parents' attention, even two years after Helen's death. But I no longer expected it to return.

My father and mother were in their bedroom, where my mother retreated after dinner each night and stayed until we left in the morning for school. I was at the kitchen table with a newspaper and a hand-drawn map of Central Asia, studying the Silk Route. A homemade bomb had exploded that week in Istanbul. The newspaper said it was the work of Armenians, though the article did not explain why. I understand now. No one on Barren Shoal owned an atlas, so Miss Finn had each of us copy what we needed from her book. Which explains how we ended up so muddle-headed about history and geography. How could we understand history if we did not know geography? I decided to add the Silk Route to our Odyssey Project, which Sofia and I still talked about even if we no longer cared enough to update our scrapbook. What still mattered was the idea.

Noah was pacing. "The men, Marta...," he sputtered. "You should have seen them. Completely amazing." It was all I could do to make sense of a few phrases here and there of what Noah was saying.

"You've never seen anything like it," he went on, moving about in fits and starts. His eyes were lit up like my own kids' eyes would get years later, when I knew they were smoking pot. Of course I knew.

"I would have seen it if you'd let me come." Not only had he left me out of the conversation, but he had ordered me away from the schoolhouse. Why was I supposed to care about a party I was not invited to? Noah did not even notice that I did not care.

He dropped into the chair. "Mr. Morrow laid out the steps for collective bargaining, which..."

"You always say that the workers should own the factories, not make deals with bosses."

"You've gotta be practical...."

"That's the word Dad uses when he's tired of saying 'no.'"

"Would you just listen, please? Everyone was passing the whiskey bottle, guys who never look each other, taking a shot, sending it on. Even Joey's brothers."

"You're excited about putting your lips on the same thing as the Pessaras?"

"It was symbolic. We're gonna be in this together, even the Pessaras." He wiped his mouth on his shirtsleeve.

"We're forming a local, just for Barren Shoal." He was poking his finger onto a picture of my newspaper, an image of a mansion on the eastern bank of the Bosporus. Talk about geography: such a thin bit of water dividing the continents.

Noah lifted the newspaper to look closer, which sent my map sailing. "Sorry about your drawing," he said, sighing pretend-exhaustion when he bent to pick it up.

"You don't have to be such a dope," I said. I smoothed out the map, even though it was not wrinkled.

"You want to hear about it or not?"

I shrugged. That did not stop him.

"Uncle David knows Mr. Morrow real well. He's the IWW man; he knew Eugene Debs!"

"What's he selling?" I do not know how or when I became so cynical, but there it was. I lived on an island where they burned dead horses. I was a girl whose little sister died in agony and whose mother refused to speak. What was I supposed to do? Walk with the faithful?

"It's about principles."

"Here's your principles: the police will move in, Dad will be fired, and Barren Shoal will still stink." I felt adult debating this business with Noah, like I was seeing into the future time when Noah and I were fully grown.

"We're allowed to join a union if we want. That's the law."

"What's this 'we' business?" This was the same question Noah put to Yorgos about going to Brooklyn. I loved throwing his words back in his face.

"It's not a trade union. Everyone's allowed in." Noah's still-changing voice cracked, which made him blush.

"They'll call you an 'agitator.' They'll never give you a job."

"I don't want a lousy job here."

"You're crazy, Noah."

He gave me one of those watch-what-you-say looks. He pulled a pamphlet from his pants pocket. "Listen up: '*By organizing industrially we are forming the structure of the new society within the shell of the old.'"*

"Says who?" I asked.

"Says the Industrial Workers of the World," he said, proudly. He slapped the pamphlet playfully on my head.

"Miss Finn says they're Communists." Or maybe it was Mrs. Paradissis. Noah had already declared himself a Trotskyite, a distinction which would not matter to the bosses any more than it mattered to me.

Noah did not bite at my feeble attempt at red baiting. "The bosses are gonna have to listen now."

"You sound like those *Daily Workers*. Which is a Communist paper, by the way, not Trotskyite." I was feeling pretty clever.

"I told you stay out of my room!" he shouted. Noah had not followed Mr. Paradissis' instructions to burn *The Daily Workers* after reading them. Maybe he should have been burning his notebook, too.

Our father stomped into the kitchen. "Nothing," said my father, slamming his hand on the table, "not one single thing is to happen in this house that disturbs your mother. No unions. No fighting. No nothing."

"Would you prefer we talk on the street?" Noah asked.

"There are no streets on Barren Shoal," I piped in.

"I'm counting on your common sense," said my father. "I can't always be here to stop your upsetting her."

"We're not always here, Dad," said Noah.

"Well you should be," my father replied. "She lost her baby, for heaven's sake."

"You think she has the monopoly on trouble?" said Noah. "The whole damn world is falling apart."

My father had never smacked any of us children before that night. One stiff word from him had always been enough to shame us. Noah's hand flew up in self-defense, his arm colliding with my father's arm on its way back down. They hung there for a moment, my father's color rising, Noah's face going white except for where my father's hand had made contact.

My father grabbed Noah's hand. I thought he was going to hit him again.

"Oh, God, Noah..." began my father.

"It's me, I shouldn't talk that way..."

My father kissed Noah on both cheeks, then on the forehead the way he did when he was blessing us.

"I never..." said my father.

"I promise, Dad," said Noah.

"Miss Finn says it's the worst thing that can happen to a person," I said when my father left the room.

"Getting smacked around by your father?"

"Children dying before their parents, you moron."

"*We're* alive, Marta."

"Shssshh!" I begged. "They'll hear you."

Noah now took Yorgos and Joey to the union hall in Brooklyn as often as they could get away. I tried imagining what the place looked like, but all I could picture was a movie palace, not the dingy storefront it turned out to be. The boys always met with Stanley Morrow, who was giving them a full-fledged education in labor movements and organizing. He lectured them; he read to them; and he introduced them around. The boys, and Barren Shoal, were on their way.

That did not mean much when Noah came home on the first morning barge a few weeks later to find my father at the dock waiting for him and me standing there waiting too, wanting to see what would happen. Noah had promised to ride the night barge back to Barren Shoal, but the boys had missed it. My father's angry concern, private as it was, was loud enough for anyone to listen.

"Morrow is using you boys. Can't you see that?"

"He's teaching us what we gotta know," said Noah.

"Your teacher here in school, Miss Finn: she ever give you any lessons about The Crusades? This Morrow fella is sending you boys on a children's crusade. You have no business doing what you're doing."

"We're not children," said Noah.

"Don't make me hurt you by telling the truth. This whole business is nothing but trouble."

"We don't have the money to get into trouble."

Noah was lucky my father did not hit him again.

"What kind of trouble takes money?" I asked Sofia that day after school. "I thought money keeps you out of it."

We were sitting in the low dunes on the far end of the island, having found a breeze that was upwind from the smokestack. Sofia was trimming my hair with a pair of scissors she had taken from Grandma Paradissis' sewing box. She was good about this task, which had formerly been my mother's. I was a pretty good sport about it too, considering that she was learning on the job.

"You are so slow, Marta."

I tugged some strands of dune grass out by their roots, strand by strand.

"Sit *straight*," she said as she cut. "They need money for girls."

The boys achieved a new status on Barren Shoal. Noah, my introverted brother, was now known by everyone. It was not as if he had been a stranger before, but now men would offer him cigarettes when they stopped to talk. People congregated in our yard after dinner. The boys were like squad mates on a small town high school baseball team and Mr. Morrow was the scout who came knocking on their doors. My father would not have liked this analogy. He might have enjoyed listening to a Giant's game every now and then or hearing about another home run by Hank Greenberg, but he thought that professional athletes were chuckleheads.

"Don't you think, Dad, that the workers need protection?" argued Noah.

"You could protect yourself better by not tom-catting around Brooklyn." My father did not go for the boys-will-be-boys attitude that Mr. Paradissis took towards their wandering.

"Look where you work every day. Look at how hard. How can you be so anti-union?"

"I'm pro-labor, Noah, but this is for adults to fight, not children."

"The men down at the plant can't be going back and forth to a union hall in Brooklyn the way we can. You're all tied down. We can move around."

"Joey Pessara has time for this? If he's not careful, he's gonna end up down a chute."

"Dad!"

"You think Boyle doesn't know? You think Boyle won't find out?"

"Morrow looks out for us, Dad. He gives us books, gets us dinner."

"That's wonderful: you can be bought for the price of a meal?"

"Do you notice anyone else giving Joey a regular meal?"

"You're the expert now on how families should conduct their private lives? That's fine, Mr. Big Shot: you go ahead and make sure those lousy brothers of Joey feed him. Then come back home and tell me about being a man."

That day, the rift between Noah and my father was blown

too wide to heal anytime soon. That meant Noah needed an ally, not that he found the idea of pulling me into his children's crusade all that appealing. But that is what happened.

He let me spend more time in his room, listening to the radio and reading pamphlets supplied by Mr. Morrow. He was practicing on me, I now know; a ready audience when there was no other. Maybe that was why he got nicer. Noah spent even more time with the boys. When my father was not at the factory, he was still always with my mother in their bedroom, the door closed. Heaven knows what went on in there. When we lost Helen, we lost everything. I know, I understand: we were not the only family to suffer that kind of loss. But why compare one family's tragedy to another's? Grief is not a horse race; everyone who suffers wears the crown.

No one asked any longer how I spent my time. I was still sleeping in the room I had shared with Helen, her empty bed inches from mine. Some things cannot be gotten used to. What was the purpose in that? I did not need to see that bed every day in order to remember Helen. I still think about her every day.

Sometimes I would doze off in front of Noah's radio and he would cover me with a blanket, tuck his pillow beneath my head, let me stay the night on his floor. We grew closer. Sofia, more than once, came looking for me on a weekend morning, only to go upstairs and find my room empty.

That spring, Noah and Yorgos also announced to our fathers that they were taking over the planting of the family gardens. The plan was to combine our yard and the Paradissis yard into one larger, better-planned patch and divide the labor. Joey would work it too, in return for food. The collective effort would result in a higher yield. The boys had learned about sustenance farming from watching newsreels with Stanley Morrow, who sometimes treated them to movies before the stinky trip home on a barge. In addition to seeing the feature film of the day, the boys saw those pro-business shorts by M-G-M and the pro-labor shorts from Warner Brothers, which included advice about home gardens. No matter how carefully Noah described them, I could not imagine what a movie really was until I finally saw one.

"Mr. Morrow says the M-G-M films are a bunch of propaganda," explained Noah, "but the Warner documentaries are full of great stuff. We just saw one about Upton Sinclair; he's running for governor of California." It turned out that this film about the writer-turned-politician was the one that gave the boys the idea of collectivizing the garden.

My father was pleased about the boys taking over the garden. He never wanted anything to do with it and my mother had lost the heart for it. Mr. Paradissis was glad to see the boys bending their brows to actual work, whatever the reason. I was excited at first about Noah's renewed interest. It seemed like a good sign. How could I know that his taking over would also mean him bossing me around? So much for his concern about the exploitation of the worker.

The first day out, the two fathers watched the three boys strip down to their undershirts, their new muscles burning in the sun. They put in zucchini and carrots, cucumbers and eggplants and peppers and potatoes and beans and tomatoes and radishes and half-a-dozen kinds of lettuces, including arugula, and escarole and broccoli rabe. There was an herb section, with basil, dill, parsley, oregano, and a bay leaf bush. In the back a few rows of corn stood like a hedge of soldiers. Noah drew a map showing Sofia and me where the Brussels sprouts and cabbages, squashes and garlic would come in the autumn. It was a beautiful map, with shadows giving dimension to Noah's precise renderings.

The only fruits that could grow in the sandy soil were strawberries and raspberries, so they put in some of those.

They enlisted Sofia and me to nurture an envelope of seeds into marigolds, which we planted to keep away bugs. The only things not collectivized were the chickens, Mr. Paradissis saying that it was one thing to share a garden, another thing altogether to look after living creatures. The truth was that Mrs. Paradissis talked to her chickens and I think Mr. Paradissis did not want other people to know. Not that other people did not talk to their chickens, too. But people talked to them about chicken concerns: how their eggs were laying or which one was pecking another, or while shooing them out of the way so the coop could be swept. Mrs. Paradissis spoke to the chickens about metaphysical things—if life was fate or life was chance; if God existed and whether it mattered—as if the cluckings of the chickens were a response. At least that was how Sofia translated the Greek.

The double garden, with the exception of the chicken coops, became the *de facto* union hall on Barren Shoal, the place where the men gathered every week. Now, on top of the old clamshell covered path, there were a couple of planks of wood resting on some old bricks, benches where the boys sat and rolled cigarettes and where the men from the factory collected after dinner. Yorgos and Noah would tell them about things they learned from the union pamphlets, the movies, and their visits to Brooklyn. What would have been intolerable had it taken place in the school house—two school boys lecturing a group of factory workers—became acceptable in the garden.

The only one who complained was Mossy Kennedy, the owner of the last remaining bar on Barren Island, where the men not playing poker would sometimes boat to after dinner. Mr. Morrow suggested that they arrange with Kennedy to send a boy over with a keg of beer. The men could bring their own glasses and the boy could collect nickels for each one he filled. This worked well enough for everyone in the warm weather, Kennedy selling beer without worrying about his place getting busted up by anti-union thugs and the men happy to be outdoors and drinking. Sofia and I were never included, of course, but we could listen from my bedroom window. Even if the men never got around to talking union, the boys always did when the others went home.

"The question is this," said Yorgos on one of those nights. "What do you want? Which is different than the question of what you will settle for, which is different than what you demand."

"We should start with what we need," said Noah.

"What who needs where?" asked Joey. "Which means what?" asked Yorgos at the same time.

CHAPTER 10

The expanded garden became a new way of tracking the passing weeks, each fruit and vegetable ready in its own singular time. Boston lettuces, parsnips, and radishes came up in late May of that warm, wet spring. Peas and beets and summer squashes were ready in June. I checked off each on Noah's harvest map as they came in, marveling at the accuracy of the triangles and circles and squares representing the approximate dates of their readiness. Then tiny sweet strawberries that we picked greedily, popping as many into our mouths as into the bowls we brought out for them. We did not care about swallowing sand with the strawberries. We imagined them with cream but were happy to have what we had. Everything thrived as it once did under our mothers, fertilized by ground-up fish, coffee grinds, and eggshells. Three kinds of small tomatoes shot up so quickly when the heat hit that we had to stake them overnight. There is nothing sweeter than a fresh, ripe tomato off the vine and we were impatient for as many as we could get.

"They take so long," I complained to Noah, when he confirmed that the best would not arrive until August.

He was sitting on one of the benches reading a newspaper that was two months old. School was out for the summer, which meant no Miss Finn, no *New York Times*. I was on my hands and knees weeding. Dune grass had found its way into everything, pushing up between the rows of carrots and parsley. It strangled the dill we did not get to fast enough. Sofia and Joey were tying tomato vines to new, taller stakes that Joey split from a piece of driftwood. Yorgos was stretched out on the other bench, his eyes closed, smoking.

"Next year we'll plant earlier," I added.

"Ground's too cold," said Noah.

"It could be a warm winter."

"Stop already about the tomatoes," said Noah. "You check the newspapers: when they tell you to plant, that's when you plant. Not a day sooner."

Noah and Yorgos, who were entering their final year of school, had pretty much lost interest in the day-to-day management of the garden as soon as they were done turning the soil and seeding. They covered up their boredom by setting me and Sofia to do most of the work. Talk about your exploitation of the masses.

"Look at this," came Noah's voice from behind his newspaper.

"What?" I asked as I tied another tomato plant to a stake.

"Not you. Yorgos. C'mere." He jiggled Yorgos' leg to get his attention. "You know about this? *The Civilian Conservation Corps*. The government's sending guys from all over—three million —to do clean up work, chop trees, clear trails. We could get jobs."

"How are you gonna chop trees when you won't even pull a weed?" asked Sofia.

"How about you shutting up," said Yorgos.

"How about not talking to me, Yorgos. Ever again. Ever."

"*Washington State*," continued Noah, "*Oregon, California.*

We could go to California."

"And do what?" asked Joey.

"Pick apples, split logs...."

"Lay tar on that new Pacific coast road," said Yorgos.

They were getting dreamy.

"What about the factory?" asked Joey.

"The hell with the factory. Come with us!" said Yorgos.

"Can't do that," said Joey, seriously.

"You got something better to do?" asked Yorgos. He lit another cigarette and flipped the still-lit match at Joey. Joey slapped at his pant leg where the match had hit and fizzled out.

"The factory, the house, my brothers," said Joey, as if he mattered as much to them as they mattered to him.

"You wanna work this shit job forever? The hell with them, Joey. And your brothers? You think they give a damn?"

"What about the three million guys ahead of us in line?" asked Joey. He drew a long line in the dirt with a tomato stake. Noah rubbed it out with his shoe.

"There's other places to live besides this stinking island," said Noah. "And better jobs than making glue."

"And people better than those stinking brothers of yours," added Yorgos.

"So you guys send me a postcard from Oregon."

That was some surprise. Joey, whose life on Barren Shoal was worse than any of ours, did not want to leave. I figured he would be glad to get away from such a hard place with a hard history. Maybe Joey knew better than us how tough it can be letting go. Leaving would mean having a real life after his parents' death. It would mean living somewhere they never lived. It would mean never again laying eyes on the last place he had seen them. For my mother it would mean a home without the bed that Helen slept in, without the stairs that she climbed up to our room. It was the same for Mrs. Aryeh, the wife of the photographer with the pigeons, who refused to leave Brooklyn after their son died of the influenza. She, too, could not give up the house where her son had lived. How could any of them give up the places that helped them to remember?

"You're a chicken shit, Joey," said Yorgos.

"Back off," said Sofia.

"Stay the hell out of this," he said, taking a short swing at her just to scare her.

"You want to spend the rest of your life eating rotten horses and tuberculosis-babies?" asked Yorgos.

Joey's fist on Yorgos' jaw made a crack I could hear across the yard. Sofia, surrounded by tomato plants, was shouting for them to stop and shouting at Noah to make them stop. Yorgos slammed Joey in the gut. They were spitting and cursing and kicking, though probably not for more than a minute. I have timed a minute on my wristwatch. It is very long time when it is a minute of something awful, never mind years of it, or centuries, or millennia.

"Noah!" screamed Sofia. "Do something."

"You guys," shouted Noah. "That's enough, guys." He grabbed each by a shoulder, but he was not strong enough to pry them apart.

Blood was running from Joey's lip and snot was leaking from his nose. Yorgos looked fine. "Get him cleaned up," he told Sofia.

"Wait out here," Sofia told me. "Grandma's sleeping."

I did not want to be left outside in the aftermath of the battle. I did not want to hear Noah and Yorgos going on about the Civilian Conservation Corps; I did not want to hear about them having a life off Barren Shoal, outside of Brooklyn, when I, like Helen, would not. I wanted to matter. I want to matter.

I pounded out of the garden, down the clamshell path and through the dune grass to the far side of the island. It was good to be alone watching the water. I have known people since, friends of Noah with waterfront property in Provincetown, who say that their depression is the by-product of always looking at the water's empty horizon. I find this improbable, what with the shifting tides and the intoxicating view of the sky, where one can see nothing and see everything all at once. But that is me. Who am I to tell someone what to feel?

Two feral cats darted in and out of the dune grass stalking the nesting plovers. One cat had the usual brown with black tiger markings and a broad, flat nose. The other, a light orange tabby, had a thicker neck, broader back, and white boot markings on its paws.

The gulls hovering overhead were making their busy gull cries, circling tighter and tighter over the cats. There was no lack of fish in the Jamaica Bay, but the gulls ate off the garbage piles anyway. I wondered if given the chance, the gulls would eat the cats. If they could eat from piles of dead horses, why not a cat? One gull was screaming louder than the others and it dove first, grazing the head of the tiger cat. The cat crouched deep into the dune grass and the gull took another pass. The orange tabby sprang up, swatting the air. A second seagull swooped down, diving into the sand and tumbling over. It was the first time I ever saw a seagull have a crash landing. Who can blame me for laughing? The gull recovered itself and hopped towards the cats, while the other gull went on screeching and diving.

The tiger shot out from the dune grass, in its mouth a tiny gull-chick, its black-pea eyes wide open and its little grey feet dangling. The gull on the ground was flapping its wings and screaming. The other gull, still airborne, circled lower and landed, but the cats were already gone.

Our house was dark when I got home. I checked in the yard to see if the boys were still there or if Sofia had returned. The only sign of them was a clamshell ashtray filled with cigarette butts.

My mother was seated in the kitchen, staring at her knees. On the table was a butcher's knife, a cutting board, and a bowl of onions.

"Hi, Mom," I said quietly. It never felt good to see her. This is a terrible thing to say, but it is true.

I switched on a small lamp on the other side of the room. My mother nodded, looking as if anything more than that small gesture would cause her pain. My once hugging, cuddling mother could not even touch me.

I sat down where I did not have to face her and slid the cutting board to my side of the table. I slit the tips off the onions, peeled back their brass skins, and chopped them into uniform pieces that would disappear into whatever we cooked them with. I ignored the streams of onion-tears on my cheeks and worked through three pounds of them. My father arrived from work to find the table covered with onions and me covered in tears, my mother staring at her knees, and the house dark but for that one small lamp.

"I got—*we* got news from Jacob today," he said, holding out a postcard. Jacob was my mother's eldest brother, the last one still in Zyrmuny, which was in Russia then. Or maybe it was still in Poland. It was impossible to keep track of the land deals being cut between the Kremlin and the Reichstag.

My mother went on staring at her knees.

"We've got to get them out of there. We've got to see about getting them papers."

No reply.

I rested my hands in my lap, knife and all.

"Rachel!" he said. "Listen to me."

He read the card aloud in Yiddish. He read the card again, this time translating it into English: *For God's sake, please, help us.*

My mother was crying now. And what did I do? Cry real tears instead of onion-tears. Does someone else's anguish become yours when you cannot help them? Better yet: when they cannot help themselves? If not your anguish, then what? It should become something, but what?

My father was on his knees, his head buried in my mother's lap, her fingers stroking the back of his neck. The card from Uncle Jacob fell from my father's hand. I picked it up and wiped it on my sleeve.

"Take Marta. Go to HIAS tomorrow," said my mother. With one of her scarred hands she rubbed his back. *Take Marta.* The first words I heard her speak in years. My father showed no surprise. She must have been speaking to him all along behind closed doors. I was angry. What about my anguish? What about my grief over losing Helen, about these last years I spent unmothered?

"That's no place for the girl," said my father. "People pushing and babies crying, like animals shoved in a barn." He had already been there time and again. After the Quota Laws, the closest that people could hope for was entry into Canada or South America, but they would have been better than Zyrgmuny. At least for now. My parents only made it through because they did it on someone else's papers. They lied. Thank goodness.

My mother swept half the mound of chopped onions into an onion soup for dinner that night, setting aside the other half for a split pea soup that she cooked later that evening. She did not speak again while doing either, but she was present in a way she had not been for so long. I wanted to ask her things, but did not. I no longer knew how. Why would I, when for so many years there had been no answer?

Come mid-week my father announced that I would ride a scow with him to Brooklyn on Saturday after his half-day shift was done, if you call working for six hours a half-day.

"What about *Tosca*?" I asked. *Tosca* was scheduled for the radio broadcast on Saturday live from the Met. I had not yet wrapped my mind around the urgency of our chore. It was hard to grasp the whole meaning of the new terror. Maybe that is why my mother wanted me to go with him. Or maybe, simply, she did not want him to be alone. How could anyone face any of this alone?

"There will be other *Toscas*," he said. The weekend before we had listened to *Tristan und Isolde*, which was not the last we would hear about Wagner in the months to come. Now I cannot bring myself to listen to Wagner. It is not just that Wagner was an anti-Semite: his music was the soundtrack for the Third Reich. I cannot worry anymore whether or not I am being fair minded about this. If Wagner is so important, let someone else listen.

"Don't you think I should stay with Momma?" Not that I wanted to be alone with my mother. But I was unsettled by the prospect of leaving Barren Shoal for the first time since Helen's funeral.

"Noah will keep an eye on things."

My mother had not done anything really crazy since that night Mr. Aryeh found her on the edge of the roof in Brooklyn. She had not done much of anything beyond cooking and staring at her knees. Mrs. Paradissis acted nutty too, spending more and more time talking to her chickens while Mr. Paradissis spent more and more time talking union. That felt different. My mother could not recover from her tragedy. But does anyone have a life spared of tragedy?

I did not tell Sofia that I was going with my father to Brooklyn or that my mother had started speaking. I was still angry that she had shooed me away when she cleaned Joey up after the fight. Silence is a meek form of vengeance, but revenge—like charity—functions best unannounced.

Sofia and I worked in the yard that morning pulling lettuces, staking string beans, hoeing soil, and feeding tomatoes. She must have assumed that afterwards I would be eating a late lunch with my father and listening to the opera, like we always did. Instead I changed into a blue skirt and a white blouse with a scalloped collar, hand-me-downs from Marie Dowd that she had gotten hand-me-downed from cousins in Brooklyn who went to Catholic school. Chances were that Sofia would see my father and me walking to the docks, but as chance had it she did not.

My father arranged for us to a ride on an empty garbage scow returning to Brooklyn, empty being an imprecise description for its condition. There was a shallow pool of fluid at the bottom that could not be gotten rid of without clearing the muck clogging the scuppers. From time to time someone powdered the barges with calcinated lime, which cut the stench, but that was rare.

The bargeman pointed out a small platform near the aft where we were could sit during the crossing. Some scavengers, who had been sitting on the pilings and waiting to ride the barge too, climbed on with us. Over time, I had forgotten about the girl in the brown dress but there she was, wearing a different brown dress and not that much taller than when I last saw her. I wonder if she stayed short because malnutrition. Or maybe she was just short. But Sofia and I had added inches. The bargeman directed the scavengers to the opposite end of the barge where the girl sat down and fell asleep.

Where my father and I sat were a couple of old, chewed up baseball bats. My father took one in his hands and banged the board beneath our feet. A rat darted out from somewhere, looked at the bat, looked at my father, and scurried past our feet and down the wall of the ship's hold. I grabbed the other bat and started pounding.

"You don't have to bang like that," said my father.

I shrugged one of those *I hear what you're saying but I'm going to do it anyway* looks.

"Suit yourself," he said. My father banged his bat a couple of times to emphasize his point and kept on banging the whole time we were crossing. The rats went on gorging themselves on maggot-covered scrap, but they stayed away from us. After a while, once he got his rhythm, my father ate one of the sandwiches that my mother had packed for us. I could no more eat on a garbage scow surrounded by the rats and horse guts than I could have eaten a rat itself. My father ate my sandwich too and I kept on banging.

A man with a cart rode us from the dock in Sheepshead Bay to a subway that milk-stopped its way to Manhattan. My father pointed out the sights when we climbed up from the subway. "Cooper Union," he said, indicating the large, sandstone building in front of us. "Abraham Lincoln spoke there when he was running for president. And Frederick Douglass, the black abolitionist who met with Lincoln at the White House. And Mark Twain, the writer. I bet you've read *Tom Sawyer*." I had not.

"They were Jewish?"

"You think I only know about Jews?"

I did not answer.

"Cooper Union is where smart, gentile boys study engineering and architecture. Jewish boys go to City College, also free. Over there, across the street, is the Carl Fischer Building. You see the name painted on the side? That's where all the orchestras in America get their sheet music. On the other side of the square is Wanamaker's, the department store, very fancy. They sell the shirts from Uncle David's factory.

"You think only Robert Moses builds New York? Turn this way," he said, guiding me by the shoulders.

"The Empire State Building!" I gasped.

"A little closer to us and to the right, a little shorter, that's the Chrysler Building. You can't see from here, but it's got gargoyles made of chrome, just like the bumpers on the cars.

"Over there, on Lafayette Street, that's where we're going. John Jacob Astor—one of the richest men ever in America—that was his library, the first in New York. He paid for the whole thing. From selling animal furs and buying real estate. That's how Andrew Carnegie, another big rich man, got the idea to build small libraries all over the city. Any town in America could get one built for free if they promised to keep it going. Another war profiteer. And another group of muckety-mucks got together and built the big one at 42nd St."

How did he know so much? While Mr. Paradissis was reading *The Daily Worker*—or having it read to him in English—my father was reading *The Daily Forward* in Yiddish. Mr. Paradissis knew a lot about labor struggles; my father knew a little about a lot of other things.

A hundred or so yards away was the HIAS building, three stories tall, built of terracotta-colored sandstone. It was a stately building with muscular arches and lead-paned windows. Surrounding the entry—the stairs to the raised lobby were inside—was a crowd of people reading newspapers, cradling babies, and talking in a jumble of languages. The sidewalk was littered with cigarette butts and paper stubs. A woman dressed in black was leaning against the building, crying; the little girl clinging to the folds of her skirt was crying too at the same time as she was looking around, her crying not an obstacle to watching the comings and goings. The voices blended into a single, monotonous hum. Here and there a phrase in English cracked through. I did not understand most of what they were saying, but it was easy enough to know the fear in their voices, the desperation in their eyes.

"Hebrew Immigrant Aid Society," said my father.

"The government?"

"Forget the government. It's a private organization that assists people. We need the right papers for the family to get to out of Zyrmuny. Here they help you make the right papers. When the people get to Canada or South America, they maybe help you get a job, find relatives, teach you English. They used to help people get settled in America before the Immigration Act, before America said *No more*."

My father got in line.

"Over there," he said, motioning toward a bench where a couple of old women were sitting, their old-woman thighs spread wide past their hips. "Take this," he said, handing me the satchel with our overnight things.

"Momma said stay with you," I complained.

"You are with me."

"All the way over there?" I said, pointing to the two old ladies. They looked like sacks of onion, their skin loose and spilling over.

"Don't be silly," said my father. When would people stop saying my worries or fears were silly? Oh boy, was I ever glad to become an adult and leave that nonsense behind.

The line inched slowly or hardly at all, people shifting forward out of restlessness until each newcomer was bunched in closely with the others. The room was filled with body smells, warm and salty and sour, and even as I grew sleepy I kept an eye out for my father's head in the crowd. Who-knows-how-much-later I woke to find my head propped against one of the old onion ladies. She was sleeping too, whistling through her lips. Her breath smelled like old plants rotting in still water. It is the smell, I now know, of decaying teeth. I raised my hand to cover my nose. The lady shifted when I moved and I caught a whiff of urine, too. How old was that woman? Younger than I am turning today, I am saying not for nothing.

A man wearing a white shirt and dark tie came out from behind the counter. On one foot was a stacked shoe meant to even out his short leg with the longer one. He limped down the line, his hip thrusting to the left with each step. "Numbers?" he asked. "You got numbers?"

He handed my father a piece of paper with a number.

"What do I do with this?"

"You wait until we call your number."

"I never got one of these before," said my father. I do not know how many times before he had been to HIAS. Enough times, no doubt, to wonder why he kept going. Or maybe, knowing my father, he could not afford that kind of thought. Giving up on the family in Europe would have been like giving up on my mother, which he did not.

"You got one now," said the man.

"They call me today?" my father pressed.

"How should I know?" said the man, limping off. "You been here before? You ever see so many people?"

We had no luck at HIAS that day, unless one thinks that getting a number that might or might not ever get called is good luck.

On the street, a man in a jacket and tie approached my father.

"Sir," he began. My father acknowledged him, the combination of the suit and the formal salutation stopping him in his tracks. This man was a number broker, a business created by the new system.

"You give me your number and I give you a receipt. When

you come back you come to me for a number. Not your old number, of course. You get the lowest number I have."

Was this free? Of course not. Was it legal? Who knows. Was it fair? With all due respect: if we are asking what is fair in life, there are some questions that interest me more than those numbers. Was Helen dying fair? Was Flat Sammy's head fair? Even stupid, disgusting Joey Pessara: was his life fair?

It was too late now to make a boat to Barren Shoal. We made our way instead to Boro Park among shoppers filling the subway car with bags of garlic and chickens and cheese. The subway car filled itself with the *whuffle whuffle* sound of open windows and the big-mouth argument of steel wheels against steel tracks.

A block from my aunt and uncle's place we ran into Uncle David, who was walking slowly.

"Look at you," he beamed, tousling my hair. "Wait just a second: I shouldn't mess a young lady's hair," he continued, making a big show of smoothing it back into place. I had not seen my uncle since the day after Helen's funeral. Not even for an unveiling, which neither Noah nor I were permitted to attend. My uncle's own hair was grey now; his skin had turned grey, too.

"How did it go?" he asked, resting a hand on my father's shoulder. He looked tired.

"Nothing but a long line," said my father.

"Come with me to this union meeting," he said. "Norman Thomas is speaking."

"I should probably...," my father started to say, indicating something about me.

"You should probably nothing. What you should do is come."

"Me too," I begged. I knew about Norman Thomas from Noah. Noah would be crazy jealous. To meet Norman Thomas: that would be something. Later on I even voted for him for president a couple of times. Better than that hypocrite Jimmy Carter, not when there was genocide in Cambodia and he ignored it. I would still appreciate an apology from him.

"You stay with your aunt and your cousins," instructed my father. "What do you know about Norman Thomas anyway?"

"That he ran for president. That he lost but got a lot of votes. That he's a socialist. That he's famous for..."

"Whoah, whoah, slow down," said my father.

My father and uncle delivered me to my aunt and then they took off for the union hall. My cousin Ruthie was out with her new boyfriend Sidney, who was taking her to a JCC dance; Flat Sammy was in the kitchen, where my aunt was teaching him to braid challah dough.

"Here you go, Sammy: you remember your cousin Marta," she prompted.

"Yes," he answered, shaking his head to say *no*. Older did not look better on Sammy the way it did on Noah and the boys. His body had gone from bad to worse, his damaged brain misfiring signals that contorted his movements more than I remembered.

"Marta will help us bake?" she asked.

"Yes," he said again, this time nodding approval.

My aunt handed me a mound of dough and told me to break it in three equal pieces, roll out the little logs like the ones in front of Sammy, and pinch them together. She guided Sammy's fingers and I followed a half step behind.

"You remember this from last time?" she asked Sammy, laying the clean back of her hand against the flat of his head.

"Yes," he said, nodding like crazy.

Sammy, once he got going, handled the dough smoothly without breaking the rhythm. We became a little assembly line around the table, making a couple of large challahs as well as a bunch of small ones. My aunt, meanwhile, turned her attention —at least some of it—to plucking a roasting chicken, singeing stubborn feathers with a wooden match.

"Be gentle with that dough, children," she cautioned. "If you overwork it, the bread will be like a sponge." Even Sammy giggled at the irony of this suggestion of gentleness as she yanked feathers out of the bird. At least I think that is why he was giggling. When we finished our loaves she checked our handiwork. I imagined Sammy working some day in a bakery, sliding dough into big brick ovens, sliding hot loaves of bread back out. He would have a job, have co-workers, have a life. He could wear white trousers and a white shirt and a white paper hat. And what would I have? Just Barren Shoal, just more of the same. I was not feeling sorry for myself; I was not full of self-pity. I was trying to understand what growing up there would finally mean for me.

"Now, the finishing touch. Marta, you break this egg in the bowl. Sammy, you beat it around with this fork. Take turns painting the egg on the outside of your challah dough with this brush." She handed me a pastry feather.

"This is the chicken's feather," said Sammy in a worried voice. He had forgotten that he had used this feather the week before and the week before that.

"No," my aunt assured him. "See how big your feather is and how this chicken's feathers are small?"

"What about the egg?"

My aunt held dinner for as long as she could until she announced, "I'm going to give those men a what-for when they march in here."

"What for?" asked Sammy.

"A what-for is...never mind," said my aunt. She prepared plates for the three of us: white meat for Sammy, dark meat for me, a little of both for her, and roasted potatoes with crisped edges, and boiled string beans. The rest she left on a plate that she covered with a kitchen towel to keep away flies.

"What about Ruthie?" I asked.

"She's having dinner with the family of her young man."

"Sidney," said Sammy.

"That's right, Sammy. His name is Sidney."

"I like Sidney."

"I'm sure he likes you, too."

Sammy was already asleep and I was half-trying to read *Hamlet* for school when my father and uncle returned. We were destined to read *Hamlet* every year now because a carton with twenty badly beaten copies had been salvaged for the school by a friend of Miss Dr. Finn who taught at Canarsie High School, one of the good schools over in Brooklyn.

"So?" asked my aunt, her voice all filled with warm expectation. "Tell."

What happened to her telling them off? What happened to her telling them to stop acting like so-and-sos while she had her hands full with us and not knowing where the meeting was or if something happened or what time they would return?

It was after 9:00. My father and uncle were tired and hungry. My aunt pulled Sammy onto the edge of her chair, holding him in place while he struggled to get into her lap, as if he could fit there.

"What important news did Norman Thomas have for the two of you?"

"Nothing," said my father.

"Not so nothing," said my uncle. "He was better than on radio. The man speaks with his eyes."

"*Double* nothing," said my father, who sat down to eat.

"What would be so terrible, our getting a little more food on the table, the way Norman Thomas says?" said my uncle.

"What kind of table?" asked my father. "You work at a cutting table. I have a butcher block and meat hooks in the ceiling. That's my table: the place where a dead horse hangs in air. You think they won't hang a man who makes union trouble? Who do you think's in charge?"

"Right now I am and I'd like to finish up here already," said my aunt, pushing plates around the table as if that alone would change the conversation.

"One minute you're supporting the union, Sol. The next you're so...what's the word?...*skeptical*."

"It's not Thomas that bothers me. I respect the man, even if he'll never be president. Even if he's a loser. It's not even the union leadership that worries me. It's those other ones, their lieutenants. They're like Boyle at the factory. Nothing in their heads but to tell men what to do. What's the difference if they're working for the bosses or for the unions? I don't like it."

"Why do you think they call it 'organizing'?" said my uncle. "Without leadership, without a plan, without someone in the field...."

"Beating up on guys who don't join? How's that different from the Pinkertons at Ford's or in Allentown?"

"Enough already," said my aunt.

"You asked," said my father.

"Spare me," said my aunt.

"It's important," said my uncle. "Important, important, important."

"You got time on your hands, David?" asked my father, his voice quiet now. "Time for the union hall, but not for HIAS, not getting the family out from that hell?"

Everyone was quiet now. My aunt scraped at something on the table with her fingernail, something that was not even there.

"We'll do both, Sol," said my uncle. He spooned more

potatoes on his plate and passed the bowl to my father. "We'll divide what we have to and do both."

Nobody spoke for a while after that until Ruthie came in from her date and my aunt took her into the other room to hear about dinner with Sidney. "Don't worry," said Uncle David, once she was gone. He straightened Sammy out in my aunt's now-empty seat and pulled it closer to the table so that it would be harder for Sammy to slip away.

I crossed my arms on the table and lay my head on them. *Hamlet* was in my hands as I fell asleep.

CHAPTER 11

We were unhappy in our own ways on the early morning trip home. My father never took his hand out of the pocket with the broker's receipt. I was still rattled by the fight between my father and my uncle, which had ended peaceably enough, but was not resolved. How can anyone with a family be surprised by anything that happens in this crazy world?

We both worked the wooden poles to keep the rats away from our feet; other than that, we were pretty quiet. The barge was filled with a hodgepodge of cow heads stripped of their saleable parts, the hinds of sheep and pigs identifiable by their tails, and who knows how many horses on which the scavengers were hard at work. How many new ways can I come up with for describing the smell?

The pier was deserted when we returned. The captain went off to sleep at the factory where Mr. Goldberg, the night stoker, had a meal waiting in return for the pint bottle of whiskey the captain brought him every week. He offered my father a drink from it, but my father turned him down.

The scavengers were not supposed to step foot on the island, so who knows where they really went. I did not think about it. The factory, which looked nothing short of diabolical when the furnaces were going full force, appeared weary under the weight of a day off. Not that the furnaces were ever fully shut down, it taking too long to get the temperature up. They were kept to a slow burn by Mr. Goldberg on his night shift and all day Sunday, meaning he was the only Jew on the island who lived orthodox and the only stoker who was not a black man.

The air on the walk home had a Sunday smell, a hollow and haunting odor made by the simmering furnaces. It was the residue of everything burned the week before and a reminder of what would be burned in the week to come.

"Where's your mother?" my father asked Noah, who was in the garden talking with Yorgos and Joey when we got to the house.

"How did the meet...."

"Noah—is she okay?" my father interrupted.

"The usual. Fine. She's inside. What happened at HIAS?"

My father took a few more steps toward the house then circled back to where the boys were sitting. Instead of finding my mother he explained about the lines, about the number broker, about hearing Norman Thomas.

"You saw him speak?" Noah's voice cracked, as if his teen-age boy vocal cords were dried dune grass.

"Thomas is a communist," said Yorgos.

Joey gave him a shove and Yorgos punched him dead on in the shoulder without even looking to take his aim. All this pushing around used to frighten me; now it annoyed me. It looked so stupid. They looked stupid. At least Joey *was* stupid. The others had no excuse.

"Shut up, you guys," said Noah.

My father told them about the crowd at the union hall, and

the noise of everyone translating Thomas' native-speaker English into Italian, Yiddish, Russian, and Polish. He also mentioned his own "debate" with Uncle David. Heaven forbid he should have called it a fight. "Uncle David and the garment workers' local are demanding new schedules so Jewish men can work Sundays, not Saturdays."

"Some of those factory owners are Jews," said Noah.

"What do you want from me, Mr. Know-It-All? They're so busy becoming American they've become Christians.

"I'm going to find your mother." He walked away.

"That shut you up but good," said Yorgos.

"He's missing the point," said Noah, "which is why we get nowhere."

"Which is what?" said Yorgos.

"That you shouldn't be forced to work on your Sabbath, no matter who you are. Even if you're not religious. The furnaces on Barren Shoal keep burning anyway, the barges are backed up in the harbor Monday mornings, so what difference does it make if the men work Saturday or Sunday."

"There's no managers here Sundays," said Joey. Only someone that dumb could be counted on for the facts.

"The Sunday men could supervise themselves. What are they gonna do, steal a dead horse?"

"People want one day when the air doesn't stink," said Yorgos.

"It stinks every day. Why is it better to stink on Saturday than on Sunday?"

"Because you're a stinking Yid," said Joey. "So joke's on you! Ha!"

"Shut up, you stinking moron," said my brother. He pulled a green tomato off the vine and threw it hard at Joey's chest. Joey turned his body so the tomato hit his shoulder blade. He pulled a zucchini and heaved it at Noah like a spear. Nothing ever changed between those guys. How long would it take before they were covered in broken vegetables and the garden was destroyed? Not even my mother, now calling from the doorway for me to come in, had the power to stop them. You would think it was a big deal that she was speaking. Not to me. What was to say that she would not just as suddenly stop?

In the kitchen was a basket of potatoes that needed peeling. I want to say this again: our mothers were forever working in those kitchens. Forget about the debate about the men working Saturdays versus Sundays. Our mothers never had a day off. Not ever.

"Come here," she said.

Her eyes were red around the rims and her nose was red too; it was obvious she had been crying.

"Closer," she said. She was still going at the potatoes.

"Where's Dad?" I asked. She was making me uneasy.

She leaned forward and, out of nowhere, kissed my forehead. This simple, unexpected display of affection was so strange. She handed me a knife. "Here," she said. "Peel."

"Maybe the union will do something about child labor," I said. If she could be affectionate now, she could take a joke, yes?

My mother laid down her potato and her paring knife, wiped her hands on the kitchen towel draped over her shoulder.

"What did you say?" she asked. Her face was so serious. I had miscalculated. So what else was new?

"Nothing."

"About the law: what did you say?"

"I was just joking."

"You know nothing, *nothing*, about the lives of most children. Your father came with a can of sardines in his pocket. You have all this. And you have us. You better be sorry."

"I am. Sorry."

It was a moment when I wished that she were still not speaking. We were so damned precious to them, Noah and I. There was so little room for making mistakes.

We worked in silence.

"What do you think about all this union talk?" I finally asked, removing myself from the center of things.

"Do I think the men should earn a living wage?" she considered. "Of course they should. And work in safe conditions? Yes I do. Yes. And should work shorter days and see a doctor when they are sick and have real time off to be with the family? Yes, again. And that someone should speak on their behalf when there's trouble with a boss? And they shouldn't lose their jobs or be thrown out of their houses when they get sick or too old to work?

"But should they demand this and that and everything else and risk being shipped back to where-ever? Where they're lucky if someone lets them live, never mind lets them work? You want fair, Marta, you go play your games with Sofia. After that, there's no fair."

What kind of games? Sofia and I had not played games for years. But I was probably no older to my mother than I was when Helen died.

She picked up the paring knife, returning her attention to her potato. "Better to know the truth," she said. "The world is a rotten place, like it or not."

I started peeling again, too. Did she see the world this way before Helen died? Yes. And she was right.

After dinner that night I went next door and found Mrs. Paradissis sewing, Grandma Paradissis sewing, and Mr. Paradissis listening to FDR deliver a fireside chat on the radio. The president was going on at length about the National Recovery Act.

"Where's Sofia?" I asked. There were not a lot of places to hide in that house, what with Sofia and Grandma sleeping in the living room and Yorgos hoarding the attic for himself.

Neither woman looked up from her sewing. Mr. Paradissis muttered something about how girls should not be out at night, not even in their own backyards.

"Did you eat?" asked Mrs. Paradissis.

"We just finished."

"Then go home," she said, with a long, tired sigh.

"Is she here?" I asked again.

"Go!" she shouted, shooing me off.

Noah and Yorgos were out back as usual, talking about organizing weekly meetings on Barren Shoal to build momentum for the union. Sofia and Joey were there too. Yorgos was saying he was tired of waiting for Uncle David's local to come through; it was time to make some other contacts. He knew of another group, he said, that he heard about from one of the barge captains. The captain would make the introduction.

Sofia and Joey were sitting off to the side sharing a cigarette. She took a drag and then asked, "How was Brooklyn?" The word "Brooklyn" floated on a current of exhaled smoke. What she was saying, I understood later on, was, *Look: this is how I am now. Sharing a cigarette with Joey.*

Sure, I was surprised. I was also disgusted. Not by the cigarettes, mind you, but by Sofia letting something that touched Joey's lips touch hers.

"Want some?" she asked, offering me the cigarette.

"Want one of your own?" volunteered Joey.

"Our parents will kill her if they catch her smoking," said Noah.

"I don't smoke," I said.

"You two don't have to do anything for your parents except

not die," said Yorgos.

"Don't you ever get tired of listening to yourself speak?" I asked. I had heard someone on the radio ask this question. I thought it sounded clever.

"Stanley Morrow is gonna drop us if he comes out here and the men aren't ready," said Noah. "And if you don't mind, girls, take off so we can talk."

"Who put you in charge?" said Sofia. She reached again for Joey's cigarette.

"Now you're a union organizer, too?" I asked her. I did not say in addition to being different, older, sexy, hanging out with Joey. Not that I minded Sofia knocking Noah down a notch. It was just that I was feeling so bothered by this whole thing with her and Joey that I needed to bother her too. None of it was any good.

"You got a problem with that?" she said.

"Go on, get outta here," said Joey. It made no sense that he would talk nasty to her when this whole thing was starting up between them, but there it was, one disgusting thing on top of the next.

Sofia tossed the half-smoked cigarette into a pile of crushed clamshells. She walked angrily in the direction of the beach, her shoes pounding the shells, the sand, the dune grasses, and anything else that got in her way. She did not talk back like she usually did when Joey was acting especially dumb or being insulting. This was Joey, after all, the boy so stupid that he could not even find Italy on Miss Finn's old globe, never mind Greece or Poland or Galicia.

"Why did you do that?" I said when I caught up with her. "Why'd you listen to him?"

"Stay out of it," she barked.

"I'm out," I said. "Watch how out I can be."

I did not wait for her to call after me so she could apologize; I did not wait for her to come after me and change the subject; I did not go back and tell her what an idiot she was being. I can talk a lot, but I know how to be silent too, until my silence is the impenetrable. I am, after all, my mother's daughter.

Sofia and I did not speak more than a few words on our walk to school the next morning, and not much more on the walk home. The week passed, me sequestered in my room after school, Sofia who-knows-where. I never asked. She never asked me either. When I was not in my room I was out walking, mostly to the far side of the island. Solitude can always be found in the face of loneliness, even on a place as small as Barren Shoal where there were not many places to be alone. The marshy side of the island, the side opposite the docks and the factory and furthest from the school house and our own houses, the side where Sofia and I had seen Joey and Marie Dowd all those years ago, had an emptiness that we could claim for ourselves when we wanted to, needed to, when we had no other place to go.

I felt grief when Helen died, but that was different, straightforward, automatic. I now understood that people were fragile, lives were fragile, and our connections to one another were the most fragile things of all. When I walked out of the backyard, when I walked away from Sofia, I felt a kind of loneliness I had never known before. The loneliness that happens when the living walk away from the living. Not that I doubted that I would see Sofia the next day or at school or whenever we crossed paths, which was often and inevitable. Sofia and I could live as neighbors for the rest of our lives, I now realized, and never speak as intimates again. Things like that happened all the time in the books Miss Finn brought us from the Brooklyn Library, usually the result of something large and awful. In real life it could also be something quiet, something unnamed or unknowable that pulled people into separate parts, separate pieces, separate places.

I poked around at the water's edge, ripples of the cool tide rising over my toes. The brown-green water turned yellow, then grey, and then clear as it rolled onto shore. It washed around some horseshoe crabs that had not been there the day before. The shells were up-ended on their backs, their innards already picked clean by smaller crabs and seagulls. I found a sliver of driftwood branch, splintered and weather beaten, and used it to turn the horseshoe crabs over so that their helmets were on top again.

I inched my way down the beach, inspecting starfish and clamshells and bits of beach glass, dried seaweed and the footprints of cats and plovers and gulls. If Helen had been there, she would have loved adding the beach glass to her coffee can. I spotted in the dune grass another piece of drift wood, shorter but smoother and less splintered than the one I held. That would work even better. I touched it with my fingers and the branch reeled and coiled, twisting itself around my wrist. I tried shaking it off, but it pulled even tighter.

I ran towards the houses screaming, waving my arm, the snake still coiled around my wrist, not knowing whose name I should call, not knowing who I was running to. I could feel the loneliness of this in my leg muscles as they carried me in the direction of everything and nothing. It is a terrible thing to not know a name to call out to. I am not afraid of snakes anymore, but I do fear that memory of loneliness.

The snake, no doubt as scared as I was in its soundless way, suddenly uncoiled itself, plunking into a dense puddle of shallow water. I kept running, crying now instead of screaming.

"Where are your shoes?" asked my mother when I blew through the door. I could smell chicken simmering in a broth of carrots and dill. The table was already set for dinner and the kitchen was clean and calm. I remembered reading how a snake could expand its torso and swallow a chicken whole, taking days to break it down in its digestive tract.

I noticed my bare feet with a kind of shame that came from not having an answer. I must have kicked them off as I was running. There were bits of seaweed stuck to the tops of my feet; there was sand between my toes. There was a carelessness my mother would have observed in this, a kind of carelessness about which she was unforgiving. Inattentiveness to those kinds of things, she believed, invited troubles. As if knowing was a way of preventing them.

"There were these horseshoe crabs and the snake and then ..." I was rubbing my arms, trying to wipe off the imaginary, invisible oil left by the snake.

She interrupted me. "Your shoes," she said.

"I'll find them," I replied. I gave up. What else could I say?

"And come right back," my mother called after me.

The next day, instead of stopping for Sofia, I left home early and settled myself in the schoolroom before anyone else, including Miss Finn. Yes, it was a terrible feeling to walk past Sofia's house. Yes, I was compounding my own loneliness. Yes, I could have knocked on her door and acted as if nothing was wrong. But I could not.

The schoolroom was especially still, as if pulsing with a hollow, empty excitement in anticipation of everyone's arrival. Miss Finn showed up earlier on Mondays than on other days, having just returned from spending her weekend at home in Brooklyn. Soon enough there would be something other than me not knowing what to do with myself.

Soon enough, through the window, I could see Miss Finn walking from the dock. Helping her with her bags and piles of newspapers and all the other packages that filled the small cart was, of all people, the girl in the brown dress. It was hard to believe but, yes, it was that same girl.

"Oh, Marta!" Miss Finn gasped, startled to see me sitting alone there in the grey light of that new morning. She set a bag down on the table and looked around, prepared for another surprise. There was none. She was still loaded down with a carpetbag and some smaller burlap bags, two of which hung from her shoulders by looped rope. "For heaven's sake: you look like you slept here."

In my rush, I had neither brushed my hair nor checked myself in the mirror to straighten my dress. More than that, I was missing the clear eye with which Sofia gave me the once-over every morning, the gaze that took care of anything that was amiss.

"I thought it was later than it is," I said. I smoothed my dress, which even I could see needed ironing.

"It always is," she said gravely. For a woman as smart as Miss Finn was, she spoke with so many clichés. At least to us she did. "Say hello to Katrine," she continued. Now the girl in the brown dress had a name. We exchanged hellos.

Miss Finn straightened the collar of my wrinkled dress.

"These need to go upstairs," she announced. Miss Finn's bags for the week were still sitting on the schoolroom floor.

I thought she meant that I was supposed to help her, so I reached for the bag closest to me. Next to it was a second carpetbag and the burlap sacks.

"No, I meant Katrine," she explained.

I felt foolish standing there holding a bag in mid-air.

"Never mind. Come, Marta. Katrine: you wait here."

I followed Miss Finn to the top of the stairs, where she had her private room. It was the room that in our identical house would be my room.

"Set those bags down here," she said, "and go back down and wait for me in the classroom. I'll be only a few minutes."

It seemed silly that she had asked me to help her only to send me away, but I was relieved that Miss Finn did not want me to stay. I was relieved, as well, that when I got back downstairs Katrine was gone.

CHAPTER 12

Our estrangement lasted for weeks, not that anyone noticed. I suppose that people were as indifferent to Sofia and me being at odds as they were to our being joined at the hip. Not that I expected them to care, but it surprised me that our friendship mattered so little. But how much do any of us matter anyway, you should pardon me for asking?

Our falling out ran its course because it had to. Who else did we have? Little by little Sofia and I returned to our usual custom of walking to and from school together, of crushing clamshells around the houses in the never-ending effort to keep the sand down. We never discussed what pulled us apart anymore than we talked about what pulled us back together. We worked hours in the garden, dead-heading flowers and weeding and tilling around the vegetables. A year passed, then another, and I was the reluctant third wheel to the now teenaged Sofia and Joey. Noah and Yorgos were making ever more complicated plans for the work-slowdown or sit-down strike, none of which had happened. Talk is cheap. Another cliché, also true.

Joey was now taking dinner two nights, sometimes three, with the Paradissis family. The thought of him at the kitchen table was disgusting. According to Sofia, these meals were in return for Joey's work in the vegetable garden. Sofia, Yorgos, Noah, Joey and I had tripled the garden's output in those two years and now there was more than enough for both families, plus some. Our parents were pleased with us; we were pretty pleased with ourselves, too. Who would not be pleased? Yet not even Noah, self-declared friend of the workingman, was ready to invite Joey to our family table. At some point my mother took to sending along extra sandwiches for Joey's lunch, though it did not stop him from scavenging. Even so, it was good to see my mother taking charge of something again, to see her acting as if there was something worth worrying over other than us. And anyway, she was doing more for him than Mr. Morrow's union, an idea that still took center stage in the boys' heads, or in the backyard, or in some conversation in Brooklyn from which Sofia and I were excluded.

I learned to keep my struggle over Sofia and Joey to myself. "Why him?" I asked her the one and only time we talked it through, months after things between us returned to normal. Sofia was trimming my hair.

"Why not?" she replied, never halting the path of her scissors. "Who is there for us? Your brother? My brother? The old men? Look how beautiful: *Finito*."

More and more Italian words, the ones from Joey's rather limited vocabulary, crept into her speech every day. Good-bye became *ciao*, cookies became *biscotti*.

"You're just boy crazy," I told her. The world itself was crazy, so why not Sofia. Or any of us, for that matter. We read about it every week in the newspapers. If I was Armenian, I would say the world went crazy in 1914, when the Turkish Ittihadists—those Young Turks!—declared a boycott of Armenian businesses. We knew what the Turks did to the Armenians—at least anyone who was paying attention, like Miss Finn was. To a Jew, the world went crazy again in January 1933, when Hitler was appointed Germany's Reich Chancellor. It was Hitler himself who connected the dots between the Armenian genocide and the one to follow. It was Hitler who said, *Who still talks nowadays of the extermination of the Armenians?* You know what? *I* do. Even today. Even if it means I digress. I still talk about the Armenians. *I* do. That is who. How can you not?

"There will be other boys," I told Sofia. "Maybe my cousin Ruthie can introduce us. In Brooklyn."

She combed her fingers through my long, curly hair, which she had been threatening to cut into a bob. "Well, I hope some of those boys are waiting for me."

"Nobody's *waiting* for us. The only thing waiting out there is a breadline," I said.

"Oh Marta," she sighed. She leaned her head on my shoulder and left it there while she spoke, her hands dropping down to her side. "Look around; what do you see?"

"Beach, sand, dune grass, sea gulls...," I inventoried. The situation was impossible; the conversation was getting nowhere. Keeping it literal meant keeping it safe.

"What kind of life will we have on Barren Shoal? This whole place is one big breadline."

"At least we're not starving." It was a stupid thing to say, what with Joey and Katrine and the others who scavenged the trash. Even so, it was true.

"Do you see yourself living here forever? Polishing shoes for your kids and packing lunches for a husband who butchers dead horses?" she asked.

"What if I do," I said. The rest of my life, the actual future, felt no closer than anyplace else, not even Zyrmuny, where my mother's family was still trapped. Sofia stood straight again. "The minute we're done with school, we'll be gone. Trust me on this."

"In your dreams. Which I hope don't include Joey."

"This isn't about that. And, anyway, dreams have power. If you were a Greek you'd know that."

No one wants to hear about mistakes they cannot stop themselves from making. I said it that one time about Joey and then I never said it again.

On a Sunday not long after that I walked to the far side of the island alone with my fishing pole. Noah was off with Yorgos and I decided to not go looking for Sofia in case Joey was there too. Being tolerant of Joey came with a price. Tolerating Joey was exhausting. The sun felt good on my arms, and there was a stop-and-start breeze from the south blowing the factory stink away from me. It was late morning, long past the best time for fishing, but I did not mind being alone. I made forensic drawings of crabs in the sand; I assembled clamshells into igloo-like hutches for the fish, so they would be on cool, wet sand but out of the sun. I wondered if maybe Sofia was right, if maybe I should get out of there. But how does one choose to stay or go? How does one decide? I know, I understand: my cousins in Zyrmuny would have given anything to have that choice. But I was not in Zyrmuny. I was on Barren Shoal.

It took a couple of hours of fishing to bring in four small flounder. I gutted them on a rock at the jetty, rinsed them again in seawater, and headed for home. I had already passed the marsh when I heard a noise coming from the dunes. Cats, I thought, raiding another seagull nest or fighting over a rat. It was a disturbing sound and I walked faster, which meant passing closer to the sounds before getting beyond them. That is when I saw the bodies in the dunes, Sofia's face, Joey driving himself into her. How many times in my short lifetime was I going to see Joey Pessara's bare behind, you should pardon me for asking?

Though I have tried—precisely how hard is a matter for debate—I have never been able to untangle sex from love. No, I am not old fashioned. In the old days young people married because their parents said that they had to, not because of love. I married Walker Lane for love and nothing more. That was the only thing he had to give me. And vice versa. But I am not so modern either. Now the young people—and the not so young people, too—seem perfectly happy to have sex with someone they do not love. It is what they do on a date after dinner, as if sex is like going to a movie. I cannot imagine why. I am a romantic, which is a very hard thing to be. There it is; that is me.

Sofia had more passion in her than she knew what to do with. She played it out on Joey; she showered it on Marie Dowd's seventh and eighth siblings, twin boys who by then were three years old, who she cuddled and tickled; she offered it to the feral cats, which she stroked and petted; and she even gave it to me. I soaked it up like fresh air.

I thought about this as I walked the long way around, where I rarely went, through the scrubbier, weedier parts of Barren Shoal to get home.

By morning I was covered in bites all over my ears and on my face in a line that ran down my jaw.

"Don't scratch," my mother ordered.

Noah reached across the table and pinched my ear. He had just returned from Brooklyn on an early barge in time for breakfast and school. His eyes were droopy, red-rimmed. He might as well have held a lit match to my skin.

"Cut it out," I told him.

"Or cut it off, Marta Van Gogh!" In one of Miss Finn's art books there was a painting of Van Gogh with a rag wrapped around his head to cover his mutilated ear. He looked like a barge scavenger, except cleaner.

"Stop it," said my mother, whose back was turned to us and who was sifting flour for who-knows-what she was baking. "You must have walked through a nest of mosquitoes."

"Mosquitoes don't nest," said Noah. "They swarm."

Where did he come up with this stuff?

I went to school, hardly able to sit, the itching around my ear and face growing worse as the morning dragged on.

"Stop fidgeting, Marta," Miss Finn scolded.

"I can't help it," I complained.

"Let me see," she said with a sigh, waving me over to her desk as if only she could authenticate my blisters. The bites were swelling and getting redder.

"These aren't mosquito bites," she announced.

I wondered if whatever it was came from touching myself in the dark.

"It's poison ivy and it's going to get worse before it gets better. Go on home. And whatever you do, don't touch it. That's how it spreads."

This was not welcomed news to a girl who liked touching herself in the dark.

The blisters split open one by one by one until they oozed like smashed cranberries. My mother packed me in cold towels the way Mrs. Dowd had packed her hands when Helen died. Every woman on the island, it turned out, had a remedy from the old country. Some said pack tea leaves onto my skin; others said to bathe me in vinegar or in bleach; Mrs. Dowd said oatmeal. Mrs. Paradissis cut a frond from her aloe plant and rubbed its slimy juice on every part of me. I was in too much pain to protest or be shy.

Sofia never came to visit in those first two weeks that I lay writing in that crazy, itching pain. My parents and even Noah took turns bringing me ice. At the worst of it, my father slept in Helen's bed so that he could watch me through the night. In Helen's bed! The three or four sips of Slivovitz they gave me every few hours kept me in a slight but extended state of drunkenness. Thank goodness.

"I've been so busy with Joey that I've lost track of myself," Sofia confessed when she finally stopped by with a plate of cookies from her mother. I was still covered in blisters but they were healing now. All Sofia wanted to do was talk about sex with Joey, think about sex with Joey, and have sex with Joey. As for me, all I wanted was to just leave my poor, itching body behind.

"If I can't count on you when I'm sick," I asked, "when can I?"

"What can I do?" she offered. "Tell me."

I was so angry with her. So angry. But who else could I talk to? Who else did I have?

"Look at me! What if I'm scarred forever?"

"I feel so awful for you," she said.

"*You* feel awful? I'm supposed to care how you feel?"

A couple of days later I was woken from another Slivovitz-induced sleep by the shrieking of the accident whistle down at the plant. My mattress was drenched from a night's worth of melted ice. The wet towels in which I was swaddled flopped to the floor. I never slept deeply for all those weeks, nor was I ever fully alert. My blisters were now in a state of suspension, getting neither better nor getting worse. I pulled on some clothes. The sores, imperfectly anesthetized by the ice, began raging again.

I ran downstairs. "Didn't you hear the whistle?" I asked my mother, who was chopping fresh ice for me.

"Come on," I said. I grabbed some ice and rolled a towel

around it. Everyone on the island had to be rushing to the plant at that same moment.

"I can't," she said.

I looked around to see what would stop her.

"I can't," repeated my mother.

She did not have to start preparing dinner. She did not have to cut up onions or chop more ice. But she could not move.

"Mom." I said it plain, just like that, and then I left her. There were others running too, including Mrs. Paradissis in her housedress and worn-out slippers. "Where's your mother?" she shouted, lifting her hem so she could take longer strides.

"Home," I called back, not slowing down to face the embarrassment of my mother being unable to leave the house, of her unwillingness to face the tragedy awaiting someone, maybe all of Barren Shoal, down at the factory.

I saw the look on Mrs. Paradissis' face. I saw what she was thinking. She had to be thinking my mother was inviting more tragedy by not coming out. If my mother stayed home, trouble would not wait; it would come looking for her, it would find her.

By the time I got to the plant men were stumbling about, their faces red and black and white with blood and grime and shattered bits of animal bone lodged in their skin. Brown smoke was pluming out of the smokestack. Heat had broken the windows and the flames were being fueled by the rush of air. There was a chorus of scared and injured men hollering in pain, and another one shouting off the names of the wounded and the ones unaccounted for. Some of the injured were sitting on stacks of bricks and planks of wood. Others had thrown themselves against the fence. Joey's oldest brother, Massimo, was among the men holding onto the fence and gasping for air. I grabbed his arm. "Have you seen my father?" He shook his head; the blood coming from his temple dripped into his eye.

Noah and Yorgos appeared, one at each end of a wood plank bearing Mr. Paradissis. Joey and Sofia had to be around too. Mr. Paradissis' shirt was ripped open and his chest was sagging where his ribs should have arced over his lungs like flying buttresses. His eyes were closed.

"Let me," said a familiar voice. Miss Finn had rushed from the schoolhouse with rolls of gauze and bottles of hydrogen peroxide. She motioned for me to hold them. "He's alive?" she asked.

What a strange thing to ask. The boys could hardly breath, never mind speak, having just run out of the factory with their eyes and mouths all full of smoke.

Mr. Paradissis moaned. "Of course I'm alive."

Miss Finn sent Noah for a bucket of water. He and Mrs. Paradissis carefully washed Mr. Paradissis' face and neck and chest so Miss Finn could clean his open wounds. Noah was so gentle with him. He soaked a piece of gauze and dabbed Mr. Paradissis' eyes and lips. He did the same to Mr. Paradissis' nose and ears. Mr. Paradissis' lips parted as he tasted the water on his tongue. The gauze came back brown and bloody.

"Do you hurt badly?" asked Miss Finn.

"Can't...deep...breath," he whispered.

"Can you spit?" she asked.

The first effort produced nothing. The next try produced a glob of mucous and brown/grey dust.

"Again," she said. More grey gunk. "But look: no blood," she said, reassured. "That's a good sign. You've only cracked some ribs."

"*I* cracked them?" Mr. Paradissis whispered, angered by what sounded like a suggestion that he had a hand in it.

"Some ribs were probably cracked," said Miss Finn, correcting herself.

"Where's Dad?" I asked Noah.

"Joey went for him."

"What? You couldn't go with him?"

"Joey's the only one they're letting past the boiler room. That's where it blew." I thought about that black man killed on the assembly line out at Ford's in Dearborn. Joey was also someone that people threw away.

"Why wasn't Dad in the cutting room?" I asked.

"He smelled something," whispered Mr. Paradissis. "Boyle said it's nothing...Sol went...the shutoff valves."

"Who's gonna stop us going after him?" said Yorgos.

"Boyle's got men over from Barren Island already... blocking...."

"So predictable, those sons of...." Miss Finn stopped herself. She touched a reassuring hand to Mrs. Paradissis' shoulder. Her hand was streaked with blood and ash. She saw this too, and wiped her hand on the side of her dress. "Come," she said, indicating that we should follow.

The heat from the fire and from running stirred up my poison ivy, like a thousand black flies were biting me. I balanced the medical supplies in one arm and slapped at the blisters with the other. When I dropped a roll of surgical gauze into of puddle of copper-colored slime, Miss Finn grabbed my elbow.

"Leave it," she yelled. "Wait over at the guardhouse while I speak to Mr. Boyle."

Mr. Boyle, covered like everyone else was with soot and grease, was shouting orders that hardly anyone was listening to. Mr. DeWitt was standing outside the guardhouse looking baffled and holding his neck. Men were carrying other men out of the building. There was still no sign of my father. The windows of the guardhouse had been blown out and the people running back and forth and around it were trampling the shattered glass. Mr. DeWitt looked like he had been thrown pretty hard. Thick red bruises were already rising over his eyes.

"What the hell happened?" asked Noah. He had to shout twice before Mr. DeWitt answered.

Mr. DeWitt shouted back something about pressure build-up blowing off a loading door. "The waste stack must've clogged with something that should've sluiced through. The heat had nowhere to go."

"Have you seen my father?" asked Noah.

Mr. Dewitt gave Noah an odd look. "Who's your father, son?"

Noah stepped closer. "It's me, Mr. DeWitt. Noah Eisenstein."

"Of course, Noah, of course." Mr. DeWitt reached for Noah. Blood came rushing down his neck when he moved his hand. A piece of glass still sticking from his neck had sliced something big. No wonder that he could barely hear.

"Let me," said Miss Finn. She grabbed a roll of gauze and went to clearing the wound. "Go boys. Hurry."

"Boyle won't let us," said Yorgos.

"He will now." This was no time to ask what Miss Finn had said to Mr. Boyle. "Just go!" she yelled.

"I'm going with you, Noah," I said.

"The hell you are," he said, and shoved me backward.

"Don't!" I screamed. "Don't touch me!" I pushed the rest of the gauze and the bottle of hydrogen peroxide into Mr. DeWitt's hands and followed Noah and Yorgos past a partly collapsed wall and a row of doorframes with no doors in them. Grey smoke was everywhere; steam was blowing hard and low, bouncing on the ground and rising. I had not been in the factory since Helen died. I remembered the horse heads in piles everywhere, but I did not see them now.

Ten feet from the entrance one of Joey's brothers was

slumped against a cauldron. He was not screaming or moaning or anything even though his right leg was split open from the shin down. Yorgos kneeled in front of him. "Vince? Listen to me. I'm gonna carry you out. Noah, let's get him up."

Vince howled when they lifted him. I closed my eyes, which made things worse, as if my hearing made up for what I could not see. I opened them in time to see Yorgos hoisting Vince over his shoulder.

"Go on," he yelled at Noah.

Noah took my hand and we ran.

If there is such a thing as a hell on earth—another cliché, another good one—the factory was hell that day, filled with the stench of burning flesh, the moans of men, the yowls of steam.

"Dad!" shouted Noah. "Dad!"

"Here," someone cried.

"I'm coming," yelled Noah. He released my hand.

It was oddly quiet the deeper we got, as if things were settling into their newly broken states. The only thing I could see through the steamy darkness was the floor. "Dad," I called, my voice trembling. "Over here," replied another trembling voice from the other side of the room. I wanted to kill Noah for leaving me. Where had he gone?

I inched across the floor through animal blood and offal that had been reduced to ooze and slime. It was everywhere now, exploded and splattered onto every surface of the room, even the ones camouflaged by smoke and steam. I knew it for a fact, even if I could not see it. As I moved, the sludge moved too.

"Dad!" I cried, wiping my mouth on my sleeve. It was no longer just about the smell anymore; it was about the taste. I can taste it even now. "Over here," he called back.

I followed the trail of his voice until I reached a shoe. I felt around for an ankle, grabbed his knee. "Oh, Dad," I whimpered.

"Marie," he answered.

I had found Mr. Dowd.

He pulled me closer, his face emerging though the grey steam. "Oh my god, girl," he said. There was blood running from his mouth. I could not see if it came from his lip or from inside.

"Can you move?" I asked.

"Maybe," he said, hoisting himself with a moan, reaching for my shoulder to steady himself.

"I don't know the way out," I cried. "Noa...!"

"Just go where I say," said Mr. Dowd. I wrapped my arm around his back and we inched forward, Mr. Dowd leading the way. I thought I heard him crying, but the whimpering could have just as easily been coming from me.

We finally got out of the cutting room and I passed Mr. Dowd off to a man who half carried him the rest of the way. I lifted my skirt to look at my thighs. I did not care who saw. The poison ivy blisters had opened in the heat and were leaking. I dropped my skirt and chased after Mr. Dowd and the other man, who led us outside.

"Where are the others? Your father?" called Mrs. Paradissis.

"Noah's still looking. Where's Sofia?" Mrs. Paradissis did not know either. Men were still stumbling out and being carried from further inside the factory. All were burned in varying degrees by steam, falling embers, or the flames shooting through the breeches in the walls. Some had singed hair; others had skin that looked like charred tapioca pudding. Everyone was coughing, even the ones who had not been battered. Noah finally emerged with my father. My father was coated in filth but he was smiling an *un*happy smile. In the face of all the pain and chaos he was happy to be alive. Noah's shirt was torn and he had a gash straight across his forehead.

"I ran when I heard it blowing," said my father. "I hid under a horse. Damn thing saved my life.

A moment later he was repeating the story to Mr. Paradissis, who was still lying on the plank, waiting to be carried home. Other men gathered as well. I can only imagine Boyle's surprise to see people sitting all over the courtyard, including men from parts of the factory that had not been rocked by the blast. Women sat too, babies in their laps.

"Look," said Noah, all keyed up. "They're sitting down on the job."

Mr. Dowd lit a cigarette. Mr. Paradissis took one though it was too painful for him to inhale, what with his broken ribs. Everyone was either sitting down or tending the injured.

"Dad!" Noah cried. "This is how it starts. Like the Triangle Shirt Waist Factory fire."

"Those girls had to jump," said our father.

"Doors are open, doors are locked."

"Settle down, Noah."

"It doesn't matter. They don't give a damn."

"150 people died," our father continued. "You can't compare...."

"This was an accident waiting to happen," cried Noah. "If they don't close down the line to clean the chutes and vents when they should the thing'll explode. It's the same thing as locking doors. And what does Boyle care? Something breaks, some guy dies, and they buy another guy to replace him."

Our father stood up. "Are you finished?" he asked. "Don't you think you've said enough?"

"You've no right," said Noah. His face was streaked with grime and tears.

CHAPTER 13

Despite the awful predictions there were only three reported deaths that first day: Mr. Douglass, one of the Negro stokers, who had been a medic in the Negro Troupes in The Great War, and two scavengers who had been squatting inside the plant. Mr. Douglass was blasted into so many pieces that there was no body to recover. What was left of his remains were cremated right there in the furnace that he had been stoking. It was never clear if the two scavengers died from smoke inhalation or injuries from the explosion. I never heard what arrangements were made for the corpses. The dozen or so other serious injuries ranged from broken bones to a case of third-degree burns, resulting in a fourth death a couple of days later. I feel especially bad about that one: I cannot remember the man's name though I can picture him, a handsome fellow with red hair and a broad chest. Why would I forget his name when I remember so much else? I have no answer.

Nobody died from concussions or infections; the other bruises and fractures were painful but would heal. There was nothing to do for Mr. Paradissis' ribs except run tape around his chest the way they did in those days. Miss Finn said he was lucky that his lungs were not punctured. We were all lucky, except for the four people who died. We were lucky that the whole plant did not blow and we were not all killed.

Mr. Boyle came to the house the next day to discuss how Mr. Paradissis could work until he was strong enough for the cutting room. Sofia and I were sitting on the stoop shelling peas, Joey was at the factory, and Yorgos and Noah were playing catch with an acorn squash from the garden. Mr. Paradissis made a fuss about coming outside to speak with Mr. Boyle. Every step, every hiccup, every burp sent a jolt of pain through his torso.

"You gave us one hell of a scare," said Mr. Boyle in a pretend-chummy voice. He offered Mr. Paradissis a cigarette, which Mr. Paradissis waved away. Boyle, a big man with fat, drooping ear lobes, always had sweat running down his face, even when it was cold. His shirt was drenched through and he kept wiping his face with a handkerchief.

"No smoking," wheezed Mr. Paradissis. He was unable to get out more than a few words without choking. "Sit up or get pneumonia." *Wheeze.* "Teacher says." *Wheeze.* "Lungs fill." *Wheeze.*

Mr. Boyle lit one for himself. "Her sister took care of my wife. Lady doctor in Brooklyn. Brought Mrs. Boyle through some kinda woman's thing, she never said what exactly."

"Eight weeks to heal." *Wheeze.* "Six if lucky." *Breath.* "Feeling lucky."

"Take a few days," said Mr. Boyle, "We'll get you back doing something. Pushing a broom, something like that."

"You crazy? My ribs is busted." We could all see the pain in Mr. Paradissis' face.

"You get paid to work, Paradissis. You get this house," said Mr. Boyle. "It's not free. That's the deal. I got no choice."

"I give you every month for the house. Everyone knows you make us."

"Forget about that. You know what I'm saying here."

I remembered how the Stavros family had been evicted when Mr. Stavros, the loader, was killed by that half-butchered horse.

"For what? Getting my chest blown open? What about the bonus you get when you don't shut down to clean the vents like you supposed to?" asked Mr. Paradissis. His wrapped his arms around his chest as if he could keep his ribs in place.

"You gotta see it from where I stand, Niko."

"Where's that?" asked Mr. Paradissis. "You live here?"

"Take it easy, Ba," said Yorgos, interrupting him.

"What the hell, Yorgos," said Mr. Paradissis. "You mind your own business."

"I'm gonna go in for you," said Yorgos. "I can cut good as you."

It was a bold-faced lie and everyone knew it. Yorgos had never butchered a horse in his life. It was a safe bet that he never even carved a roast chicken.

"Start Monday and we'll be squared," offered Mr. Boyle. Who knows why Mr. Boyle would let Yorgos jump the seniority line like that, never mind go in at all? I like to think it is because Mr. Paradissis said something about Boyle shaking down the men for housing money when they were supposed to be getting the houses as part of their pay; I like to think it is because Boyle worried that his little scheme would be exposed to the bosses, though they were probably getting a piece of it too. It just might be that Boyle felt something for Mr. Paradissis and how badly he got hurt. Or it might be that it was easier to take Yorgos instead of training a new cutter from the ranks and evicting the Paradissises. Do I know why people do what they do? We want to know, we think we know, but we know nothing.

"Tomorrow," said Yorgos. "I'll start Thursday."

"I won't have broken ribs forever. You got school."

"We'll talk later," Yorgos told his father. It was best to quit while they were ahead, the way people say. Boyle could call off the deal if he wanted to.

I do not know when Yorgos started at the factory, only that he arranged for a meeting in the city on that Sunday afternoon, which meant him and Noah jumping a ride on the last barge back to Brooklyn on Saturday night. Yorgos made it plain that he was tired of waiting for Mr. Morrow's local to come through. The barge captain, Parson Otis, set up a meeting with the other union and Noah arranged for the boys to stay the night with our cousin Ruthie, who had moved to the Lower East Side when she married her young man Sidney. This gave the boys all Saturday night and Sunday morning before they had to be at some private social club on Mulberry Street, where the heads of the local unofficially gathered.

I sat with Noah while he gathered his things. He said that Joey was pretty upset that they were not taking him along. "There's no room at Ruthie and Sidney's place. I told him we'll be jammed up enough as it is." While he stuffed a change of underwear and his toothbrush into a bag, he explained how he and Yorgos would use their free time to explore Greenwich Village.

"John Reed and Emma Goldman went there with the bohemians," he said, fired up by the importance of his mission.

"Why'd they bring Bohemians?" The Nazis had been stirring up trouble in the Sudentenland from the moment that Hitler grabbed power the year before. Plenty of those ethnic Germans living there were only too glad to join in on the Jew-beating. So what else is new?

"Not *the* Bohemians; just *bohemians*, artists and musicians."

It was so hard to understand Noah. Now I understood less,

if that was possible. "So you're going to be a bohemian." I was not asking a question; I was trying on the label.

"First you walk in someone's footprints and then, who knows, maybe you follow in their footsteps."

The boys really did spend Saturday exploring Greenwich Village, I would later learn. On the walk from Ruthie's apartment on Rivington St., they passed by the storefront on Mulberry where Yorgos had arranged for their meeting. The storefront window was mostly painted over with the same forest green paint used for the door, the window boxes, and the fire escapes. In small black letters at waist height were the words *Private Social Club* stenciled neatly by a very steady hand. The very top of the window, where it was clear, was the only place light could get in.

"This doesn't look so good or official or nothing," said Noah.

"You said you're done waiting for Morrow," said Yorgos.

"I'm just saying that...."

"Let's see what *they* say," said Yorgos.

They kept walking and soon they were drinking beers on the corner of 7th Avenue and 4th Street in a bar that was closed by Prohibition, secretly re-opened as a speakeasy, then re-opened as a bar again when Prohibition was repealed. At least that is the story the bartender told them and that Noah told me. The man guarding the door—I do not know if they were called bouncers then—asked who they were and where they were from before letting them in.

The boys nursed the one round of beer that they could afford. Another couple—a man and a woman—who were seated at the other end of the bar drinking martinis insisted on buying them another round. The woman was perched on the stool closest to the small dance floor at the back of the room. She had dark, naturally wavy hair that she wore long, and olive-complected skin that made Noah figure she was Spanish. The man, paler by comparison, was tall and thin with longish blonde hair that kept slipping over one eye. The woman's makeup was immaculately applied. Her musk-red lipstick matched her nail polish. She was wearing double-roped pearls around her neck and a black dress. The man was wearing a suit and tie and had clean hands and trimmed fingernails. They ordered pints for the boys and a bowl of cocktail nuts for them all to share. They ordered another round of martinis for themselves.

To one side of the dance floor was an upright piano played by a solemn-looking man, his head turned away from the bar as if it hurt to rotate his neck. A second musician switched back and forth between saxophone and bass.

The man in the suit asked the boys where they were from and when Noah said Barren Shoal the man said, "The horse factories?" He offered them cigarettes from his monogrammed case.

Yorgos explained how a whole community of factory workers and families lived on Barren Shoal and how there had just been a huge explosion and fire, lots of men hurt, a couple died. He did not mention the scavengers.

"You mean Barren Island?" said the woman. "I never heard of any Barren *Shoal*."

"That doesn't mean it's not there," said Noah. Which has been my point all along.

"Stinks pretty bad?" asked the man.

"Why is that always the question?" Noah replied.

The woman stubbed out her cigarette. "Don't let Gray bother you," she told Noah.

"What do you think happens to the horses no one wants anymore?" Gray asked her. "They chop them up, melt them down, and the greasy wheels of commerce keep turning."

"Come on," she said to Noah. "Gray can lecture himself

silly while you and I dance. I'm Lois. And you are?"

"That's Noah; I'm George," said Yorgos.

Noah grinned. "That's right: Noah and *George*."

Noah had never danced with a woman other than my mother, who had not danced with anyone since Helen died unless she and my father danced in their room, which I doubt. Noah raised his hand to remove his cap but Lois said, "Keep it on." That struck him, he would tell me, as particularly strange. He worried that maybe it had something to do with the smell of Barren Shoal. He thought it was stranger than her asking him—*telling* him—to dance. Stranger than Gray ordering yet another round of beers and cocktails. Noah told me that watching Lois drink martinis was the first time he heard the word "glamorous" inside his head.

Lois took the lead after Noah stepped on her toes a couple of times. Now Yorgos—pardon me, *George*—was drinking martinis, too. When Gray and Yorgos approached so that Lois could choose her next partner, all four of them ended up dancing in a circle.

Lois was Gray's "skirt," as they were called then. She was the woman who made it safe for a man like Gray to move about the world. She came to it honestly. It was on Gray's white elbow that Lois could pass as well. Gray, with his unaccounted for and unlimited supply of cash, had long ago extended his hand to Lois, just as he was now doing to Noah and Yorgos. I cannot say what he saw in Noah and Yorgos other than that they had stumbled into a bar where he was a regular and they were not.

The next thing Noah remembered was Gray giving him a calling card and Lois writing something on the back with a pencil she borrowed from the bartender. No one had ever given him their card before. Who knew anyone that had cards?

Noah and Yorgos somehow found their way back to cousin Ruthie's place on Rivington St., Noah so drunk that he was certain they were in Brooklyn and Yorgos only clear enough to remember that the apartment was over a store that sold nuts and dried fruits. Hanging in the windows, he remembered, were strings of figs just like the ones the Paradissis family wore on the boat over from Greece.

They finally found the building a half-block in from Essex Street, where the recently or soon to be covered open-air market— Noah's telling changed back and forth over the years and I never bothered to find out—was already coming to life. Men were unloading live chickens from New Jersey and sides of beef from the meat market on West 14th St. Essex Street itself was already lined with two-wheeled wooden pushcarts loaded with everything from apples to underwear. I do not remember where the merchants parked the carts at night or what they did with the unsold produce, or where they got their merchandise in the first place. It is hard to know what it is I never knew versus what I have forgotten.

Sidney, cousin Ruthie's husband, had given the boys a key so they could let themselves in. In the same pocket, Noah found the calling card with Gray's telephone number. On the back of the card was a number for Lois, the thing she had written by hand. "What am I supposed to do with this?" he asked Yorgos.

"Hell, boy: it's a trophy."

He figured that this was Lois' number at work until he dialed it a few days later. Lois' sleepy voice answered, instead of the switchboard operator he was expecting. He was so startled that he hung up without speaking. He had assumed that Lois and Gray were married, though the precise nature of their relationship eluded him. What surprised him even more was later finding out that neither Gray nor Lois had jobs. He did not know a single person who slept late in the morning other than Mr. Goldstein, who saw to the factory's furnace at night.

The meeting on Mulberry Street was set for 10:00 a.m., but

Noah and Yorgos left the apartment with Sidney after breakfast. Sidney, who was first generation American born to parents from Minsk, had a high school diploma and a steady job in the clerical department of the Metropolitan Insurance Company on Park Ave. and 25th St. At night he took courses at City College where, class by class, he intended to earn a degree in engineering. Noah and Yorgos agreed to walk Sidney uptown. They were lucky to be so young, to be able to walk right through a hangover.

There was more life on a single block of the Lower East Side than on all of Barren Shoal. Sidney pointed out the old, overgrown Jewish cemetery between the elementary school and a neglected, four-story brick house on 2nd St. "There are little graveyards like this tucked all over Manhattan," said Sidney. "There's one on 11th St. with headstones from the 1700s.

"Some people say the first Jews came with Columbus in 1492," said Sidney, "which, otherwise, was not a banner year for Spanish Jews. The English also kicked out their Jews around then, but didn't burn them the way Torquemada did. Shylock didn't appear out of nowhere, you know. Shakespeare was a Jew-hater like the rest of them, but a step up from the mob. He hated us as people instead of hating us as sub-human. It was the kind of thing that placed Shylock—and Shakespeare, for that matter—on a different moral scale."

How can there be more than one moral scale on which things are measured? If you need more than one, it means that none are complex enough for our very complex human condition. It means having greater scales and lesser scales for greater or lesser people. Why is it possible to be so disgraceful?

The history of Jew-hating goes on and on, and our parents had told us plenty. My goyishe friends insist it ended when Nazi Germany collapsed. This is their careless way of denying that Jew-hating is resilient. And that they might be guilty of it themselves.

Interesting, you think, that I am willing to call them friends? I refuse to let their ignorance drive me away. What is the worst that can happen? Nothing worse than what already has.

Am I saying too much? Am I being impolite? Should I care?

I will not worry until at least one of them admits to an anti-Semitic thought. On that day I will reconsider everything. I am 80 years old and still waiting.

The noise level further up 2nd St. was staggering, even though the Yiddish theaters running as far north as 14th St. would not open for hours. Sidney brought the boys to Schacht's Appetizing, where the smells of whitefish and pickled herring were intoxicating. Noah, still hungover from the night before, had to step outside, but Sidney and Yorgos scarfed down their bagels and lox in a few big bites. They turned again on 9th Street, over to 4th Avenue and its row of bookshops. Outside, in front of each store, people were browsing through cases of used books. How fine it must be, thought Noah, to browse through books on the way to work. He thought about our father walking to the factory, about there being nothing between our house and his work other than the unavoidable smell.

The old Astor Library, Sidney told them, home now to the Hebrew Immigrant Aid Society, was one block over on Lafayette Street. Noah told Sidney about our father spending more hours in vain than anyone should have to at HIAS trying to get the family out of Zyrmuny.

This walk was all it took, according to Noah, for his universe to grow larger. "Someone takes you along one day," he later told me, "and the things you believed impossible, because someone said they were, as if their saying it made it so, are the things you're doing. You're doing the impossible. You are walking down a street in the city because you can, looking at whatever and whoever you want in any which way you want and for as long as you please. And nobody cares a damn about what you're thinking, so you don't worry either. And you don't worry about what they're thinking, especially about you. Nobody notices you have a hangover; nobody notices if you're walking north or south; nobody can tell if you like girls or you like boys. Maybe they notice if you are wearing a black felt hat and pais and a beard. Or a yarmulke. Or if you have black skin." Noah was wearing dark blue pants and a grey newsboy cap over his short brown hair; he had the same olive-complected skin as our mother. "It was one of the best moments of my life," he told me, "all because I was walking down a crowded street and nobody cared."

A couple of hours later Noah and Yorgos were back at the Mulberry Street social club meeting with two representatives of the Longshoreman Union, one of who was doing all the talking. The other one sat at another table playing solitaire. The third table was empty. "The point is this, fellas," said Mike Sierra, a black-haired, overweight man whose flat nose had been broken at least once. "The stevedores don't mix up with the municipals. The municipals means civil service, which means the city, which means someone else's turf. If you think I'm gonna wage a union battle on account of thirty-seven glue workers, you're younger than you look."

"First off, they don't work for the city on Barren Shoal."

"All trash workers do."

"They're not garbage men."

"Excuse me: glue guys."

"It's a rendering plant. Half of them are butchers."

"So hook up with the food workers union."

"This is not some kind of Upton Sinclair thing," said Noah. "They don't trim meat. And they're not garbage workers either."

"So what the hell are they?"

"What the hell difference does it make what they are?"

asked Yorgos. "You guys run the docks. If you say a barge don't get loaded, no one loads it. If you say a barge don't dock, it don't dock. What more do you need?"

"To know what's in it for us."

"Thirty-seven members and a toe-hold in Jamaica Bay," said Noah. "When the city develops a port there—wait five years and you'll see, it'll be the biggest commercial port on the eastern seaboard—you'll control it from start to finish instead of watching from the bleacher seats, eating peanuts instead of steaks. Not just the docks but the...."

"Why in hell should we go through you?" asked Sierra.

"Because if you don't, someone else will. We've got people in there; you got no one."

Noah and Yorgos returned to Barren Shoal at dawn on Monday with a promise from Mike Sierra to make an exploratory trip to Barren Shoal. They brought a stack of blank membership cards that Sierra wanted signed in advance as a gesture of good faith.

They also returned with Joey, of all things, who had managed to sneak over to Manhattan without their knowing. I could hear them arguing with him in the yard before I even got out of bed. At least they had the good sense not to grill Joey on the barge ride back over or at the dock.

"Where the fuck you been?" asked Yorgos.

"I got a meeting too," he said proudly.

I tip-toed to the window to listen better.

"Oh yeah? With who?"

"None of your fuckin' business."

Yorgos kicked some dirt at Joey.

"With my brother."

"Which damn brother?"

"Massimo. And the longshoreman."

"*We* were with the longshoremen," asked Noah. "Who does Massimo..."

"On Thompson St."

"What'd they want?" said Yorgos. "How you know they're longshoremen?"

This time Yorgos kicked Joey in the rear.

"Enough already with the kicking," said Noah.

"Were they brown shirts?" asked Yorgos. "Were they wise guys? Where's Massimo now? Why'd he bring you? Why didn't he come back with you?"

"Just about how you can't get no union interested. They asked other stuff I don't know."

"About what?" asked Noah.

"About Barren Island. If there's union talk over there, too. They told Massimo to get me outta there so they could take him out for a girl. They said they would bring him back by speedboat. I went myself to the dock and slept on the barge."

"Told him to keep *you* outta the way or all of us?" said Noah.

"I don't know. I don't remember." The more they asked him, the more he got confused.

"I'll fuckin' kill you if you ever go there again without my say so," hollered Yorgos. "You hear me? And you tell me every damn thing that Massimo says. I swear I'll kill you. Now get away from me. You stink like hell."

"Should we tell Mike Sierra?" Noah asked Yorgos.

"You're gonna talk with that gorilla Massimo and find out? He don't think we're worth pissing on. If we gotta worry, we'll worry. Either they're gonna kill us or drag us in. Or nothing. It could be a big nothing. They might have something else cooking we don't know crap about. If they wanna talk, they know where we live. And I got nothing else for Sierra until he comes over."

"What about those cards?"

"Just because I told Sierra I *could* get them signed don't mean I will."

"Don't be an idiot. These longshoremen don't fool around," said Noah. "They bust up fascist rallies with knives and cracked heads. Maybe they talk union, but they also talk about who's just over from Italy because they shot a bunch of brown shirts outside some church in Naples."

"That's why we want Sierra, you retard, and not some pussy union that'll make nicey-nice with the bosses."

"What about Stanley Morrow?"

"What the hell, Noah? It's two years already and he's never set foot on Barren Shoal again. He's another one who thinks he's too good for us. He thinks Barren Shoal is a stinking disease."

"You don't know crap about what Morrow thinks."

"Morrow thinks we're just a step up—a very small step—from the scavengers. That's what he thinks."

Yorgos was proud about getting an introduction to Mike Sierra through Parson Otis, the barge captain who brought his father *The Daily Worker*. He was proud about getting the longshoremen interested in Barren Shoal. As Noah tells it, Yorgos was already scripting a future for himself as a union boss, someone who would hold meetings at social clubs on Mulberry Street over little cups of espresso.

"We don't know a damned thing about Mike Sierra. It's one thing to go through Uncle David. It's another to deal direct. We don't know what the hell we're doing." Noah had not told Uncle David about talking with another union.

"The bosses know Sierra, at least by reputation. That's what matters."

"What about the men at the plant? Shouldn't they choose?"

"Who's to say otherwise?" said Yorgos. "You, Noah? When you've got DeWitt's old dick in your mouth?"

Noah turned red. I could see it all the way from my window.

"It's not like that," said Noah.

"The hell it's not. Which is why from today on, other than opening it to suck off DeWitt's shriveled up prick, you keep your fuckin' mouth shut and let me deal with the unions."

One minute they were talking union and the next Yorgos was blackmailing Noah. Yorgos did not say how he found out about DeWitt, but Noah understood that he had to leave Barren Shoal. He did not know how; he did not know when. But that was when he knew.

Mr. Paradissis had plenty to say when Yorgos came home from the factory that night, all of which he shouted in Greek. We could hear their voices going back and forth until Yorgos slammed out the door. Noah, Sofia, and I were already in the yard.

"What's your father so worked up about?" asked Noah.

"None of your goddamned business, you little faggot." Yorgos threw a mean glance Noah's way. Then the moment passed. "I'm on the inside, working my butt off, while you're at school planning a revolution."

"Joey's been on the inside even longer," Sofia reminded them. They ignored this the way that we all ignored the faggot comment. It was the first time I remember hearing someone use that word. I somehow knew what it meant, but did not think that Yorgos was doing anything other than calling Noah a bad name. I did not put it together with what I read in Noah's journal about Mr. DeWitt.

"We're not planning a war," said Noah. "It's about reform. You can't just sit on the crapper reading *The Daily Worker*. We've got to be in there with the union—I don't care which one—if we mean to get it done."

"What's this *we* business?" said Yorgos. "I don't see you picking up the butcher's knife."

"Boyle won't have me in the factory or I would be. You know that as good as me."

"So make your father quit and you take his place."

"Fat chance. Who's to say Boyle would take me?"

"All the Pessara boys are in: Massimo's in, Nick's in, Vince is in. And Joey here, right Joey? Why not the Eisensteins, too?"

"All four of them together earn only twice what a cutter does."

"Says who?" asked Joey. Nobody answered.

"Boyle gets four huge guys for next to nothing plus one, tiny house," Noah continued.

"I didn't even ask about money when I started," Yorgos realized. "You think he's gonna pay my father's wage?"

"Don't bet on it."

"How are we gonna eat?"

"Ask Joey."

Two weekends later an unfamiliar motorboat moored at the pier. The captain neither blew a horn nor rang a bell to announce its arrival, nor did anyone appear on the dock to greet it. Joey was poking around like he did every day, even Sundays, as if going through garbage was a religious ceremony. The captain politely asked Joey where he and his companions might find "two young fellows named Noah and George."

"I told them I don't know no George," reported Joey, "but if they stayed put I would get them Noah. I wasn't bringing no strangers around. One's a hot mama, big hat, fancy looking. You shoulda heard 'em crossing the water. I didn't know what was coming so fast."

"Well screw me," said Yorgos. "How the hell'd they find us?"

"Who?" asked Sofia.

"C'mon, Noah. You other three: wait here."

"The hell I will," said Joey. "I'm the one that's come for you."

"First say who they are," insisted Sofia.

"I'll stay back," offered Noah.

"No sir," said Yorgos. "You get your butt down there with me."

There was no way that Sofia and I would wait at home, not when strangers appeared. We never had visitors on Barren Shoal. Either you were there all the time or you were never there at all. We hung back until the boys were way down the road. Then we took off after them, always keeping a hundred yards behind until we caught up with them at the water.

Gray and Lois were just like Noah described: Gray was tall and blonde and pale; Lois had dark, wavy hair. He was wearing a seersucker suit; she was wearing a long-sleeved white blouse, a yellow linen skirt, and a broad brimmed hat that shaded her face. Even their boat was handsome: a triple cockpit mahogany hulled runabout, like the ones on the society pages. No wonder they crossed the bay so fast.

"George! Noah!" Lois took off her straw hat and was waving wildly when, suddenly, she flinched and dropped to her seat, as if something had stung her in the eye. She fanned the hat in front of her face, pausing only to remove a handkerchief from her purse.

"How did you find us?" cried Noah.

"What are you doing here?" called Yorgos.

"We thought it would be one hell of a fine day for a picnic," said Gray. "Grab this, George." He passed a box of ice to Yorgos.

"And for Noah," he continued, handing over three bottles of gin and a bottle of vermouth. "Now Lois, dear, please remove yourself from the boat and bring the basket."

"I will do no such thing," said Lois, crossing her legs and getting more comfortable, all the while still fanning herself. "That basket is grotesquely heavy and that dock is grotesquely dirty. And what in heavens is that awful smell?"

"That's from the horses they bring ..." Joey started to explain.

"No need to enlighten us," Gray interrupted. "Grab this basket, if you will, and we'll set off. There is a shore here, yes? Perhaps soft sand like we enjoy in the Rockaways?"

Sofia, who was standing at the edge of the conversation, squeezed between Joey and Gray. "I'll take the basket," she offered.

"I bet you can, little lady," said Gray.

"She's my sister," said Yorgos. "She's Sofia."

"And as strong-minded like her brother," replied Gray, addressing his remarks to Sofia. "And this would be?" he asked, turning to me.

"Marta. Noah's sister."

"Aha! Which leaves only...."

"I'm Joey."

"And whose brother might you be?"

"You don't wanna know," said Yorgos. "And they don't neither."

"I don't know about no picnics," said Joey.

"Well this is your lucky day," Gray continued. "Welcome to the first annual Barren Shoal Invitational Seaside Picnic and Cocktail Extravaganza. Lead on, George."

Lois was still sitting in the motorboat. "How do you stand this awful...."

"We've come all this way, Lois. We've brought all this food. Not to mention three extremely fine bottles of London gin to share with George and Noah. And now their beautiful sisters and their handsome friend."

"Oh, brother," said Lois, sighing.

"You *do* drink gin, I hope?" Gray asked Joey. "Because you will be soon enough."

"Now be a dear, Lois, and get out of that damned boat. And remember your hat." Gray held out his hand to help Lois; Noah reached over to steady her onto the pier. "Hates the sun, Lois does," said Gray. "Turns her brown as a bean.

"Let's be off, then, shall we?" he continued. "The air here *is* rather fetid."

"Yeah," said Joey. "Smells real good on Sundays when there's no horses in the furnace."

Yorgos thumped the box of ice at Joey's feet. "You wanna come, Stupid, you can carry this."

Yorgos and Lois led the way, followed by Gray and Noah, then Sofia and me, and finally Joey at the rear. Yorgos and Lois were laughing, but Noah and Gray were serious, tilting their heads to better hear what the other had to say. What could be more serious, it turned out, than Noah asking Gray for help? He had decided to apply for jobs to the Civilian Conservation Corps and the Works Projects Administration. He asked to use Gray's mailing address so that our parents would not know. Or Yorgos. Or anyone.

"What's all this," asked Mr. DeWitt when we passed the factory gatehouse. He was standing outside, his arms folded across his barrel chest and a half-smoked cigar between his lips.

"None of your damn business," said Yorgos.

"Family friends come to visit," said Noah.

"Mighty fancy friends," said Mr. DeWitt. "Rubbing

shoulders with the quality?"

Noah blushed up to his ears. "It's not like that, Mr. DeWitt."

"Like what?" asked Gray.

Noah told me long after how rough it was to realize who he was and what that meant, especially on Barren Shoal. Not that it was easy anywhere else. This was long before the whole Civil Rights time, the whole hippie time, and that riot at the Stonewall bar that, by the way, is just two doors down from the bar where the boys first met Lois and Gray. Coincidence? Fate? This was the 1930s and Noah suffered. Not that the suffering has ended. People hang on to cruel ways.

Lois stepped in. "There will be time, gentlemen, to resume this conversation, but we must press on before the ice melts." She stroked Noah's back and nudged him forward. Joey lifted the box of ice; Yorgos grabbed the food basket.

"What was *that* about?" Sofia whispered.

I shrugged. "How about we ask *George*?"

"This is rather charming," said Lois, when the rows of cottages where we lived came into sight. "Your own little Cherry Grove. Albeit a touch more rusticated."

"No cherry trees here," said Joey. "Just beach plums, strawberries, blackberries. Beach plums and blackberries ain't ready yet. Strawberries is come and gone."

"I believe they have," replied Lois. She adjusted her hat to better shade her. "To whom do these bungalows belong?"

"It's where we live," replied Yorgos, warily. "My family over here, Noah's next door. Joey and his big brothers on the other end."

"His parents are dead," added Sofia. "The influenza."

Saying "influenza" was like saying "the war": everyone knew this meant the epidemic, just like everyone knew that "war" meant The Great War.

"How dreadful for you, Joey," said Lois. "And how lucky that you have older brothers to look after you."

Sofia and I winced, but said nothing. Nor did Yorgos or Noah.

Thank goodness no one from our families saw us passing. What made me understand that these worlds should never collide? Was it when Lois described our houses as "charming"? I might not have been worldly, but I was not an idiot. Our houses were just a half-step up from shacks.

We continued down to the beach on the same path we took to go fishing, to gather clamshells, to disappear. It was the same path that I walked year after year with Sofia and Noah and years ago with Helen. Now, for the first time, I imagined what the island looked like through someone else's eyes. I imagined the quiet beach and the sad, little schoolhouse; I imagined the vegetable garden and the outhouses; I pictured the gatehouse, and the factory, and the men going to work. I saw Katrine and Joey stripping meat from a dead horse; I saw my father butchering what was left of it.

I could not stand what I saw. I closed my eyes. I was dazed by the smell. Even on Sunday, with the fires banked and the loading shoots empty, there was always the smell.

I ran to catch up with the others. Lois and Gray had seated themselves on the big driftwood log at the water's edge. The others were sitting on the sand. "Shall we begin?" said Gray, sounding both impatient and eager. "The best quality, dry London gin, not that awful Canadian bootlegger swill. Thank heavens Roosevelt put a stop to Prohibition. Talk about your New Deal! Ha! Though I confess that there was something much—how shall I explain it—*freer* about drinking in speakeasies with so many sorts of reprobates. Who among them wasn't breaking the law!? It was stunning. Now, sadly enough, we've been abandoned again to our own indiscretions, to our bathhouses and bars."

215

"They don't know what you're talking about," scolded Lois. "Gray means...."

"It means he's a fairy," said Yorgos, interrupting her. "A stroll in the park for Gray means Vaseline Alley."

"As opposed to you, George, who frequents New York's finest teahouses?"

Yorgos laughed. "Fat chance. That would be Noah."

"They drink plenty of tea at Yorgos' house; Noah's too," added Joey. He did not understand the "fairy" comment. Or Vaseline Alley, or teahouse, or bathhouse. Then again, neither did Sofia nor I.

Noah blushed.

"Of course they do, darling," said Lois. "Now why don't you try one of my cigarettes." She offered Joey her case; when he reached for it she pulled back. "Here," she said, reconsidering. "Let me." She opened the case, removed a cigarette, lit it with her matching silver lighter, and handed it to him, careful that his fingertips never touched hers. I cannot blame her; his hands were filthy. "Please, Gray; please continue."

"Now where was I?" asked Gray, ignoring the tension. "Ah: dry vermouth, of course. The Supreme Court of Appeals of Turin, I'll have you know, has made it illegal for cafes to sell a martini cocktail unless it is confected from Martini & Rossi vermouth."

"That's in Italy," said Joey.

"Exactly so, dear friend." Gray held the gin and vermouth bottles side by side, as if they were finely cut, leaded crystal.

"Quality gin and vermouth are imperative because, unlike a gin & tonic, a martini contains nothing to camouflage the taste of an inferior gin. And why dilute a superior gin with tonic water? Have we been posted to the sub-continent? Are we traders in Indo-China? No, my friends, no, and therefore unlikely to succumb to that devilish malaria mosquito."

"There's no malaria on Barren Shoal," said Joey. Lois' cigarette was dangling from his lips; a thread of smoke was rising into his nose. "Just mosquitoes. Not all mosquitoes are malaria."

"You've got one hell of a memory there, Dr. Schweitzer," said Noah.

"My name is Joey. Joey Pessara."

"Why do you know so much about malaria, Joey Pessara?" asked Lois. She was still dabbing her handkerchief to her nose. Her hat was pulled down as low as it would go.

"We talked about it when Mr. Boyle put up the gate. Where you met Mr. DeWitt," explained Joey.

"I see," she said, sounding interested but not curious enough to ask what one thing had to do with the other. "Well, you don't look like a doctor to me anyway. You're more like a movie star with those Hollywood looks of yours."

"You got a cold?" Joey asked, suddenly so self-conscious that he changed the subject.

"Not at all, Hollywood," said Lois. "Oh, this?" she asked, referring to her handkerchief. "The odor, you certainly understand, is...."

"This ain't nothing," said Joey, perking up. "You should get a whiff of it on a regular day, when the heat's up and them work horses is dropping dead in the streets like bugs and the barges are loaded full and the furnaces can't burn 'em fast enough and...."

"Knock it off," said Noah. It was hard to tell what made Noah more uncomfortable: Lois and Gray seeing us and Barren Shoal and smelling the smell, or us seeing Lois and Gray and how they dressed and how they spoke. It was one thing for Noah to breach their world, even if invited; it was something else for them to trespass into ours. To them this was a grotesque place of sickening smells. For us it was home, never mind how bad it smelled or looked to anyone else.

"Might I continue before the ice melts?" asked Gray.

Lois held her handkerchief to her nose with one hand and offered her cigarette case to Yorgos and Noah with the other. I half hoped she would offer one to Sofia and me; I was relieved that she did not.

"The quality of ice matters as much as the gin, since it will melt somewhat while I'm mixing. The melted water is a concealed but vital component that marries the gin and vermouth. If the ice is made from inferior water, the quality of the martini will be utterly compromised.

"The lemon, as well, should be fresh, preferably with a thick, stiff, glossy skin. As stippled and rich as a lemon in a Dutch still life."

He extracted an unblemished lemon from the food hamper.

"That's a Dutch lemon?" asked Sofia, eager by now to hear anything that Gray had to say. And why not: he was charming; he was well-spoken. He and Lois were like no one else we knew. They were urbane. They saw Noah and Yorgos, I imagine, as provincial. Maybe that was the allure. I cannot imagine what they thought of Joey or Sofia or me. I will not attempt to speak for them; it is exhausting enough to speak for myself.

"Excuse my poor manners, young lady," said Gray. "The Dutch painted exquisite still lifes in the 17th century: flowers, fruits, fish, game. You shall go, one day, to the Metropolitan Museum of Art. You will see the magnificent lemons of 'Still Life with a Glass and Oysters.' It is beyond amazing. It is sublime. But that is for another day.

"Now, then: necessary tools include a shaker, proper glasses, a measure, and a freshly sharpened paring knife." He produced these like a magician, like a surgeon, like a veteran drinker. "A martini should be served in a proper glass. Bear in mind that the traditional glass has functional aspects: its shallow, conical bowl forces one to sip the drink rather than tossing it back in large, vulgar gulps; the stem allows one to avoid holding the bowl, which would transmit heat to the drink, causing it to warm prematurely. Unfortunately, we have with us today only four martini glasses and, therefore, no solution but for the boys and for the girls to share."

"I can run back and get some," said Yorgos. "Just regular glasses, nothing fancy."

"Perhaps this is a perfect mission for Hollywood."

"They don't got glasses at his house. They drink from empty tins."

"Then off you go, George: posthaste."

Yorgos trotted away through the dune grass. Gray continued his lesson.

"Just prior to mixing, carefully carve a thin slice from the peel of the lemon. Cut just deeply enough to include a bit of white pith to give the twist some stiffness; avoid cutting into the yellow pulp of the fruit. Now gently set the twist aside.

"Noah, please: get the shaker out of the box of ice. The glasses can remain there for now. Fill the shaker half full of ice. Pour two-thirds of a pony of vermouth into the shaker, coating the ice." Gray raised the measuring glasses to eye level. "Then tip two jiggers of gin into the shaker.'

"A pony!" cried Joey, laughing and slapping his leg. It had taken a moment for the word to sink in.

Gray scowled. "Affix the lid of the shaker and agitate in a vertical motion for 10 to 15 seconds. Remove the glass from the ice, holding it in a clean bar towel to avoid spoiling the frost. At last, carefully strain the mixed martini from the shaker into the glass.

"Hold the strip of lemon peel horizontally, one inch above the surface of the martini, yellow side facing downward. Gently but firmly squeeze along its length, expressing the volatile citric oils onto the surface of the drink. Holding the strip by its ends, twist it into a corkscrew shape, briefly tug on the ends, then squeeze it back into shape. Only then should you gently drop the twist into the glass.

"And that, my loves, is a martini." He handed the first one to Lois and started on the next. "I sense that we will be ready for those supplementary glasses at the very moment George reappears. Now girls, be dears and retrieve the delicacies from the basket. Beneath the tablecloth you'll find a hundred little cucumber mint sandwiches, herbed cream cheese sandwiches, and ham watercress sandwiches."

And so there were. Not that we actually counted. Is it ungrateful to say that these sandwiches were not worth the bother? Not that I minded eating them, except the ham, which I bit into and swallowed in a gulp, my penance for throwing caution to the wind and eating pork. But they seemed like a whole lot of trouble for not a whole lot of taste.

Yorgos reappeared with the jelly glasses. Sofia and I volunteered to use them, but Gray would not hear of it.

"I could have sworn you girls were paying attention: *a martini should be served in a proper glass*. The boys shall flip a coin to see who gets the jelly glasses."

This was easier said than done: none of the boys had any money and Lois and Gray had nothing smaller than dollar bills.

"Wait a second!" cried Joey. "We can pick straws!" He jumped up and pulled out a clump of dune grass.

"Utter genius!" cried Gray, as Joey ripped three pieces of dune grass into equal lengths. He bit off the end of just one to make it shorter. "Lois, dear: would you adjudicate?"

Lois held the grass while the boys selected.

"Hollywood wins!" she cried. Joey, of all people, would

drink from a bona fide martini glass while Noah and Yorgos drank from junk.

"Now Lois, again please do the honors of the first taste," begged Gray.

"Brilliant!" announced Lois. "Let the games begin!"

Joey had trouble managing his wide-mouthed glass. He threw the drink back instead of sipping. A good amount of it splashed down his face and his throat.

"Oh shit," he said, wiping his mouth and neck on his shirtsleeve.

"Gimme that," said Noah. He grabbed the martini glass from Joey and poured half of his own drink into it. He handed the jelly glass to Joey and kept the martini glass for himself.

Gray mixed a second round. I did not need another. Just a few sips were all it took for the drink to go to my head. I felt happy sitting with the group, pleased by how handsome and beautiful everyone was now that Gray and Lois and their martinis were here.

Gray was telling a story about the wild parties at the Dark Tower, A'Lelia Walker's famous Harlem salon at her 136th Street townhouse, when Mr. DeWitt appeared from over the dunes.

"Join us," called Lois. She raised her hat and waved to him.

"Over here," shouted Noah, patting the sand next to him.

We must have been quite a scene, what with the gin bottles and tea sandwiches and Gray talking about drinking bathtub gin with the poet Countee Cullen, which was also when he met Lois.

"Where in hell you think you are?" hollered Mr. DeWitt. "What in hell you doing with these kids?"

"What are *we* doing?" asked Lois, smiling knowingly. She looked at Noah, who was looking at Mr. DeWitt.

"It's okay, Mr. DeWitt. They're just visiting, like I told you before," said Noah. "A surprise visit."

"You might be visiting with them, but they're trespassing."

"According to whom?" said Lois.

"According to me. And I'm the gatekeeper. So pack up your fancy selves and your fancy boat and get the hell outta here."

"Look, now: you saw us earlier and said nothing about...."

"I'm saying it now."

If there were rules about visitors, none of us knew them. Why would we? Who ever came to Barren Shoal?

Gray looked at his watch. "Perhaps Mr...." Gray stumbled for his name.

"DeWitt."

"Possibly Mr. DeWitt has a point. This is as good a time as any for us to be getting along." He stood up and dusted off the seat of his pants. "Granted, it will take a few minutes to tidy up."

"That's what seagulls are for," I said, though it was probably the martini speaking.

"Shut up, Marta," said Noah.

Joey reached for the sandwiches. "Those ain't going to no gulls." He stuffed a handful into his mouth and the rest into his pockets.

"You have some appetite there, Hollywood," said Gray. "Perhaps we'll dine again sometime soon. With these lovely young ladies, of course." Both Sofia and I blushed.

"Not around here, you won't," said Mr. DeWitt. "You oughta be ashamed, loading them up with those silly sandwiches and swanky drinks."

I do not know if Lois and Gray felt ashamed, but Yorgos and Noah were humiliated. They did what Mr. DeWitt told them to do without defying him or threatening to expose him. It could have gone the other way, but it did not. DeWitt had won. Sofia and I followed suit. As for Joey, maybe he was just too stupid to feel humiliated. Lucky him.

Yorgos, in the weeks that followed, changed his walk from a wise guy to something more determined. Sofia reported that Mrs. Paradissis put dinner on the table when Yorgos came home from the plant instead of when Mr. Paradissis announced he was hungry. She now gave Yorgos the first pull on the bread, the largest serving of potatoes, the best piece of meat when they had some. Even so, Yorgos' skin turned ashen. His face looked like it was dusted with lime powder.

"You're looking like hell," Joey told him before a month had passed. We were all in the garden after dinner.

"Hey, brother: I been working the ovens of heaven," said Yorgos.

There was a new camaraderie between Yorgos and Joey that left Noah behind.

"And I've been sifting the fruits of the Garden of Eden," said Joey, equally self-satisfied.

Sifting the fruits? Where was Joey was getting this stuff?

He was getting it from an ad in *The Daily Worker* announcing a rally at Union Square. The quote was from Eugene V. Debs. The boys planned to attend.

"Maybe Debs will be there," said Joey.

"Only if you believe in ghosts," said Yorgos. "The guy died in '26."

"Mr. Morrow said Carlo Tresca might be speaking," said Noah.

"You still wasting time on Morrow?" said Yorgos. "Sierra told you to lay off them."

"He's my uncle's friend. And he said Tresca might come. He worked with Debs on the Sacco-Vanzetti case, for chrissake." Uncle David, when he heard about them meeting with Mike Sierra, called them idiots for talking with "the syndicate." He said that Stanley Morrow was a good man, invested in Barren Shoal already. But to what effect? A couple of years had gone by; the boys were tired of waiting.

"Wrong, asshole," said Yorgos. "Tresca worked on it; Debs was in jail. He sent money. What the hell: Debs ran for president from jail."

Mr. Paradissis exploded when he got wind of their plans to attend the rally. "You outta your cotton picking mind!" he hollered in English, wincing in pain and holding his ribs. He was outside checking on his beehives. "If Boyle gets word of you boys going to hear Tresca, we'll all be on the next boat outta here before you can say kiss my ass."

"Nikolaou!" said Mrs. Paradissis, who rushed out to see why he was yelling. This was one of the rare times that Sofia's mother addressed Mr. Paradissis in front of us by name. Formalities mattered a lot to people who had so little.

"No one's got to know, Ba," said Yorgos.

"Maybe someone sees you, who knows you, who knows Boyle. He puts two and two together, and boom, you're done, *we're* done, no job, no house, no nothing."

"We're three guys, Dad. Everyone expects us to go tom-catting in the city."

Mr. Paradissis grumbled something in Greek.

"You can't stop me, Dad," said Yorgos.

Mr. Paradissis slapped Yorgos across the face. "I wouldn't dream of it."

Noah got in touch with Mr. Morrow to find out where his group was meeting in Union Square. Yorgos said there was no way that Sierra would be there if the communist clubs were coming. When my father heard the rumor about Tresca speaking, he decided to go over that day for his bi-weekly visit to HIAS. "You'll come too," he informed me. "Dress nice, okay?"

"But Dad," I complained. I did not have heart to stand on that line again and hear all those sad stories. So many lost souls felt unbearable. Who knew that the worst unbearable was yet to come?

"You already got plans that day?" he asked playfully.

The barge trip to Brooklyn went better than usual. Not even the stench of rotting garbage got in the way of a cooling breeze. The boys pounded their rat sticks in unison. Joey, whose voice had already changed from a boy's voice to a tenor, began scat singing to the beat.

"What's that he's singing?" asked my father.

"It's 'scat,'" said Noah.

"As in *The rats better scat*?"

"As in Louis Armstrong. Ella Fitzgerald. As in *jazz*!"

"Which you know from what?"

"From the radio, man!" Noah drummed the syllables on his thighs.

"*Man, schman.* Just keep banging those sticks and leave the jazz-mattazz to the radio. What happened to this being an important day when you hear your big hero Tresca?"

"If he shows," said Yorgos. Joey was still singing who-knows-what and Noah was dancing with just his feet.

"If I can't dance, I'm not going to the revolution," Noah crooned.

"Says who?" asked Yorgos. He banged his stick near Noah's feet.

"Says Emma Goldman, that's who."

"You boys think politics is some kind of party?" asked my father. "People are getting beaten to death, thrown in jail, thrown out of the country."

"You still think misery's at the heart of everything," said Noah. "I think it's joy."

Rumor had it that Tresca would be speaking at 5:00 p.m. Dad worked it out with the boys to meet up on the southern end of Union Square at 6:00 p.m. in front of Klein's Department Store.

We split up at the subway at Astor Place. My father and I walked the half block to HIAS, where the line was snaking out the door. People looked angry or anxious or empty, as if standing there, hoping to come to someone's rescue, was more exposure of their humanity than they could stand. My father found the man who sold numbers, exchanged his receipt, and got a stub that moved us ahead in the line. We stepped inside.

A man in the lobby was lecturing a small group of people who, unwilling to risk their places in line, had no choice but to listen. "*...the fall of the Roman Empire, the fall of the Hapsburgs, the Herero and the Namaqua, the collapse of the Ottoman Empire, Azerbaijan, Uzbekistan, Turkmenistan, the upheavals in Macedonia and Serbia....*"

I tugged at my father's sleeve. "What's he talking about?"

"What does she teach you in that school?"

"*...Genghis Khan, King Leopold of Belgium, King Ferdinand and Queen Isabelle,....*"

The man was getting louder and people across the room were looking around to see what was going on.

"*...Russian Civil War! The Fall of Rome! The Thirty Years War! Russia's Time of Troubles! Napoleonic Wars! French Wars of Religion!*"

Two men in shirtsleeves came out of an office and grabbed the man, who by now was yelling at the top of his lungs.

"*THE AN LUSHAN REVOLT, THE FALL OF THE MING DYNASTY, THE TAIPING REBELLION, THE AMERICAN*

INDIANS, THE ARAB SLAVE TRADE, THE ATLANTIC SLAVE TRADE, THE GREAT WAR...."

He struggled to throw them off. A third man approached and spoke to him as he yelled.

"*THERE ARE DATES, THEY HAVE NAMES; THE MASSACRES, THE PEOPLE, THEY HAVE NAMES!!*"

It could have happened to anyone in that room. Anyone could have gone nuts waiting in line, but not my father. He did not look one bit bothered. Perhaps anyone who lived with my mother could do the same. Including me.

The man was still yelling when my father's number was called and the wooden floor boards creaked under our shoes and we were seated in swivel chairs in front of a man named Schwartzbart, on whose desk my father spread a piece of paper with the names and addresses, neatly printed, of the brothers and sisters and parents still living in Zyrmuny. We had been in line for barely thirty minutes. Make that two years and thirty minutes.

Mr. Schwartzbart reached for a stack of printed forms from shelf behind him. Carefully, with a kindness I had never witnessed before in the lettering of a word, he wrote the names of each person.

"Occupations?" he asked.

"Children?" he asked.

"Health status?" he asked.

Two of my mother's sisters had been diagnosed with tuberculosis but had survived, depending on your definition of survival. In their letters they each described the other as being chronically thin, chronically tired, chronically weary, and chronically pale.

"Tuber..." my father started to say.

"Shssh," Mr. Schwartzbart interrupted. He looked over the top of his eyeglasses and tapped his pen to his lips. "Garden variety illnesses from which everyone recovered?"

My father nodded.

A drop of ink had leaked onto Mr. Schwartzbart's lower lip and dried there. Neither of us mentioned it.

"How many will you sponsor?" asked Mr. Schwartzbart.

"That list," said my father, touching his fingertips to the official piece of paper.

"You're talking ten people here," said Mr. Schwartzbart, "not counting the grandparents."

"My family, sir," said my father. "We're talking about my family."

"How are you going to put up twelve people, only two of whom have had jobs? How will you feed them?"

"Mr. Schwartzbart, with respect: I thought that's what *you* do. Find a place to live, find a job."

"Yes, Mr. Eisenstein, we try. But tell me: did we help you or did you manage?"

"No, my brother-in-law helped," my father answered. He lowered his eyes.

I can still see him pondering, wondering if there was only one right answer that he had already gotten wrong.

"So, tell me: how many can *you* sponsor. Your wife's parents, yes? They'll live with you, the grandparents to your children, always room.

"Two for you then and ten for us," Mr. Schwartzbart said with a sigh. He smoothed out the completed form that was not even wrinkled and slid it to the side of his desk.

"Please," said my father. "Do the best you can."

Mr. Schwartzbart stood; the conversation was over. He extended his hand to my father, who clasped it and held on. "We always do the best we can," said Mr. Schwartzbart. "What else can we do?" He used his free hand to cover my father's hand and left it there for a somehow comforting moment.

CHAPTER 14

We walked up Astor Place to Broadway, passing stores selling hats, selling shirts, selling shoes. There were other stores selling nuts and dried fruits; dried mushrooms were looped on strings, like the dried fig necklaces that the Paradissises wore on the boat from Greece. It was easy to believe—at least on a brief walk up Broadway—that we were living in abundance. It was certainly nicer than thinking about scavengers and barges, or the fact that we were seven years into The Great Depression without a sign of it ending, or that the only promise Mr. Schwartzbart could make was to try.

HIAS, it turned out, was six easy blocks from Union Square. The closer we got, the better we could hear the din rising from the park. Soon we could see the backs of people who were facing a simple, unadorned platform that had been set up above the crowd. Hundreds, maybe thousands were already gathered. Lots of them were carrying placards: *In Unity Is Our Strength* or *We Demand 8 Hour Work Days*. Others were wearing buttons for the I.W.W. or the A.F. of L. Most of the signs were in English, but plenty were in Yiddish or Italian or Chinese. People disagreed about religion and politics, but not about full employment. Who wants to starve? The Depression had circled the globe, Spain was on the eve of a civil war, and those stupid Italians had embraced Mussolini, who changed from a socialist to a fascist because it suited him. Jews and anti-fascists were being gunned down at will in Germany and Austria. We read about it in the newspapers; we heard about it on the radio. Japanese troops were slaughtering Manchurians and raping Nanking on the other side of the world. Must people suffer so that life can have meaning or to prove it has none?

My father assessed the scene, his hand salute-like on his brow to block the sun. A few policemen on horseback were circling the square. Others walked through the crowd, twirling their nightsticks. Party members were selling political pamphlets and *The Daily Worker*. Vendors were selling soft pretzels, hot dogs, and apples.

"Let's go home, Dad," I said. I was finally at one of Noah's meetings, but it was crowded with noisy chaos. It looked like anything but fun.

"Where the heck are they?" my father wondered as he scanned the crush. Union Square was already two-thirds full and people were still coming.

"Look, Dad: more mounted policemen." Another half-dozen were crossing into the park.

"If they're not here at 6:00, I'll wring Noah's neck. I'm not spending all night searching for him."

It was only 1:30. The speeches had already begun and a man in overalls stood at the lectern: *We gather today from all shades of labor opinion, from the right to the left, but we can agree on this: let the workers' strength be the answer to Spanish Fascism. Help the democracy of Spain fight the Fascist Party.*

"Noah says England's already betrayed Spain."

"Never mind Spain right now. Let's get out of here," said my father.

He led me out of the park past more shops, some closed for good, some with their lights off but their doors propped open to show that they still had something to sell. No one could afford to leave lights burning when no one was shopping. I think of this as the literal darkness that preceded a greater darkness, the one that had already overtaken Europe and China and Ethiopia.

We walked back to the subway down a corridor that stank of old air and sewer gas. People on the platform looked busy, and bored, and hot. Some of them were fanning themselves with newspapers. A man eating a hot dog leaned over the tracks. He bowed his legs so that loose strands of sauerkraut dropped on the rails instead of his suit. Watching him was like seeing a car wreck on a highway. He was disgusting; I could not stop looking.

My father found a subway map and traced one of the lines with his finger. His chin relaxed. He counted the number of stops to the destination he had not yet revealed. His eyes lost their worry. Mr. Schwartzbart's office and Union Square fell away.

An express train arrived and more people fanned out wearing buttons and carrying banners. My father motioned me to a seat next to a plump, young woman holding more pillows than she could manage. He stationed himself in front of me, gripped the passenger strap overhead, and steadied himself with an easy sway as the train rocked back and forth. I could feel the press of people from every direction, even the ones nowhere near me. One of the woman's pillows was soon resting across my lap. The man on my other side cleaned his teeth with a matchstick. Somewhere was a baby in need of a diaper. Barren Shoal was not the only place that smelled awful.

"This is us," my father said at 34th Street. He reached for my hand, which I gladly took against the rush. We passed Macy's, which stayed busy despite The Depression. We passed bars and newsstands, past men loitering, past vendors selling apples, past carts selling shaved ice.

We walked a few blocks before stopping in front of a glass-plated display case.

"Well?" he asked, with a satisfied grin. "*Tosca*!" That is what it said on the poster. *Tosca*. Hanging inside the case was a plaque with red lettering: **TODAY**. "Come on," he said. We joined some people standing in a neat line at the box office window. We inched our way forward. Then we were in the Metropolitan Opera House, the old Met on 39th and Broadway, taking our places with the others holding standing-room tickets. It was that easy.

Elegantly dressed people passed us on their way to their seats. They looked away from us. I suppose they pitied us just like we pitied the scavengers.

"Does Mom know?" I asked.

My father shook his head. He smiled as if to say *we are conspirators*.

"And Noah?"

He shook his head again. "I'd told your mother that I'd bring you if we finished in time at HIAS."

"We're not going back?"

He draped his arm around my shoulders. "Stop asking so many questions. Look at where you are. Isn't this something?"

We settled in against the back wall of the orchestra section, in one of the crowded little spots reserved for standers. The air was heavy with perfume and cologne that I now remember as Chanel and Shalimar, but that is my memory filling in details it could never have known. The audience rustled in their seats until the orchestra members entered the pit. I had heard live music before: *klezmer* clarinetists and fiddle players and a girl in my aunt and uncle's building who actually had a piano at home because her mother gave lessons. But never in a concert hall dark with expectation.

A restless hush announced the conductor's arrival. The audience broke into applause, already happy about a thing that had not yet happened. The beautiful house fixtures dimmed; the stage lights came up. I tightened my grip on the ledge. It is hard to convey: we imagine something, and we imagine as well that the very thing we have imagined is impossible. Then, suddenly, it surrounds us. The thing I had thought impossible was now true. I was attending an opera at the old Met. Such a special building should have never been torn down. Nor its neighbor, the old Pennsylvania Station. What is left to say about such reckless destruction?

The instruments, like perfume and cologne, transformed the air. I was hearing *Tosca* with my whole body now, not just my ears. When the music trembled, I trembled. When Angelotti rushed into the church of Sant'Andrea della Valle, my pulse rushed right along with him. When cannon fire warned of Angelotti's escape from the fortress, I grabbed my father's hand in fear. It was damp with sweat. Our own beating hearts had become instruments as well.

At intermission, my father found a pretzel cart on the street. The vendor asked if I wanted mustard, but this whole street-food business was as new to me as the inside of the Met. My father pulled a loop off the pretzel and handed it to me. The mustard stung my sinuses. I hoped we did not look as disgusting as that man on the subway eating his hot dog.

"I want to explain this union business of Noah's," my father said. "It's not that I don't believe in their cause. You understand that, don't you?"

"It's between the boys and the unions," I said. The pretzel was burnt where it had been sitting on the coals. I flicked off some ash.

"And between Mr. Paradissis and Mr. Dowd and Yorgos and Joey and DeWitt and every single person who lives on Barren Shoal. And even Miss Finn, who goes back and forth to Brooklyn. It's between the union bosses and the factory bosses, the planning commission and the mayor. I don't disagree about the principles. But I don't want Noah getting hurt. And I don't want him hurting us."

I took another bite of the pretzel. Big grains of salt stuck to my lips, stinging them. Noah was right. My father was right. No matter what they did or did not do, there would be no guarantees.

"Can we get a drink, please?"

"There's a fountain inside by the restrooms," he said. He cupped his hand under my elbow and we crossed the street. We joined the line inside for water. "People get so wrapped up in things that they can't see the forest for the trees. You understand that saying?"

I nodded. The line inched forward.

"Here's another saying: pick your battles wisely."

I nodded again, half-listening. There were now just two people ahead of us.

"Think about *Tosca*," he continued. "People think it's enough to love opera for the singing, for the spectacle. But don't let that distract you from the story. You've always got to keep an eye on the whole story. You got to at the opera; you got to everywhere."

"Sure, Dad," I mumbled as I leaned over to drink. The first warning chimes for Act II were ringing as I slurped.

There were empty seats in the orchestra section now, but when I suggested that we take them, my father scowled, as if I was suggesting that we steal them.

"If you want you can take a look-see at the orchestra pit. And don't bother the musicians!"

I was heading down the aisle when I heard familiar voices. There, seated a few rows down, were Lois and Gray. Of course they would have opera tickets; of course they would have orchestra seating; of course their seats would be on the aisle. If they saw me what would I say? That I was standing in back with my father? That we would be standing the whole three hours while Lois and Gray sat comfortably? I felt plenty small enough around them already. I turned back up the aisle before they spotted me.

My father, surprised to see me, said, "I thought you wanted to—"

"Changed my mind." This was not a respectful tone to take with my father, but there it was.

I leaned against the low wall separating the standers from the sitters and kicked off my shoes, my socks now the only thing between my feet and the thousands of pairs of shoes of the thousands of people who walked through the Met every week. I did not regret, just for that day, how teenage girls then wore socks with dresses. My feet were tired from so much walking. Not even Puccini could stop my toes from hurting. I will not pretend that being uncomfortable did not matter. But, really, it had no meaning compared to the fact that I was standing in the same concert hall where the music was being made. Hearing music is not like reading a book. At least, not for me. I cannot read a score and hear it in my head. Yes, we had a radio, which was wonderful. But the difference between music live and on the radio is like the difference between Michelangelo's *David* in person and the postcard. I know because I went to Italy after the war, after we were married. And then I saw it in person. Me, Marta Eisenstein Lane from Barren Shoal, visited Florence.

"Now *there's* a fashion statement." The house lights were up for intermission when Lois appeared beside me. Gray was smiling over her shoulder.

"Lois, hi. Hi, Gray." I slipped back into my shoes.

My father leaned around to see who was speaking. "Going to introduce us?"

"Lois, Gray, my father: Mr. Eisenstein."

"Then you are Noah's father as well," said Gray, while they shook hands.

"You know my son...."

"Through a union meeting, Dad. They know Noah and Yorgos from a meeting."

I knew what he was thinking: *How do they know Marta? Marta's never been to a union meeting.* I do not know why I felt safe to lie about them, but I did. And wiser.

"We visited your island a few weeks ago, Mr. Eisenstein," said Lois, who was much wiser than me. Better to be in charge of the facts than let my father hear gossip.

"Then you must know my brother-in-law, David...."

Would you believe that I was literally saved by the bell? Crazy, yes? But sometimes things really work that way. A bell chimed for the next act and Lois and Gray, after quick good-byes, hurried to their seats. It was a great little flash of feeling lucky.

It was hard now to keep my attention forward and not on the backs of Lois and Gray's heads. Who were these people? How did they have the money for the best seats at the Met and fancy London gin? What did they want with Noah and Yorgos? What would knowing them mean for Noah?

The stage filled and the story moved forward. Thinking about the opera was the same as thinking about anyone: it was about who wanted what and why. How could Tosca doubt the devotion of Mario, the artist who loves her? How could she believe the empty promises of the brutal Police Chief Scarpa? When she sings that she "lives for art," is she refusing the burden of seeing what is happening around her? Was there something that Noah was not seeing? Were Gray and Lois sincere or was there something that they wanted?

"You've had your big day," said my father when the curtain fell. He removed his glasses and wiped his face with a handkerchief. "Your first opera." The rest of the audience was now on its feet applauding. The curtain rose again and the supporting singers returned to the stage. The principal singers came on stage followed by the conductor, who signaled the orchestra to rise. The applause of the audience grew wilder. I could see Lois and Gray clapping like mad.

It was hard letting go of the opera just because the singers, restored to life again, were gathered on stage. I wanted to believe for a while longer in what was unbelievable. I was having my day. I closed my eyes. When I opened them, Lois and Gray were gone.

Back at Union Square, hundreds of policemen now circled what had grown into an enormous rally, leaving only two breaks in the line where people could enter or exit. Those openings were flanked on either side by dozens more police on horseback. The moment that one horse shifted its weight from one set hooves to the other, a rippling effect went down the row. Another would shift and then another until it reached the end and they stopped. Then a different horse would shift its weight and the rippling would begin anew. The rippling effect spilled into the crowd, with people pushing away from being trapped.

"This isn't good," said my father. He craned his neck, rocking up and down on his toes to see better. "Noah," he called into the crowd. "Noah!" Pointless yelling like that, but what else could he do?

The person at the podium had just invoked the Scottsboro Boys, the very mention of whom whipped up the crowd. Not that there were a lot of black people in the crowd, but everyone knew that those young men were railroaded by the all-white Alabama juries. On the other hand, you know how they liked their lynching parties down there, so the jurors went disappointed too.

My father waited for the crowd to settle before calling Noah's name again.

"Hold it down," shouted a woman. "This ain't a racetrack."

"Is that Tresca up there?" my father asked, ignoring her scolding. "Who's speaking?"

"No Tresca. This one's from the Y.C.L. Or maybe the Y.S.L."

"You don't know which?" asked the man next to her. He was holding a tattered *8 Hour Work Day* sign.

"Oh, what's the difference," said the woman, waving him off.

"Young *Communist* League or Young *Socialist* League: it's all the difference in the world," said the man, who must have been her husband.

"At least to them it is," said the woman.

"Don't be such a know-it-all," said the man. "I was here on Unemployment Day 1930. The Y.C.L. people, they should have been happy with the turnout, but no: they had to march to City Hall. Made a mess of everything. The police started swinging, people got hurt. You think the party organizers care that we got busted up? Forget it: they were happy!"

They must have had this argument a hundred times before.

The woman rolled her eyes. "If you would've...."

My father pulled me past the couple. "Come on. We've gotta find the boys." We weaved through the crowd, me holding onto the hem of his jacket. People were packed even tighter closer to the platform. My father kept asking them to let us through, but he pretty much elbowed us forward.

"Take it easy," said a large man with a red face and sweat-dampened hair, who reminded me of Mr. Boyle.

"I've got to find my son," said my father, pushing past him.

"That's what you get for bringing children where they don't belong."

"He's not a child," my father replied, elbowing his way ahead.

"Then he's old enough to find his own way home," called the red-faced man.

Sure enough we spotted Noah approaching the podium, of all things, looking gawky and handsome in his newsboy hat and loose jacket. A man at the microphone described how the protesters would now hear from "some young people already learning to carry the weight of the movement." The crowd kept pushing closer and now the police were moving in too. Someone started singing "The Internationale" and others joined in. Something exploded. *Pop, pop, pop.* The police were swinging their nightsticks, batting people on their shoulders and backs until they fell to the ground.

People were shouting, panic-pushing to get away from wherever they were standing, slamming against one another from all directions in a desperate attempt to get to the street. Others were pointing to the roofs of the office buildings at the north end of the square, to a row of policemen resting the barrels of their rifles on the parapet walls. Others still were pointing deeper into the crowd where a loud fight broke out at the same time as the gunshots fired overhead. The people pushing to get out of the square were colliding with some men pushing to get closer to the fight, some of whom were pulling sticks and clubs from under their coats. All sorts of metal objects—knives and chains and pistols—caught the sunlight before they disappeared into the brawl. More *pop, pop, pops* triggered a different kind of screaming, the kind that comes with pain. I knew the difference. I never forgot my mother screaming in horror while Helen was shrieking in agony. All it takes is a child screaming for me to hear that moment all over again, the same way the stink of a passing garbage truck lands me right back on Barren Shoal. I know my senses are tricking me, but it is like phantom pains in a missing limb. And who would tell an amputee that what they feel does not hurt?

Whatever was peaceful about the rally vanished, changing a well-behaved crowd into an unpredictable mob. It made not a bit of difference who was honorable or who was corrupt or who had the highfalutin cause, at least not in that moment when anyone's gun killed as good as the next one. Would I feel any better if Noah or my father were killed by a protester's pistol instead of a cop's? I should think not. And who could tell who was who? Maybe the men with the knives and clubs were demonstrators or maybe they were agitators sent in to stir up trouble. Or maybe they were undercover cops. We will never know.

From the tight little circle where the men were fighting came something small and dark, soaring into the air trailed by a thin, broken streak of fire. It rose a few feet over the mob before landing and exploding right where a band of anarchists were holding up a banner. The bang of the explosion was followed by the shrieks and moaning of the people hit by the blast and by the *pop, pop, pop* of more gunfire.

The injured who could walk stumbled about like drunks, wiping debris off their faces with their bloodied hands and torn shirtsleeves. Some were crawling away on their hands and knees and others stayed where they were, crying for help, crying for their mothers, crying for God. A woman holding a baby stood frozen while the crowd swarmed around her. Blood was running from her lips over her chin and down her neck. She wiped her fingers across her bottom teeth, some of which fell to the ground. A man covered in dust and dirt approached her and dabbed the blood from her lip with his thumb. It was the same man who had been standing next to us a few minutes earlier, the one with the *8 Hour Work Week* sign. He wrapped one arm around her shoulder and other behind her knees, lifted her off the ground, and walked away slowly as the crowds pushed around them. His wife walked ahead of them, clearing the path as best she could by swinging the sign from left to right. "Just like 1930," he shouted to my father as they passed us. I held onto my father's arm, scared that we would be separated. "Except now it's my daughter that's bloody, not my wife."

The mounted policemen were now walking their horses into the crowd. This triggered a new wave of shouting and screaming. A protester lunged at one of the horses, reaching for its bridle and causing the horse to rear on its hind legs. This was following by more shrieking from the crowd, neighing and rearing by the horse, and a bone-shattering scream from the protester when the horse came down on his foot. The policeman, who must have been one hell of a horseman the way he stayed on that horse, you should pardon me, added his two cents by using his billy club to crack open the protester's head. Literally. I cannot say for certain if what I saw spilling from his skull was blood or brains or something else. The inside of a horse head I knew about, but not a man's. A gang of the trampled man's friends pulled the policeman down from the horse and threw him into the crowd, which obliged by kicking the policeman to the ground, where he disappeared.

Another man grabbed the horse's reigns and pulled him away. Most everyone made room for the horse the way crowds always do, the few exceptions shoved aside by the horse itself as it followed the man leading him. People were as afraid of those horses as they were of guns, and for good reason. Look at all the years of hell, you should pardon me, that Flat Sammy lived through on account of the horse that kicked Aunt Sara. The only horses that could not hurt us were the ones going to Barren Shoal.

Thank goodness there were no police dogs at Union Square, the way those sheriffs used them on the marchers in the '60s, ripping them apart like rags. You would think that people would have learned after seeing the way those Germans used the poor Shepherds and Dobermans in the death camps. I say poor because people teach them to be terrible, these dumb creatures that our ancestors went through all that trouble to tame. I am still waiting for humanity to improve. We can make everything better except ourselves.

The man leading the horse handed up the reins to another mounted officer, after which he disappeared back into the crowd. Like I say: there was no way to know who was who. And since one agitated horse leads to another, the other horses were now stomping and rearing up and landing hard while the policemen on foot grabbed whoever was close by and beat them. Not just the young men, who were at least strong enough to fight back, but women and old folks, too. Instead of things quieting down, they got worse. People were shoving so hard to get to the streets that they were trampling the others who had been whacked to the ground or who stumbled and fell. A short man wearing a stained newsboy cap just like Noah's bumped against me, sending me skidding as if the ground was ice. Someone had left a mess of blood down there.

The man in the dirty newsboy cap—I do not know who he was or why he did it—threw a punch that landed on my father's chin. My father grunted when he knocked the cap off the man's head. Then he shoved the man out of his way and climbed onto the stage. My father threw another punch, this one at Noah, who was standing still with his arms wrapped around himself, despite the noisy chaos of the gunshots and the Molotov cocktails and the stampede. My father punched Noah, it seemed, so that no one else would climb up there and punch him or worse. My father's fist landed squarely on Noah's jaw and I, in that instant, remembered the old story about my father getting the job on Barren Shoal from the man with the scrap cart in the garment district. My father had punched that man too after the man told my father to steal a bolt of cloth from under Uncle David's nose. It is not lost on me that my father went from punching a stranger to protect a family member to punching a family member to protect him from strangers. Punching a stranger over an insult sounds pretty foolish, if you ask me. As for punching Noah, well who could blame him: if that is what it took to save Noah's life during a riot, then so be it. I wish I could be a pacifist, but I am not. It is a luxury that I cannot afford.

My father pulled Noah from the podium by his jacket collar, leaving Noah's hands free now to punch the policeman, who slammed his billy club across Noah's shoulders and into his gut. Noah doubled over and vomited on the policeman's legs. The policeman tried jumping away, but there were too many people crowding the stage. He and Noah were tumbling to the ground in a vomit-covered pile when my father grabbed Noah by the collar again and pulled him to his feet. There was blood soaking through his jacket sleeve. I landed between two Chinese men with signs I could not read, which they were swinging to keep the policeman at bay as he staggered back up. When the policeman reached for his gun, one of the Chinese men knocked it from his hands. The gun went off, followed by more screams. A bullet pierced the sign and struck the Chinese man's cheek. Blood spit from his mouth in red clots.

My father dragged Noah and me out of there like we were puppies. The Chinese man and his friend were right behind us. If I could have closed my eyes I would have. I am not a person who gets thrills from seeing other people hurt or scared. Nor have I learned any better why some people do. People do terrible things because that is what people do.

My father did not let go until we were out of the park and all the way over by the Automat, where Joey and Yorgos had been watching the riot the whole time. When I looked behind me, the Chinese men were gone. There were no police in sight.

"What the hell is going on?" cried Yorgos, pulling Noah out of my father's grip. Noah looked green in the face and was holding his stomach. His lip was split and his coat sleeve was stained with blood.

"Get Noah out of here," said my father.

The five of us walked in a huddle surrounding Noah: Yorgos and Joey on either side of him and my father and me right behind. Noah was crying. He told them about the explosion and the police and the gunshots. He told them he had been about to address the crowd.

The doors were still open at the shops we had passed hours before. The injured and the just plain scared found safety among the merchants selling hats, the merchants selling shirts, the merchants selling shoes. Some looters found what they wanted as well. So what else is new?

"Where were you guys?" my father demanded. "You were supposed to stick together."

"We were gone a minute," said Joey, still working on a half-eaten sandwich.

The only shuttered doors were at the shop selling cheese and dried fruits. Through the glass I could see two men with bats and a third with a wide, long knife—the kind used for cutting those big wheels of cheese. People were banging their fists on the doors in outrage or desperation or who-knows-what as they passed by, but no one threw any bricks or tried to break the doors open. People were still running from a fight, not looking for one.

"Why'd you hit me, Dad," cried Noah, wiping his bloodied

lip on his shirtsleeve.

"What the hell were you doing up there?" My father was shouting so loud that other people, even the ones rushing away from the police, looked over.

"You should be proud of me," said Noah. "They asked me to. They got my name from Mike Sierra. They asked me to speak."

My father passed him his handkerchief. "Are you some kind of jerk? Are you *trying* to be arrested? Thrown in jail? Thrown out of the country? Is that what you're going for?" He was still shepherding us away from Union Square, farther south on Broadway, back in the direction toward HIAS, toward the quieter subway station we had used that morning to go uptown.

"They can't throw *me* out of the country," said Noah. He was bragging in a foolish, hurtful way, as if this somehow made him better. "I was born here."

"*Here*? Where? Exactly what do you think 'here' means?"

"I'm a citizen. It's my birthright."

"You can get that out of your head fast." He grabbed Noah's arm. Noah moaned and turned pale and then green, like he was going to be sick again. "What?" my father barked, like he was giving an order, not asking a question.

Noah pulled his jacket away. The bloody fabric had a tear in it, beneath which there was a tear in Noah's shirtsleeve, beneath which there was a tear in his skin. It must have been his adrenaline racing around in all that chaos that kept him from feeling the wound. He was damned lucky, you should pardon me, that he was only grazed by the bullet and not killed by it. It was his left arm, so close to the heart.

My father tore off the ruined shirtsleeve and tied it into a tourniquet. You might think it would be hard to rip a sleeve off a shirt, but Noah was not wearing the kind of good shirt that Uncle David cut. The cheap shirts that Noah made do with would have fallen apart had he yawned wide enough.

Noah wiped his bloody fingers on the makeshift tourniquet. "You're wrong, Dad," he said. "A birthright's like air and water. I'm entitled. Anything less isn't normal. It's my right."

"They cut your toes off if they want. Because they *feel* like it. Or because they feel nothing for you at all. Never mind you're *entitled*. No one gets entitled to nothing. That's *normal*."

The crowd thinned out south of Union Square. It was quiet, as if the riot had never happened, as if the streets had sucked everyone up and everything out of them. It was getting dark and people were walking quickly, including my father and the boys. Here and there a gaslight had been lit early. It was hard to keep from falling behind.

"And just where've *you* been," Yorgos asked me when we stopped for the traffic light at St. Marks Place. The way Yorgos spoke, it was as if I had abandoned Noah, not he.

"Opera," I said, out of breath. Imagine how hard it had been for those opera singers to get enough air, even with those big, enlarged lungs, when I could barely catch my breath from rushing! I never learned to breathe right anyway, the way singers do. It is part of the legacy of growing up on Barren Shoal. Who felt safe to take a deep belly-filling breath, never mind one after the other after the next?

Yorgos laughed at the mention of the opera. "That's damned nice, Marta: Nero fiddles while Rome burns."

"That's just a story," I said. "Ask Miss Finn."

"You think this is some kind of fairy tale? An opera? People got shot today. For real. We coulda been killed."

"Not you and Joey. You were too busy stuffing your faces."

Noah barely spoke on the trip back to Barren Shoal. We Eisensteins are so good at that. He refused the cigarettes that the boys offered. When Joey resumed scat singing to the beat of the rat sticks, Noah told him to "shut the fuck up." Those are Noah's words, not mine. At one point he threw his stick at a rat that would not be frightened off by the pounding. The rat lay stunned for a few seconds before scrambling away. One of the rats—there was no way to tell one from the other or if this was the one that Noah had stunned—poked its head back out from behind a horse hoof and ran. It stopped in its tracks when it neared Joey in order to nibble something off his shoe. Yorgos reached into a pocket inside his jacket, pulled out a knife, and stabbed the rat a bunch of times. When the rat finally stopped twitching, Yorgos wiped the knife on the corpse and kicked it on the pile of horses. No one even flinched.

A bright red cherry appeared on Noah's chin where our father had hit him; there were also three pale impressions where the knuckles made contact. Noah stood quietly cradling his wounded arm. Too quietly. After all those years of my mother's silence, I do not have the stomach for anyone else's. I tried telling him about *Tosca*.

"Not now," he said, when I began describing how, in the second act, Scarpa manipulates Tosca, who is too self-righteous to even notice when she is being used.

There was certainly plenty of that going around. Noah was polite and quiet and angry, like someone shooing a fly from their plate at a holiday dinner.

By the time we reached the halfway mark across the bay, Joey was using his stick to poke around the fly-covered horse cadavers, jacking up their legs and letting them drop. No one cared until Joey poked his stick beneath a horse's tail. Yorgos grabbed the stick, threw it into the bay, and kicked Joey so hard in the rear end that Joey stumbled over the horse and landed on another.

Everyone settled down again, quiet except for the steady

pounding of our sticks. So much silence. What do people do with all of the silence they keep inside themselves? Is it comforting? Contemplative? Cowardly?

The barge captain, Parson Otis, was drunk as usual and too busy talking to himself to pay us much notice. I wondered what he would tell police when they came for Noah, which they would certainly do. What would they do when they found him? Arrest him, of course. What else would they do to him on the trip from Barren Shoal to Brooklyn? From the police station to the courthouse; from the courthouse to the prison? He had punched a cop. Now every cop in New York would feel entitled to kill him, never mind slap him around.

The barge churned closer to home. The sky over Barren Shoal was dark but for the single red light atop the smokestack, which served as a beacon for the airplanes landing across the water at Floyd Bennett Field. Funny thing, that light: planes never landed at night, but the light glowed anyway. A little further off I could see the similar lights on the smokestacks of Barren Island. Behind us were the lights of Manhattan, draping a pink glow over the island like the pale rose umbrella of a moon jellyfish, the kind that washed into Jamaica Bay in late spring.

CHAPTER 15

The awkward silences of the barge crossing and the walk along the sandy loop road ended at home with the door closed behind us.

"You'd no right to stop me, Dad," insisted Noah. "I keep telling you: this island is an accident waiting to happen. There'll be another explosion, a worse one, more people blown to pieces."

"What should I do when my son's getting bashed in the head by a cop? Or gets shot by who-knows-whose bullet? Stand by and admire his principles?"

My mother was in their bedroom, as usual, still avoiding everything she could. Working through Helen's death took her so long that she never fully moved on to what came next. For my mother, there was no next. She must have known we were home by then, what with my father and brother hollering loud enough that anyone could hear.

"That's why we have to organize, so you don't have to." Noah was standing at the sink washing his wounded arm. It was bleeding again now that the tourniquet was off.

"Stop already, stop it!"

Each waited to see if the other would let it go. But why would they? My father was angry and terrified; Noah was angry and terrified and bleeding. Neither had something different to offer. They were stubborn and stuck, going round and around.

"A 'right' is an idea," said my father. "A 'protest' is an act. Between an idea and an act are the New York City police, who will bust in your brains if they can find you, never mind arrest the bunch of you, throw you in jail, who knows what. What gives you the 'right' to that?"

Noah's face was shimmering with sweat. His arm hurt more as his excitement wore down. "The same reason you got on the boat in the first place. Because I have to; because I can."

Maybe other families do not talk to each other this way, do not talk about these kinds of things. Mine did.

Sofia came across the way to see what was wrong.

"I'm not listening to this again," I told her on the way upstairs. "I won't be their audience." Words like "forbidden" and "selfish" rose through the floorboards. *Not in my house*," my father shouted just before the back door slammed and the house went silent.

Sofia sat on my bed, hands in her lap, waiting for me to get past whatever it was that was making me too angry. Neither of us ever sat on Helen's bed. Except for that time I was so sick with poison ivy that my father slept upstairs, no one ever did.

"Yorgos says Noah was amazing until your father punched him."

"Yorgos wasn't even there! He was over by the Automat with Joey, stuffing his face." I do not know why I needed to defend my father, except that I could not stand Sofia defending every stupid thing that the boys did. "My father was afraid Noah'd get arrested!"

"Your father is afraid, period."

"Shut up, Sofia," I said. "Would you just shut up."

I pulled off my shoes and kicked them across the room. One landed on Helen's bed.

"What are you doing?" This time she spoke harshly.

A quiet moan leaked out of me as I dropped onto my bed.

"Tell me about the opera," she said, the harshness suddenly, unpredictably gone. Nothing is predictable. There is only what happens.

"How'd you hear about *Tosca*?" I wanted to be the keeper of my own secrets. Yet one more thing we cannot control.

"Like I said: Yorgos told me everything."

"You and Yorgos are friends now? I don't believe this." I shook my head. I was losing track of Sofia, of one of the few things I thought I knew.

"And now the opera's some big secret?" she asked, throwing one of her cold looks of doubt.

"You're the one with secrets."

"You wanna tell me about the opera or what? If not, fine. If you do, c'mon already."

There was no point in doing otherwise. Why resist the desire to tell what follows in beauty's wake? It was not like we got so many chances. I told her about the tuxedos and the costumes, the perfume, the scenery, and the lighting. I told her about Lois and Gray and the awkward introductions to my father. But how does one describe sound without speaking in notes?

"You know that the story makes no sense, don't you?" said Sofia, when I finished Act II.

"Just let me finish." I said. "Finally, when the firing squad appears, Tosca coaches her lover, Mario, on how to fake his death. The soldiers fire and Mario falls; the soldiers go off. Tosca kneels by Mario, urging him stand up so they can escape, but he doesn't move. Tosca discovers that instead of the blank bullets Scarpia promised to use, the rifles were loaded with live ammunition. Mario is dead. No pretend dead; for real dead. Realizing this, Tosca leaps to her death."

"Because Mario's dead or because Scarpia duped her?"

"Don't know. Maybe both."

"Union Square sounds a lot more exciting, if you ask me," said Sofia.

I would have described it again until I got it right, but that would be like an accounting of an infatuation. Its story is tedious when it happens to someone else.

"So tell me: what don't you understand?"

It was warm upstairs even though the day had been cool. Certain things that Miss Finn had taught us, such as that heat rises, were not as mysterious as they seemed. Usually it was the other way around: events were more mysterious than expected.

She grabbed one of my bare feet and held it tight. "Such as I think I'm pregnant."

"What?" I could not even think about doing what it took to get pregnant, never mind imagine being pregnant. With Sofia's announcement, all that changed. How could it not?

She nodded and squeezed harder.

"You can't marry Joey!" I wish that I had said something else, but it is easy to wish that when it no longer matters.

"Oh god," she said. "I can't marry Joey." By then she was sobbing.

We were out the door long before anyone else Monday morning and long before the police boat arrived bearing Miss Finn and her carpetbag of clothing, bundle of newspapers, and the groceries to last the week. Joey was already sifting through a recently arrived barge, as was the girl in the brown dress, Katrine, who was scavenging with the other regulars. I cannot imagine that year after year she wore the same brown dress; it is just that this is the only dress I can picture her in.

Miss Finn was startled to see us waiting at the dock. She told Katrine that she did not need help getting her things to the schoolhouse. It was the first time I heard about Katrine always helping Miss Finn. Joey could have mentioned it, but never did. Katrine looked a little pained as she turned back to the barge.

"Come in a bit," Miss Finn called after her. "Girls?" asked Miss Finn, inviting us to account for the mystery of our early morning appearance. It was awkward, all of us standing there, but somehow Miss Finn understood its importance. She handed her carpetbag to me, the newspaper bundle to Sofia, and took the other parcels herself.

We followed Miss Finn up the sandy path to the school and waited quietly while she fumbled with her keys and unlocked the door. Plovers and starlings were chirping and we could see desperate groups of gulls, always hysterical, swarming to the barge. I thought how I might remember, later on, the morning light on the undersides of things as much as I would remember anything else about that day.

Miss Finn finally remarked about how she appreciated our help, but could not stop wondering what brought us out so early. I nudged Sofia in after her, which was all it took to tip Sofia into tears. Miss Finn began putting things away in the classroom and the kitchen and on the shelves along the steps leading up to her private rooms. Sofia and I stood at the doorway, Sofia still quietly weeping.

"Are we expecting an earthquake, girls?" asked Miss Finn, as if only something as grand as an earthquake warranted notice. "You're supposed to stand in a doorway if there's an earthquake, yes?"

"There aren't earthquakes in New York," I said. It was a stupid conversation to be having when Sofia was right in front of her crying, but I suppose that Miss Finn was waiting for Sofia. Besides which, I was wrong. Of course there are earthquakes in New York, just like there are earthquakes everywhere.

"There's a fault line running right through New York State," said Miss Finn. "Not like the ones where your family is from, Sofia. Greece and Turkey—all of Asia Minor—a huge fault runs through it. The whole history of western civilization has been suddenly turned upside down a number of times because of earthquakes."

Tell her, I said, mouthing the words. If we did not stop her, Miss Finn would chronicle each and every one.

"Tell what?" asked Miss Finn. She rested her hands on her hips the way that our mothers did when they grew impatient.

"Go on," I said, nudging Sofia in Miss Finn's direction.

"Marta, why don't you unpack these things," said Miss Finn, pointing at a canvas bag filled with small, brown paper bags. A bunch of carrots and stalks of celery were poking out along with some fat, white leeks.

"And this?" I asked when I lifted the other bag as well. Glass jars inside it clinked together. *This one must be cooked things*, I thought.

"I'll take care of those," Miss Finn said, snatching the bag from me and setting it back down, the bottles clinking again.

"I can't do this," Sofia whimpered over the clinking of bottles, the rustling of bags, and the other minutia of the groceries. She turned as if to go, then turned back again. "I don't, I can't."

"Come," said Miss Finn, extending her hand. Sofia did not take it, so Miss Finn came closer. She placed her hand on Sofia's shoulder. "We'll talk?" she asked.

Sofia looked at me, not Miss Finn, but she nodded.

"It's better if we go upstairs," said Miss Finn. "Marta, you stay here." The exactness of her instructions made it plain that I should not wander to another room, even though the only other room was the classroom.

It was hard being parked in Miss Finn's kitchen doing nothing, wondering what it was that Sofia had found her way to saying. I thought about our so-called hygiene lesson from years ago, and how Sofia had been intrigued and I had been put off. Same story, different girls. It took me longer to see the point, but I was catching up. What, it should be some sort of race?

I sat at the cold little table, rested my head in my hands, my palms against my brow, and closed my eyes. I emptied the visible world of everyone and everything until I was emptied from it as well. All that was left after that was the smell of Barren Shoal.

There was no mistaking the cry that broke my...what should I call it? Daze? Stupor? Reverie? In Sofia's cry I heard a question that traveled to something larger than her, then back to her again as if it contained an entire conversation. Not a cry like Helen's wailing nor like my mother's, but something her own. I suppose there are millions of ways to cry in pain. Never mind suppose: I know it. Anyone who reads a newspaper knows. Or hears a man howling in the HIAS lobby.

A door opened and closed, followed by the sound of footsteps. Miss Finn blocked my way.

"Sofia's not feeling well," she said with a worried smile.

"Will she be okay?" I stepped back so I could see her better. I could not ask her if Sofia was pregnant before knowing for sure that Sofia told her.

"I'm sure she'll be fine. Why don't you work at your desk and I'll put these things away." She placed her hand on my shoulder, gently but firmly pushing me across the kitchen.

She guided me into the classroom and into my seat, like I

was some sort of mannequin on wheels. She sat down in the chair next to mine—Sofia's chair—and said that Sofia and I were invited to her house in Brooklyn the following Saturday. She would speak with our mothers and arrange everything. And that I should go about my business; that everything would be fine.

After she left, I could hear the sound of glass jars clinking around in her kitchen, and then the sound of her voice in conversation with Katrine, who must have been waiting outside the whole time. I thought she had gone back to the docks.

My marvel at Miss Finn's invitation to Brooklyn was accompanied by a sense of unease, as if a large mechanical wheel was turning our lives. Not the busy wheels at the factory oozing grease, but a mechanism that was cold, deliberate, and precise in its intentions.

Sofia slipped into her chair an hour later, sliding it so close to mine that our arms brushed as we turned the pages of the prior week's newspapers. The room had filled. I could only hope it was as comforting to her as it was to me. The world was asking something more of her than it had just a week earlier, and I could feel it knocking harder on my door, too. We were growing up slowly and then—how suddenly—we were growing up a lot.

On the front page of my newspaper—I do not know what date it was from—there was a headline about the National Industrial Recovery Act being declared unconstitutional. I had not thought about it much when the bill was passed by Congress, but now, two years later, I was old enough to make a leap from a Supreme Court ruling in Washington to its direct effect on Noah, Yorgos, and Joey, which by then meant its effect on all of Barren Shoal.

I could hear it in the garden debates over which union was the right union; I could hear it in the desperate sounds of their voices. Who would not be after so much time? Too much time when things all over were going from terrible to worse. Yorgos was still leaning towards the tough guys from Mulberry Street, who Noah said were fascists; Noah was leaning towards Stanley Morrow's anti-fascists, who Yorgos said were communists. When Joey accused them all of being a bunch of big-shot bosses any way they looked at it—I think he was right—the other two knocked him around playfully, though they were training for a bigger, more brutal fight.

"Noah," I now whispered loud, trying to get his attention across the classroom. I pointed to the article about the newly decommissioned Recovery Act. I asked one of the Dowd kids, who was seated across from me, to pass it over.

"Now you see why we were in Union Square, whether Dad believes us or not," he said, reaching for the paper. He had grown too tall to tuck his knees beneath the school desk, and they banged against the underside. He had grown too big for everything about Barren Shoal with a suddenness that showed on his face not as anger, but as the discomfited posture of someone counting subway stops only to realize that he has boarded the wrong train.

"They're gonna take away fair working hours, minimum wages, collective bargaining, the unions," he said. He was ready to step up on the stage again at Union Square. "If we go on strike here, on Barren Shoal, no one's gonna write about it in the newspaper. No one's gonna give a damn." His voice strained with frustration. "We've got to make noise where people will hear it. It's our time." He snapped his fingers, emphasizing his point. He had never been good at doing this, but now his fingers flew like he was clapping small, wet stones. Miss Finn, who had been ignoring our whispering, could no longer overlook it.

"Is there something you'd like to share?" she asked in the same weary voice of a thousand schoolteachers who came before her, who would follow after. Now that Yorgos was working at the factory, the idea of the "you" was noticeably smaller. If it shrank any further, how many of "us" would be left? Marie Dowd would soon be leaving for Hunter College; Noah would be leaving for somewhere too, though he had not said so. I just knew. Once the signs begin showing, it is impossible to not see them everywhere.

"The National Recovery Act," said Noah. "They've taken that away too."

"Who is *they*?" asked Miss Finn, never one to let it go when we were imprecise.

"The Supreme Court," said Noah.

"And therefore?" she asked again. "Accurate articulation," she reminded him, "leads to accurate thinking." What she did not take into account is that propaganda is the most skillful articulation of all.

"Workers have lost everything," said Noah. The tips of his ears turned red when the whole class looked at him. "Business can go back to doing whatever it wants. The regulations are overturned; the protection is gone."

"You speak as if these were rights that people are born with," said Miss Finn, echoing our father's words from the other night.

"'*The inalienable right to life, liberty and the pursuit of happiness.*' Inalienable. Meaning we're *born* with it," said Noah. Noah believed in the Declaration of Independence and the Constitution. He took them personally, the way he took most everything. "I'm not going to live on Barren Shoal forever doing homework."

"Though you will tomorrow," said Miss Finn, with a chuckle.

"Like I said: not forever."

"So this is only about you?" she said, pushing him.

Noah's ears got that about-to-burst red look again. "It's about all of us. Right now, right here, even in this classroom."

"Is anything about everyone?" she asked.

"Yes," he stammered. "I don't know. Maybe not."

"Perhaps it's best to settle down and think about that."

I thought about it too, though obviously not in the way that Noah did. I am certain that Sofia thought about it as well, as did every chronically curious child in that room. How could we not?

Another letter arrived from my mother's family in Zyrmuny, a battered envelope already yellowed like old newsprint. My mother sat at the table, carefully slitting it open with a kitchen knife. She read it, set it down on the table, and gently smoothed it with her scarred hands.

"So?" asked my father.

She looked at him. "'*For God's sake, help us.*' That's all."

You would think that this was not the kind of plea someone would need to write twice; you would think there would have already been some help for them; you would think that what was happening would not have happened, should not have happened; you would think that there would have been a way to stop the insanity. Except nothing insane was happening in Europe; there was no epidemic of mental illness, no black plague of psychosis. People had choices. The choices they made were disastrous. They were unforgivable.

"I'll go back to HIAS," said my father. Not a week had passed since my father talked with Mr. Schwartzbart, who had made no promises, who had said nothing about time, which could be any amount at all, or even which country might take the family.

"You don't think he's seen a hundred letters just like this?" said my mother.

"If he's seen a hundred, it won't kill him to see a hundred

and one."

"They'll be murdered whether Schwartzbart sees the letter or not."

My father pounded his fist on the table. "What do you expect?" *Pound, pound.* "He said he'll do the best he can."

Which was not true. I was there; I heard him. The best was what my father had asked for; Mr. Schwartzbart said he would try.

"And now? What? We still wait?" said my mother.

"You have a better idea?"

It is 65 years later and still no one has the answer.

Everything that we ate for dinner that night we harvested from the garden or pulled from the sea: a couple of sweet flounder that Noah caught in the bay; fried zucchini blossoms stuffed with minced eggplant; sliced tomatoes with basil. For dessert my mother made rice pudding that we ate warm right from the oven. My father was digging into his second serving when Noah said he was going out, which meant he was going to meet up with the boys and do whatever it was they did until they finally quit being out and came in. I had hovered around Sofia after school that day, but she did not want to talk about the prospects of being pregnant any more than my parents wanted to discuss the situation in Zyrmuny. Silence had been silently agreed upon for both problems. Is that how it happens? You stay silent about this and silent about that until the worst possible things become easy to be silent about too?

I slipped out of the house after dinner. Anyone would have guessed I was going next door to Sofia. I walked, instead, past the Paradissis house and up the sand road to the schoolhouse to find Miss Finn. There was enough moonlight that night for me to see the eyes of the rats skittering across the road and the feral cats chasing them. As I approached the school, I saw Miss Finn leaving. I was about to call out when I realized it was Katrine, not Miss

Finn, walking down the road toward the factory.

I do not know what went into my decision to follow her, which I did so quietly that she never noticed me over the usual sounds of the tide, the cats yawing, and the night sounds of the factory. It is a lousy thing to do, to spy on someone like that. Though I have never done it again—and I have certainly done worse—it is not a moment that I am proud of. And still, I would not do any different if I could do it over.

Katrine was walking briskly, one of Miss Finn's canvas grocery bags slung over her shoulder. Upon reaching the dock, she emptied the contents of two jars onto a garbage scow, then turned around and walked back up the road. I jumped into a shadow, listened to the water rats moving about the docks, breathed in the stench from the scow and the furnaces, and saw the new ashes drifting from the smokestack across the factory, then downwind into the bay. I counted Katrine's footsteps until I could no longer hear them, until I was certain she was back at the school.

She and Miss Finn would see me for certain if I went home the usual way. If I went through the brush instead, I would have to walk through the poison ivy beds. I removed my shoes, grabbed my dress and pulled it high around my waist. Then I dropped into the oily, scummy shallows and waded until I was far past the schoolhouse and in the water closest to home.

CHAPTER 16

When I stopped by for Sofia in the morning, she was telling her mother that she had cramps and needed to miss school. Yorgos was long gone to work and the house, which should have been settled into the new quiet of the day, was filled with turmoil.

"What a terrible girl!" cried Mrs. Paradissis, evidently more upset by Sofia mentioning cramps in front of her still-recuperating father than she was about Sofia feeling unwell. Unwell. That was the code word. Do girls use it anymore?

Mrs. Paradissis glared at Sofia and tipped her chin twice in the direction of Mr. Paradissis, leaving no doubt about Sofia's blunder. Mr. Paradissis, who was paging through *The Daily Worker*, paid them no mind. Some frantic seagulls were passing overhead, marking the arrival of another barge; the mean stench of the factory meant it was going full blast.

"I...just...can't...go," Sofia moaned. She was bent over at the waist, gripping her legs just below the knees, and gagging.

Grandma Paradissis looked up from her stitching, smiling her toothless smile. Grandma could not hear what Sofia was saying, but Grandma knew she was saying something.

"*Porta o Theos*," Grandma muttered, lost in whatever it was she imagined she had heard. *God willing.*

Sofia rushed off to Yorgos' room, slamming the door behind her. Mr. Paradissis, who had promised every year to build a room upstairs in the eves for Sofia and Grandma, shouted at his wife to tell Sofia to not slam doors. Grandma Paradissis resumed chanting *Porta o Theos* and shooed me out the door.

Joey was standing boot high in a scow when I passed by the dock, shoveling something in a green-black state of purification into the wooden cart that would transfer it to the sorting room, where the carcass would be hoisted away from the other, already desiccated bones and rotting flesh so that another team of men, which included Yorgos, could haul it to the cutting room. That is how it went all day, every day. Joey was taking short drags off the cigarette clenched between his long, stained teeth. The cloud of tobacco could not keep away all the gnats and flies fighting to nest in the corners of his eyes.

"What are you looking at?" Joey hollered when he noticed me.

He smirked and thrust his hip in my direction. He could have been an Elvis Presley, that Joey, if he had any talent for being anything other than a creep. The fact that he was sinking in rotting flesh meant nothing. Joey was an ass, if you do not mind my saying so. I would have ripped out his throat had I been close enough, or strong enough, or been able to go through with it.

"What are you looking at?" he shouted again. He was resting a foot on the haunch of a putrefied horse. He cleared his throat and spat a yellow glob of saliva into the water.

"Nothing, Joey," I said. "What I'm looking at is absolutely nothing."

Everyone was so preoccupied with what mattered to them

most that no one could see the changes in what mattered to others. Sofia was absorbed by her possible pregnancy, and who could blame her, though no one beyond Miss Finn and me knew why she was so weepy. Her moods were explained away as a girls-being-girls thing, meaning that girls were not only allowed, but were expected to be unpredictably emotional. Miss Finn was busy finding an answer for Sofia's situation; Mr. Paradissis was consumed by the pain in his still-healing ribs; Noah and Yorgos and Joey were obsessed with the struggle to unionize the plant; and my father was struggling to get our relatives out of Zyrmuny while keeping Noah out of jail and my mother on this side of sanity. Nobody—there is not an ounce of melodrama in this, I swear—no one was keeping an eye on me. But this happens all the time. Anyone can slip through the cracks.

Miss Finn gave us a whole assortment of arithmetic problems, penmanship exercises, and maps to draw that day. I did not touch them. How could I do anything but imagine how Sofia felt? I answer with another question: How could I not?

I passed the day eavesdropping on the other lessons, staring out the windows, daydreaming. I smoothed out some paper that had been used on only one side and drew a picture of a garbage scow. I left out Joey and Katrine and any of the other scavengers who, at that very moment, were sifting through the one tied up at the pier. Drawing people was too hard. I outlined and shaded the bow and stern, the bilge and the deckhouse, and the fat posts on which the longshoremen knotted the ropes. I drew the cargo hold and the cargo itself. All that was sneakily tossed onto the scows meant fewer horses and far more of everything else than was ever meant to be there. A pile of putrefying horse heads could easily disguise all of this unidentifiable stuff as it decomposed into the oozing, amorphous mass.

I left my seat once to use the outhouse. I felt detached and determined as a sleepwalker; I was there and I was not there. For lunch I peeled a hard-boiled egg that I ate in a couple of bites. Yes, it was too much all at once; yes, pieces of egg stuck in my throat until I could not breathe. Noah slapped my back to stop my choking.

"Where've you been all day?" he asked. His question, like him, came out of nowhere. His attention had been focused on Marie Dowd after she got news that week of her acceptance into Hunter. Noah was probably calculating how Marie could become his emissary to that new world.

"Where have *you* been?" I said, coughing out little bits of egg into my hand. I raised my eyes in Marie's direction, implying some kind of design on her that Noah never had. "I've been right here. All day. Doing nothing."

"Joey's in trouble," said Noah. *Slap, slap, slap.* "Breath deep, Marta."

I coughed some more and sneezed whatever was left in my throat onto Noah's shirt. If Noah knew about Sofia, that meant Yorgos also knew. After Yorgos murdered Joey, he would kill Sofia as well. It was impossible to imagine otherwise.

"Thanks a lot," said Noah. He brushed away the bits of egg and wiped his hand on my skirt.

"What are we gonna do?" I asked, still struggling to swallow. I slapped his hand away from my skirt.

"Who told *you*?"

"Sofia." I could feel the heat of my blush rising, which turned me even redder. It was not like she could hide this forever.

"How does she know?" he sputtered.

"*What*?" The remnants of egg were gurgling in my throat. The sulfur smell was disgusting.

"Quit it, Marta. This is serious. Some union guys are trying to track him down. Remember those guys he went to see with Massimo?" Noah was so anxious to say what he wanted that he forgot I had said something else.

"You got what you wanted, for the union to come to Barren Shoal."

"These guys that control the ports are waging their own little turf war now that they think we're getting somewhere with organizing," he said. "They're going nuts."

"You wanted a union; now you've got two. I'd call that a blessing."

"Shut up and listen. Joey, that moron, he doesn't know what he's doing and got all chummy with the guys who handle the garbage who, it turns out, take orders from some other guys back in Italy. It's all got something to do with a fascist syndicate against the communists and I don't know what, except that one of the barge pilots said there were guys in suits on the dock in Brooklyn who he'd never seen before talking about coming over in a few weeks."

"To Italy?" I did not know the word *schadenfreude*, but it must have been invented to describe siblings.

"Are you gonna be serious or what? C'mon already."

What I had thought was the smell of eggs was the smell of Noah being scared. His sweat smelled rotten-sour instead of its usual boy-sourness. If some men in suits had been looking for me, I would have been scared out of my skin too.

The captain evidently explained to the union men how it was impossible to hitch a ride on the barge unless they lived on Barren Shoal, a long-standing factory rule meant to keep out "agitators" and do-gooders from the settlement houses. He could not tell if they were from the garbage union or the longshoremen. The guys in suits roughed the captain up, after which he gave them the name of a tugboat that could bring them over. So much for the rules. The barge captain, with his split lip and swollen jaw, was the one who told Yorgos, who told Noah and Joey that they were coming.

"What do they want with Joey? The guy is useless."

"They wanna beat the crap out of him, which they'll do unless we slip him outta here first. I don't know if someone saw him at the Union Square rally or something else. I don't know who they are; I don't know why they want him. Yorgos says they're trying to get to Massimo. They might even kill him. Or at least mess him up bad enough so Massimo knows they mean business."

"Why not just go for Massimo?"

"Because there's no point messing up Massimo when they can smack around Joey. They want something from Massimo, which they won't get if they bust him up. They're sending a message."

"So they're coming? Are they coming now?"

"The barge captain said not for a few days. They want to make sure Joey's good and scared waiting. And to give Massimo time to come around."

There were people—Mrs. Dowd, for one—who were born and raised and had grown into adults on Barren Shoal and had never left, not once. When did leaving Barren Shoal become so easy?

"What are you gonna do?" I asked.

"I don't know. But we gotta get outta here."

"What are you saying? Who? Where?"

"I don't know. I've gotta figure this out."

"Joey's brothers—can't they help? Shouldn't Massimo fix this?"

Could the Pessara brothers have gotten a decent price for Joey, they would have sold him. No wonder their parents named him Joey.

Miss Finn made quiet preparations to take Sofia to Brooklyn and for me to go along with them; Noah and Yorgos made quiet plans to tell Mike Sierra they needed help; my father made his own plans for another trip to HIAS. We all ended up on the barge together on a glum day, none of us saying where we were going or why, everyone so absorbed by their own concerns that none of us paid attention to anyone else, or to the other boats in the bay, or to the seagulls trailing our wake, or to the light and steady rain.

The water was rough and little whitecaps were swelling and splashing and breaking against the barge and onto us. Lucky for us the barge was empty and riding high. I pressed my forearm against my mouth, glad that the smell of salt on skin could camouflage the smell of almost everything else. Sofia, who had not been off Barren Shoal in the ten years since the Paradissi family arrived, spit up her breakfast over the side. No one said a word, including my father, who volunteered his handkerchief.

Miss Finn met the barge at the dock in Brooklyn, where my father and the boys said polite hellos before setting off to their own difficult meetings on Astor Place and Mulberry St. The plan was for my father to meet us back at the dock in time for the final barge to Barren Shoal.

Miss Finn's place in Brooklyn was a sturdy brick house with decorative masonry in geometric patterns that looked Egyptian. Set between the sidewalk and the house was a flower garden flooded with pale blue running hydrangeas, petunias, and white roses. Do roses and hydrangeas blossom at the same time? At least that is how I remember them. The copper window boxes were filled with pink, double-begonias that Miss Finn absentmindedly deadheaded with one hand while she searched for her keys with the other. At the top of the steps, like sentries on either side of the door, were two marble urns overflowing with ivy and lavender.

"Try this," said Miss Finn. She pinched two stems of

lavender and held them beneath our noses. "People dry it and sew it into sachets to freshen drawers."

"Uchh," said Sofia, pushing Miss Finn's hand away. She threw up on a blue hydrangea. It was amazing that she had anything left after vomiting on the barge. She wiped her mouth with my father's handkerchief, which she folded to hide the newest yellow stain.

"You two wait here," said Miss Finn, pointing to a mahogany bench in the foyer. At its foot was a small, brilliantly blue and burgundy wool carpet.

As we were taking our seats, a man entered through the still open door and greeted Miss Finn.

"This is Sofia and Marta. Girls, please meet Mr. Whitmore."

Ray Whitmore was tall and lanky with a pink, sunburned complexion. He was wearing a plain, clean shirt and blue work pants with a crease pressed down the center of each leg.

More brief, polite greetings were exchanged. Mr. Whitmore explained that he had seen us walking up the street and came by to return a shovel he had borrowed. "And to drop off *The New Masses*. They ran MacLeish's speech."

"Mr. Whitmore is the one with the green thumb around here," said Miss Finn. "There wouldn't be flowers without him. Or healthy rose bushes. Thank goodness for Ray."

He asked if Miss Finn would be attending some sort of gathering that night. Word of a surprise guest had gotten around, someone come all the way from Spain.

"We can discuss that later," said Miss Finn. She tapped a finger to her lips, a sign that he should drop the subject. "When I know better about the girls and their schedule."

Sofia looked at me with a knowing grin. It was good to see her smile; I smiled back.

"Is that your boyfriend?" I asked when Mr. Whitmore left. It was not the kind of question I would have asked on Barren Shoal. But we were in Brooklyn now.

"For heaven's sake, no, he's not my boyfriend" she said, laughing. "He's a boy from two doors down. He's your brother's age."

"But you called him Mister," I reminded her.

"I've been calling him Mister since he was a little boy, when he was a patient of my sister's," she explained. "It is a way of making children feel grown up, less frightened."

"He looks a lot older than Noah."

"Some people just do, but this isn't really the time."

"It'll be okay," I said to Sofia while Miss Finn stepped away to another room. It sounded unconvincing. She took my hand and rubbed her fingers across my thumb, pulling the nail back a little as her own, larger finger passed over it.

"That's a big, fat lie," she said. "Nothing about it's okay. Either I'm pregnant or I've got a tumor." She smiled weakly, stroked my hand again and started to weep.

Miss Finn returned with her sister, the woman we had referred to for all those years as Miss Doctor Finn. She was close in height to Miss Finn, but dark-haired instead of blonde and with a paler, smoother complexion, broader hips, and a wider mouth. She was pretty in a quieter, more elegant way than Miss Finn, though I would be happy to look like either of them. She had a professional demeanor. This is not to say that she looked masculine, which is how people always described professional women in those days. She appeared preoccupied, quiet; she appeared efficient.

"I think you'll come into the library, Marta, while Sofia is with the doctor," said Miss Finn. She spoke in the teacherly way that made commands sound like choices, even when they were not. She did not even introduce me. The doctor led Sofia in one direction; Miss Finn led me the other way.

The library floor was cushioned with a thick carpet like the one at the front door, only many times larger. Its gold tone changed as we crossed it, though it was obviously only one color. I kneeled to smooth the impression left by my footsteps.

"These are silk rugs, hand-woven by young girls somewhere in Turkey, back when it was still the Ottoman Empire. They were my great-grandmother's."

"She worked in a rug factory," I noted. A historical tidbit to share later with Sofia.

Miss Finn laughed. "For heaven's sake, no." She reached for a picture frame on an end table, where it was sitting next to an elaborate clock with a rose-colored, porcelain face with cherubs in place of numbers. "This is my great-grandmother," she said. The photograph was of a beautiful, heavy-set woman with a mass of white hair combed up in an old-fashioned braid that rested on the crown of her head. "She lived with us when we were little girls, after my great-grandfather died. My sister has that gorgeous hair *and* her wide hips. I, as you know, have neither."

On another small table were a glass of milk that someone had already set out and a plate of perfectly uniform bakery cookies on a blue and orange faience dish with latticed edging. I had never even seen pictures of this kind of finery, never mind the real thing.

"Find something to read, Marta. There's lots here to keep you busy." She pat my shoulder and disappeared before I could ask after Sofia.

I ran my finger over the leather spines of the complete works of Twain, Trollope, and Balzac. Directly across the room were a tan leather set of books by Mark Twain and a black bound set by Dickens, who I had never read though I knew the story of *Oliver Twist* the way everyone did. The book I selected started somewhere in London during something called Michaelmas, which was new to me. The only Christian holidays I knew about were the Greek Orthodox ones that Sofia and her family celebrated, but I figured it was something like Christmas. I never guessed that it was the day in England that quarterly rents were due and accounts settled. Whatever the case, it was so hard to keep the story straight that I put it aside in favor of the magazine that Mr. Whitmore had dropped off. I turned to the article that he had mentioned, something about the mounting troubles in Spain, and American writers standing up to fascism. Soon enough I dozed off. I dreamed about a baby, about pulling my nipple from his mouth and him grabbing for my breast with his tiny fingers while his mouth quivered in that fuzzy zone between sucking and crying. The next thing I knew, Miss Finn was taking the magazine from my sleepy hands.

"He's a poet, you know, MacLeish," said Miss Finn. She began to recite:

A poem should be equal to:

Not true.

For all the history of grief

An empty doorway and a maple leaf.

For love

The leaning grasses and two lights above the sea—

A poem should not mean

But be.

"From his poem 'Ars Poetica,'" she explained, "his statement about how poetry works."

"His article is about the Italian Fascist Party and the Spanish Fascist Party and...."

"A poem *is* something, an article is *about* something," she said. "Writing one does not exclude writing the other, as you can see with MacLeish. Some people think poetry and politics don't mix. Nonsense. Try telling that to the ancient Greeks. But that's a conversation for another time. This might be better." She exchanged *The New Masses* for a book of 19th century botanical drawings by Clarissa Badger. Who could forget a name like that? "There's paper and soft pencils on the desk beside the atlas. You can look up the places where the plants and flowers grow."

"Where's Sofia?" I finally asked. Miss Finn had been gone for an hour and had returned with a cheese sandwich for me and a cup of tea for herself.

"She's fine," said Miss Finn, with a brave chumminess that I could hear right through. "Don't look so sad. She's just resting."

"She still throwing up?"

"She needs some rest." Miss Finn sat for a while, sipping her tea while I ate.

More time passed. The house was quiet except for once when the doorbell rang and I could see Miss Finn through the corner window, declining to take a pamphlet from a young man dressed in a shirt and tie. I moved closer for a better view. The street was deserted except for that boy Ray Whitmore, who was hammering dents out of a garbage can. I watched him shoo the other boy away, stamping his foot like he was chasing off a dog. The boy with the tie could have been a Jehovah's Witness; he might have been from the German-American Bund. I never asked. Just before 5:00 p.m., Miss Finn came in to say that Sofia would be spending the night. She pulled out a sheaf of notepaper.

"I've telephoned Ray to ask him to bring you to the dock to meet your father. I'm explaining in this note that Sofia is still unwell and that it is best if she stays here tonight and tomorrow night. She can return to Barren Shoal with me come Monday."

I watched anxiously as Miss Finn wrote. I had not laid eyes on Sofia since she went off with the doctor hours earlier.

Minutes later Ray and I were out the door, walking to the streetcar. It was not until we had taken seats that he spoke.

"You shouldn't worry about your friend," he said. "The lady doctor is as good as any."

"I know," I replied, not that I knew anything of the sort. I have plenty of women doctors now—my internist, my ophthalmologist, my radiologist. But who would have imagined such a change? We are all lousy prophets.

"Who's coming from Spain?" I asked.

"Miss Finn wouldn't like my talking about it," he said.

"It's her boyfriend?"

"She's told you about Ernesto?"

I did not say yes, but I did not say no.

"He's back for more money, more guns."

"Can't someone else bring them over?"

"Sure, once they understand why. Ernesto will tell it better because he's been there."

"Isn't he afraid?"

The streetcar jolted to a stop. Ray grabbed my arm to stop me from hitting the seat ahead of us. The conductor was now yelling at the driver of a horse-drawn fruit cart blocking an intersection. The cart was filled with bananas and peaches and pears—seven pears for a dime, twenty bananas for a quarter, three pounds of peaches for 15 cents. Cheap. Then again the streetcar cost a nickel. Nothing is ever cheap for people with no money.

"I don't really know the guy," said Ray when we started back up. "Hell, I don't even know his real name; Ernesto's his *nom de guerre*—but no one talks about it."

"Why doesn't he use his real name?" I asked.

"Protects his family. Protects his friends. You think the big deals in Washington want us over there?"

"You going to Spain?"

"As soon as they'll take me."

"Do you have a nom de guerre?"

"If I did I couldn't tell you."

"You could die."

"Not a good enough reason to stay home."

"They take girls?"

"Nurses, ambulance drivers. You know how to drive?"

"I could be a nurse."

"No on-the-job training," he said. "You need experience."

"You've soldiered before?" I asked.

He looked at me hard.

"You're pretty clever. But you're not old enough for Spain."

I thought about Sofia, if she was okay, if she was upset that I had left her. I wondered if she had been put to bed in a beautiful room with another oriental rug. I did not know enough what to wonder about.

"Maybe I can help here," I said.

"Well maybe you can."

Ray delivered me to the dock and my father, explaining that he was Miss Finn's neighbor and that Sofia was not well, had stayed behind. He shook hands with my father and gave him Miss Finn's note. My father was in no position to question Miss Finn's judgment, never mind put up an argument. And on another day he would have been angry that I was escorted by a boy he had never met. But he was tired from his own day of disappointment, one in which Mr. Schwartzbart had no good news.

"It goes to show that you can't plan an adventure," my father said in a feeble attempt at sounding lighthearted. "You can have an adventure or you can make a plan. You can't do both."

I reminded him that he said this when Yorgos showed up without Noah or Joey.

"They're staying with Mr. Morrow," said Yorgos.

"What the h—"

"Look, Mr. Eisenstein: your brother-in-law brought Flat Sammy with him to the union hall today. Noah said he'd take Sammy to the movies if there was time, but the meeting was still going when I left."

"The deal was that you all stay together," my father bellowed. "Why can't you guys get it right?"

"I got some things going on at home, Mr. Eisenstein."

Mrs. Paradissis got hysterical when she heard Sofia was staying in Brooklyn, as did my mother when she heard that Noah was there as well.

"Why didn't you wait?" said my mother, angry at what she so obviously saw as my father's abdication of his duty.

"We would have missed the barge; we would've had to stay in Brooklyn, too," he said. "And what if DeWitt was too busy with the poker or whatever to come down and tell you? You wouldn't know what happened to us. What then?"

"These people where he's staying—you know them?"

"It's already done. Now stop."

Sofia was wearing the same opaline pallor on her face as Dr. Finn back in Brooklyn when the police boat docked on Monday morning. She showed neither surprise nor delight at my waiting for her. One of the officers carried her down, after which he helped Miss Finn onto the dock. He then passed her bags to Katrine, who, it was evident, had managed this routine before. A man on the police boat wearing a suit and tie observed the scene as well. He had a handkerchief tied over his mouth and nose, as if that could protect him from the smell.

Miss Finn handed a canvas bag to Katrine, who slung it over her shoulder. She passed the week's newspapers to me. Behind us, the police boat sped off across the narrows to Barren Island.

"Of course you'd be here, Marta," said Miss Finn. She

groaned a little as she lifted a heavy bag, all the while holding Sofia's arm.

"Should we get the other bags?"

"Katrine will catch up," said Miss Finn.

We walked quietly down the path to the schoolhouse, Sofia between Miss Finn and me. It was the empty hour between when the factory opened for the morning and the students arrived at school. The only sound came from bottles clinking in the bag she shouldered on the side away from me.

"Feeling better?" I asked Sofia.

I wanted to ask if she had seen Ray Whitmore again or Miss Finn's boyfriend Ernesto, but I did not dare. I wanted to know if Ray had mentioned anything about me getting involved. Barren Shoal was about waiting, whether it was for my mother to speak, or Sofia to stop being with Joey, or for the union to step in, or for the relatives to be rescued from Zyrmuny. Pitching in for the Spanish cause was something to do. Ray Whitmore was something to do. Everyone had something. Now I did as well.

"Let's just be quiet for now," Sofia said.

I looked over my shoulder and saw Katrine watching us from the dock where Joey was already picking through a barge. I was always torn between wanting and not wanting to know her, between being repulsed by her and intrigued.

"Are Noah and Joey back?" asked Miss Finn.

"Last night on a Sunday barge," I said. Barges lined up on Sunday nights so that their loads wouldn't stink up Manhattan.

Joey had managed to evade the thugs looking for him, at least for now. If he knew anything about Sofia's situation, it did not show.

"Is Ernesto coming here?" I asked.

"How do you know Ernesto?" she asked.

"Ray told me that he is—"

"Never mind what Ray told you. Better that you should walk Sofia home, make yourself useful."

So much for Miss Finn's little lecture about poetry and politics.

When I returned to the schoolhouse, Katrine was in Miss Finn's kitchen rinsing bottles with soapy water. Here was my chance to speak to her. But what would I say? What do you say to a girl who survives off the waste of dead animals? Who sometimes sleeps on the barge?

My own restlessness in the face of Joey's new role in Sofia's life and waiting for the call from Ray was buried in the work Miss Finn gave me as long-range preparation for the entrance exam to Hunter. After her luck with Marie, she decided that I should take it too. Who knows if any of us were really so smart—Marie or Yorgos or Noah or me—or if it was just that Miss Finn liked to think we were. Maybe it made her feel better about herself. Or maybe it distracted her from worrying about Ernesto, who I somehow understood had returned to the fighting in Europe. Whatever the case, she managed to tip the odds in favor of our getting in by getting us prepared. I read *Hamlet* again like everyone did, but I also read *Macbeth* and *King Lear* and *Julius Caesar* in the big Riverside Edition that she lent me. That book was so heavy that I did not have a hand free for Sofia's when she finally returned to school. I scoured Miss Finn's newspapers for stories about Spain; I listed to radio reports about the riots and strikes in Madrid. I read the names of the dead. How would Miss Finn know about Ernesto if that was not his real name? I read Sophocles and Aeschylus and Euripides, and after everyone else who was old enough finished them, the *Odyssey* and the *Iliad* for me. Helen, it turned out, was not only my sister, but was the face that launched a thousand ships. Our Helen had become a mythological figure as well. How could she have been otherwise, having died so young? I read about Galileo and about the Renaissance, which meant I read about Humanism. I wrote an essay about the ascent of individualism coinciding with Copernicus explaining that the earth revolved around the sun. How about that! I was really something. When I asked Miss Finn about Homer's journey and the ancients' knowledge of the roundness of the world, she said something about the contempt people have for what others have long known. I wanted to ask her if Ray had returned to Spain with Ernesto, but the moment was never right. I wondered if that was why I never heard about helping the cause.

My essay won a citywide prize, which my parents knew nothing about until Mrs. Paradissis said something to my mother, having heard about it from Sofia. The school board wanted a photograph of me with Miss Finn for the newspapers, but no one on Barren Shoal owned a camera. My prize from the school board was a copy of Thoreau's *Walden Pond*. I do not know who chose it or why, but it was the first book I ever owned. I grew tired of it later on—Thoreau making a big deal about the wilderness when civilization was just down the road—but I was never without it that year, always carrying it for company on my Walden Pond-inspired contemplative walks around Barren Shoal. Like Thoreau, I thought about nature, including its cruelty and violence. He observed black ants killing smaller red ants; I thought about the fascists. Noah worried about the workers; I worried about the Spaniards. And so on.

There was a terrific nor'easter that spring and when the storm passed there was a new driftwood tree on the beach, a comfortable bench for long stretches of sitting. A nearby stand of dune grass made that lonely section of the island smell a little sweeter than other places. Sometimes I wrote in my marble school notebook; other times I drew nothing especially memorable. I was a doodler. At some point I decided that I would become a naturalist like Thoreau and asked Miss Finn if she could bring her book from Brooklyn, the one that named all the plants. She instructed me to take clippings of what I found, "so you'll have samples to go with your descriptions."

I clipped beach plum fronds and dune grasses; gathered seaweeds with dappled edges and tubular seaweeds that popped and sprayed their salty perfume when I squeezed them. I collected mysterious plants not native to Barren Shoal that washed up on the shore. These would smell good at first; then they would turn and stink like a turtle swamp until they finished drying. My sketches became reasonable replicas, but they were nothing compared to Noah's.

"What is that smell?" Noah asked the day he found me out back shaking sand out of my notebook. He was about to hop a barge to Brooklyn for a union meeting.

"Samples," I said, as if he was stupid not to recognize that. "They're drying out."

A black fly was buzzing around my ear. As I brushed it away, I dropped the notebook.

Noah grabbed it. "You think this is important? Collecting weeds?"

"You could take me to the union meeting." I had not mentioned the business about Ray and the Spanish Civil War or even Miss Finn's Ernesto. Why would I share my new interests when he excluded me from his? Having this new secret made me feel superior, sort of like having a nom de guerre. I had a cause de guerre.

"In your dreams."

"You have a better idea?"

"How about growing up."

"Like you, Noah?" I was, of course, which meant the joke was on him. Or on me. Okay, fine: on all of us.

CHAPTER 17

Our neighbors on Barren Island were given thirty lousy days to pack their belongings and get out. The mystery man with the grey fedora on the police boat that brought Sofia and Miss Finn to Barren Shoal appeared again a few weeks later to nail evictions notices on every cabin door. This included the house of a man named Gunyan, 74 years old, who was born on Barren Island and had only left it a dozen times or so in his whole life. And there was Mrs. Fishkill, who owned two milking cows. And at least fifteen families with infants under the age of one. At least that is what people said.

News of the Barren Island evictions spread as fast as the stink of burning horses on a windless day. Some people ripped up their notices before word got around about how destroying official documents could get an American thrown in jail and an immigrant thrown out of the country. The teacher at P.S. 120, Miss Jane Shaw, fought with the city school board and then Robert Moses himself to keep her grade school open through the end of the term. Miss Shaw was one of the few people to ever take on Robert Moses—the City

283

Parks Commissioner/Roads Commissioner/Housing Commissioner and signatory of the eviction notice—and win. Commissioner Moses agreed that the children could finish the school term. Who knows how she got him to consent to this? Maybe the schoolhouse did not matter in the overall scheme of things.

Noah slipped over to Barren Island with Yorgos and Joey for purposes of "reconnaissance," as they called it, when the wrecking crew arrived. I would call what they did looting or grave robbing, though it was not exactly that. My grandson would call it recycling, since no one was coming back for the stuff they had abandoned. These were mostly things in need of serious repair, including a small rowboat with a crazy gash in its bow. Even so.

An all-island emergency meeting was called for Friday night in the Barren Shoal schoolhouse. Word was passed from house to house, neighbor to neighbor. Everyone would gather once Mr. DeWitt sent word that the managers were off the island for the day. That would be 6:00 or so.

Yorgos jimmied open the lock without bothering to ask Miss Finn's permission or even letting her know. With the exception of Sofia—who offered to stay home with Grandma Paradissis but in truth was still in no mood to see anyone, never mind be in a room with a hundred people—everyone was present. Everyone was not a lot of people but included my mother, who had attended no gathering of any kind since Helen's funeral.

Noah, of course, said the only recourse was an island-wide strike. What did he know, with his foolishness about his own ignorance?

Mr. Dowd was the first to take him on. He was no taller than Noah, but his forearms were as wide as his hands. He had a broad face and a thick chest that gave him stature. "What kind of 'we' business?" he asked. "WE go on strike while you go to school? Some sacrifice, Noah." Most of the men laughed, but others looked mad.

Mr. Dowd accused Mr. DeWitt of being ignorant when he said that the city would have to expand and modernize the plant on Barren Shoal to handle the overflow. "Who put that cockamamie idea in your heads?" asked Mr. Dowd. "Boyle puts up a fancy gate and you think he's getting modern?"

"The Barren Shoal factory will be the only game in town once Barren Island's closed," answered Noah before Mr. DeWitt had a chance. "Don't you see what that means for us?"

"Power," said Joey, as if he was answering a question on a radio quiz show. Massimo cuffed him on the head.

"Only schoolboys can call this a game," said Mr. Dowd, "so sit down and keep your mouth shut."

"What else are they gonna they do with all the dead horses they've been sending there?" said Yorgos. "Burn 'em in Union Square?"

"If German university students can burn books in front of their opera house, why not horses in Union Square?" said Noah. Nothing sounded impossible after seeing the pictures of those book burners in the papers.

"We've got them by the balls," said Noah, "and we can twist them." He must have remembered that our mother was in the room because he blushed and shoved his hands in his pockets. "You'll see," he said, struggling to regain his composure.

No one on Barren Shoal had anyone by the balls or had anything else, including the means of reasoning their way to a happy conclusion. People who are surprised by the cruel exercise of power rarely do anything about it. Even the smart ones. That is why they are surprised again and again. My father knew this; Mr. Paradissis knew it and so did Mr. Dowd. You could read it all over their faces.

"You're all wasting time," my mother interrupted. She was

standing by the door next to Mrs. Paradissis, who was wearing her good scarf draped around her shoulders as if she was attending church. They were never close friends, really, but Mrs. Paradissis kept a kind eye on my mother after Helen died. Maybe it was her way of warding off the other eye, the evil eye. Maybe she had been watching out for her all along. That is one of those things we never know for sure; I mean who is watching out for who or if we are being watched out for at all.

"All that matters now is how long before they also close Barren Shoal," my mother continued.

This was the cold question everyone was waiting for someone to ask, but no one expected it from my mother. How can I know what other people were expecting from her? It hardly takes a big leap of imagination: after Helen's death, people were surprised by even a "hello" from her. I could see it in their faces. Even with us she mostly spoke of factual, familial matters when she finally spoke again: who should sweep and who should dust, when dinner would be ready, whether the soup was sufficiently peppered, who my father might talk with about visas. She could also say cruel things, ugly things that changed nothing, especially the things that she should have left alone. No, I do not repeat them. It was hard enough hearing them, never mind my giving voice to them. No, I will not.

But now she was addressing the room as if she had never disappeared. Maybe to my mother the evictions from Barren Island were no different or distressing than the daily facts of scheduling meals and searching for visas. What is more factual and personal than people being forced from their homes?

"Every one of you, first thing tomorrow morning, you'll open your doors to see if some noise you hear is a man nailing the notice," she went on. "Your heart will hurt on account of this letter you're waiting for. You won't even feel safe without it. You'll sleep bad tonight and tomorrow and the night after. Your things will be packed before they tell you you're going, even if your clothing is still in drawers and your dishes are on your shelves. You'll worry that this man is coming back even when you're too busy to worry. Because he is. And you know it. Not a doubt."

The factory on Barren Island closed right away. Children attended school but the men who did not leave for the rare job elsewhere sat idle. Gossip about stupid and brutal bar fights spread quickly, there being nothing important left to fight over. Pretty soon it was an island of women desperate for their husbands to find work, even when it meant pulling children from school.

The last of them left a couple of months later on a ferryboat sent by the Port Authority, which was also headed by Robert Moses. How could one man have so many big jobs in the middle of a depression?

On their final day, I stood up to my knees in Jamaica Bay, casting for flounder in the brown haze of the afternoon, watching them leave. It took all day for the people and their things to be loaded. Then, without fanfare, a horn blew, the engine began grinding, and the ferry pulled away. The ship, which was packed in haste and grief, listed to the starboard, the side from which the passengers could best observe Barren Island. The captain's voice came over a bullhorn telling people to spread to both sides of the ship or it would sink. There was some shouting about this, but most people stayed put. The captain came on the bullhorn again. The yelling from the crowd got meaner; the sounds of a fight erupted. A man was leaning over the railing hollering. Someone was frantically splashing in the water. A powerboat sped by, heading out of the bay into the ocean. A ship's mate from the ferry threw over a lifesaver and rope and pulled the person—man? woman?—on board.

The crowd spread out and the ferryboat gained its equilibrium with its now silent passengers.

That would have been well and fine were it not for the fact that suddenly it was me losing balance. At first I thought the wake from the speedboat was dragging me over. I pulled back on my rod to catch my balance and caught a glimpse of something on the line. I pulled again. Up through the shallow water came a sea raven, the ugliest fish I ever laid eyes on. It had a mean, spiny head and spiny dorsal; its mouth was bright orange like preserved apricots, with skin the mottled brown of apricots dried in the sun. It thrashed in the shallows as I reeled it closer. I gave it some line and it pulled away fast. Then it swam close enough on its own for me to see again. I cut the line, a coward's release. The raven sped off, a length of fishing line trawling after it and my only hook lancing its mouth.

The cottages on Barren Island began coming down the following Monday, the wrecking crews working as many hours as there was daylight. Noah and the boys slipped over every few days to see if there was anything new worth taking. One night Joey's face was streaked with dirt when they came home. He looked like he had been crying. He said that all the vegetable and flower gardens over there had been trampled. Dogs that could not move with their families were killed by small caliber bullets to the brain. Some house cats had been left in a pile, probably suffocated. Feral cats were still roaming the island, getting fat on the mice and rats that the demolition chased out of hiding.

The boys were also shaken up a few days later when they came home from a trip to Manhattan, bloodied up pretty bad after crossing paths with some club-wielding German Bundists up on 85th Street. They called Lois and Gray, who told them to come down to their apartment in Greenwich Village, where they got cleaned up and bandaged. It was Noah's first time on an elevator.

He had expected it to open onto a hallway, like in buildings in Brooklyn. It opened, instead, into a large and elegant apartment. It was a day of one surprise after another.

After seeing Joey so cut up and swollen—worse than from any beatings from his brothers—Sofia stopped fibbing about how much time she was spending with him. I suppose it was inevitable. We never discussed it. Being assaulted by the Bundists did not stop Yorgos from smacking around both Joey and Sofia like he had any number of times before, but no one said anything about that either.

Noah got his school diploma the same week that the people on Barren Island were packing. He had no job prospects—there was certainly no work for him on Barren Shoal—and he had applied to City College too late to begin in the fall. There was a celebration party anyway for him and Marie Dowd, who had done everything the way Miss Finn had told her to and was heading off to Hunter. My father and Mr. Paradissis built the barbecue pit they had been talking about for years, setting mismatched, discarded bricks into mortar they bought from Mr. Boyle. He could not just give them some? That stinking so-and-so. They hoisted a piece of fire-escape metal on top of the bricks—something they got from a junkyard in Brooklyn—to use as the grill. It took both men plus Noah and Yorgos to lift it into place.

It was a wonderful, hot night and there were all sorts of fish to eat, potatoes roasting on the coals, and a salad of early lettuces from the garden. The air was cleaner, what with the Barren Island smokestack idle now. That made things pretty terrific, even if it was heartless to say so. My mother did not interfere when Noah passed me his glass of beer, my first ever. We formed a quartet with Joey and Sofia and tried singing "You're the Top," everyone making up the lyrics because no one remembered more than a couple of words and it did not much matter what we threw in.

Cole Porter would not have cared. We did much better with "For All We Know," which is so much shorter. And sadder. No one messes with that. Even Miss Finn showed up. The bigger surprise was Ray Whitmore, who came along, she explained, to escort her back home that night in the dark. I did not know if he was still in New York or had gone overseas and returned. I had not seen him since that day in Brooklyn with Sofia, though he had been on my mind. Or the Spanish Civil War had been. I never thought about one without thinking about the other.

Miss Finn was wearing a delicate white cotton dress, a straw hat, and a red silk scarf around her neck. It lifted gently from her throat when she cheered our singing. She was so elegant. Ray was wearing the same plain shirt and blue work pants that I remembered from when we met him at Miss Finn's.

Miss Finn introduced Ray to the boys, explaining that they had been trying to get a union serious about Barren Shoal and had been through all sorts of trials and travails and had no better luck than Ray was having with the International Brigades. She also introduced him to Marie, "the other guest of honor."

"Most people would give anything for a life without struggle, but not my boys," said Miss Finn. "I wonder if it's something in the drinking water. Ray, have you been coming to Barren Shoal without my knowing?"

"We never seen this guy before," said Joey. "I woulda known."

"I'm teasing, Joey," said Miss Finn. "My little joke."

Yorgos rolled his eyes and cuffed Joey playfully on his chin. Joey raised his fists.

"Take it easy," said Yorgos. "My little joke, too."

Joey looked puzzled. "What's so funny?"

"No one meant anything by it," said Miss Finn, trying to soothe him. She seemed pleased that the boys would play along.

"So why don't you say what you want?" Joey was still baffled.

"Oh, Joey: when will you learn?" said Marie. She patted him on the head like he was just another Dowd child.

"Are you union?" asked Sofia. She made no sign of knowing Ray and he did not remind her.

"You gotta have a job, which I don't," said Ray. "Wall Street folks made sure of that." He glanced at Miss Finn. She stared back hard; her face looked like ten different ways of saying *No*.

"These are union boys," Ray reminded her. "They're okay."

"That's up to you," said Miss Finn. "But keep it about your business, not anyone else's." I imagined that she was referring to Ernesto, but she could have been referring to anything. Ernesto was the only secret I knew.

She crossed the yard to greet our mothers.

Ray seemed younger without Miss Finn in the picture. Instead of looking like one of her friends, he looked like ours.

"I've been writing pamphlets and collecting supplies for the Abraham Lincoln Brigade," he told us. "You know about that?"

"I could help with that. I won an award for my essay...." I began.

"You're a communist?" asked Yorgos.

"If you say so," said Ray.

"How about this," asked Yorgos, "how come you guys never come to Barren Shoal? Too busy recruiting the coloreds?"

"Good question," said Ray. He sounded amused, not angry.

"So what do I win?" asked Yorgos.

"All I got."

"What's that?"

"Time to answer your questions."

Yorgos laughed, I was happy; all was good.

"C'mon," said Noah. "There's lots of food, beer."

We tramped down to the beach with our plates and glasses, hoping it would be cooler than by the house, what with the crowd of people and the homemade grill and the June heat. We settled in where we had once picnicked with Gray and Lois, this time with grilled fish, potato salad, and beer instead of finger sandwiches and martinis. That had been a lesson; this was a party.

The sand was damp, as were the driftwood logs that we leaned against. The moisture was cooling through my dress.

"You'd think there'd be more of a breeze down by the water," said Ray, who fanned himself with his hand.

"Stinks bad here, all right," said Joey.

"I got an earful about that from Miss Finn," answered Ray. "She told me to clam up about it."

"Nothing to say," said Noah.

"What d'you think?" Ray asked me. It was about time he noticed.

"This is Barren Shoal, take it or leave it. Yorgos and Joey got jobs here. Our families have houses. Nobody starves," I said.

"So why the unions?"

"I didn't say it was perfect," I told him. I sounded testy. "I said—"

"He's trying to back you into a corner," interrupted Noah. "By the time he's done, you'll be a card carrying member of the YCL."

"I'm not trying to back anyone into anything," said Ray through a mouth of potato salad. "I'm asking her a question. Admit it: Barren Shoal is damned peculiar. I've heard of company towns, but never company islands. And this company town, island, whatever it is—it's in the middle of New York City."

"Nowhere near the middle," I said.

"You know what I mean. It's like the company is the government and the city doesn't exist."

"The city sends Miss Finn to teach," I reminded him.

"Because the company doesn't want you going off-island every day and bringing back trouble."

"You know that for a fact?" I asked, "or is that what you think?"

"We go to the city all the time," said Joey.

"The bosses don't know the half of it," said Yorgos. "They'd jam us up good if they did."

Ray nodded. "That's my point."

"So how come you're not with the unions?" I asked.

"I know some Wobblies. That's how I got to the Lincoln Brigade. Lots of old Wobblies joined up."

It was one thing to want a union so Barren Shoal would be better. It was where we lived. It was another thing to worry about Spain, about people Ray had never met and a life he would never lead. I am not saying that one was more important than the other. I would have thrown everything I had into the union if they had let me. But Ray's altruism was something else. It was terrific, but it was also an indulgence. Going to Spain would be an adventure. Not that there was anything wrong with that. It was romantic, but that also took the shine off what was right about it.

"Hey, you," someone called. One of the Dowd kids was walking towards us. "Your mothers say you should come back to the party."

"I don't have no mother," Joey shouted back at him.

"That's not my fault," yelled the kid.

"How about I beat you up anyway?"

The party was going strong back at the house.

"Where have you been?" asked my mother.

"Eating," I said.

"Your mother asked where," said my father.

"You think I didn't see you talking to that boy?"

I could not say which was more surprising: that she had noticed me at all or that my curiosity about Ray was obvious. So much for guarding secrets.

"Noah was with us."

"That's besides the point," said my father.

"What *is* the point?" I asked.

"You're not a little girl anymore. *That's* the point," said my mother.

"Are you saying I can't talk to him?"

"Is he Jewish?" asked my father. Can you believe it? Oh, why not. It is the same question I asked my own children thirty years later.

"We were talking, not getting married."

"Remember that," said my father.

I caught up with the others, who were gorging themselves on big pieces of a lemon sheet cake. Joey had helped himself to the scholar's cap and tassel made out of chocolate.

"Want some?" he asked. It was already melting and he licked the chocolate that was oozing between his fingers.

"Thanks but no thanks," I said.

"How about cake?"

I turned quickly and my chin landed squarely in the piece that Ray was offering. The others laughed harder than the moment deserved. At least it felt that way, the laughter being at my expense.

"Not funny," I muttered.

"Sure it is," said Sofia.

I grabbed the cake from Ray's hand and smushed it in her face.

"You're right," I said. "Hysterically funny."

She wiped a big piece of it away from her mouth. Her lips curled into grin.

I took off.

Sofia chased me around the yard, weaving through the tomato plants and the string beans and an assortment of Dowd children of all ages and the fathers smoking until she finally gave up. Out of breath and gasping for air, she handed the used piece of cake to Joey who, of course, ate it.

The other boys said nothing either except for Ray, who had been laughing and cheering us on.

"If you wanna help the Internationals come to Brooklyn, help roll bandages we send over with the volunteers."

Days passed—not weeks, but just days—before the first dump trucks could be heard filling the shallows between Barren Island and Floyd Bennett Field with landfill. What a silly, misleading name for trash. The bulldozers came every day, no matter the weather, to drive the landfill further into Jamaica Bay. It was not long before Barren Island was an island no more. It was merely another piece of land jutting into the water.

Life on Barren Shoal became measured by the comings and goings of work crews to the newly created extension of Floyd Bennett Field. Noah said something about seeing if he could get work there, but Mr. Paradissis said a few choice words to him about being a collaborator. Noah discussed it with Stanley Morrow, who declined to weigh in on the matter. Morrow told Noah to stay focused on Barren Shoal, so Noah dropped it.

Noah became obsessed with eviction notices that he was certain were coming soon. He and my mother discussed them for hours: when they might come, who would bring them, why it was inevitable, how much time we would have to pack. The situation was awful, yet it was good to see her interested in something again. The strangest thing of all was that other people dropped the subject from public conversation as if that would make it disappear.

"Mr. Morrow also says it's time to make a move on the factory," announced Noah. "He says the local is really ready now to back us up, especially after everything that happened to Barren Island."

"Who says we want them?" said Yorgos. "It's taken them a hell of a long time. Forget about Morrow. It's Mike Sierra or nothing."

"We still got work in the plant, Noah," reasoned Joey. "What else you want?"

"I got nothing," said Noah.

My father continued making fruitless trips to HIAS, as if there was still a chance of saving anyone who could not save themselves. Noah and the boys continued traveling to the union hall in Brooklyn and the rallies in Union Square, from which they often came home with black eyes and split lips. They did not act concerned about being arrested. Noah said someone from Morrow's union promised him a job, but there were no jobs anywhere.

Unlike the boys, I did not leave Barren Shoal, though I finally wanted to. Sofia could sneak around with Joey without drawing much attention, but what could I do? Ask my father to bring me to see Ray Whitmore? Ask Miss Finn to arrange a rendezvous? Girls in my day did not do that, not the kind of girl that I was. Ray became a conversation I had with myself. He was the secret I kept, even from him.

After Noah explained it, I understood the irony of reading the moldy copy of *Robinson Crusoe* that he had found in the Barren Island schoolhouse. Noah said I could borrow it if he could borrow my Thoreau.

"Lakes, islands, get it?" he said.

"Get what?" I asked.

"Imagine you're Crusoe, an imaginary man at the center of your own universe, and you're lonely. Or you're Thoreau, a real man circling the center, and you're just as alone. In either case you want to stay alive. So do you try to stay where you are or do you go?

"You expect an answer?"

"Never mind," he said. "Just take the book."

It turned out to be pretty terrific, the way Crusoe reinvented everything from what little he had. It was crazier still that Crusoe was a nicer man alone than he was when Friday appeared. Correction: calling it crazy is too easy. Crusoe chose to make Friday his slave. And it is choice that makes us human, even a character in a story.

Like Crusoe, I sketched every species of plant and grass that grew on our island, as well as every object that washed up on the beach, and every animal and insect that crawled across the sand. I drew the marram grass and heather on the dunes, and the glasswort and sea lavender in the waters of the muddy shore facing Long Island. When I ran out of paper I snuck into the schoolhouse and helped myself. I took the key that Miss Finn hid on a nail beneath a loose shingle. Having opened that door once, I felt free to open it whenever I needed. I never mentioned the key to the boys, who still jimmied the lock to get in. Why would I?

On the bookcase behind Miss Finn's desk stood a volume of botanical drawings by Albrecht Durer, Franz Andreas Bauer, Gerard van Spaendonck, and others. No women artists, even though we are supposed to be so crazy in love with flowers.

I am done with being told what to like.

I worked my way up to birds, though without much success. Only later, with the aid of a Roger Torey Petersen book, could I say with authority how Barren Shoal hosted muted swans, cormorants, snow geese, Canadian geese, gadwalls, snowy egrets, great egrets, herons, roseate terns, sandpipers, red knots, dunlins, piping plovers, a couple of kinds of gulls, warblers, and grackles. I love saying these names. By the end of the 20th century, the plover and tern in Jamaica Bay were on the endangered or threatened species lists. I bet plenty of others are gone for good.

I made studies of rock crabs and mud crabs, including forensic studies based on a couple of claws or the back of a shell. I pulled in butterfish, yellowtail, and hogchokers, sketching them too before scaling and gutting them. I still brought quahogs and surf clams to Mrs. Paradissis, even if Sofia insisted that crushing them was a task better left for children.

"Which children exactly?" I asked, one of the few times we were now alone. Sometimes I would forget what she had been through that winter. Sometimes I wondered if she had forgotten too. That was probably me wishing we could all forget, as if any good would come from forgetting.

There was a new restlessness on Barren Shoal, a feeling of agitation I would have embraced had I any thoughts about what to do with it. The boys fed themselves on this tension, ready to tussle with any palpable feeling.

Yorgos had grown worse than anxious. "What now?" he would ask impatiently. The racket from the dump trucks at the marshes would end for the day, Joey would gnaw on leftovers from Sofia, and Yorgos would ask, "What now?" Noah would read aloud from Mr. Paradissis' *Daily Worker*, the only newspaper around now that Miss Finn was home in Brooklyn for the summer, and Yorgos kept asking, "What now?"

On every front there was nothing until one evening Noah said, "Look at this. Isn't that Miss Finn's Ray?"

I was pulling weeds, though the garden barely needed

tending. It was better than imagining eviction scenarios or Sofia with Joey. I never did make peace with that.

Sure enough, in *The Daily Worker* was a photo of Ray waving goodbye to some Lincoln Brigade volunteers. They were shipping out to join the Spanish Civil War. He had a real big grin on his face and a *Friend of the Abraham Lincoln Battalion* pin on his shirt.

"He's a communist," remarked Noah.

"That's only what Yorgos said. Ray just didn't say that he wasn't," I said.

"The guy's red," said Yorgos.

"Aren't you?" I asked.

"I'm union," said Noah. "And a socialist if I've gotta be anything."

"I wonder if he'll come over again," I said.

"You know they won't let him," said Noah. "The graduation party was a one-shot deal."

"I liked him," I said. It felt good saying it.

"Marta's got a boyfriend," said Noah, chuckling.

"It's not like that," I protested, tugging the newspaper from his hands.

"Oh yes it is," teased Noah.

"Ray could be a socialist," I said. My feelings for Ray, the ones that continued to multiply despite having met him only those two times, made no more sense to me than did the passion that Sofia had for Joey or Noah had for the unions. Or maybe even for Mr. DeWitt. But there they were.

"It doesn't matter, Marta. Ray's okay. He's an anti-fascist."

"And a gardener," added Joey. "Like us."

"Imagine that," said Noah, grinning. "Two things we all agree on."

Agreeing about two things, even important things, was no

guarantee that anything might come of my schoolgirl crush. I knew better. Even so, I was glad to have one.

"Forget about that. The point is that we're not going down like sheep the way they did on Barren Island," said Noah.

Noah had his cause just like I now had mine. I had Ray.

"Sheeps and horses are what they burned on Barren Island," said Joey, without a trace of irony. "We do horses and cows."

"Very funny," said Yorgos, "except we eat the sheep now, too."

"Right," said Joey through a mouthful of chicken, though it was unclear what he was agreeing to. Joey could go either way on anything as long as he was included. Or eating.

"What could those poor dopes do? The city threw them out," said Yorgos.

"What city? There was a person's name on the eviction papers. A living, breathing person. Robert Moses. He signed them. *He* made it happen. *He* takes the power, he's gotta take the blame."

The boys spent the evening debating strategies for convincing Commissioner Moses, coercing Moses, even kidnapping Moses, though he was too big for anyone to take on and they knew it. Mayor LaGuardia had tried and failed. President Roosevelt, too. To this day I do not understand how Moses managed all that power, but he did.

That was the last I heard about Robert Moses for a while. It was officially summer, a hot one that came on the heels of a heat wave in May. Instead of politics the boys turned their attention to baseball and Noah's radio. It was too hot to listen inside so they turned it to an open window facing the yard.

Lots of people came by to listen to the games. Everyone cheered for the Dodgers and booed the visitors and no one owned up to rooting for the Yankees, though plenty must have because DeWitt was always around to collect their bets. The men brought sandwiches or plates of cold chicken and marinated seafood. There was no bar on Barren Island anymore—for heaven's sake: there was no Barren Island anymore—where the men could buy beer, so they bought bottles of spirits from the barge captains or drank homemade wine. Barren Shoal could have been anywhere in America in those days. Or at least anywhere in Brooklyn.

That summer Miss Finn, for the first time, sent over newspapers from Brooklyn every week so that we could follow the fighting in Spain and China, the legislative barbarities in Germany, as if the Nuremburg Race Laws were not bad enough, and the unrelenting heat wave that had become a national disaster. The Herald-Tribune printed photos of buckled roads in Minnesota and families sleeping outdoors in Detroit public parks. The randomness of suffering corresponded to a world that was forsaking reason.

There were no other pictures of Ray, but I studied the papers anyway—even *The Daily Worker*—so I would be ready when I saw him again. I knew little about the Communist Party before that. Even now, long after my brief affair with them came to a dismal and disappointing end, I can understand their appeal. They stood up for working people, for poor people, even for the blacks when no one else did. At least on paper. It was a lot more than the big muckety-muck capitalists were doing. Too bad the reds became muckety-mucks too.

As for seeing Ray again, it was not so complicated. One night in early July, Noah and I were listening to a radio story set in a London church in 1915; whole families were rolling bandages for the English soldiers fighting in the 2nd Battle of Ypres.

"That's what Ray said we could do," I told Noah.

"Attend church in London?"

"Why are you such a dope? Roll bandages for Spain."

"Why would I do that?"

"Because they'll need them. Because there's gonna be war.

And because Mom and Dad might let me go with you."

"Where?"

I wrote a letter to Miss Finn that night and gave it to one of the bargemen, along with three pennies to cover postage. I got the pennies from Noah. I did not ask where they came from. I wrote that Noah and I wanted to help Ray and could she please ask him where we could do this and how. An answer came a few days later.

"Ray says come to Brooklyn. A warehouse near the docks. We can go on Sundays. No one will even care."

"What about Sofia?" asked Noah.

"She won't notice," I said.

"I mean why can't Sofia go with you?"

"Because then Joey will come. Would you use a bandage rolled by Joey?"

Noah laughed. "Captain Otis will take you. He's a big drunk. Just slip him a little something to whet his whistle."

"You'll send me on a barge with a drunk captain? And with booze that I get how?"

We returned our attention to the radio story. Word had arrived from Flanders that the Germans were now using chlorine gas. Barrels of baking soda were delivered to the church so the parishioners could prepare packets of powder. The soldiers soaked wet cloths with it and covered their faces until the fumes passed.

"You've got a point."

"What?"

"The barge, the bandages. And look," he said. From some odds and ends he stored behind the radio he unearthed a bottle of gin. "From Gray and Lois, a present for a rainy day."

I did not look a gift horse in the mouth by asking what changed his mind.

We slipped out early the following Sunday. Noah spent the trip to Brooklyn at the side of Captain Otis, who happily sipped on better gin than he probably ever had in his life. He and Noah talked the whole time about this and that, about the barge and piloting ships. By the time we docked, Otis looked surprised that I was on board.

The address sent by Ray was a ten-minute walk from the pier. The children playing in the street paid us no mind, nor did the men on line for the soup kitchen at a church. At the far end of the street was a small building, the upper floors of which looked like people lived there, what with laundry hanging on a line out a window. The street level had no windows, only a set of double doors like on a factory or a warehouse.

I was surprised by how clean it was inside: just a couple of tables and some floor-to-ceiling shelving along the walls. The only one around was a woman, who we startled.

"We're looking for Ray Whitmore," said Noah.

"Ray sent us," I said more gently, though I was already disappointed. I had been imagining a big greeting.

"You the kids from the garbage island?" she asked. She was a pretty woman, wearing a button-down shirt and khaki slacks much like Ray's, like some kind of uniform. Only movie stars wore slacks in public, like Marlene Dietrich. But we were in a stark room near the Brooklyn waterfront, not Hollywood.

"We're Noah and Marta Eisenstein from Barren Shoal," said my brother.

"Barren Island?"

"Barren Shoal, next door. It's just like Barren Island but smaller."

"I thought I knew everything about New York, but Barren Shoal's the fish that got away."

"Well, look at who's here," said Ray, wheeling in some boxes on a dolly.

Noah and Ray shook hands and Ray patted me on the back.

When his hand was gone I could still feel it where he touched me. The pretty woman was Dolores.

"She's in charge; she knows Hemingway," whispered Ray. Was Hemingway the kind of person that another person could meet? "It's a big deal that you came. Not everyone can recruit two volunteers, never mind one. She may not look it, but Dolores is impressed." We were the only ones in the room. "You won't meet the others," Ray answered the obvious question. "They come in twos and threes so no one outside catches on."

"Sounds subversive," said Noah, grinning.

"We're helping freedom fighters, not the Boy Scouts."

"We never had a troop on Barren Shoal," joked Noah. "Offends their code of cleanliness."

Dolores did not smile or laugh with us. I thought she looked exotic and mean.

"Come by me," said Ray, leading us to a bolt of cloth and a sack of tobacco at the end of the table. "We're rolling bandages and packing tobacco. When you get tired of doing one, you switch to the other."

"Ray's like a veteran out of uniform," said Dolores, laughing. "He got bossy the minute he started."

"And packing tobacco is my rest cure."

Their friendly banter reminded me of Gray and Lois, except they were debating bandages and tobacco instead of martinis and finger sandwiches. They spoke in a code that only they understood, the way my parents spoke in Yiddish when they wanted to leave us kids out. Not that it made any difference. They were having fun *and* were doing something serious. We could have used a big dose of that on Barren Shoal, what with the boys so serious about the unions, my parents so serious about Zyrmuny, and Joey too stupid for Sofia to rag on.

"Ignore Dolores," said Ray. "She's just jealous because I got two volunteers and she's got none."

"Whoop-de-do," said Dolores, waving a piece of muslin like it was a flag.

"If the show's over we'll get started," said Ray. Noah and I drew closer. "Bandages aren't one size fits all. You have to make 'em twelve yards by four inches, eight yards by three inches, eight yards by two and a half inches, five yards by two inches, and three yards by two inches. This here is soft, unglazed muslin. You have to tear it, not cut it, into strips. You sew the strips together with flat seams. When it's long enough, you roll it tight, tight, tight and burn the loose threats with a match. Here's a pencil for writing the size on the outside so the medic knows which is what. It's the tearing that'll get to you. You'll see. You'll get tired."

We measured and tore. Ray also stitched. Noah rolled wool socks, pair by pair, from a basket filled with them, all brown, all as close to the same size as hand-knit socks can be. Dolores was at the other end stitching extra pockets into the lining of surplus WWI army jackets. It was a remarkable thing, Noah and me sitting on a couple of stools at a table with Ray Whitmore. Without anyone making speeches or asking why we were there or insisting on some schmaltzy pledge, we became volunteers in the struggle against the Spanish Fascists. All we had to do were things as simple as the things we did at home, as simple as folding laundry, darning sheets, and packing lunch.

Noah and I returned the next Sunday and the Sunday after that. Captain Otis was happy to oblige us for a few sips of gin. School was out, it was summer, and I had nothing better to do than pack tobacco and wonder about Ray. I imagined us having long conversations about the fate of Europe; I imagined us going to the movies or even to the opera, where we would bump into Lois and Gray, who would insist we join them for cocktails at intermission. But at the worktable, sitting close and feeling unsure, all I knew was to follow.

There was plenty to discuss as we worked. In the warm weeks of June there were radio interviews with the U.S. Olympic team. On July 9th, the mercury hit 106 degrees. There has never been a hotter day in New York City, at least not on record. The fighting in Spain broke out in earnest a week later. Our work took on new urgency. Dolores made sure of that. The harder she worked, the less she spoke to Ray; the less she spoke, the faster I sewed.

If my parents were worried about us when they found out, they never said so. Rolling bandages was safe work, not like going to rallies or walking picket lines. The only one who made a fuss about it was Mr. Paradissis, who hailed us as patriots and comrades.

"You think maybe Sofia goes with you sometime?" he asked one evening.

"She's not interested," I replied. We were gathered in the garden, listening to the Joe Louis/Max Schmeling match at Yankee Stadium.

"You ask her?" he asked.

"She'd say no."

"Not nice, Marta. You ask."

Sofia and Joey were standing not ten feet away.

"If she wants to come, she'll do the asking."

"*Girls,*" he said, disgusted.

Everyone listened to the fight that night, even people like me who thought that a prize fight was a dirty dogfight. Everyone was brokenhearted when Schmeling knocked out Louis in the twelfth round. Well, maybe not everyone. Plenty of Americans rooted for the German, the same as plenty joined the Bund. I confess: I was delighted when Louis beat Schmeling at their rematch two years later. For as much as I hate fighting, there were some punches I wanted thrown.

Dolores turned off the overhead lamps at the warehouse during the heat wave and we worked in the dim light from the windows. Ray brought a fan and had blocks of ice delivered. The fan cooled the room with the help of the chill surrounding the melting ice; we collected the melted ice water for drinking. We took turns standing in front of the fan for a few seconds for a cold gust of air to the face. We had nothing like that on Barren Shoal, which stank worse than ever from one day on top of the next of crazy heat. Maybe it also stank worse because we were going back and forth to Brooklyn instead of never leaving.

I was always a little afraid of Dolores, but over time she acted more friendly. Her voice was stern, but she would crack a little smile when she spoke to me. That little crack was all I needed to put me at ease. When she asked me to wait in front of the building for a package on one of those horrendously hot days, I was glad to oblige. Not that I would have known how to say no.

The package was a waxed paper bag like the ones for tobacco.

"Give this straight to Dolores," said the man who brought it. It was so hot out that it was hard to breathe. "From your hands to hers; no one else's."

Had he not made such a big deal about it, I would not have wondered. Back inside, Ray was helping Dolores fold jackets. Ray was taking them to someone who would deliver them to the next person on the long chain of people who smuggled supplies.

"I've got it," I said, waving the packet.

Dolores jumped, tipping the stack of jackets onto the floor. Ray stooped to get them and I rushed over to help.

"Don't sneak up on people like that," said Dolores. Ray laughed. "It's not funny," she scolded. "It might've been anyone."

"Don't be such a worrier," said Ray.

"Don't *you* be such a smart aleck or I'll assign you to leaflet duty," said Dolores. Now she was the one laughing. "And you," she said to me without a smile or a laugh or anything, "gimme that."

We returned to our work, me watching Dolores out of the corner of my eye.

She opened the packet with a penknife, counted out some $20 bills, and slid them into the pocket she had sewed into the lining. I had never seen a $20, never mind a stack of them. Then she stitched the lining closed.

"It's for Spain, silly girl." Of course she knew I was watching.

"American money?"

"Nobody wants *pesetas*. At least not people selling guns."

We had all heard about the riots in Madrid and the labor strikes. We had all heard about the fascist vigilante groups gunning down peasants. Anyone who did not know did not want to know. But I had never thought about smuggling money, about buying guns. Who could imagine such things?

"I know how to sew," I offered.

"Tired of tearing bandages?" teased Ray.

"Aren't you?"

I sometimes worked beside Dolores after that, re-stitching the seams of the jackets after she slid in the money. We didn't sew many—not even one a day. We had to pull out the entire lining and re-sew it so that all the thread was identical and unbroken. It was meticulous, time-consuming, important-feeling work. Each little jacket felt like we were saving the whole, huge world.

On August 1st, Jesse Owens, grandson of a slave, marched in the opening ceremonies of the 1936 Summer Olympic Games in Munich. Owens won a gold medal for the 100-meter dash and a second medal for the 200-meter dash. All of us listened to the crowd going wild. After earning a third gold for the long jump, he took an arm-in-arm victory lap with Luz Long, the German athlete who won the silver. When Owens broke a world record by winning a fourth medal as a member of the 400-meter American relay team, Noah asked about the two Jewish boys, Marty Glickman and Sam Stoller, who had been scheduled to run. Word got out later that Avery Brundage, head of the U.S. Olympic Committee, agreed to remove them from the team at the request of the Germans. Glickman, later on, became a sportscaster. Stoller disappeared from public life, evidently utterly humiliated. No wonder. How could one man stand up to the terror that the world was bending over to appease?

Brundage instructed his American athletes to not become involved in "the present Jew-Nazi altercation." *Altercation*? What the hell was he talking about, you should pardon me? He wrote this in a U. S. team pamphlet after the Nuremburg Laws had been passed and Jews were no longer allowed to teach school or practice medicine or hold German passports. I say, to hell with Brundage, the same man who alleged that there was a Jewish-Communist conspiracy aimed at keeping Americans out of the Olympics. This Brundage being the same man who later on, as president of the International Olympic Committee, insisted that the games go on at the very moment when terrorists were massacring Israeli athletes at the 1972 Olympic Games in Munich. I repeat: to hell with Brundage. I make no apology for my language or my thoughts. Avery Brundage should rot in hell.

When the medals were presented to Owens and the U.S. national anthem rang out over the Munich stadium, the German chancellor stormed away. There was a snippet of Hitler's voice on the radio that day, a stupid, screaming crow just like Father Coughlin. So much for Brundage placating Hitler, who flat out refused to present a medal to Owens. Hitler did exactly as he pleased. Jesse Owens, it should always be remembered, came to the defense of his Jewish teammates, publicly protesting Brundage's decisions and telling the coach that the Jewish boys should run. That was a hell of a lot more than most did, you should pardon me. Riskier, too, him being a black man and hated almost as much in Germany as a Jew. The Germans would have killed Owens had the whole world not been watching.

On the other hand, that did not stop the killing later on. I have tried to understand this, but what do I know. And even then, even then...what is there to figure out? Why make it complex when it is so simple? Pardon me for repeating myself, but people do terrible things because that is what people do.

CHAPTER 18

It got harder to buy groceries and such after the store closed on Barren Island. More of the things people needed were brought over by a small boat, which meant people were told to ask for less. Everyone ate more fish, which meant more fishing. The boys started coming out more often, as did Sofia. As the landfill project linking Barren Island to the mainland came closer to completion, the shallows surrounding Barren Shoal rose higher as well, flooding the marsh grasses and drowning some of the better fishing spots. Mr. Goldstein, the widower who worked the night shift stoking the furnaces to keep them burning and who doubled as the island's *kosher* butcher, announced he was going to live with his daughter's family upstate, where his son-in-law had a job trimming leather at a factory in Gloversville. The day before leaving, he taught my father how to properly slit the throat of a chicken, drain its blood, and remove its innards. Cleaning fish is one thing, butchering chickens another. Oh, never mind. What does it matter?

Noah, through a stroke of dumb luck, inherited Mr. Goldstein's job at the factory. Now all three boys were working, the very thing everyone said would never happen. Grandma Paradissis died in her chair one evening after supper, another victim of the heat wave. It was a couple of hours before anyone noticed, her teacup still full and her needlework on her lap. The rigor mortis had already set in. All the neighbors attended a funeral service in the yard; Mr. Paradissis accompanied the body to a cemetery in Queens, where a Greek Orthodox priest could officiate. It was the first time Mr. Paradissis had left the island since arriving.

The family went into mourning and paid more attention to Grandma Paradissis in death than they had when she was alive. Maybe she had not asked for attention. Or maybe that was just their way. Why are there always so many questions? They were unable to go to her grave every night like they would have at a cemetery, so the family walked instead to the water, where Mr. Paradissis would say something in Greek and everyone would cry. There was something about the orderliness of it all that was mind-boggling, especially given that the Paradissis house was so loud and chaotic.

"Do you miss your Grandma?" I asked Sofia one night during the long, official period of mourning. She was trimming beans for the meatless meal they would eat on the designated vegetable night, as opposed to the night on which they ate only pasta. The rules for Greeks around death and mourning went on forever. I suppose they do for everyone, as if grief is the food that keeps people alive.

Sofia sighed. "It's not like she did anything other than sit on the couch and sew. But somehow the empty place is bigger than the space she took up. That's how it goes." She drew a big circle in the air with her paring knife. Her face quivered; she tried to stop herself from crying. She did not succeed.

Noah still came to Brooklyn on Sundays, but soon announced

he would drop me at the warehouse and return for me later. His factory job was all the excuse he needed to separate from me and from Ray, whose only work was rolling bandages and dreaming of Spain.

He went off to see Lois and Gray.

"Who?" asked Ray.

"Friends. I dunno. Maybe union." Lying about them was easy, a pleasant surprise. And besides, what could I say? That they had fancy seats at the opera and a mahogany speedboat and drank fancy gin? Lois and Gray were Noah's secrets for all the reasons people keep secrets.

Dolores was working on a coat, Ray was ripping bandages, and I was packing tobacco. They made idle chatter; they gossiped. I had imagined serious conversations about Mussolini's invasion of Ethiopia or the return of the Rhineland to Germany. People, it turns out, go about the business of being people no matter what. Nothing stops their blather: not illness, not earthquakes, not wars.

"Anyone thirsty?" Dolores asked after a spell. Even after the worst of it ended, the heat that summer was nasty.

How else to say this: the *very* first time that Ray and I were alone—I do not count the day Sofia had her abortion—he kissed me. He leaned over, pressed his lips to mine, then returned to the bandage he was rolling as if he kissed me every day. No warning. No nothing. My first real kiss.

"You like that?" Ray asked.

"Sure," I said, though I was too surprised to feel much *except* surprise.

"If you want me to kiss you again you gotta say so." He spoke with such confidence that I smiled and just like that I kissed him back. It was hardly enough of a kiss to go crazy about. Who knew it took time to kiss right, never mind kiss well? Not that I am complaining. Some good things keep getting better. Like loving, you should pardon me. Every good time picks up where the last good time left off.

"Your smile means yes?" he asked.

I smiled again; he kissed me again. Imagine my surprise when my lips opened. Imagine my surprise that I could feel him pressing against me. That was surprise enough. I was glad for the cold lemonade that Dolores returned with minutes later. I was glad that Ray behaved like nothing had passed between us. Silly as it sounds, I needed time to recover.

Later that week, in the first minutes of dawn when there was only a tinge of sunlight, I heard the boys moving about in the yard. What were they doing out there at 5:30 a.m.? I slipped into my dress and quietly followed them to the vacant side of the island. When they reached the water they dragged from the rushes the abandoned rowboat they had rescued from Barren Island. I dropped flat on the damp sand and watched them from behind a low dune. The gaping hole on the port side of the boat had been crudely patched with scrap wood and tar.

Yorgos passed around a bottle of the whiskey and the boys each drank a ceremonial shot. Joey manned the oars and Noah launched them from shore with a push. There was some subdued hooting and whistling from the rowboat, a quiet celebration that was amplified as it traveled over water.

They had not gone far when Joey pulled in the oars. As best I could tell, they were just bobbing along on the incoming tide, talking quietly. I stayed low behind the dune, my head propped on one arm, the cold dew clinging to my skinny legs. Nothing had happened yet that made it worth having left a dry, warm bed, but if I walked away now the boys would see that I had followed them. They would make me pay for that.

A half hour passed before a garbage barge piloted by

Captain Otis pulled into sight. Joey took the oars again and rowed a little closer. It seemed strange that the captain was alone on the barge without any scavengers but there it was, no one but Captain Otis and a flock of seagulls for company. Maybe someone else was supposed to be with him. Maybe the boys knew that Otis would be bringing the barge alone that day. They certainly knew they could count on him to be drunk. Noah never recounted all the details, not wanting to involve anyone else when things turned to trouble. Not that it made any difference, but it means something to have the facts.

Yorgos and Noah stood up to hail the captain while Joey struggled to steady the rowboat. Who knows what Captain Otis made of their being there. Or how much he would have cared if he were not already drunk. A man who drinks that much is always just picking up where he left off. Yorgos offered Otis a bottle while Joey roped the rowboat to the barge. Noah hoisted himself aboard, followed by the others. The captain busied himself with the bottle as the boys relieved him of his command.

Joey took the wheel while Noah jumped around to chase off the rats. Yorgos grabbed a launching pole and tied something to it. A breeze passed, unfurling what turned out to be a flag fashioned from a pillowcase. The symbol on the flag was...a horse? A cow? Whatever it was it was something on four legs. It was hard to tell now that the sunrise was glaring off the water.

There was plenty to wonder about while the boys maneuvered the hijacked barge, yet it was the creature on the flag that held my attention. I crawled further up the dune for a better view. The arm I was resting my head on had fallen asleep but it suddenly woke, a thousand pin needles rousing it from its brief death. Was there really a difference if the flag had a horse or cow or dog or sheep or pig? Of course there was. Everyone wants to name what moves them.

I spotted footprints in the dune where the plovers always nested. A thin shadow curled between a pair of them, a snake track that disappeared into the dune grass. At the edge of the grass was a long, narrow, pale piece of paper with pencil marks on it. I crawled closer, hoping to discover the details of the boys' plot the way it was done in radio stories.

Another breeze moved up the dune, raising the tail end of the paper and snaring it on a twig. I crawled closer and reached. The paper did not contain the boys' secrets. It held, instead, the translucent traces of tiny scales on a perfectly intact two-foot-long snakeskin. Even the orbits and mandible were visible.

I now imagined things in motion. The sun, having finally appeared on the horizon, revealed the great impatient rising light. The breeze lifted the snakeskin yet again, this time long enough to expose the nest of newborn snakes sleeping beneath it. You would have thought I would have learned by now to put up with the snakes on Barren Shoal.

Next thing I was rushing to the shoreline. "No...ahhhh!" I hollered. "No...ahhhh!"

"Marta?" he yelled back.

"There's a nest of snakes," I hollered.

Noah grabbed the pole with the homemade flag and waved it back and forth. "It's independence day!" he roared, rousing the gulls from the surrounding trash.

The barge sat idle for the better part of that summer morning before two Harbor Patrol police boats arrived. Neither vessel approached the barge. Perhaps this was their protocol. It is just as likely that they could not stand the stench that became steadily worse as the day warmed. Captain Otis, for his part, jumped ship the moment the police boats appeared, splunking right into those murky waters of Jamaica Bay. This created an unexpected problem for the boys. Turning the barge about had been easy enough for Joey in open water; docking, if and when they decided to, was a different challenge.

It became a problem for Captain Otis as well when neither of the police boats moved in to rescue him. Instead, the men on the boats began clapping and whistling as if Otis was a racehorse they had placed bets on. The captain, who had finished the better part of the whiskey, had to swim for ten minutes before reaching the closest boat. Someone finally tossed out a life ring and dragged him aboard.

"They's pirates!" he blathered over and over.

I could hear the boys laughing at that. I laughed too. Just imagine them as buccaneers on the high seas instead of some guys on a glue barge in Jamaica Bay!

As if on cue, a swarm of seagulls took flight, drowning out Captain Otis. They made a spectacle of themselves, swooping and diving and circling again, inspecting the police boats for a possible meal. One of the cops pulled a gun on the gulls and shot a couple right out of the air. The bullets he used were large enough to shatter them.

Sofia was out of breath when she found me on the beach.

"Mr. Boyle says no barges get into the bay until the police figure out what's going on. No work today. No pay. He says the police know it's the boys. He didn't say what else they know. Your father says don't tell your mother. He says to tell you she's unhappy that you and Noah were already gone when she woke up."

"Where is he? My father?"

"At the factory in case Mr. Boyle changes his mind and lets them in." She described how the men spent the past hour outside the locked factory gates cursing the boys. "Mr. DeWitt is taking bets on whether another barge will be allowed to dock today. And Mr. Boyle says if the factory finally opens and the men aren't waiting at the gate, they're fired."

My father was not at the factory for long. Another police boat came and took him out to the boys, telling him to say what they were doing was driving my mother crazy. The police had not bothered to find out that my mother was long past the point of going mad. What she needed was the vestiges of madness driven from her.

The police would have taken Mr. Paradissis as well had they found him at the factory or at home. They did not look for him in the guardhouse, where he and Mr. DeWitt were still taking bets and arguing over whether to get word to Stanley Morrow or Mike Sierra. The boys needed help, but they could not decide whose. It was a good thing that the police did not find Mr. Paradissis, who could barely speak to his family without shouting, never mind a cop who wanted to arrest his son. Mr. Paradissis would have ended up in handcuffs.

My father's voice went back and forth across the water in a heated debate with my brother and his friends. First he sounded angry, then plaintive, then angry again. Whatever sway my father had meant nothing in the face of their resolve.

"Ohmygod, there's your mother," said Sofia. "Oh god, there's my mother too. Over there, Marta, on the dune. Look!" She waved so they would see us.

My mother struggled to keep her balance through the dune grass. She had not been to the beach since Helen's death. Who knows what doors of grief were being opened. I wished I were back in bed, dreaming any terrifying dream with its promise of being a dream from which the dreamer awakens.

A fourth boat arrived, this one carrying newspaper reporters and photographers, some of them holding handkerchiefs over their mouths and noses. If they had been like the rest of us, if they had come to stay, they would not have made such a fuss about the smell. They would have pretended not to notice until, finally, they could stand it. The photographers were balancing their clunky 4x5 Speed Graphics, calling for the boys to look up for the camera. My mother, who was standing with us now, raised her arm slowly and waved as if they were calling to her. One of the photographers waved back. It was Mr. Aryeh, from my aunt and uncle's building in Brooklyn.

"Help them," she cried. "Please help us!"

"There's nothing to do," Mr. Aryeh yelled back. If there had been a way to help, he no doubt would have, but it was too late. There was no fixing Barren Island or Barren Shoal or anything else that needed fixing. The boys were in the middle of the bay. They had hijacked a barge. They were in trouble. These were facts.

There was more confusion now, with Joey steering the barge in lazy circles and the police shouting at the boys to hold still, and the reporters and photographers cheering them on. Yorgos yelled for one of the cops to approach the barge alone.

It was unclear what either side wanted in return for doing what the other asked.

A tugboat entered the harbor bringing another barge captain who could take the wheel from Joey. Someone called out on a bullhorn.

"Let him on now and we'll call it a prank, boys," shouted the officer.

Yorgos cupped his hands around his mouth and hollered back. "What if we say no?"

"We call it a crime."

The negotiation came to a quick deadline. We could hear the police talking across the water about leaving the boys on the barge until they ran out of food and water. The boys let it be known that they had jugs for rainwater, plenty of biscuits and bread, and fishing lines.

To hear my father tell it, the hijacking opened floodgates for every disgusting joke a human being could make about another. Do you think my father shared the cops' jokes with us?

"*Just imagine*," he said when the police returned him to the dock and he found us down by the beach. He declined to repeat them with Sofia and me around. "Imagine a cop telling a joke about a garbage boat hijacked by an Italian, a Greek, and a Jew."

"And you standing there," said Mr. Paradissis, disgusted.

"You think they cared?" asked my father. "So they maybe insulted me, insulted my family. You think this bothered them? Like they give a damn?"

"Acch," said Mr. Paradissis, spitting a great, wet glob into the water. "Where in hell is Stanley Morrow, the stinking bastard. What the hell they want with our boys? What the hell your brother-in-law and Morrow get out of this? Just a lot'a talk. A lot'a nothing."

"Like they got any better from Mike Sierra? What you think about that?"

That evening we could see the fire over which the boys cooked fish. Joey, of course, made out fine. I am not being spiteful, just honest.

By then the scene on the beach had turned into a carnival. Whole families came down after the men finished their suppers, the fathers smoking, the little ones splashing barefoot through the shallows, the older children told to mind the smaller ones so that the mothers could talk. It was more than my own mother could take.

"Get us out of here," she told my father. Yes, I know: it was the same plea as the one from the family trapped in Zyrmuny.

The names of the boys were in the newspapers that Miss

Finn sent the over the next day. A photograph of the barge, credited to Mr. Aryeh, ran in *The Post*. The other papers ran photographs of the police boats and the man with the bullhorn. He was wearing a suit, it turned out, not a uniform. The boys were described as "suspected anarchists or communists, with ties to the Wobblies, the Italian Fascists, and the international Zionist movement." The newspapers kept referring to them as immigrants, even though Yorgos was the only one born in a foreign country. As for Noah and Joey, being the sons of immigrants made them foreign enough.

Later that afternoon, Gray and Lois showed up in the mahogany runabout. Gray throttled down as they approached the barge, the engine *put-putt*ering to an idle.

"Don't get any closer," ordered the man with the bullhorn.

"We know these boys," Gray called across the water. "We can talk sense into them." He and Lois had seen the pictures in the newspapers.

"Back away or I'll take you in for conspiring to receive stolen goods."

What kind of stolen goods? Dead horses?

Gray piloted the runabout over to the Harbor Patrol, where we could see him and Lois trying to reason with the officers. Lois had her wide-brimmed hat pulled low and was holding her handkerchief to her nose. Gray pulled out his own handkerchief and wiped his brow. Lois raised both of her arms, palms to the sky, as if to say, *We're trying to help! Let us help!* This was followed by more finger-pointing at the barge, more gesturing towards the shore, more palms raised to the sky.

Gray motored away from the barge and closer to the beach where my parents were standing with Mr. and Mrs. Paradissis, Sofia, and me. I have no idea where Joey's brothers were; I do not remember seeing them that day. My mother walked into the water as they approached. Gray throttled down completely.

"What are you doing?" cried my father.

My mother kept walking until she was waist-deep in the bay.

Miss Finn, who was tracked down at her sister's house by Mr. Boyle, successfully reasoned with them to give in after winning from the police a guarantee that the boys would not be arrested nor lose their jobs. The boys handed over control of the barge the next afternoon. I had hoped that Ray would come with her, but no luck. I had not seen him since that day he kissed me. Nor had I told anyone, not even Sofia. Everyone had their secrets; I had mine.

Miss Finn managed to win a pledge for a face-to-face meeting with Commissioner Moses. She did this with the help of Jane Shaw, the Barren Island schoolteacher who had that small success with him about her school. But who in hell did Miss Finn think she was dealing with, you should pardon me?

Yorgos was fired right away despite all guarantees to the contrary. It was a lucky thing that Mr. Paradissis' ribs were pretty much mended. He was strong enough to return to work, even if he was still wincing and cursing when he belched or sneezed. Mr. Boyle took him back, saying he did not want the bother of breaking in someone new. Noah was fired as well from the job he had barely started. On top of that, there was still talk from the police about coming over to arrest them. To our amazement, no one mentioned the brawl at Union Square. We had been so afraid for Noah; it turned out they did not even know he had punched that cop. For the time being, at least, none of the authorities seemed worried about the boys escaping the island. Who in their right minds would help them?

There was no meeting with Robert Moses, of course. He probably knew nothing about the episode other than what he read in the papers. If that. Noah and the boys, not even Miss Finn— none of them understood how little they were, how insignificant they were to anyone not directly affected by the biggest thing they had ever done in their lives.

Mr. Morrow sent word to Noah that the union wanted nothing to do with them anymore. Noah showed me the note that came over by barge: "Who the hell you think you are, trying some lame-brained scheme without running it past the local. Nothing but lug-headed, punk kids who need to learn how to follow orders." So much for all those years Noah followed Morrow around like a puppy. If the boys heard anything from Mike Sierra, they kept it to themselves. No one came to help them; not then, not ever.

There was talk about firing Joey too, but without Yorgos and Noah there to lead him by the nose, he could do no harm. At least not to the factory. Before Joey went back to work, his brothers beat the crap out of him—not slapping him around, mind you, but beating him good—at Mr. Boyle's behest. They bragged about it, as if to say that they were tight with Boyle. One of Joey's eyes remained half closed forever, the nerves in the eyelid permanently damaged. Boyle made a point of telling everyone that the Passara brothers had been glad to oblige.

There was a lot of sulking in the days and weeks that followed, everyone waiting for arrest warrants and eviction notices that never came. Being afraid was enough to keep everyone quiet and miserable. The boys were placed on probation on condition that they stayed put. If they got caught leaving the island they would go to jail.

This meant going to Brooklyn by myself. My father would not hear of it. A week passed, then two. Ray wrote to ask if I was coming back. Another letter that came over on the barge. He had read about the hijacking in the papers. He said he missed me; he wrote that Dolores missed me too. There is missing and then there is missing. Dolores, to be sure, missed my help. From Ray I wanted the wanting kind of missing.

"It's not fair," I told my father. "Noah's on probation, not me."

"I didn't say it was fair," he replied. "I said it's not proper."

"I'm not alone; you know where I am."

"Better you should visit your cousins, help your aunt if you want to go somewhere."

"I'm helping plenty by rolling bandages, not tomcatting around like Noah."

"Don't ever speak that way. Girls don't tomcat. And Noah doesn't either."

He was right. Noah was not much of a liar. This was the boy, after all, who left his French journal lying around for anyone to see.

"Can we make a deal?" I begged.

"I don't bargain with my children."

"What if Noah walks me to the barge and meets me when I get home?"

"It's not Barren Shoal that worries me."

"Ray can meet me at the dock in Brooklyn and bring me back when we're through."

"Who is this Ray that I should say yes?"

Who was Ray? Ray was my purpose. This is what people do. We decide on a purpose; we expect others to understand and cheer us on. Or at least not stand in our way. But why do we expect what we can barely do for ourselves? Because we are desperate to find the courage we lack.

"Ray's the boy from Miss Finn's street. You met him at the graduation party."

"It's not right."

"You don't think it's right to help the Spanish?"

"I should've said I don't *reason* with my children, never mind bargain," he replied. "Just make sure this Ray doesn't let you travel alone. Not one step."

I threw my arms around his neck.

"I love you so much..."

"Go on already," he said. "And don't tell your mother."

Noah was still out of work when school reopened in September. Having no prospects or plans, he announced he was volunteering to fight in Spain.

"With Ray?" I asked. Ray was now a part of our lives the way that outsiders enter the folklore of small towns. He was part of my life because of the way we kissed on the way to the dock and the way he draped his arm around my shoulders as we walked. For the time being, that was plenty.

"Who says Ray's going to Spain?" said Noah.

"Nobody's going to Spain," cried my mother.

"Over my dead body," said my father, at which point my mother slammed their bedroom door and did not come out for three whole days except to use the outhouse, which she did infrequently, like she was some kind of camel.

Ray had not left for Spain. He was still in Brooklyn, two doors down from Miss Finn. He was still in the warehouse on Sundays. He and Dolores still spoke in code. That was okay: we had our own code, Ray and I. I even asked Miss Finn about Ray going, but she said the decision was not up to him. If not him, who? I would no more ask about that than I would ask about the source of the money. I had my own worries. I was torn between dreaming of Ray fighting in Spain and being heroic, and wanting him safe in Brooklyn, close by, meeting me on Sundays.

Marie Dowd left that fall to live with a cousin in Brooklyn Heights and attend Hunter College. Miss Finn read Marie's letters aloud to us. I had never written a letter of my own before, but I worked up the courage to write to Ray. I asked Miss Finn to deliver it that weekend so he could read it before seeing me on Sunday. It was hard to talk with Dolores around. Miss Finn smiled in a coy, knowing way. I said that I wanted to ask him more about Spain, that it was difficult to speak at the warehouse in front of Dolores, who would think I was stupid. If I had asked anyone else to mail the letter, the whole island would have been talking. Besides which, it cost pennies to mail a letter, pennies I did not have.

Ray handed me his reply on Sunday. I still have his letters in a box of other things from back then, including a couple of pages from the Odyssey Project and some botanical drawings. I never look at any of it, but I cannot throw it away. Someone else will have to—my children, I suppose—but not yet. Ray had this to say:

> You ask if I'm a communist. Is there a right answer? No, I'm not a party member. Nor am I a member of any other party, union, league, or church. I support actions, not ideologies. Ideologies are always disappointments; they demand that we believe in them unconditionally. Actions don't require that kind of devotion. I don't need to be a communist to know that no man should starve while another grows fat. Nor must I attend Catholic mass—the religion into which I was born—and take Holy Communion in order to treat another man as I would treat myself. I do not trust the Communist Party any more than I trust the Catholic Church. The consolidation of power in the hands of the few is always dangerous, especially when the actions of those who govern cannot be questioned by those they govern.

I wrote back asking how it was possible, then, for him to be involved in the Spanish cause when so many members were communists. On Sunday he handed me his next reply:

> The writer Archibald MacLeish says, "The man who

refuses to defend his convictions for fear he may defend them in the wrong company has no convictions." There's a difference, Marta, between allies and friends. Alliances are constructed upon agreements; friendships endure despite disagreements. Don't confuse the one with the other. It'll break your heart.

It became impossible to not think about Ray, no matter what. Maybe it was the same for Sofia about Joey; maybe she could not help herself. The harder I tried, the more important he became. Noah had the unions, my parents had Zyrmuny, Sofia had Joey, Ray had the Spanish Civil War, and I had Ray. Everyone needs a purpose, including me. Does anything make us feel more alive?

I wrote back saying I hoped we could talk about it on the coming Sunday and on all the other Sundays to come. I handed him my reply the following Sunday when I got off the barge. He opened it right there.

"You're a hell of a girl, still coming after everything that happened with the boys."

"I don't worry about defending my convictions with the 'wrong company,'" I said.

"Very clever," he said with a knowing grin.

When we got to the warehouse, he steered me into one of the alleys that flanked either side. He was still clasping my hand when he kissed me. My lips opened just enough, then opened more.

He released my fingers and rested his hands on my shoulders. He kissed me again and slid one of his hands across my breasts. I pressed my mouth closer. When his fingers found one of my nipples through my thin cotton dress, I moaned.

On the Saturday after Thanksgiving, Gray and Lois appeared at the dock in their speedboat. Joey hustled off to find Noah. The very official letter they carried came addressed to James Peck, a name Noah had evidently invented for himself. It was from the Civilian Conservation Corps and was sent in care of Gray. Noah had applied again on one of those days he left me at the warehouse. I could guess what he was thinking: a fellow named James Peck would get picked faster than a fellow named Noah Eisenstein. He was right. Only people who routinely choose Pecks over Eisensteins would think that using an alias is cheating.

Instead of going to Spain like he had been vowing to do, Noah was to leave in a week for a job with the CCC cutting trees in Washington State and Oregon. No one from the police had ever checked on him after the hijacking, so he reckoned they never would. The new application was a secret. Or not telling us was a lie. One gives birth to the other—yes? But which comes first? Oh, these baffling little chickens and eggs. If we could answer that grade school question we would know the answer to everything.

Noah took what little clothing he owned and stuffed it into a bag along with his journal and his pencils. Had he been able to fit his radio, he would have taken that too. Gray and Lois came back for him in the speedboat and got him to Pennsylvania Station.

He said goodbye and then he was gone.

On Sunday I rode the barge to Brooklyn because not going would have been harder. Ray took my hand on the walk to the warehouse, but I did not care. He tried to guide me into the alley, but I shook him off. When he put his hand on the small of my back, I opened the door and took a seat by Dolores.

"What's eating you?" he asked.

"Cannibals," I replied. With that, I took the jacket Dolores was stitching and I sewed.

CHAPTER 19

Noah wrote every few weeks. The first pieces of mail were lonely letters postmarked from Washington State, where he was clearing rubble along the Columbia River to make way for the Grand Coulee Dam. He worked there long enough to write a bunch of times but he never included a return address for the fishing camp where he was staying. Did he honestly think the NYPD would trace a piece of mail across a continent to arrest a boy who hijacked a garbage barge? If they had wanted him in for punching a cop, they had plenty of chances and they never came. Noah was another piece of junk they were glad to be rid of.

In his early letters, Noah asked for details about Joey's recovery from his brothers' beating and Yorgos' luck finding a job. He asked for news from Europe. He also asked after Ray and about our work at the warehouse. Without a return address there was nothing to say, not even that, after my pushing him away for a couple of weeks, Ray and I had returned to our routine, no explanations required. Besides which, I had not even told Noah about me and Ray.

Then came a worrisome silence of two months, after which a letter arrived from a logging camp in Oregon. Noah reported that the work was hard but he was keeping up. The weather was wet and always cold; there was oatmeal every day for breakfast and potatoes and beans for dinner. In one letter, he described rigging a fishing pole from a red oak branch and buying line made by a local the old-fashioned way, out of horsehair with catgut leaders. After that he added freshwater trout to his diet.

Later on he was sent to California, where a crew was clearing a road buried by a mudslide. A dozen houses had been forced into the Pacific; two shotgun shacks were still wedged between the cliffs and the boulders below. Noah described how a few more pieces pulled away every time the tide came in until the houses finally collapsed.

California had more of everything—people, food, sun—and he sounded happy to be there. He heard Upton Sinclair address a group of loggers one night at a tent revival. He read *The Jungle*, which brought back the smells of Barren Shoal. He confused Upton Sinclair with Sinclair Lewis, which turned out fine because he read *It Can't Happen Here*, which he said was terrifying, what with Charles Lindbergh playing footsies with Hitler and the economy taking another dive. By that point a Jew in Germany could not be a dentist anymore. The Nazis were now going after the homosexuals, too. Of course it could have happened here; it still can. Nothing has changed since antiquity, from the times of Antiochus. Every Jew must be ready to live as a Maccabee. I make no apologies for saying so. The facts stand.

There was enough work to keep Noah in California forever. He befriended another boy from the east named Tyson Johns, whom he described as a handsome fellow, 6' 2" to Noah's 5' 10", with bright eyes and an easy smile. Tyson lived with his family on a chicken farm in South Jersey until the bank called in the paper when the Johnses missed some payments. The farm was auctioned for a pitiful sum, made more pitiful by the fact that Tyson's parents were unable to raise it. His father and brothers worked the same land now as tenant farmers. *They need to make cash*, wrote Noah, *so Tyson came out here.*

The only baby born that fall on Barren Shoal was another Dowd. This made number eleven. I wonder if the word *no* was in that woman's vocabulary or what Mr. Dowd would have done had Mrs. Dowd refused him. Maybe she did and he climbed on her anyway. Or maybe she liked being pregnant and nursing and the whole to-do. I liked it well enough myself for my two, but I cannot help thinking he was killing her. When the baby died of a fever my mother went silent again, as if was Helen dying all over. I did not hesitate when my father asked if I wanted to visit my aunt and uncle for a weekend.

Instead of riding the garbage barge, I went to Brooklyn on the police boat with Miss Finn. The plan was for me to ride back with her on Monday morning; I do not know how Miss Finn got the police to agree, but they did. Maybe her sister, Miss Doctor Finn, had helped out one of their wives or a girlfriend at some time or another. They were not friends but had learned to be allies, just like Ray explained.

On Saturday, my cousin Ruthie took me to see *The Life of Emile Zola*, my first movie ever. Sidney was at work and Flat Sammy howled when Ruthie told him he was staying behind, that the movie was for grown-ups.

"Marta's no grown-up," he wailed.

"She certainly is, but would you mind telling me when that happened?" asked my uncle as he helped me into my coat. "Overnight? On the sly? When I wasn't looking?"

Jews loved Zola because he defended Alfred Dreyfus. I loved Dreyfus because he was played by Paul Muni, my celebrity crush before the end of the first reel. Ruthie said that Muni was Jewish, a Galitzianer just like our family. That sealed the deal.

Ruthie and I ate popcorn while Dreyfus ate bug-infested gruel in the Devil's Island prison. We wiped our hands on paper napkins; Dreyfus got dysentery. We were completely absorbed; Dreyfus was finally pardoned. Time and history zipped by, which is pretty terrific for a character living in an unjust world.

On Sunday, instead of my going to the warehouse, Miss Finn insisted on taking me to the Brooklyn Museum. I was delighted that Ray came too. I think it fair to say that he came to see me, not the art.

"Good to see you again," Ray said, as if speaking to an acquaintance.

"So what," I replied.

"You're in a lousy mood," he said, purposely falling behind Miss Finn.

"It's okay that we're a secret; it's not okay to pretend you barely know me. And besides, it's not as if Miss Finn doesn't know I volunteer."

With Noah gone, I had no patience for being treated like a little girl. We had long been a confederation of children, even after Helen died. Without him I could not stand it. Being an only child was too lonely and I resolved to not be one. Helen was gone; Noah was gone. Therefore, I was an adult.

"The entrance used to be a wide set of steps, like at the Metropolitan Museum," Miss Finn explained as we walked in. "Three years ago the Municipal Art Commission decided that the steps were 'undemocratic' and demolished them. They didn't make the entrance democratic; they made it ugly."

She led us to the Egyptian collection. "Look at these steps the Egyptians climbed at their temples. Their priests and rulers were perched at the top so they could look down on the suppliants who brought offerings. *That* was undemocratic. But who was looking down from the steps of the museum? No one but the other visitors who had entered the same way. It's the private collectors who make art unavailable and elitist, not public museums."

"They should've ripped out the steps of the U.S. Capitol while they were at it," said Ray.

"Who exactly are you referring to?" asked Miss Finn. As always, she demanded specifics.

"Whoever decides these things, that's who."

"Perhaps you should tell them."

"I don't matter a damn."

"*Mr. Whitmore*," said Miss Finn in a scolding tone.

"And won't till I ship out."

"You're still going to Spain?" I asked anxiously. My being annoyed did not mean I did not care.

"I better be."

"Never mind that," said Miss Finn. "You're standing in front of one of the most celebrated tablets in the collection. The head on the left is the king, on the right the queen."

"Heads without bodies," Ray observed coolly.

Further along was a statue of a man and woman, seated in an embrace.

"That's more like it," said Ray. "A guy with his arm wrapped around his girl; a girl with her arm around her guy. She's even smiling."

Miss Finn gave him an appreciative look.

"Speaking of smiling, I need to find a Ladies Room," she said. She was so good at changing the subject when things got prickly.

Ray and I waited in the Egyptian gallery for Miss Finn. He tried to kiss me, but I held him off.

"I want to go too," I announced.

"Catch up with Miss Finn," said Ray.

"Not the bathroom, stupid. Spain."

"Anyone with half a brain wants to go."

"I'm serious."

"Except you're not," he said. "I mean you're not going."

"You don't get to decide," I said. "You can't even decide about yourself."

"We've discussed this. Are you a nurse? Can you drive an ambulance?"

"There must be something I can do," I said. "Rolling bandages isn't nothing."

"Stay here. Keep reminding folks."

"No one'll forget you."

"This isn't about me."

"But it is. I'm trying to tell you."

"Oh, Marta."

"Don't say my name that way."

"How should I say it?"

I blushed.

"Oh, Marta," he said. "You're sweet."

"Don't."

"I'm flattered. Truly."

"I'm not trying to flatter you. I lo—"

"No, no, no," he interrupted. "You can't. Not that way."

"What about everything and—"

"I'm not the only guy you'll ever kiss. But that doesn't mean you're in love with me. I'm the guy you're learning with. If anything, you're in love with the *idea* of me."

"That's ridiculous."

The only thing I could feel was my mouth moving.

"You've confused me with the person going to fight the Fascists."

"What about the boy who plants flower boxes, and smuggles money? The boy who *touches* me?"

"You hardly know me."

"I know what makes you laugh, what you believe in..."

"The FBI knows more than that."

"What's the FBI know?" asked Miss Finn, now in earshot.

"Nothing," said Ray. "They don't know a goddamn thing."

"*Raymond*," said Miss Finn. "The walls have ears. Even in museums."

We did not go to Brooklyn for the holidays that fall, nor did I return to the warehouse. Brooklyn was a purpose that had disappeared. It had been so easy for Ray to dismiss me. It was more humiliation than I could bear.

After a time I had some success in not thinking about him, just enough to feel miserable when I did, as if I had to forget about him all over again every time. I did not move into Noah's room like I thought I might, but I sat there a lot doing homework, listening to the opera, to Walter Winchell, even to Father Coughlin. Then my father received a letter from Mr. Schwartzbart to please come. On a beautiful blue Saturday in April, I accompanied him to Manhattan.

"The young lady," said Mr. Schwartzbart, motioning to me, "should wait outside." He waved me away with the handkerchief he had been using to blot his face.

People were crowding by the bulletin boards and waiting in a doorway for their numbers to be called. I took a seat on the bench in the hall. I only had to wait for ten minutes.

One of my mother's brothers, it turned out, had been conscripted into the Soviet army. The chances of him returning alive were as close to none as Mr. Schwartzbart could say without saying there was no chance at all. The other brother was working in a munitions factory in a labor camp in Poland. The chances of *him* returning were less than zero. In everything but fact he was already dead. Unless someone went from America to Galicia and married the two brothers' wives, there was no way that U.S. emigration would allow the unskilled women and their children into the country. But no one could marry them until they were legally widows. Which they were in a *de facto* way, even though this was agonizing to admit. My aunts and cousins were stranded. My grandparents, who might have tried escaping on the Trans-Siberian Railroad to Harbin, where they had people, stayed to help care for them.

"What am I going to tell your mother?" asked my father. He was already steps ahead of me, crossing Lafayette St. to 4th Ave. He was not really asking me; he was asking the air. And why not? Was there anyplace else to look for answers?

He slowed down at the crosswalks to wait for me, taking off again as soon as we reached the other side. At Union Square, where 4th Ave. merged into Park and we entered the subway, I thought about Noah jumping up at the rally the year before and my father dragging him off the platform. It would be easy to say in hindsight which one of them was right, but it would bring me no closer to the truth. When we got off at 34th St. I thought about Tosca as well. I still have questions swimming around in my head about protests and opera, about politics and art, but I had such hopes for them.

At 39th St. we turned west and paid a surprise visit to Uncle David, who was now in a shoe factory where he got work as a cutter when the shirt factory, also on 39th St., shut down. The factory was a block away from the Metropolitan Opera House. So many things took place on 39th St., of all the hundreds of streets in New York City. What did it mean? It meant nothing. It was simply a fact. At the shirt factory, Uncle David had worked his way up from cutter to stitcher to pattern maker. Now, at the shoe factory, he was a cutter again.

The one and only time Uncle David got lucky that I ever heard tell of was the day the shirt factory closed. Uncle David and some of the other workers were milling about in the street, wondering how a factory could go from extra hours one week to out of business the next. A man he knew from the subway, who not only worked on the same street in Manhattan but who lived the next block over in Brooklyn, told Uncle David to come upstairs, there might be an opening in the shoe factory where he was a foreman. Uncle David, who had the softer hands of a garment worker, soon acquired the thicker calluses required for cutting shoe leather. To hear my Aunt Sara tell it, his fingers bled at night right through the calluses. How was it possible for him to bleed at home without him bleeding at work on the leather? I did not dare ask.

We rode up the big freight elevator, one large enough for the horse-drawn carts that carried goods onto and off the production floor. The same horses, of course, which would sooner or later end up on Barren Shoal.

Our entrance created a minor fuss. Just a couple of years earlier, before the new labor laws, no one would have thought much of a girl walking through a factory, especially one who had been kissed. No more. Not that this prevented minors from doing piecework at home, just like farm children milked cows and dug potatoes. Families had to eat, social progress or not. And now for the biggest cliché of all, but also the one and only thing I know for sure: life is hard. I apologize, but there you have it.

The shoe production floor, unlike the reducing plant, smelled of things being made, not things being boiled beyond recognition. We passed stacks of uncut leather, tins of aged glue, and thick, oily rounds of shoe polish as beautiful as wheels of cheese. Uncle David, in his vest and tie, was at a table cutting. My father did not dare interrupt before he finished the piece he was working on.

My grandson, the anthropologist whose name is also David,

has written many scholarly papers on the nature of work, but has never made a thing in his life that did not start with pre-cut pieces. This does not take into account, of course, the toil, the many hours he bends his brow to his studies. Besides which, I love my grandson. But my David has never worked a job where he has to wash his hands *before* he goes to the bathroom, never mind wonder if there is a place to wash at all. They say writers should write what they know. So should scholars. David cannot know what it is like to stand on his feet all day until he has stood there, his arches aching and the balls of his feet swelling and not enough time between one week to the next for the swelling to disappear. He cannot know what it is like to bend over and stitch until the eyes sting. No one can until they have done it day after day. Year after year. It is not only a matter of wearing down the body. Knowing that one's days will be spent at the cutting table or sewing machine affects the heart, the brain, and the soul. Summer jobs do not count because summer jobs end. My grandson, of course, disagrees. I cannot blame him. Nor would I have it any other way. Nobody wants their loved ones to suffer.

Uncle David asked his boss if he could clock out ten minutes early, it being almost lunchtime anyway, and the boss said something about not coming back ten minutes early to make up the time, that the time would come out of his pay. My uncle said something about what *he* could do in ten minutes that the boss could not do in ten hours and my father said *David* and gestured in my direction, as if I understood their innuendo. Why not say what they meant to say? Even if what they said—like most of what most people say—was stupid. I do not say this with malice, but there is no virtue in concealing what I think. At the risk of repeating myself: I am 80 years old now and can say what I want. Even when I repeat myself.

"I'll give you the nickel tour," said Uncle David, leading us away from the foreman.

"Look, David, I've got to...." my father began.

"News can wait, can't it, Sol?" My uncle understood that things had gone from bad to worse. "You've got to start somewhere, no matter your calling. With shoes you start with the skins, a skill dating back thousands of years and never a pretty one on account of how bad the raw skins smell. The only way to work them soft is to smoke them, which stinks them up worse. Leathers come to the factory from all over the country, so they look different depending on what the animals are eating. The hide of a cow eating hay in Colorado looks different that the hide of a cow eating corn in upstate New York. You've heard the saying 'you are what you eat'? This is truth for cows, never mind people."

And for Joey, of course, you should pardon me.

"We buy the tanned pieces of leather—whole skins so we know exactly what they are—on wood flats like this one from a jobber. He gets them from a tanner or maybe a middleman, depending on the size of the operation, some outfits having consolidated on account of business being so slow. They get the hides raw from places I don't even want to think about."

My father was standing so close to Uncle David that their shirtsleeves were touching. David coughed a little to clear his throat, maybe worried he had insulted my father by insulting his trade. "Never mind all that: it's once the skins get to the factory that the crafting begins," he continued. "This is good leather here, but not the best. Top-of-the-line leathers give you shoes soft as gloves. I won't even tell you what they cost because you wouldn't believe me anyway and you'd go home and tell your mother that Uncle David is a liar and she'd give me some kind of argument, putting those highfalutin ideas into your head about the price of a pair of shoes. Feel these." He slipped off one of his own shoes and held it out to me. "Go ahead, feel the leather."

Not like gloves, but almost. "I made these by hand from a top-grade skin I bought direct from a salesman. Out of a job now, that guy, except for the sample skins he was able to take with him when his boss folded. The samples tell you something about the grade of the lot and the quality of tanning. That way the factory knows what it's buying before taking a shipment."

The cordovan-dyed leather shifted colors from bright burgundy to almost black when he tilted it under a light. He took a moment to admire his own handiwork and coughed some more. "This poor sales guy must have an apartment filled with samples because he's on the street every day, selling them by the piece for next to nothing. The skin I took has enough that I also made a pair for Sammy. Who says the shoemaker's children go barefoot, eh? The lady downstairs complained she could hear Sammy walking, his step is so heavy in these new shoes, but they make him happy. A little happiness isn't so terrible for a boy like Sammy. What do I do? I talk to that lady, make her a pair of shoes, and now she's happy too. Why make things hard when you can make them easy. Am I right, Sol?"

"We need to talk," my father replied.

Across the room were rows of cardboard boxes stacked high against a wall. There were hundreds of them, waiting to be packed with shoes.

"I'm explaining something, Sol," said David. "This factory mostly makes ladies' shoes, plus a little of this and that. Every shop has its specialty: some only ladies, some for men, others the children. But with how things are now, so many out of work and no one with too much money except the people who buy custom-made, you got to cut everything just to stay open. Now look around," he continued. He was unstoppable. "You see eight different departments, eight different specialties, maybe ten people in each group. There used to be more, maybe twice as many, before the layoffs."

Nine men were working in staggered stations at a long wooden table. Each of the stations was illuminated by an incandescent light bulb suspended from a long, black cord. Dusty metal lampshades reflected what little light they gave.

"Here's Mr. Linder, our master cutter, from Leipzig. He handles every single skin like it's an angel in the making. He can show the biggest oaf how to make an angel, too. The second seat is Mr. Goldberg from Warsaw, a jigsaw master who gets more out of a single piece of skin than almost anyone, even if he can't show anyone else how, not if his life depended on it. This young fellow here," he said, stopping in front of a man who looked close to his age and kissing him on the cheek, "this is Mr. Singer, our floor manager, the same man who got me this job, my subway companion, originally from Kielce."

Mr. Singer wore a shirt and tie; he had a stain of indigo ink above his lip, just like Mr. Schwartzbart at HIAS. He was wiping his hands on a cloth.

"You missed a spot," I said, pointing to my own lip to show him where.

"A permanent stain," said Mr. Singer.

"I'm...." I did not know what I was. Sorry? Embarrassed? There was no reason to feel anything, but I felt both. Just because. That is what I mean by being younger than Sofia in every way. I did not even know how to be comfortable being wrong, even about things that hardly mattered.

The stitching department contained more long tables with more dangling bulbs. This was where the upper sections were sewn.

"Miss Tsipkin from Bialystok, Mrs. Babel from Odessa, and Mrs. Kopelev from the Ukraine are the senior stitchers, responsible for all these other fine ladies as well as the stock fitters in the next row, who prepare the soles. The lasting department, under the watchful eyes of Roth from Tarnopol and Zweig from Vienna, is where the uppers and the linings are attached to a last—this wooden shape is the last—so the sole section can be fitted to the upper in the next department by the bottomers. It's in these two departments that trouble makes itself known. Roth and Zweig make certain it's fixed. You don't throw away shoes and stay in business.

"Finally come the finishers, where the shoes are polished and the heel and toe pads go in and the name and brand of the shoe gets stamped on the sole. If it passes the watchful eyes of the finishers, which it better because Mr. Singer spot-checks them too, it goes on to the treeing department for laces and buckles and bows and all those little touches that the ladies like. Sturdy isn't enough: people like pretty. Including poor people. And why not?

"In the old days, one worker was responsible for each pair of shoes, start to finish. 'Whole garment,' they called it, like a tailor used to make a whole shirt or even a whole suit of clothing instead of breaking it out to cutters for jackets and legs and so on. As if people come in parts that someone assembles. Those days are gone except for tailors who work for society people. For them, only custom-made. The owners say the machines work faster and they're right, but no machine makes a better shoe. Which is a whole lot of talking that gets us nowhere.

"Are they stitched or are they cemented?" Uncle David continued, further delaying the reason for our visit. "Stapled? Nailed, like the old days? The truth is that glue, no matter how strong, never holds like stitching. Every shoe you see here," he said proudly, "is sewn by a lady who knows the sound of her Singer machine like the cry of her own baby. She hears trouble before she sees it. Maybe a thread gets knotted or the needle splits or runs off track. If she doesn't stop fast, the whole shoe can get ruined."

"Enough already, David. We've got to talk," interrupted my

father.

"Go on," Mr. Singer told my uncle. "The young lady can wait over here by my desk. There are things about shoes that I can tell her too."

My father pulled Uncle David away to where I could see them but not hear.

"Did you know that people in northern Europe, by the end of the Stone Age, were sewing animal skins together to make leather thongs?" asked Mr. Singer. While he spoke he turned part of his attention to a short stack of papers, cross-checking style numbers against size numbers to make certain, he explained, that they did not stitch too many size 4's, a small size for ladies, and not enough 6's and 7's, the most popular sizes. "All the shoes, all the clothing was made by hand until spinning and weaving machines were invented in the 1700s. A Frenchman invented a sewing machine in the early 1800s, but he never got success in the U.S. The tailors and seamstresses were against it. At least until Mr. Isaac Singer—my namesake but no relation—introduced a foot-powered machine for stitching simple seams. Plenty of folks objected, but the fact was the Singer sewed a stronger stitch. That's how we ended up with factories. That was only fifty, sixty years ago. Not so long."

I remember my parents turning fifty, never mind me today turning eighty. Another platitude. But what can you say about mortality that has not been said?

Mr. Singer rolled up the stack of papers, knotted a piece of black thread around them, loaded them into a pneumatic tube, and closed the cylinder trap.

"Press," he said, pointing to a brass lever.

I pushed it down and the roll of production sheets sped straight up the tube from Mr. Singer's desk into another tube braced against the ceiling. We watched the roll racing through short glass tubes sandwiched between the longer brass tubes until, finally, it arrived at the office on the mezzanine.

"Lots of sewers owned their own machines, even at the small factories," he said. He pulled another stack of papers to the center of his desk. "They had to, like a carpenter owns his own tools. When I was a boy, you would see people on the Lower East Side carrying sewing machines on their backs. People worked so hard, like mules. Lots of men and women sewed in their apartments; children, too. A family would take turns so that the one machine never stopped except when everyone sat for the evening meal, if even that. They couldn't afford to stop. The machines were expensive, the families were poor. Now we got this Depression. But we also got the International Ladies' Garment Workers' Union in 1900 and the Amalgamated Clothing Workers of America in 1914. No more children working in factories; no more barricaded doors; no more Triangle Shirt Waist Factory fires." Mr. Singer's voice choked as if those women had been trapped in that fire last year.

"What if a factory closes? What good is the union then?" I asked. After all, it was Mr. Singer, not the ILGWU or the ACW, who found my Uncle David a new job.

"Smart girl," he said, with a smile and a shrug. "When the union can't help like they want, we do how we can."

My father and Uncle David were solemn when they returned to Mr. Singer's desk.

"Our brothers," Uncle David said to Mr. Singer. "One into the army, the other in a work camp, their families still in Zyrmuny."

Mr. Singer's whole being turned solemn, too.

Their faces said that certainty, which could hold out the promise of security, could also hold out tragedy.

Miss Rosen interrupted for Uncle David and Mr. Singer to come help, something was wrong with her sewing machine. "Why do they make me work the machine that always jams?" she complained.

My uncle and Mr. Singer laughed; the natural color returned to their cheeks. "Some people," said my uncle, tilting his head toward Miss Rosen. "*Always* rotten luck no matter what machine they get. This one's got troubles like flies to honey."

"You mean bees to honey," said Mr. Singer.

"Bees *make* honey. Why would they look for it? It's those flies you've got to watch out for."

What is there to say about my mother's response to the news from Mr. Schwartzbart? Her despairing was predictable by now, though no easier to live with.

"What did you expect?" she asked my father, as if he was at fault for thinking the situation might turn out better. "You think the world's a decent place? Maybe that's why you like living on Barren Shoal, where you got plenty of sand to stick your head in. Pull your head out! Did you think you could save the whole family? Even one? The world is rotten; people are rotten. You just think it gets better with your American Revolution, or your French Revolution, or your Russian Revolution. Ideas change, but not people. People stay rotten."

After making this declaration, she shut herself away in their bedroom for two days. She only emerged in the middle of the night, when I could hear her moving around in the kitchen. Cabinets opened and closed, utensils clanked in the sink. The bucket she used for mopping scraped against the floorboards as she dragged it along.

Where did my mother think this put her in the scheme of things, if every time she grieved she abandoned us? She would likely say this made her a rotten person, but that is too easy. My poor mother. We knew she loved us. She was afraid of how much she loved us, as if that makes it any better. I could not curse my mother so I cursed Noah, wherever he was, chopping trees or shoveling landslides or doing whatever he was doing that day in California instead of being home in this new, rotten mess. And I cursed Ray Whitmore, who would not let me love him. And I decided to return to the warehouse, if they would have me. Forget waiting around on Barren Shoal for something to rescue me, I thought. No one and nothing was coming.

Miss Finn delivered a letter for me and Dolores replied saying that of course they would welcome me back.

Ray was not at the warehouse when I arrived, the first time I made the entire trip by myself. For days I had steeled myself for seeing him. Dolores did not volunteer his whereabouts nor did I ask. I was too proud. Nor did Dolores ask why I stayed away or why I returned. I pulled up a stool and resumed sewing as if I was never gone.

Uncle David had his first heart attack a month later, not bad enough to kill him but bad enough to retire him for good. He was 45 years old plus or minus a couple of years depending on who was saying, my uncle or my aunt, who did not want anyone to know that she was a year older than him. What a silly thing to be ashamed of.

Uncle David's brother Sam had one in his forties too. Men in those days had heart attacks, not midlife crises. Who had time for a crisis when there was a Depression at home and fascists in Europe? And before that the Cossacks. And before that the Tsars. And Torquemada. And the Romans and Haman and Pharaoh. I bet that no Cambodians had midlife crises in the Pol Pot years.

Today, Uncle David would get an angioplasty like Noah did last year at age 83, in and out of St. Vincent's Hospital in twenty-four hours along with a whole gang of WWII veterans who spent the evening playing bridge at a card table near the nurses' station. Some crazy life.

My mother blamed Uncle David's heart attack not on diet or genes—as if the blame for anything can be assigned to just one cause—but on the working conditions at the shoe factory, even if they were decent by the standards of the day.

"What do you expect?" I overheard her saying to my father, "a man his age on his feet all day, stooping over a table."

My mother, of all people, went to Brooklyn to watch over Flat Sammy while Aunt Sara traveled back and forth to Coney Island Hospital. Uncle David's brother Sam was still too weak from his own heart attack to come up from Philadelphia. Cousin Ruthie, I suppose, was too busy with her married life with Sidney. I have no idea what the real reason was, though I would prefer whatever kind of certainty that comes from knowing. My mother slept on the living room couch—Flat Sammy on the floor beside her—knowing that Aunt Sara would take all the help she could get when Uncle David came home.

My mother did the marketing, the cooking, the laundry, and the cleaning. She kept Flat Sammy in the kitchen with her where he went on playing with paper cutouts, even though he was old enough now to shave. Without Uncle David there to shave him, my mother did that too. She baked intricate, colorful cookies, and cleaned chickens and did things she had barely done since Helen died. I know because my aunt told me.

It took two young men from the building to carry Uncle David upstairs when he was released from the hospital. According to Aunt Sara, Uncle David arrived soaked with sweat from the effort of holding on. Flat Sammy threw himself into his father's arms, almost knocking him off his feet before the men got Uncle David settled into a chair.

The already cramped apartment became a hospital ward. Windows were shut tight to keep the heat in and the soot out; no one was allowed to visit if they had a cold. They could not even come if they had a cold sore. It is a wonder that no one died by suffocation; it is no wonder that my mother went up to the roof after dinner every night for air.

I would like to know what Mr. Aryeh said to her one night and what she answered on all the nights that followed when they must have sat on the parapet wall, the pigeons cooing themselves to sleep after Mr. Aryeh swept out their coop and refilled their food and water troughs. I asked my aunt if she knew what my mother was doing up there but she said no. She even asked my mother if she had taken up smoking, but my mother said no. Who knows if this was true. I would not blame my aunt for protecting my mother. Or for protecting us from the path that brought my mother back to us. Was there a romance between my mother and Mr. Aryeh? Was there something else that came from two people talking? Whatever passed between them accomplished all that falling in love can do.

The photographs Mr. Aryeh made of her during that period changed her. I saw only two of them, but those were enough. One shows her in all her despair, chin and brow cast downward and hollow eyes wide open. She is staring away from the camera as if she is looking away not only from the lens, but from the past and the future as well. In the second photo, her eyes are addressing the camera and her expression is firm and elegant and fragile. Her mouth is poised in the silent quivering that takes place between speaking and having just spoken.

These two photographs are in their original cherry wood frames that my mother kept on her dresser for years and that now sit on mine. These photographs are everything I need to know about whatever passed between my mother and Mr. Aryeh. For a time—not right then, but after—I assumed that this had everything to do with the physical aspect of their intimacy. My mother reemerged in the weeks to come as if her absence had been a mere episode, even though I knew it and remember it as epic. This was before my own life had taken enough turns and I learned a different way of looking at those pictures, when I saw the subject and the photographer and the mysterious place that they shared. If this is not about intimacy then nothing is.

My mother, having already been in Brooklyn for two weeks, got a message to my father that she would be staying on a few days longer. Our household routine on Barren Shoal was as close to normal as we could manage. My father prepared breakfast while I packed sandwiches for lunch. I was also in charge of dinner. Mrs. Paradissis provided loaves of fresh bread; Sofia helped me snip beans and peel potatoes. The period of our estrangement faded away. I did the laundry on Saturday morning when my father was at work so that he never saw the washtub, as if I was now in charge of Helen's memory. My father washed his own underwear, I washed mine, and we each hung them to dry in the privacy of our rooms. I ironed on Saturday afternoons when the clothing was still damp, listening to the opera with my father, who put his own things away when he came home from work. I missed my mother and I dreaded her return.

On Sunday I returned again to the warehouse where there was still no sign of Ray. Another fellow was there ripping muslin bandages. Dolores introduced us, but I did not catch his name. I saw him many times after that but never asked and never cared. We would say hello and go about our business.

It was a relief to be with people and not care. Neither of them mattered to me in a personal way. Being with them was a vacation, not that I had ever taken one. Now I know that people do crazy things on vacations: they go swimming in the dark; they jump into lakes with their clothing on; they jump in totally naked.

As for me, I stole. That was me jumping into the water. I took a little money here and a little money there. Every time I worked at the warehouse, I took a little more except every so often when I skipped a week. If you think I am ashamed, think again.

It was easy.

Dolores slid ten $20 bills into every jacket that we stitched. $200! Who had that kind of money? I returned the first twenty I took just to see if I could. That was harder, the bill all crumpled from the trip to Barren Shoal and back. After that I kept what I took.

I pinched a bill here and a bill there. Some weeks I took nothing, just in case. Back on Barren Shoal I slipped the money between the pages of the old Odyssey Project that nobody touched anymore. It would have been faster to take one whole packet, but that would have left some poor soldier high and dry—maybe even Ray—not to mention maybe getting caught.

I no longer had Ray, but I was getting rich.

My mother again sent word that she was spending another night in Brooklyn, and then another and so on until a month had passed. My father went to the factory, I went to school, and on most Sundays I stole $20 bills because I knew how. I would steal enough to buy passage for ten people from Zyrmuny to someplace else. Not America, I understood, but somewhere.

"I'm taking you this weekend to see your mother," my father finally announced. Who knows what went into this decision? So many decisions are made about which we know so little. Including why one day is a better day for stealing or why we decide to steal at all. It is no wonder people are frantic to come up with an explanation for everything.

"Sammy slept in Uncle David's pajamas while he was gone," were my mother's first words when she saw me. How crazy was that after not seeing me for four weeks? She was up on the roof, sitting next to Flat Sammy on the parapet wall, where they were cutting paper dolls from a newspaper. Sammy's scissors were tethered to his pants by a string. My mother was wearing a pink housedress that belonged to my aunt. My mother never wore pink after one time when Mrs. Dowd told her it made her look sallow. It was green, according to Mrs. Dowd, which brought out my mother's eyes, forget that the one good dress that she owned, the one she wore to Helen's funeral, was navy blue and beautiful.

It was useless to guess what she wanted me to say in return. That I had slept in her nightgown? I had not. That I missed her? I had not. That my single, humiliated appeal to Ray—and his kind and condescending rejection—hurt me in ways I was unprepared for? That I had longed for a mother's reassurance? Why bother. My mother, having quarantined herself since Helen's death, made it impossible to recognize the ways that I needed her. Impossible for her. Impossible for me.

My mother and Flat Sammy went on trimming paper dolls until Mr. Aryeh emerged from the pigeon coop, where he had been checking the tags on his birds.

"This is my Marta," my mother said by way of introduction.

"Of course I know Marta," he replied, smoothing the feathers of the pigeon in his hands. When he said that he knew me, it was not just that he had seen me before. He knew about me. Not about the thief I had become, but a girl seen through her mother's eyes.

"You like pigeons?" asked Mr. Aryeh. He stepped back into the coop, set down the bird he was holding, and returned to the assembly line inspection of the others, adjusting the tags with a pinch of his needle-nose pliers.

My mother and Mr. Aryeh had pulled a shroud of exclusivity over whatever was passing between them, but they were the elephant in the room that my father and uncle never spoke of. Now they were the elephant on the roof.

"There aren't many pigeons on Barren Shoal," I replied. "Mostly seagulls."

"Which don't compare to pigeons."

"They're not afraid of people either."

Mr. Aryeh smiled. "A good point. But you can't train them to deliver messages, can you?"

"The only thing a seagull delivers is...."

My mother cleared her throat. She finally noticed me enough to slap me on the wrist. Flat Sammy cleared his throat too in pure imitation.

Mr. Aryeh laughed. "I get your point. Pigeons, though, they're pretty smart. Even so, it happens every once in a while that a pigeon gets lost and another pigeoneer returns it. Sometimes someone holds it hostage, shakes you down for a ransom, or returns it with a mutilated wing or a knife cut in the beak. People do pigeons how they do each other. I can't explain it.

"You want to see a guy go crazy, you watch a pigeon man get back a cut bird. What did the bird do? Nothing. Pigeons are very sociable. It's a bird; it sees other birds, it flies to them. But some guys don't want their pigeons mixing with another guy's pigeons, so a bird'll come back with a marker, maybe something not so nice, something so you know where it landed. Then you got to decide what to do: do you wait until one of *his* birds strays so you can take a piece of *its* wing? Do you keep the guy's pigeon and switch tags with a bird you wanna get rid of? Do you let it go so it doesn't dishonor your flock by association?"

Mr. Aryeh raised the wings of a homer; the bird shifted its weight from one pink foot to the other. "The stakes are high when your heart's in it. A couple of months ago a guy from Greenpoint called to say he had one of my birds. Way the heck the other side of Brooklyn. Nice fella, immaculate coop, open sky to Manhattan. Italian guy. His wife set out cookies and coffee. She said stay for dinner, they were ready to sit down, noodles with green sauce, pesto from basil she grows in boxes beside the coop. Who knew? All along I thought Italian sauce was red. We end up trading a couple of birds. I don't see this guy ever, us living at opposite ends of Brooklyn, but now he's a friend. We send messages via the birds. We got plans to trade again. It's good to bring new blood into the flock, mix things up with a well-cared-for bird. Makes the birds stronger. Good for everyone all around."

My father finally appeared on the roof and the men shook hands through the open door of the coop. He tousled Sammy's hair and gave my mother a peck on the cheek.

Mr. Aryeh went on, with a wrapping-things-up rise in his voice. "A bird gets lost, and now, maybe, you're in the middle of a tragedy. Or maybe you're about to make a friend. This is what everything boils down to: you never know. The old proverb is true: about nothing you never know nothing. You can't predict; you can't plan. But you just go on planning anyway, because that's how people do."

My father took a seat next to my mother. She moved closer, finally leaning into him. Flat Sammy looked up from his cutouts, blew some air kisses at my father, and returned to his rough scissoring. My mother gently kissed my father's cheek.

"I'm going to stay a few days longer," she said.

Down on the street a wagon was passing, bottles clinking as its wheels passed over the ruts. I remembered the milk wagon from the night of Helen's funeral; how I was a girl on the street in her pajamas; how I was throwing away a confession to a crime my mother never committed.

"I know you're staying," answered my father.

"Then I'll be home," she said. She brushed a pigeon feather off his pants.

"That'll be good," he said.

"Come on, kids," Mr. Aryeh to Flat Sammy and me. "Let's get the camera and make some pictures."

My parents, to my astonishment, were still sitting on the parapet wall when we returned with Mr. Aryeh and the camera gear. How often did I see my parents sitting, just sitting, instead of making something, fixing something, reading something, planning something? How about never.

"Can you stay in one place if I tell you?" Mr. Aryeh asked Sammy.

Sammy nodded, though who knew what he was agreeing to. Mr. Aryeh gave Sammy a box of rejected photographs and a pair of scissors, telling Sammy to cut the people out from the pictures. Sammy was essential to the process, intently cutting out figures while Mr. Aryeh used him as a model.

Mr. Aryeh was a patient teacher. After setting up the tripod, he folded it down so I could open it again and lock it myself. He laughed when I splayed its legs and the thing toppled onto Sammy, who thankfully laughed too. To my further delight, Mr. Aryeh handed me the big 8x10 view camera, talking me through each step of mounting it on the tripod. A welcome peacefulness settled on Sammy while the technical problems were being solved around him. Then Mr. Aryeh took the light meter hanging from his neck and draped it around my own. He showed me how to take meter readings from Sammy's left cheek, his right cheek, and directly in front of his face, the sun always behind me where it belonged.

I exposed two images that day. The first was of my parents. The second was a self-portrait made using a shutter release cable, the trigger hidden from view in my hand. I have kept them both, rare souvenirs. Of course I wanted someone beside me; of course I imagined Ray. Or Ray and me rolling into a pile of $20 bills like a big old bed of leaves. I have witnessed enough to believe this happens to most everyone: we become stuck on someone not because they are perfect or we are perfect together, but because the feeling is. It was not the idea of Ray that I fell in love with, the way he said on that humiliating day at the Brooklyn Museum. It was the sensation of loving him, which had changed everything. I confused it with the creation of the universe, as if nothing existed unless I did. A girlish thought, but not dumb. It will not exist when I die, this universe as I know it. Do not worry about me. I am okay. I would be running out of time if all that mattered were the future, but it is not.

My parents stayed on the roof when Mr. Aryeh led Sammy and me back down to his street-level studio where the film holders could be safely unloaded in the darkroom. The room had no windows. Heavy black fabric, similar to the camera hood, hung over the door, preventing light from leaking in. Sammy moaned in the absolute darkness, so I took his soft hand while Mr. Aryeh talked us through the process of pulling each sheet of film from the holder and passing them through the trays of different solutions.

"Developer," he said. "Eight minutes. Stop bath, just a quick wash through. Fixer, takes off the excess silver, makes the image permanent. Then you rinse in cold running water to wash off the chemicals. Ten minutes. Twenty is better. That way the film lasts. And your image lasts on the film."

"Lasts how long?" By now, despite the darkness, I could see him performing each step.

"Forever, maybe. At least that's what they say. Forever if it doesn't get damp and you keep it stored in a cool, dark place, and you don't handle it much and get it dirty. Otherwise the image goes and the film crumbles."

"Goes where?" asked Flat Sammy.

"Aha!" cried Mr. Aryeh. "The family savant!"

"What's that?" asked Sammy.

"A genius."

"No," said Sammy, giggling. "I'm slow."

"Okay, then," Mr. Aryeh agreed. "A slow savant."

When enough time had passed, he switched on the lamp. Both sheets of film were hanging from a line of string over the sink. Wooden laundry clips held them in place while they dripped, dripped, dripped. Shadow was light and light was shadow, just like everything ends up eventually.

"Magic," Sammy whispered.

"Alchemy," said Mr. Aryeh, "except better than gold. What's gold got to do with being a human? A picture, though, a picture is something. A big something. So now you kids go eat lunch. Come back in an hour. It's so hot in here that the film should be baked by then. I can't teach you everything, but today is a start, yes?"

I tugged Flat Sammy upstairs to the apartment. My aunt, who was putting the finishing touches on a bowl of chicken salad, motioned to a loaf of bread. "Cut sandwiches for the two of you, please, and for your uncle."

Uncle David was sitting in the living room, his feet resting on an ottoman, his eyes half closed.

"Aunt Sara said bring this for you," I said.

He cocked his head. "Is that Marta?"

I never saw a man eat a sandwich so slowly, as if eating was a chore. He would take a bite, put the sandwich back on his plate, then start to chew. As if the sandwich weighed more than he could hold. Flat Sammy plowed through his sandwich and I ate quickly as well, wanting that awkward meal to be over.

"Go on, you two," said my uncle. "I'll finish later." He set his plate on the little table beside him and closed his eyes.

"Come on, Sammy," I said after we returned our plates to the kitchen. Only thirty minutes had passed since we had left Mr. Aryeh but I knocked on his door anyway. He answered, a napkin tucked into the collar of his shirt.

"You kids again? So soon?" He checked his watch. "Look through these while I finish eating," he said. He handed a box of photos to each of us. "You have your scissors, Sammy?"

Of course he did, attached by a string to the waistband of his pants like a pocket watch.

Sammy rifled through a box of extras, outtakes and rejects, some of people who came every year for a new portrait for their parlor, or the bedroom, or to be mailed back to Europe with a couple of American dollars.

Sammy went to work with his scissors, as focused in his attention as a diamond cutter working a stone. I sifted through my box photo by photo, though who knows what I was looking for. I must have looked at a hundred in the time that Mr. Aryeh ate his big plate of sour cream and boiled potatoes and drank his cup of hot tea.

"It will take years to become a photographer," he said, "but you can learn. You got years?"

CHAPTER 20

Dinner was an abbreviated affair, what with my father and mother sequestered on the roof next to Mr. Aryeh's pigeon coop, the flock locked in and muttering like tipsy men at Mr. DeWitt's poker games, Flat Sammy in the living room with my uncle, a folding table between them, and my aunt with me in the kitchen. Mr. Aryeh had slipped away to his own dinner and heaven knows what conversation with his wife about my mother.

Mr. Aryeh had not asked after Noah and the boys, nor did he mention the hijacked barge. In addition to working for the newspapers, he was now working weekends for the police department taking mug shots. His portrait work was falling off as local families lost touch with loved ones in Europe. What kind of lost touch? Thousands of people had already disappeared, shoved to the east by the Germans and to the west by the Russians, and shoved around in every way by the Poles. German and Austrian Jews with money were boarding the Tran-Siberian Train to Japan and passenger ships for Shanghai; others were walking to Marseille and to Thessaloniki—where Sofia's mother was born—to hire boatmen who would smuggle them to Palestine. The relatives in Zyrmuny, who had barely a cent to their names, could not know how fast my hoard of $20 bills was growing. They could not know —nor could I tell anyone—that help was coming.

"What do you hear from Noah?" my aunt asked when she got me alone in the kitchen. She set down a plate with a chicken leg and boiled potatoes for me, and a plate with the chicken neck, the back, and the liver for herself.

"That he's not coming home from California," I said.

"Is that so?" she asked, startled.

"He writes about all these big plans for when he gets back, but that's just him dreaming."

"More potatoes?" she asked. My aunt had careful eyes. "So *he* doesn't say that he's not coming. *You* say it."

"Sofia and I invented this Odyssey Project when we were little, scrapbooks of all the places in the world we would visit. We went on making them even when we were old enough to know it was make-believe. It's like that with Noah. Cutting down trees, being gone from the police. As if that makes everything okay. It's just more make-believe, what he's doing out west." We had abandoned the Odyssey Project years ago without even discussing it. It was not something we decided. It just happened. Then it came to life again, the perfect safe place for cash instead of girlish dreams.

"But look at him, all the way in California," she said. She chewed on the backbones, making a sucking sound that sounded good. "Maybe it's make-believe, but it's also a fact."

My aunt apologized again and again for sending us off with a bag of apples instead of the usual overload of leftover roast and puddings and what-have-you. "Had I only known you were coming," she complained. She looked at my father. Then she looked at my mother. Then she looked at me. What on earth was she searching for? What kind of clue or sign was she looking for after all these years when there were fewer answers instead of more?

I was relieved to get away from that sullen apartment and from my mother's perfunctory good-bye. A quick peck on the forehead, an invisible smudge wiped from my face. My father tucked the bag of apples under his arm and held my hand for the quiet walk to the streetcar. Gaslights were being lit for the evening and the sky changed from pink to blue to black. A few minutes later, through the streetcar window, I saw a family huddled beneath a burning street lamp. The woman's eyes were little explosions of panic that she was stoking by slapping her palms against her hips. Surrounding her were dilapidated wood crates overloaded with blankets and pillows. Her husband was sitting on an equally ramshackle chair; his face was buried into the back of a small boy who was staring at nothing. My father was looking out the window too. He pulled me closer.

At the pier he arranged for us to ride an evening barge to Barren Shoal. At the head of the dock was a vendor selling beef hotdogs from a steam cart. My father gave him the once-over and me one of those *Why not?* looks, though we had already eaten dinner and had the bag of apples to tide us over. The hotdog man split open two rolls and stabbed the dark pink franks from the steam cabinet with his knife. We each ate one loaded with sauerkraut, then shared one with onions in greasy red sauce, a spot of which got on my shirt even though I bent at the waist to eat the way my father did. And like the man I had seen on the subway. I had not eaten on the street since that pretzel at the opera years before. My mother, of course, would have been revolted by the whole enterprise. It is hard to imagine that she ever ate on the street. Never mind hard: how about impossible.

"Good?" asked the man.

"Good," replied my father.

"Good?" asked my father.

"Good," I answered.

"Good," said the man, as if for that moment the only thing in the world that mattered was a hotdog. He folded down his umbrella, rinsed the top of the cart with water from a jar, and rolled off to the stable where street carts also parked.

The usual crew of pickers was on the barge that would carry us back to Barren Shoal. The fat corpses of horses not fully picked over looked lavish. I wondered about Katrine, the girl in the brown dress who I had not seen for a long time. Thinking about her had something to do with the family I had seen from the streetcar. I looked for her among the pickers working in the dark. After that, with everything happening so quickly, I did not think of her again.

My mother really did come home a few days later. I did not know she would be arriving when she did, or if my father knew and withheld the information, or if, in fact, he did not know either. I cannot say what difference knowing would have made. After all, it was not until she was gone that I saw how comforting her absence could be. The house was emptier for sure, but easier without all those daily reminders of what she was not. Not that this delighted me: we were supposed to have a mother who we could leave, not a mother who could not stop herself from leaving us.

I arrived home from school and there she was, working at the kitchen table, the thin curtains pulled back to let in more daylight.

"It's been a while since we had brisket for dinner," she announced into the dead air, never taking her eyes off her knife.

I did not tell her I had made a brisket the Sunday before any more than I would have said I was stealing money. Or that I touched and had been touched by a boy named Ray. The bowl beside her was filling with chopped onions, an amount which had taken me three times longer to chop just days ago. There was always the risk that anything could set her off.

"I stopped on the way back," she said, meaning she shopped at the same good butcher in Brooklyn where my father had stopped a week earlier. It was her only acknowledgement about being away. "Keep chopping while I brown this meat," she said, the familiar tone of instruction now returning to her voice. "Wash your hands good first."

She spooned some rendered chicken fat into a roasting pan, struck a match beneath the pot, and the fat began to sizzle. Then came the searing sound of the meat on the hot pan, so hot it browned the down side almost instantly. She hovered over it, long fork in hand ready to turn it. Then the searing sound flashed again when she browned the other side, the house filling with the sweet aroma of onions and meat, as if her cooking could drive away the odor of rotting flesh, the mystery of her absence, and everything else that was morose, or confusing, or mournful. I craved it, this food that overpowered the smell of the factory. I wanted everything that was corrupt and putrefied replaced by the sweet. Better to be guilty of romanticizing than to never imagine things better than they might ever be. How else would we know what to hope for?

A few days later she went next door to thank Mrs. Paradissis for the bread and other things she had sent over during her own absence. This was not such a big deal but for the fact that my mother had not set foot in anyone else's house on Barren Shoal since Helen died.

She was gone for the better part of a late afternoon.

"Here," she said when she returned, a plate of Mrs. Paradissis' melomakarona cookies in hand.

"Honey cookies," I said.

"Melomakarona," she corrected, as if she knew about them

all along. "Just baked."

"Mrs. Paradissis doesn't bake cookies on Wednesdays," I said, guarding my turf with a degree of authority that far outweighed the importance of the thing I was protecting. "She bakes bread on Wednesdays."

"Well, today we baked these," she assured me. "I told her how much I'd enjoyed these in the past—I can't remember when I last ate one, can you? Next thing I knew, she had the sack of flour on the table and I was draining a honeycomb and chopping nuts."

She again offered me the plate. The honey not absorbed by the cookies pooled around them.

"It's almost dinnertime," I said.

"So what, go on." Her voice was still flat, but she was there.

It only takes a shift of a few degrees to make a world feel the new tilt of its axis. I was still shy around my mother after that, not certain what to make of her having changed overnight. Or having changed in the month that she stayed in Brooklyn. The fact is that whatever made this possible must have been stirring about inside her; she had probably been changing for months, maybe even years. Now she wanted catching up about everything. She wanted a full report about things that happened in the weeks she was over in Brooklyn, but she also wanted to know about things that went back years.

"Tell me about the union, Marta. Your father doesn't talk about it anymore, at least not to me," she said. We were in the yard taking down laundry. That clothesline was a pretty silly place to hang clean clothing, now that I think about it. Not that we had a choice, but no sooner was it washed then it was flaked with soot. "Your father's still convinced that he could have stopped Noah from leaving."

I did not have a whole lot to report. With Noah in California and Yorgos now living in Astoria and going to school, the subject of the union rarely came up.

"Last thing I heard is that two groups came over to talk to the men. Everyone made a big deal and Joey served homemade wine. Then a fight broke out."

"Help me with these sheets," she said, handing me two corners.

"A man from one group called someone from the other group a fascist. Then everybody got into it. 'You're a fascist. You're a Trotskyite. You're a wise guy. You're a commie.' They're supposed to be getting a union, but instead they were beating each other up. Mr. Dowd got his nose broke!"

"It makes no difference," said my mother. She walked towards me and joined her two corners with mine.

"Both eyes got black and blue."

"None of this matters. Who wins. Which union. Everyone wants to be the boss."

I reached down for the two corners created by folding the sheet in half.

"And what about this boy?"

I said nothing.

"Ray," she said.

"What about him?"

"I saw you writing those letters. I heard your teacher say he was going away."

Dolores never spoke of Ray at the warehouse and I saw no point in drawing attention to myself by asking. I had no idea what he was doing or where.

"You'd have to ask Miss Finn," I said.

Not that I imagined she would. But hearing Dolores or Miss Finn say that Ray was in Spain would be dreadful; it would be just the thing to make me care more instead of less. What is crummier than still caring after being rejected?

"You miss your brother?" she asked.

"Uh-huh," I said, raising the new corners to again meet hers.

"And Sofia: does she miss Yorgos?"

"We don't talk about it."

"You girls talk about everything."

"He used to smack her around. Why should she miss him?"

"What should she do? Not be his sister?"

"Be happy he's gone."

"Don't say such a thing. Not ever."

"It doesn't matter that he was bad to her?"

"That's family," she said.

"I'd rather be beaten by a stranger."

With Noah and Yorgos gone and Joey slowed down by the beating he took from his own brothers, our lives settled into a different rhythm. Sofia studied the movie magazines that Miss Finn now mixed in with the newspapers. Perhaps she had always brought them over for the older girls; we were the older girls now. As for me, all those weeks of stealing made me jumpy, even if stealing was easy. The longer it went on, the likelier I would get caught. The greater the likelihood of getting caught, the jumpier I got. Instead of $20 a week I now took $40. Why not? I was trying to save lives.

Noah wrote letters every month, sending them under the pseudonym James Peck so neither the police nor anyone else could track him down. How he came up with that name he would never say, not even later when we were both grown and he would swear he honestly could not remember and I would swear back that I did not believe him and he would say believe what you want. To this day I cannot say why it mattered to me, but it did. Maybe it had something to do with all the mysteries that Noah and so many others meant to hide.

He wrote mostly about the site where he was working: about the beauty of the Pacific West; about how boring is to eat rice and beans, beans and rice, and fish, fish, fish—even more than we ate on Barren Shoal; how his buddy Tyson had convinced one of the camp guards to go deer hunting in the hills and they shot a buck; about how Tyson dressed the deer with a bowie knife and they grilled the meat, liver and kidney and all, over a wood fire. Anything they did not eat—mostly innards, but also the hooves, and the snout, and the kinds of things the scavengers would have gladly hauled away from the garbage barge—they hurled into the brush for the buzzards.

After months of mystery and being on the move, he wrote that he would finally be staying in one place long enough to receive mail. I wrote back the very same day and told him about Yorgos moving again—this time to Staten Island—to work at the new dump called Fresh Kills and how he came to visit every few weeks at what he now called Old Kills. I said nothing about Ray; I said nothing about my little larceny or my plot for getting our relatives out of Zyrmuny. The first part felt like it was already cursed and I was afraid of cursing the other. Better to go it alone; better to not screw things up like the boys, who had gotten nowhere other than beaten, fired, and exiled. There was already plenty enough of that in Zyrmuny.

A few days later I sent a drawing of places and things from Barren Shoal that would mean something: a clamshell, a tuft of dune grass, a window frame from our house, the school, and the factory, the small things representing the whole, meaning the whole of Barren Shoal. And I changed my mind about telling Noah about Ray. *I'm so impressed*, he wrote back. *It takes a hell of a lot of courage to love someone, never mind tell them. I'm sorry it didn't work out, but it will. With someone else, someday. Promise.* It was a promise he was in no position to make, but so what? I took my consolation where I could get it.

The more we wrote, the more I missed him. He missed us too, but not enough to come back to New York, where surely Gray or Lois could have found him a place in the Village. It was only Barren Shoal that he could not come to because people would know him. Anywhere else in New York he could be anyone he wanted to be.

"Why do they need guards at this camp?" asked my mother, when I read to her about the hunting trip. "Now Oregon's a prison?"

"He's in California, Mom. The guards watch the camp so no one can get in and make trouble or steal."

She wiped her hands on a rag and pushed some hair off her brow. "Who can believe this? First Noah's hiding from the police and has to go all the way to California; now he's being protected by the police. And they call me crazy."

The measure of a good life is not whether or not we live in some kind of Eden; it is how we compensate for the fact that we do not. Joey, after Noah and Yorgos were gone, took to spending time with Mr. Paradissis, who taught him how to make wine from the grapes now growing wildly on the arbor. Mr. Paradissis took this project to heart, what with the bar on Barren Island long gone and the people on Barren Shoal having more reasons to drink than ever. Joey's role in this enterprise included keeping the seagulls away from the grapes. He dreamed up a jamboree of sorts. Joey, who could barely speak after his brothers beat him so badly, devised a contraption out of the broken tools that were left behind on Barren Island. He strung these from the arbor using fishing line, creating wind chimes that surprised human beings as well as gulls. Little kids stopped by after school to play the tools and make a crazy mixed-up racket. The people who lived nearby got pretty fed up with the noise until the first harvest of wine was ready. After that everything was forgiven. The same neighbors who were complaining became customers. My father even asked Mr. Paradissis to concoct something sweet, which he did by adding his honey. This was not truly *kosher* wine because it was not officially blessed by a rabbi, but my father used it regardless to make a *Kiddush*.

Joey, after a day at the factory shoveling maggot-infested animal parts into carts, spent his evenings washing wine bottles, chasing away birds, and mashing grapes. I do not know if it was the wine itself or something else, but he seemed happier. Mr. Paradissis appeared happier too. What was there not to like? Mr. Paradissis had a helper who, unlike Yorgos, did as he was told; Joey now took his meals inside at the table, across from Sofia, where he did not have to worry that someone would grab away his plate or interrupt dinner with a beating. Joey, even before the rest of us, found his calling.

A portion of my father's salary now went to keeping Uncle David and Aunt Sara and Flat Sammy in their apartment. Uncle David was not strong enough to keep an eye on Sammy all day if Aunt Sara went out to get a job, so she took in sewing to supplement their tiny relief checks and what little my parents could give. Things would have been even harder were Ruthie not married or Noah not off in California. That meant two less mouths to feed, not to mention Helen, which no one did. Things would have been easier had I shared my booty but for the fact that they would have made me return it. No matter. They would be happy when I turned the money over to Mr. Schwartzbart and saved the family in Zyrmuny. They would give me a hero's welcome.

As for me, on top of thieving I was busy preparing for the

exams that could get me into Hunter. Nights found me in the schoolroom, away from the noise of Joey's bootlegging and bird chasing and the sad hum of my father listening to the radio in Noah's room, writing yet another letter of appeal for visas. On those evenings the schoolroom smelled of autumn, the new winds from Canada valiantly driving against the factory smells. I had spent so much of my life in the schoolhouse by then. Ten years is a whole life to a girl. I was looking at that room with new eyes now, as much for who was gone as for what was still there.

I paced the room one restless Saturday, touching books and pencils and the globe on Miss Finn's desk in search of something to cool my fingers, as if there was anything in that room that did not retain heat. The globe was the same one that Sofia and I had been turning since we were children. Of course Ray had to be in Spain by now. He might be with Miss Finn's Ernesto; he might be facedown in the brush, a bullet through the back of his head. He was wrong about my being in love with the idea of him, but the idea of him was how I now measured things. *Does it feel worse than Ray?* I would ask myself about this thing or that, not *does it feel worse than Helen?* Helen was something that happened; Ray was something that happened to *me*.

With a tip of my finger I sent the globe spinning counterclockwise, not clockwise the way Miss Finn had instructed, "in order to replicate the rotation of the earth on its axis." I turned it faster and faster until the globe achieved liftoff, spinning across the room, smashing into a window pane, shattering it, dropping down to the shelf below, knocking over a display of sea shells with name cards attached to them, and finally falling to the floor and rolling under a table. Turning it counterclockwise, I learned, not only ran contrary to science; it unscrewed the globe from its base.

Aside from breaking the window, the globe itself was dented and its surface material cracked, leaving the Baltic states something of a mess. No, I was not concerned that day with geopolitical metaphors. The same would have happened no matter where the globe landed. My only concerns were replacing the window and repairing the globe. On the bookcase behind Miss Finn's desk was a dictionary, a thesaurus, and an atlas of the known world. I decided to draw a replacement for the damaged section and glue it into place. Not without Miss Finn knowing, of course, but it would be ready to hand over when I offered my confession. I had no ideas yet about finding a new piece of glass. I thought about using money from the Zyrmuny fund, but then everyone would know.

I flipped to the map of Europe, which only barely resembled the borders of the countries on the globe.

"Of course not," said Miss Finn, when I owned up to the situation. Being a thief had made me gutsier. "Look at the publication date of the atlas. 1913. A gift to me from my parents for my 13th birthday. By 1914 it was inaccurate. Just like this globe.

"A globe, a book, a map," she said, smiling. "They represent things for a moment. Look at the maps Columbus used. How could he imagine he was going to India and end up in North America? Because of the maps. Just wait until you read *War and Peace* and see what a mess the cartographers got Napoleon into, never mind Tolstoy."

"You don't care about the globe?"

"Of course I do and yes, you're going to do your best to fix it. But it's a globe that you made a mess of, Marta, not the world."

Barren Shoal, on the other hand, was thriving. Production increased to take in the rendering that had been handled on Barren Island. Five families were relocated to Barren Shoal. Nestled in among the Dowds, Eisensteins, Paradissises, and Pessaras were now the Smiths, the Johnsons, the Woods, the Whites, and the Hansons. One day there were five empty cabins on Barren Shoal and the next day there was laundry drying out on the line. My mother was wary.

"Why are they doing this," she asked, "moving in Protestants with Catholics and Jews?"

"And Baptists, and Eastern Orthodox?" said my father, bothered by my mother's fears and suspicions. "They're just happy to have jobs."

"Such a step down for them," said my mother, coolly.

"There were mostly Irish and Italian on Barren Island, too," he reminded her.

"So how is it that only Protestants got the jobs here?"

"What's your point?"

"I'm just seeing what's in front of my face," she said, angry now.

My mother was not the only person looking for signs that the U.S. would take a sharp right turn into bed with the Nazis. Joe Kennedy, the paterfamilias of *those* Kennedys, was appointed ambassador to England and became, as the German ambassador described him, "Germany's best friend in London." It made me sick to have to vote for his son in 1960. I did it, I held my nose, but I was not happy. Better than voting for that rotten Nixon after what he did to poor Helen Gahagan Douglas, red-baiting her that way. "Pink down to her underwear." That is how Nixon described her. Such a disgraceful way to speak.

Lives reorganized themselves; things were not what they had been nor what they were going to be. Some of the men from Barren Island had gotten work on the clean-up crews way out on Eastern Long Island after the big hurricane in September. I hoped that Noah would be among the WPA boys trucked out there, but that was just wishful thinking. They brought in boys from New York City, not California.

My parents argued and the Paradissises argued about the

terrible things happening in Europe. Hitler was deporting Polish Jews from Germany; Metaxas ordered book burnings in Athens, among other things.

"If Roosevelt doesn't know what to do about this Hitler, how should we?" asked Mrs. Paradissis.

"Stalin will make a move," Mr. Paradissis assured them. "He's not gonna sit this out."

"Like he did with Franco?" I asked sarcastically. Ray popped into my mind like a Jack-in-the-box. The International Brigades were getting walloped in Spain, with casualties way out of proportion to their numbers. Was this my fault? By then I had stolen $800—the price of a new car—and heaven only knew where Ray was.

"The Soviets are sending supplies to fight the Spanish Fascists," said Sofia.

"Stalin don't give a damn about Spain," said Mrs. Paradissis. "Or Greece. Just trouble for Russia."

A labor union local was the only cause anyone on Barren Shoal had been willing to fight for; now it was just a handful that stayed involved. When Yorgos and Noah were on Barren Shoal, the men could say that they were trying to keep the boys from making things worse. With the boys gone, the men had no one to hide behind. Most of them stayed home. Sometimes my father went to a meeting, sometimes not. Mr. Paradissis never missed a meeting, so Joey never missed one either. Mr. Paradissis even tried tying his wine sales to attendance, but just got everyone mad.

At the end of October, when I should have been studying trigonometry, Sofia and I sat in Noah's room on an unusually warm night listening to Orson Welles' radio broadcast of the "War of the Worlds." It is pretty thrilling to get excited about something that is not true. Every now and then, for a few seconds here and there in the dim light, we would forget the facts and become gloriously scared. We would poke our heads out into the warm autumn air and check the sky for flashing lights.

In the middle of the broadcast, Joey rushed up to the window, banging on the glass. "There's Martians," he said, breathing hard. "They landed in Jersey. They killing everyone with heat rays."

Sofia sighed. She motioned for him to come inside.

"We gotta take cover," cried Joey. "They's killing cops in Jersey."

"It's a radio play," I said wearily. The fact that Joey was getting stupider did not shrink my contempt for him.

"You think some Martian's gonna come all the way to Earth so he can invade Barren Shoal?" asked Sofia. Even she was getting fed up.

"Hide on the barge," I told him in a conspiratorial voice. "They won't come looking there."

Joey's lips twitched as he considered this. "I'll slip you on," he said, proud and determined. "Come find me."

With the program over and Joey still scouting out an escape by barge, Sofia offered to quiz me on the trigonometry problems I needed to master for my upcoming exams. Did we take NY State Regents exams then, or was there a city requirement for math? Some things I am glad to forget. What is trigonometry, anyway? Just a way of measuring angles? It could have been so beautiful, a way of knowing what happens to the whole when a single part is moved. What an interesting idea if that, in fact, is what it is about. But what do I know?

"Come to Hunter with me," I begged Sofia. "You've done all the work."

"It's plenty enough I'm doing these damn questions."

"Don't be stupid," I said.

"You're turning into Marie," she said, a warning tone in her voice.

"Huh?"

"It's one thing to be a snob. It's another to be an out-loud mean one."

Maybe I was a snob, thinking I could go off to college like Marie Dowd, turning her back on everything and anyone at Barren Shoal. How many months had passed since she visited?

"Don't be ridiculous," I said, though the thought of disappearing from Barren Shoal—or of Barren Shoal disappearing from my life—was not at that moment unappealing. What a thing it would be, I thought, to forever get that stink out of my nose.

"See what I mean?" said Sofia.

The world did not need my help messing things up. Chamberlain came back from Munich in September and announced "peace in our time." Nazi foot soldiers, under orders from the Gestapo and cheered on by ordinary Germans, were unstoppable on Kristallnacht in November, smashing windows of Jewish-owned shops and painting terrible words on Jewish homes, and burning synagogues, and beating up ordinary Jews walking down the streets, and arresting prominent members of Jewish communities throughout Germany. How did Father Coughlin explain this on his weekly radio broadcast? He declared that, "Jewish persecution only followed after Christians first were persecuted." He was saying that the horror of Kristallnacht was retribution; he was saying that Jews got what Jews deserved. This priest, from his radio pulpit in Detroit, revealed things about Christians and Christianity that I wish I never knew.

All the Jewish children were expelled from the German public schools a few days later. Jews could no longer be doctors, or own land, or receive national healthcare. German-born Jews had already been stripped of citizenship back in 1935, no matter how many generations of their families were born in Germany. Having everything taken away overnight is one kind of torture; having things ripped away in increments is another. Anyone who believes that every unhappy family is unhappy in its own way should understand that every act of cruelty is cruel in its own way. There is nothing to be gained by comparing them.

Like all Holocaust deniers, Father Coughlin turned the truth inside out and upside down. I listened to his famous November 20 radio sermon alone in Noah's room: "Although cruel persecution of German-born Jews had been notorious since 1933, particularly in the loss of their citizenship, nevertheless until last week the Nazi purge was concerned chiefly with foreign-born Jews. German citizen Jews were not molested officially in the conduct of their business. The property of German citizen Jews was not confiscated by the government, although a few synagogues and stores were destroyed by mob violence."

Who was he kidding? Evidently millions of his listeners, who did not understand that every German Jew was a foreign Jew from the moment they were stripped of citizenship. Books had been burned, business burned, Jews banned from owning land or editing newspapers; Jews were being beaten in the streets. And what would his listeners have cared anyway, after the way he roused them by masquerading his bigotry as anti-communism.

Every word of it was a lie.

And listen to me now, trying to discredit his lies as if I could change the minds of anyone who wants to believe them. By comparison, my stealing all those $20 bills was the sanest thing in the world.

In January 1939, in his anniversary speech to the Reichstag, Hitler announced that if Germany went to war—never mind an invasion by H. G. Wells' Martians—the Jews of Europe would be annihilated. It was a promise, simple as that. From then on my mother traveled with my father every week to HIAS as if he had not already done all that could be done to get whoever they could out of Europe. I stayed home and prepared dinner, the opera playing in the background. What was the point? My parents had no money to ransom the family. They had nothing but prayers. I, on the other hand, would have a thousand dollars in just a few more weeks. Imagine that. A thousand dollars meant more to me then than a million dollars could mean to me now. Not even ten million. Mr. Schwartzbart could do a lot more with a thousand dollars than he could with a thousand prayers or a thousand heart-felt thank-yous. It was disgraceful, but it was a fact, even if a life is something you save, not something to buy.

In March of 1939, Germany completed its occupation of Czechoslovakia. On April 1 the Spanish Civil War ended in defeat for our side. I had no idea of Ray's whereabouts. I only asked Miss Finn if he was okay.

"Ray?" she repeated. "Ray Whitmore?" She looked surprised.

"Is there another Ray?" I asked.

"You haven't spoken about him in ages," she said.

"He told me not to."

"That's a strange thing."

"I wouldn't know," I said.

She reported that Ray was fine.

"Shall I send him your regards?" she asked.

"Not if he's fine," I replied.

By the time Dolores closed down the warehouse, I had a thousand dollars in hand. I went one last time to say good-bye. Dolores, to my surprise, threw her arms around me and cried.

"You're the last good thing that Ray Whitmore did for me, honey," she said through her tears. "I loved him, you know. You can't understand, but you will. You'll get your heart broken, too."

She pulled away and wiped her face with a strip of muslin.

"Ray's a passionate guy. He was passionate about me, and I loved that. He's passionate about justice and freedom and Spain, which I love too. It turns out he's also passionate about money and about other women. I can share a lot of things, but not that. I don't know which was worse: finding out about him and that whore Marie Dowd or that he'd been helping himself to the money."

I turned bright, bright red. My cheeks sizzled.

"How do you know?" I asked.

"I caught him red-handed with Marie. That's how. It was all the evidence I needed. I know you care about Ray. Even about Marie. But a rat's a rat. Now he's a rat with the number five carved on his forehead. Everyone'll know." She tapped her fingers on the penknife she used for opening money packets.

"Know what?" I asked. I could not believe it. Had she really cut him? Heaven knows what she might have done had she heard that I was in the mix.

"That Ray is a member of a fifth column; the only state he's loyal to is himself."

I should have confessed—only about the money, of course—but how could I? Ray deserved to be punished for how he treated me. *And* for betraying Dolores. As for Marie, she might have known about Dolores and not cared. Or me. Or maybe not known at all. But Dolores would have attacked Ray no matter what, even had she only known about Marie and not the missing money. That was how I lived with myself; that was how I convinced myself to let Ray take the fall. Besides, Dolores was entitled to a little revenge on Ray for messing around with me, whether she knew about it or not. Or so I believed.

It was not my finest hour.

My cheeks stayed hot the entire ride home. Not even the spray on the crossing could cool me off. There were plenty of rats on board, real rats, all of them getting fat from dead horses. I pounded a stick to keep them away, not that they scared. I could feel them moving through the piles of horseflesh, greedy and determined.

On Sunday April 30, German Jews lost their tenants' rights. Thousands were thrown into the streets, only allowed now to rent from Jewish landlords.

On the following Sunday, I rode the barge again to Brooklyn. No one asked where I was going or why. The furnace was banked for the day, there were no new barges to be emptied, and the red light at the top of the smokestack was blinking as always. A few scavengers were resting near the stern; some hopeful seagulls were watching from above. The barge captain did not ask after Noah, nor had Mr. DeWitt in all those months since Noah fled Barren Shoal. Not only had Noah-the-person disappeared, but the topic of him vanished too. Maybe that was better. It kept Noah safe. Being safe was all that mattered.

I arrived at HIAS, got my number, and waited in line with the usual sad crowd of angry, frustrated, and frightened people. What else could they be? Plenty were talking about the Evian Conference in France, which was supposed to address the crisis of Jewish refugees but did nothing. Lots of countries attended, plenty expressed sympathy, none condemned the Nazis, none lifted their Jewish quotas. Like Chaim Weizman said: the world was divided into places where Jews could not live and places we could not enter. Most of it still is. Can a Syrian Jew live anymore in Syria? Is a Jew welcomed in Indonesia? The only people who do not believe this are not Jews.

An hour later Mr. Schwartzbart, who came out to get some air, saw me standing in the crowd.

"Where's your father?" he asked, looking around.

"I'm by myself."

"Since when does he send you by yourself?" He guided me into his office with what felt like grandfatherly concern. I did not know my grandfathers, but I like to imagine them caring for me not because they had to, but because they could not help themselves.

I pulled the money from my pocket. It was folded into one of the packets used for tobacco. I waited for Mr. Schwartzbart to become ecstatic. I could have waited all day long.

"Where'd you get this?" he asked, alarmed.

I explained that it was given to me by some anti-fascists, but only if I promised to not say where it came from.

"They said it's all the same, whether they help republicans in Spain or Jews in Zyrmuny. It is, isn't it?" Ray had said something like that to me as a reason for why helping the republican cause was as worthy of my own time as helping Jews. It served him right that I turned his logic around. As far as I was concerned, Ray owed me.

Mr. Schwartzbart sat quietly, thumbing the stack of immigration forms on his desk. The streetcar rattled up Lafayette St. and the subway rumbled beneath us.

"I suppose it is," he said, finally breaking his silence. "I hope we have better luck with our fight. But we must involve your father."

"You don't know him," I begged. "He'll give it back." Not that I believed this was possible. Who would he give it to: Dolores, who I did not know how to find outside the warehouse? Ray, if he ever dared show his face?

Mr. Schwartzbart took the packet and held it up to the light as if sneaking a peak at its contents.

"So what difference does it make?" he repeated. He laid the packet on the desk and folded his hands over it. "We help who we can help. Why look a gift horse in the mouth?"

Not a question we ever asked on Barren Shoal.

In early May, spring came to Barren Shoal. When my children ask what it was like to live in war times, I tell them people live the same as always until they no longer can. One would think they would know this, having lived through Vietnam and all that news on the TV. But they mean something else. Losing the war in Vietnam did not mean the Viet Cong coming to New York in order to kill us. The Nazis would have brought SS to America; Americans would have signed up. They would have built camps here. And so on. My children want to know if I was afraid. "Of course I was afraid," I tell them. But I will not describe my nightmares. That is too much.

Do miracles happen? I think it was hard work that got me into Hunter.

To celebrate our graduation, Miss Finn announced that she was taking Sofia and me to the World's Fair, which had opened in Flushing Meadow in April. I was glad she did not suggest another barbecue like the one when Noah and Marie finished school. I was relieved when my parents did not either. I was happy about Hunter but still sullen. Never speaking about Ray had not cured my being brokenhearted. Nor was I interested in making nice to the many Dowds who littered the island.

"It will be a day of surprises, I promise," said Miss Finn.

The more Sofia and I talked about why it was just we two Miss Finn was taking, the more I grew convinced that Miss Finn had some secret plan up her sleeve.

The secret she was hiding, I decided, was Noah.

Once it came to me, I knew in my soul that he was passing through New York as part of a thirteenth-hour effort to fight the fascists in Spain. Noah, of course, would be joining up with the remnants of the Abraham Lincoln Brigade. Yes, it had officially disbanded but some had stayed behind, hiding in the Pyrenees and aiding the underground. Perhaps Ray was there, too? Wondering did not equal wanting him, at least not that I was aware of. But he had a place now in my personal history, which meant I would always be curious.

Noah, with all that Spanish he learned in California, could get across the border. He and Tyson: they would be sailing out of New York Harbor. Where better for us to meet than at the World's Fair, crowded with thousands of people from all over America, never mind from all over New York, and Noah tanned and stronger and not looking like himself anymore and nobody else from Barren Shoal around to alert the police or our parents. What better time for me to tell him about the money, about Mr. Schwartzbart, about Zyrmuny?

I thought a lot about what Noah wrote: *I can't wait for you to meet Tyson.* Another piece of the puzzle fell into place. Noah was playing matchmaker, of course; they were also stopping in New York so that Tyson and I could meet. He was trying to help me get over Ray.

Sofia trimmed my hair. Thirty cents would have bought me a real cut in Brooklyn, but that was a fortune. A funny thought, especially after handing over a king's ransom to Mr. Schwartzbart. Our mothers had cut our hair when we were little; as we got older we cut it for each other. Noah even cut my hair a few times. He said cutting hair was a whole lot cleaner than being a dead-horse butcher. He had such a steady hand, holding the crown of my head with one set of fingers and scissoring with the other. He became so enamored of his own handiwork that he thought he might become a barber.

There was something of an embarrassed pleasure that day in letting Sofia pull the coarse brush through my hair, me seated backward on a kitchen chair staring at the wall. With my eyes closed, I imagined being in a real salon, all heady from the perfumed shampoos, and the noise of the fans overhead, and this person talking to that one and some new, sad girl pushing cuttings with her broad broom. I asked Sofia to try parting it in the middle, or parting it on the side, or twisting it up into a French knot. Who knows how many other styles she tried out of the movie magazines.

"How about a roll?" she asked.

I shook my head.

"A wave?"

No again.

"A bob?"

"Eewww."

"What *do* you want?" she sputtered, waving a rolled-up magazine in my face.

"How about not going too wild. How about remembering that we live on Barren Shoal and that everyone's broke and we're about to go to war."

"How about you sit quiet and let me start somewhere."

CHAPTER 21

The 1939 World's Fair had nothing to do with anything that resembled, reflected, or even hinted at anything in our lives on Barren Shoal. It was a gigantic, gleaming stage production of everything modern, as if everything old could be replaced by something that would always be new. No one knew that new things would come faster and faster until it did not matter anymore how long anything lasted. I bought a 4x5 Speed Graphic view camera in 1943 that I used for fifty years. If I buy a digital camera today, it will be obsolete by tomorrow. I will have to replace it in a couple of years. If I live that long.

I looked for Noah everywhere not merely because he might turn up anywhere, but because the life he had now looked nothing like his old one. It stood to reason that neither would he. Instead of the slender, brown-haired boy who won second prize in the *Brooklyn Evening Eagle* All-Borough High School Students Arts Contest for the drawings he made of Hollywood movie stars, I looked for a muscular 25-year-old with forearms as strong as the solid shank shovels he used for digging roads. I looked for him in the Theme Center, which was so jammed that children cried when their parents moved a step forward in the lines. I looked for him in the grey shadows of the Trylon and at the Perisphere, which the line circled so many times that it was impossible to keep track of which people I was seeing for the first time and who I was passing again. I scoured the crowds in the moving rings around the Democracity diorama, with its perfectly laid out city and town and roads and waterways, where there was not a single garbage barge, or steam pipe, or track of grease trailing from a truck, or a boat, or a cart, or a car, as if every kind of effort was pure efficiency, as if no action resulted in a reaction that was not usable. Had I a better idea of what Tyson Johns looked like, I would have watched out for him too.

I had dressed that morning in a pleated skirt and blue sweater set that Noah would recognize from before. I had filled out the sweater in the year and a half since he had been gone. It was a hand-me-down from Marie Dowd—how is that for a kick in the pants?—who had inherited it from who-knows-who. I looked like the young woman I had become.

"There are a few things I would like you girls to see today," said Miss Finn. "After that you'll choose. Fair?"

What could we say? That it was *not* fair?

She drew us close to study a special pull-out section from *The New York Post*. She had been saving it since opening day on April 30, and had drawn stars at the exhibits she wanted to visit.

The desire for the unflawed was everywhere in Flushing Meadow, as if engineers, bricklayers, and electricians were recreating the universe in their own images, meaning the ones they held in the minds' eyes. Near the Perisphere was a statue called "The Astronomer" by Carl Miller, who, according to the descriptions that Miss Finn read aloud from the newspaper, was "a Chicago artist who built 'civic sculpture.'" An interesting idea except for the fact that art intended for the broad public is supposed to be 'uplifting' or 'inspiring,' which pretty much guarantees that it won't be. Yes, girls? Look at the Washington Memorial, which is what? A whole lot of nothing. Like Mt. Rushmore, which is more silliness. Built to bring tourists to the Dakotas to do what on earth? Look at big faces? The Lincoln Memorial, mind you, is another thing altogether: the approachable figure of Lincoln sitting rather than standing; the Gettysburg Address and second Inaugural Speech etched into the walls; the inference of democratic wisdom confirmed by the colonnades; its overall resemblance to a Greek temple. Compare the Lincoln in Washington to the Lincoln in South Dakota and you'll see the difference between honor and idolatry."

"Look at that thing!" said Sofia, pointing across the way. She was laughing at a giant, sculpted George Washington of the way he was supposed to have looked at the 1789 Inauguration. "It says on this plaque that the 1939 World's Fair marks the 150th anniversary of the first inauguration of 'the perfect father of a once-perfect nation.'"

"First they build that awful obelisk in Washington and now this: 'perfect father'?" said Miss Finn. "A rather religious accolade, wouldn't you say? And what is intended by 'a once-perfect nation'? Does this suggest that it has been perfect in the past but no longer is? Is that disloyal? Is that merely imprecise writing? You know who built the first obelisks?"

"The Greeks," guessed Sofia.

"The word 'obelisk' is from the Greek word '*obelus*,' meaning a spit, but the structure as we know it is Egyptian. Which would you prefer as *your* monument: Lincoln's Greek Temple or Washington's Egyptian obelisk?"

"Lin—"

"Of course you want the Greek one. And Marta?"

"'Once-perfect nation'?" I asked, repeating Miss Finn's question.

"Don't blame the messenger," said Miss Finn. She bent over to more closely examine the plaque. "I'm merely quoting James Earle Fraser, who also designed the Buffalo nickel. In case you are interested."

"Hey, look!" cried Sofia.

Noah. Finally. I turned to embrace him.

But not Noah. Not even close. Just two guys ambling past. Behind them were two more guys, the second pair wearing brown slacks and brown shirts and swastika armbands. They were eating big, soft pretzels.

"German soldiers," I gasped.

"Americans, no doubt," said Miss Finn. "Bundists, Sturmabteilungen, Storm Troopers, big shots ever since their big rally in February at Madison Square Garden. Plenty of Americans are Nazis."

"Noah got jumped that night on 86th Street," I told her. I hoped that Noah would not appear just now and use his new CCC muscles to avenge himself. The last thing we needed was for Noah to get into a street brawl, get arrested, get found out.

"What do you do with a man like Fritz Kuhn?" said Miss Finn. "How does an American man stand in front of crowd of twenty thousand Americans at Madison Square Garden, in the middle of New York City, and announce that white gentiles are 'the true patriots'? That kind of man...that kind of man could run for office and get elected because no one would stop him. They adore him. Fritz Kuhn isn't the problem. It's the twenty thousand other Americans who cheered him and saluted him in Madison Square Garden."

We fell quiet. It was impossible to press her about Noah when two Nazis had walked by so closely that I could see the salt grains on their pretzels. Two young men who for no good reason wanted me dead. When I tell that to people now, to younger people like my grandson, they reply with a patient smile that makes me know that they think I exaggerate. They still want to believe that the danger was only in Europe. They do not imagine the consequences of things turning out otherwise. And the non-Jews? I have never heard a Catholic wonder aloud if their parents or grandparents listened to Father Coughlin on Sunday nights. Millions of them listened. I bet you even the Dowds.

Maybe it never crosses their minds because their families, their fathers and grandfathers, fought against Japan and Germany, not England and France. None of them, not Joe Kennedy's children or Lindbergh's children, had to defend their fathers' infatuation with Hitler once America went to war. But Joe Kennedy and Lindbergh hated Jews before the war and still hated us after. Fighting Hitler did nothing to change that. And what about today? People who say we Jews should think about this less are the ones who should think about it more. I am not paranoid nor am I crazy. I am eighty years old and have seen what I have seen.

We were all there together: the Hitler Youth were strolling around Flushing Meadow eating pretzels, while Miss Finn was leading Sofia and me on a tour of public sculpture. Give the people bread and circuses, pretzels and Trylons. The hell with virtues; the hell with reason. Forget about Greek ideals and Egyptians temples. Sedate us with spectacle! The Roman Emperors were right: keep the poor fed and everyone entertained. Bread and circuses two thousand years ago—bread and circuses today. Never mind the Enlightenment's belief in human reason, in human rights. The Enlightenment was the single greatest anomaly in human evolution. I do not mean great in size; I mean great as in magnificent, as in brilliant. Yet an aberration, nonetheless, in the history of ideas, which has been more about controlling people than freeing them.

Ray Whitmore was right: ideologies are worthless. As Rabbi Hillel said: *What is hateful to you, do not to your fellow man. This is the law: all the rest is commentary.* I love that: *all the rest is commentary*. He was not the only one who thought this: Confucius said it, and Jesus said it, and Baha'u'llah all said it in their own ways, too. *This* is what matters, not useless, high-flown ideologies. But who listens? Is anyone listening?

"Look at this one, girls," said Miss Finn, drawing us close to a scruffy bronze of Walt Whitman, his legs set to look like he was walking. She faced the Whitman statue and spoke:

> I have said that the soul is not more than the body,
> And I have said that the body is not more than the soul,
> And nothing, not God, is greater to one than one's self is,
> And whoever walks a furlong without sympathy walks to his own funeral drest in his shroud,
> And I or you pocketless of a dime may purchase the pick of the earth,
> And to glance with an eye or show a bean in its pod confounds the learning of all times,
> And there is no trade or employment but the young man following it may become a hero,
> And there is no object so soft but it makes a hub for the wheel'd universe,
> And I say to any man or woman, Let your soul stand cool and composed before a million universes.

One, then two, then a cluster of people stopped to listen, including a hunched man so old that he could have been a water boy for the Union Army. Old enough to know Whitman himself. The man rested his hand against the leg of the statue while Miss Finn continued:

And I say to mankind, Be not curious about God,
For I who am curious about each am not curious about
    God,
(No array of terms can say how much I am at peace about
    God and about death.)

I hear and behold God in every object, yet understand
    God not in the least,
Nor do I understand who there can be more wonderful
    than myself.

Why should I wish to see God better than this day?
I see something of God each hour of the twenty-four, and
    each moment then,
In the faces of men and women I see God, and in my own
    face in the glass,
I find letters from God dropt in the street, and every one
    is sign'd by God's name,
And I leave them where they are, for I know that
    wheresoe'er I go,
Others will punctually come for ever and ever.

"From "Song of Myself,' " said Miss Finn, pausing to collect
herself. "Number 48."

"That the whole thing there you spoken?" asked the old
man.

"Heavens, no. It's very long."

"People used to recite the whole Odyssey," said Sofia.

"Not teachers from one-room schoolhouses on Barren
Shoal."

"You from Barren Island? What a stink, all those dead

horses. You a actress?" asked the old man.

"No, sir," replied Miss Finn.

"A poet?"

"No, sir, I was reciting a poem by Walt Whitman," she explained.

"'Why should I wish to see God better than this?'" the old man repeated. With that kind of memory *he* should have been the actor. "I'm counting on seeing a better God than this one if I see Him at all, I can tell you that. Because the one I know is a war criminal," he muttered.

"What Whitman means is that...."

The man did not hear her. Or did not care. He shuffled away.

The Fair reached its epiphany, so to speak, at the General Motors complex, outside of which formed the longest line of the day, way longer than any line ever at HIAS where my parents were standing at that very moment. Everyone was there for the Futurama.

When I saw this impossibly long line—we would have to wait an hour or more for our turn—I understood that this was the place where Noah would find us. All that he had to do was walk the line. What an excellent strategy. What a brilliant surprise.

Kids were leaning against their parents' legs, half sleeping on their feet; women were fanning themselves with Chinese sandalwood folding fans, or with church fans printed with proverbs on one side and a blonde Jesus on the other; men were wiping their brows with handkerchiefs.

A half hour passed; Miss Finn suggested that Sofia and I go for a stroll. Sofia looked tired and impatient. I felt that way too.

"Just don't wander far, girls," said Miss Finn.

Of course not, I thought, though I liked the idea of making Noah wait for us rather than us waiting for him. He had been gone for so long.

Sofia and I were somewhere other than Barren Shoal together for the first time since her abortion. We deserved something better than that; we deserved something fun. And it *was* fun seeing all the men in jackets and ties—other than those idiot Nazis, of course—and women wearing gloves, girls in dresses and boy in knickers, as if we finally had tickets for the good seats at the opera.

"Ohmygod!" I shouted. "*There* he is." Finally. There was Noah, way down the walk just before it curved around the back of the General Motors building, where it ran parallel to the Grand Central Parkway.

Sofia craned her neck. "Where are you looking? Who?"

"Noah! Look!"

Sofia could have been a track star at a big school with a sports program, but I outpaced her that day, fueled by adrenaline and desire.

"Noah!" I hollered. "Noah!"

"Hey, hey," Sofia yelled as I ran down the line. "Wait up," she was still calling when I threw my arms around him and squeezed him and kissed him on both cheeks and ruffled his hair.

"You'll have to excuse my friend," said Sofia, pulling my arms away and laughing. "We don't know what's gotten into her lately and now she thinks it's okay to kiss boys she doesn't know. We think it's something in the water."

I wish there had been something in the water to offset my humiliation.

That caught me for a second. I had never said a word to her about Ray. Then I realized she was just making talk.

The boy straightened his jacket. He was from Rochester, he told us, sent by the Eastman Kodak Company to work at the company exhibit. He stepped back and looked us over before pressing two guest passes into Sofia's hands, as if my kissing him made him owe us something in return. Then he dashed off.

"What ever were you thinking?" demanded Sofia.

Miss Finn, who had been watching the whole silly encounter, rushed over to see what was the matter. "She thought she saw Noah," said Sofia, repeating my explanation. "She thought that's why you brought us here. That you'd arranged a secret rendezvous with Noah. That he was coming through New York on his way to fight the fascists in Spain."

"Oh, girls," she said. "The war against the Franco is lost. At least for now." She led us back to our spot in line, which the people behind us were guarding for her. "It's not Noah who's going to fight the fascists. At least not that I'm aware of, though I wish he had. It's me. I wanted us to have a special good time before I say good-bye."

"You?" we asked together.

Try as I might, I could not fold my mind around this one. Miss Finn, the woman who buried all those aborted fetuses on the garbage barge, was now off to Europe to fight the Nazis? Did she have to take a stand on everything?

"You're going to Finland," I said, as if I was not surprised and had expected this all along.

"Why on earth Finland of all places?" asked Miss Finn.

"Because of your family, where you're from."

"Where did you ever get that idea?"

"From my mother," said Sofia. "Finn as in Finland. Like Napolitano as in Joey's uncle Sal Napolitano from Naples."

"It's Finn as in Finnenberger, from Prague. Clipped and trimmed by a clerk at Ellis Island. I'm going to Prague."

"To do what?" Sofia asked.

"Whatever I can."

"Why you? You're Catholic, you're American."

"Because someone has to help and right now that someone is me," said Miss Finn.

"Everybody's trying to get out," said Sofia, as if there was a conspiracy afoot. "Why in God's good name would you go?"

"So maybe a few less people will die, maybe some will get out faster."

I thought about Sofia's abortion; about all the other abortions that Miss Finn and her sister performed for those women in Brooklyn; about Miss Finn's refusal in our health lessons to call a fetus a baby but how, when pressed, she would not say whether or not they were the same thing.

Complicated. Miss Finn was very, very complicated.

"What about Ray?"

Miss Finn laughed. "Ray's not going anywhere, at least not yet. Ray's a good talker, but it will take a draft to get Ray into uniform. At the end of the day, he's too happy here to go far from home."

"He's not in Spain?"

"Ray? Oh, Marta, he's in Brooklyn, where he's always been."

"But when I asked, you said he was fine. After Franco declared victory. Don't you remember?"

Everyone keeps a list of worst moments. There are the obvious ones, like a dead sister. Add to that particular betrayals. Ray had betrayed me not only with other women, but by staying behind in Brooklyn. He had played me for such a fool. Maybe he pulled it off because he was right. Perhaps I loved the idea of him once loving him for real was off the table. Now that was gone too. There are so many things we know about people, about ideas; there are things we cannot. Why is this so difficult to live with?

When we returned to Barren Shoal that night on the garbage barge, we could see a bonfire blazing.

"What on earth?" said Sofia.

All sorts of people were milling about when we docked, including my father and mother looking as ashen as ashes really look.

"Oh, baby," said my mother.

"Momma?"

"Look," she said, shoving the piece of paper into my hands.

We can think we are safe, we can think we will dodge the bullets, and maybe we can. We can convince ourselves that we are as insignificant as we are told we are and not worth going after, but none of that matters. They come after us exactly because they see us being as worthless as they have made us believe we are. We could have talked ourselves blue in the face after the letters came, but no one was going to talk our way out of being evicted. The notices came from Robert Moses, who still had the *chutzpah* to sign his name. You would think he would have been ashamed, would have kept his identity a secret from the people he evicted from Barren Island and Barren Shoal, and later on from the Bronx, this man named Moses.

Just like Barren Island before it, Robert Moses needed Barren Shoal for his master plan of New York. We needed it too, but nobody was asking any of us about *our* master plans. People who did not live there, people like my aunt and uncle, thought this was a blessing in disguise. But Barren Shoal, despite its stench and isolation, kept our families off the bread lines and coal lines and relief lines all those years. It was where we lived in our own little houses with a speck of land, small as they all were. How many ways and how many times must I say this? Barren Shoal was home.

Everyone drifted to the schoolhouse the next morning: Sofia and her parents, Joey and his brothers, the Dowds and all their children. Miss Finn came too, packing up books and rulers and pieces of chalk and anything else she could fit in a few boxes. Instead of it all being used by a new teacher who would come to Barren Shoal to replace her, the boxes would go to one of the segregated schools in Brooklyn.

"Those Negro children," she said, "get worse than nothing."

"What's worse than nothing?" I wondered.

"Broken, page-missing, raggedy books that the white schools don't want anymore."

"At least that's something," said Sofia.

"What's the point in reading a story that's missing a page?" Miss Finn continued. "You might as well read the back of a soap carton. And that's the point," Miss Finn continued. "Those Negro children *won't* know any better. It's deliberate. I don't mean ripping out the page, though it might be. But not fixing what's broken: that's a conscious and deliberate choice. It's a choice to be cruel."

CHAPTER 22

Some of the men took up a vigil at the factory gates. Mr. Paradissis brought along some homemade wine. After the men emptied a few bottles, Mr. Dowd stood up and shouted that it was Mr. Paradissis' fault about the evictions, saying that if he had not gotten the boys all worked up with his *Daily Workers* and his talk about bringing a union into the plant and such nonsense, none of this would have happened. Mr. Paradissis, according to my father, accused Mr. Dowd of being a company goon because he refused to take going on strike seriously.

"If Dowd was spying for Boyle he would've gone along with a strike so he could finger the guys who were for it," my father said when he came home. "Nonsense, anyway. Who cares if we strike when they're closing it down? At any rate, Paradissis threw a bottle at Dowd, missed his mark, the thing broke, and Dowd threw the neck back at Paradissis. He got one ugly gash on his hand."

"You should've stopped it," said my mother.

"You know what? Nothing wrong with them getting angry. Not anymore."

My mother was not impressed. "It doesn't take a whole lot of guts to get angry at your friends. Lot a good that does them."

"Maybe it got them all the good it's gonna get. You think if they throw a bottle at Boyle the plant will stay open? It'll get them shot dead. That's what they'll get."

Mr. Paradissis and Mr. Dowd did not fight again that we heard of, but their anguish and rage bristled and spread, especially a few days later when the plant shut for good without any fanfare whatsoever. The furnaces were allowed to burn down. Even without being fed, they smoldered for days.

The men gathered again at the gatehouse that night and each night that followed as if to play cards, except no one played. Beyond that, no one protested the evictions, there being no one to protest to aside from Mr. Boyle, who left Barren Shoal before the furnaces even cooled for a job as an inspector at the 14th St. Meat Market.

I asked Miss Finn for one final favor, to get a letter to Lois and Gray. I asked a favor of them as well: would they please get me to Manhattan. Lois and Gray were the only people I knew with a boat; they were also the only people who would not insist on knowing why.

They pulled up a few days later in the mahogany runabout. We did not know when to expect them, but we could hear them crossing the bay. Gray was wearing a seersucker suit, just like he did at the martini picnic. Lois' hair was pinned back beneath yet another broad-brimmed hat.

"Darling," cried Lois, extending her hand to me. "Get into this boat right this minute and tell us everything."

So I was wrong about them not asking.

Gray sped off before I settled into my seat. A garbage barge was the tortoise to the runabout's hare. It was all I could do to say *hello* and say *yes, everyone at home was fine*.

"What's all this urgency about getting to town?" asked Gray.

Who calls Manhattan "town"? People like Lois and Gray, who have enough money to know the best of it.

"I need to see someone," I replied.

"Someone? Or *someone*?"

"He means someone special," added Lois. "You know, darling: a young man."

"Sure," I said. I was not about to tell them about stealing $1000. Instead I told them about Ray. It was easier to admit I was a fool than a thief. Correction. It was more expedient. Not that I worried about what they thought. After all, my intentions were gutsy, which would impress them. It was the desperation of it all that was so painful, and the fact that $1000 was so little to them. Should I have asked them for the money instead of stealing it? Interesting question. Should they have offered? A more interesting question.

"How dreadful," said Gray when I finished telling them about everything but the money, including about how Ray was involved with Marie and Dolores and me at the same time. "And typical. A fellow like your Ray gets to dash from woman to woman to woman, and the only ones who get upset *are* the women. His pals must think he's the bee's knees. I, on the other hand, would be branded a pervert for doing the same with men."

"Have you forgotten, darling? You're a 'pervert' with even one man."

Gray smiled broadly. "And a cheater on my charade of a marriage, not that I don't love you, Lois."

"Of course you love me: I'm the most elegant skirt you've ever had."

"And you, dear Negress, have never passed as beautifully as you do my arm."

"Are we shocking you, Marta?" asked Lois.

It took a few seconds to dredge up my courage. "You're a Negro?" I asked.

They burst into laughter.

"And you're married?"

I understood that they lived together, which was odd enough —they had made that clear at the martini picnic—but I had never put them together. All of us are blind when it suits us.

"You do what you have to do, dear," said Gray. "You do it in order to live another day."

So I told them about the money.

Not only did Lois and Gray deliver me to a pier in Manhattan, but they escorted me to HIAS which, it turned out, was in walking distance from where they lived.

"I wish you the best of luck, dear," said Lois, after which she kissed me on both cheeks. I had never been kissed before by a black person. At least not that I knew of, unless it was by another Negro who looked white. Think of me what you will; I will not pretend it was nothing. I had never been kissed Continental style either, on both cheeks. Not that the two are the same, but they were two new steps that would help me walk away from Barren Shoal.

"Thanks a million," I said.

I grabbed each one in a brief hug, then opened the door and slipped inside. I pushed through the crowd of people and up the hallway to Mr. Schwartzbart's office

"Hey toots, you can't go in there," a man called after me. "You gotta get a number!"

My fingers were already wrapped around the doorknob when the man grabbed my arm.

"Where do you think you're going?" he snarled.

"Mr. Schwartzbart!" I cried. I banged on the door, hoping he could hear through the open transom. "Mr. Schwartzbart!"

The door swung open. Seated behind Mr. Schwartzbart was as sad-looking a family as I have ever seen; sadder than the homeless family I had seen on the street; even sadder than the pickers on the barge. They did not look at Mr. Schwartzbart; they did not look at one another; they did not look at me. All four kept their gazes locked on their knees.

"Never mind, Danny," Mr. Schwartzbart told the other man. "Let the girl go."

Mr. Schwartzbart walked me further up the hall, out of earshot of the people in his office. "What's this about? Is your father okay? Is your mother sick again?"

"They're shutting down Barren Shoal. And I need to know where you're sending them. The family. How will they find us when we're moved?"

"Do you speak German?" he asked in a hushed voice.

I frowned.

"Yiddish?" he asked.

"A *bisl*." A little.

"Come inside."

The sad family was sitting stone still. They did not appear injured. They did not even appear frightened. They were beyond that. They wore the sadness that keeps people lonely in a room of those who love them.

The only thing Mr. Schwartzbart said that I understood was my name. The parents nodded in my direction; the children did nothing. We all understood that we were to wait while Mr. Schwartzbart stepped out.

He returned moments later with the man named Danny, who said something else in German. The family filed out behind him, but not before the father shook Mr. Schwartzbart's hand. Mr. Schwartzbart covered the man's hand with his own, just like he had my father's hand all those years before. And, like then, he held it for a long moment.

"Sit, young lady," said Mr. Schwartzbart when we were alone. I took the chair beside his desk, the one where my father sat when they first filled out the papers.

"Did you take a good look at those people?" he asked.

"The ones who just left?" I said.

"They're Germans. From Berlin. He's a lawyer. She teaches violin. Very successful. Very charitable. Their parents were Berliners. And their grandparents. Her father was awarded the Iron Cross in the Great War. They had a house on Krausnickstrasse; he had an office with partners; she had a conservatory room at home where she instructed the children of other middle-class Berliners.

"Last year they sold the house and everything in it for pennies, because that's all anyone would pay a Jew. Thank goodness they began withdrawing from the bank when the troubles started. Thousands of deutsche marks, which they hid in so many places that they had to dig up their whole garden when their papers came through. What did this get them? On a train from Berlin to Paris, then a train to Marseille. From Marseille on a boat to Morocco. From Casablanca a boat to Portugal. From Lisbon a ship to Brazil. From Rio de Janeiro a ship to Canada. From Halifax a boat to Portland, Maine. From Portland a train to Boston. From Boston a train to New York, where they have people. You want to know about your relatives from Zyrmuny? So do I. But I don't. I wish I did. I wish I could tell you some news, but I can't."

"But my money...."

"...is in a pool of money that we use to get out whoever we can, however we can. Maybe even your relatives from Zyrmuny."

"It was *my* money!"

I jumped up from the chair.

"Sit down, Marta. Not yours. It was never yours. No one gives $1000 to a poor girl from Barren Shoal."

"But I gave it to you!"

"Go on, then. Report me to the police."

I sat down.

"Believe me: I know this is difficult. Do you remember what you said? 'It's all the same, whether you help republicans in Spain or Jews in Zyrmuny.' At this very moment, a thousand dollars can't get your ten people out of Zyrmuny. But it can help someone. Maybe. We do what we can. When we can. And maybe next time someone else's money will get to Zyrmuny at the same moment that someone else is willing to sell visas."

"What if we were rich? Like those people in your office."

"If they were rich enough they would have left long before. Maybe. Those people aren't Rothschilds. They spent everything they had getting out. But listen: money is no guarantee. This is the hardest thing you'll ever learn, so you better start now: there are no guarantees. None at all, financial or otherwise. Zero. Never. Zilch. Do you hear me? No guarantees. Stop searching for them, stop believing in them, stop hoping for them, stop praying for them."

The furnaces were still cooling on Barren Shoal—they had been burning practically non-stop since the 1850s!—when my mother and I finished packing the towels and linens and the handful of items that went into what we called our wardrobes. Everything we packed was ironed first, including a dress that had been handed down from Marie Dowd to me and from me to Helen. That little wool dress was a dress that Helen had worn. There was also a pair of her small socks. My mother packed Noah's few remaining things with mine and Helen's things with her own.

It was impossible to predict the life that was coming, never mind the final moments of the life we were leaving behind. Who would be there to watch us drag our boxes down the sandy road to the dock? Or to pick through what we left behind, the way Noah and the boys had scavenged the books and tools and rowboat from Barren Island? Who would be there to watch our boat pull away the way we watched the ferry leave three years earlier? Who would care about our leaving the way we cared about those people? Who but us cared at all?

Expectation made everyone count and re-count the days as if anyone needed to be reminded that time was running out. For all that I remember, I cannot remember how much time passed between the arrival of the eviction notices and the day we left for good. There were arguments over whether the last day counted as a day when we still lived on Barren Shoal or as a day when we no longer did. But that was like arguing with water running down a drain.

The final day arrived as if everything took place without warning. How many ways can I describe being unprepared? All that matters is that we had to go.

The seagulls were screaming hysterically when the garbage barges did not arrive. They hovered over the ferry in disbelief as the morning sky grew brighter and the big clouds, like a bouquet of pink and blue hydrangeas, were drained of color. The dock stank of rotting things that had been oozing into the pilings for decades. It also smelled of panic.

All those years of planning and hoping and scheming on Barren Shoal had nothing to do with what others had in mind for us, the things we did not even know how to imagine. The people who believed that Barren Shoal was safe after Barren Island was demolished never stopped believing, even when they were dragged onto the ferry by policemen. Other people, including my mother, stopped believing Barren Shoal was safe from the moment they arrived. My mother never thought we were safe enough from anything, safety being a relative term and the thing it was relative to forever shifting. She was right, I suppose, which does not change the fact that she was a little crazy. What kind of way is that to live, afraid all the time as if the only things that matter are the things we are most afraid of? Perhaps she never had the luxury of wondering about that, the luxury I have right here, right now, this very moment.

Our garden was bursting by then with tomatoes and eggplants that we harvested to take along, and so many zucchinis that we had to leave for the rats. The factory—after all that brouhaha over whether or not to have a union and which union was the right union—was already being razed by picks and hammers that we could hear as we crossed the water. Half of us spent the slow ride to Brooklyn watching Barren Shoal disappear behind us. The other half of the people on the ferry—Sofia among them—had a view of Brooklyn growing larger.

I barely said a proper good-bye to Sofia, what with all the sorting and packing and crying. Not that we did not talk about what was happening. But as for saying good-bye, every time the subject came up it left us breathless. Literally. What could we say? With what words, in what language, with what meaning? When we docked at Gravesend, there was mostly chaos and crying and time for little more than a hundred quick farewells to people I had known my entire life.

As for Barren Shoal itself, the island disappeared not long after. No exaggeration. The combination of the ongoing landfill project for Floyd Bennett Field and the suffocation of the salt marshes from an oil tanker spill caused irreparable erosion. The tanker made it to the Esso refinery in New Jersey without breaking up, but not before leaking who-knows-how-much crude into the waters off Long Island. With the salt marshes gone, there was nothing left to protect the sandy soil from the tides or the annual nor'easters.

My parents and I moved into an apartment around the

corner from Aunt Sara, Uncle David, and Flat Sammy. I slept in what would have been the dining room behind a curtain that my mother hung for privacy. My cousin Ruthie and Sidney lived five blocks away, where they had moved from Rivington St. when they started having children. Brooklyn Heights, where Miss Finn lived, was almost as far away from where we lived now as Manhattan. Not that it mattered. She left for Europe the week before Labor Day, just days before the Germans invaded Poland. Jane Shaw, the Barren Island schoolteacher, died two weeks later, meaning that neither knew what happened to the other, just like millions of people.

The pain of missing everyone and everything took up cold residence in a previously unspoken-for hollow in my chest. I did not know that I had room for more pain after Helen died, and more again after I let Ray break my heart. It turns out there is always room for more.

Hunter College was no longer a possibility for me, not because anyone said I could not go. And not only because the classes sounded like dreary repetitions of the subjects I studied with Miss Finn. I did not go to Hunter because I could not go. I had never been afraid of those kinds of things before, but for a while I was afraid of everything. So much for the courage that came with my short-lived career as a thief. I hear what I am saying: for a time I became as fearful as my mother. Noah was gone, then Miss Finn was gone, the $1000 was gone, and now we were gone as well. Our whole life on Barren Shoal was gone not by choice but by circumstance, which meant it had everything yet nothing to do with us. I had believed that knowing things made knowing about them worthwhile. But to what end? Islands disappear anyway. So do people.

My parents were brokenhearted when I announced my decision to find a job instead of starting school. My father took it especially hard, his hopes for Noah already dashed by the invention of the mysterious James Peck.

"What makes you so certain you'll find a job anyway?" asked my father.

"What kind of job?" asked my mother.

"A lot of good school did those university boys who burned the books in the Berlin Opernplatz," I replied.

"You're not half as smart as I thought if you compare yourself to them," said my father, who was equal parts disgusted and distraught.

The biggest surprise of all was barely a surprise given who I was and the traceable history of those still around me, however brief and incompletely traceable that turned out to be. I found a job in the garment industry of all places, just like everyone in the family before me, as if some impossible and incalculable force of destiny was in play. Even if I do not believe in providence, which has been my whole point all along.

I was assigned to assist a photographer. I carried dresses and hats and gloves back and forth from the design houses to the studio. My father got a job in the shoe factory on 39th St. as a cutter, my Uncle David having sent word to Mr. Singer on his behalf. It was the first time I knew of that he did not come home smelling of rotting flesh. Now he smelled of boot polish and glue.

I worried for a time about Noah finding us if he ever returned to New York from wherever he was—Oregon, Washington, California, Spain, who-knows-where next. Later I decided this was silly; at one point or another one of my letters would catch up with him, which one finally did. Soon he was sending mail to the new address. My father wrote to the relatives in Zyrmuny as well. It was too late. No one ever heard from them ever again. Not even Mr. Schwartzbart—despite how angry he made me on that terrible day—who tried to save everyone he could. It was not until 1998, almost sixty years later, that we finally learned of their fates. A new, huge directory was now made possible by the Internet. The Nazis and their cohorts kept impeccable records. The relatives who were not killed right away were sent to a concentration camp. They worked as slaves in a Krupp factory, where they either starved to death or died of typhus.

My grandson found a second cousin of my grandfather through the Internet, a clarinetist who returned to Warsaw after the war to look for his parents and who decided to stay, there being plenty of work for woodwinds during the post-war jazz craze. When the Russians moved in, he became a teacher in a conservatory, married a Catholic woman, and kept his survivor stories of barns and cellars to himself. The clarinetist, ten years older than me, was the only one, to our knowledge, who survived. He saw his father beaten to death in the street outside their house when the SS came for the family. His mother and sisters were pistol-whipped and shoved into a truck and gassed. The clarinetist, who was sneaking back from a girlfriend's house after curfew, took his chances and ran. If only all of those who ran had such good luck. Maybe another survivor will turn up like they sometimes do, squeezing through the otherwise impenetrable weight of the twentieth century. They had better do it fast.

I had been working for two years in the photo studio when Pearl Harbor was bombed and my boss was drafted. He recommended me for his job, explaining that he was entrusting to me temporary custody of his position. He never came back. Not only did he not come back to the studio, but he never made it back from the war. I felt awful about this for a long time, as if his death made my job dirty. For a long time I thought that my supervisor felt awful about it too, which is why my title remained "assistant" instead of "manager." It never crossed my mind that I did not get the title—or the pay—because I was a woman. I never thought about it until the feminists came along. It took me that long—twenty years—to first wonder.

There was no one who was not touched by the war, no one who did not lose people. Instead of being swept into the vortex of absolute sadness like my mother was yet again, I volunteered, writing letters to troops overseas on behalf of loved ones who were illiterate. I was also an air-raid warden in the building on 39th Street. I had no idea what Ray did; I could only assume he was drafted.

There is nothing to be gained by beating up myself about Hunter. Or about the money I stole. What I did was wrong, even if I did it for the right reasons. And there is nothing to be gained by making my life sound harder than it was. We understood exactly what would become of us if the Nazis came to power in America. Phooey on those Europeans who insist they did not know. It is one thing for a person to try for survival when people all around them are dying. It is not for me to judge; I was not there. It is something else altogether not to notice the very thing at the tip of your nose. Or to pretend. To pretend not to notice the smells that blew in from the death camps at Auschwitz-Birkenau, Belzec, Chelmno, Jasenovac, Lwów, Majdanek, Maly Trostenets, Sobibor, Treblinka, and Warsaw. Or pretend not to notice the stench of the dead at the work camps. Do I have to name them too? Do you want to ask about the smell?

If the residents of Brooklyn could smell the smoke from Barren Shoal and Barren Island, then the people of Germany and Austria and Poland and Croatia and Belarus and Ukraine smelled the stench of the death camps too. They may fool themselves and one another, but they cannot fool me. They might believe their own lies after all this time, but you cannot forgive someone who is unwilling to acknowledge their crimes.

After the war, when it seemed like everyone wanted to dress

their wounds in money and fashion, I got work photographing models. I made a name for myself before all the men returned; I got good enough to earn some real money. That is how I met Walker, who was an art director just back from overseas. Six months later we were married. Sofia, of course, was my maid of honor.

Noah came back from the army in one piece, thank goodness, and moved to an apartment on Grove St. in Greenwich Village, around the corner from Lois and Gray. He jumped on the fashion bandwagon too and soon became the celebrated designer James Peck. Tyson survived the war as well, after being stationed in North Africa where he picked up an intestinal parasite that almost killed him. When he was finally released from the V.A. hospital, Tyson moved into the apartment on Grove St. too.

When I shot Noah a startled look about this news he said, "What about it?"

Once again I stumbled, like I had so many times before. "I just thought that...."

"Don't think too hard, Marta. Tyson is going to be my personal assistant. It's the only way they'll let him in the door, though he's every bit the designer that I am. The rag trade welcomes our kind, but not if he's a black."

"Then how is it you met him in the CCC? I thought the Negroes had their own camps."

"What do you want me to say? Yes, the camps were segregated. Yes, Tyson was assigned to our camp. We don't know why and we didn't ask. We were just glad that they let him alone long enough to get out of there alive. We got split up when we got drafted. He was sent to a black battalion; I was sent with the whites."

That was the only conversation we had about typecasting homosexuals in the fashion world until many years later, when he asked me where else I thought he might work and not have to always worry about being gay.

"After all," he pointed out, "working in fashion is a family tradition."

"Working in a shoe factory isn't exactly high couture," I said.

"I'll leave that up to you," he replied.

He never said anything to our parents about his life with Tyson, which was probably for the best. I confess that it took me some getting used to, longer than it should have, but I did. I miss them so much now. It is terrible to be one of the last ones alive.

Sofia, who I worried was gone from my life after Barren Shoal, got a job in the gift wrapping department at Lord & Taylor on 5th Avenue, right around the corner from my studio. Pretty soon she was the manager, then the manager of customer complaints. After two years she had heard enough whining, so she quit. She found work as a scent tester for a French perfume company that relocated to New York following the war. Imagine Sofia making what was left of this world smell beautiful.

She got married soon after to a scent salesman named Peter, had kids, and moved to a nice house in New Jersey. We saw less of one another after that, but visited by phone every week. We even took all our children one Sunday to the Metropolitan Museum of Art. Gray and Lois and Noah and Tyson came too. We did, indeed, see "Still Life with a Glass and Oysters." Only in a painting can a lemon last so long.

When her little one started school, Sofia got a job in one of the big new factories that sprang up along Route 3. The whole bunch of them made artificial flavors. If she had been a little younger—given her penchant for chemistry—she might have been one of those kids mixing up LSD in the basement. Which, it turns out, her middle one did, which is why she moved the whole family to her father's village in Greece: to keep the middle son out of jail and the older boy out of Vietnam. After the junta in '67, things got hard for them; when the colonels were overthrown, things got better. They could travel again and she and Peter went on vacations with Walker and me to France and to China. We finally got to see the Forbidden City and the Great Wall and all those places that we talked about when we were little girls making the scrapbook for our Odyssey Project. How about that.

Ray, I learned from Yorgos, married Marie Dowd. I expected to run into them one day, what with all those Dowds roaming New York. I never did. Yorgos said that Ray was wounded on Normandy and had an ugly "S-shaped" scar on his forehead. It was no surprise that Ray lied about the scar, just like he lied about so much else. It was probably easy to persuade everyone that a 5 was actually an S. People like Ray lie whenever it suits them, until the truth completely disappears.

I did, however, run into Miss Doctor Finn while Sofia was still working at Lord & Taylor. She told me that Miss Finn had died of typhoid in a concentration camp. That was a terrible blow.

I visit Sofia and Peter for a few weeks every year, my visits longer now that I am alone. I never imagined I would survive after Walker died, but here I am. Sofia comes to America every year to see her children, who all moved back. It made no sense to stay in Greece, what with the draft dodger amnesty and the statute of limitations, never mind the lack of opportunity. We speak more now than ever. I know that this cannot go on forever, but I am too busy reckoning with this day, and all the days that came before it, to become terrified by the days that are still to come.

I like to row on days like this. My kids bought me an inflatable boat and a small air compressor that I keep in the car. I plug the compressor into the cigarette lighter and in less than ten minutes I am in the water. Some people say I am too old, but it is silly to insist that I not do what I can do. I fish a little, or at least pretend to. I do not have the patience I once had; baiting a line gets harder with creeping arthritis. I bring a portable radio and listen to NPR or, on Saturdays, the opera. It is sponsored now by a different oil company, the same one that helped destroy the salt marshes around Barren Shoal.

As it turns out, no one—not one single person I have ever met who did not live there—has ever heard of Barren Shoal without my telling them. My children, I suspect, will handle this differently when the telling is left to them alone. For the time being, at least, we still speak about it amongst ourselves. It is a reference point for all that has happened to us since.

I have a sextant in my living room, a beautiful one made from brass and polished mahogany just like the runabout that brought Lois and Gray to Barren Shoal. My kids gave me the sextant too, the year after they bought me the inflatable boat. They like to think it would matter, somehow, if I could find the exact site of Barren Shoal. They think that finding it among the channels and beaches of Jamaica Bay would somehow make a difference.

Precisely the difference they are looking for is a notion they cannot explain. I suppose that measuring the coordinates might be useful to someone who has never been there, who needs more help in remembering than I do. But not me.

As for you, ask what you want. Had you been there, the way you are supposed to be everywhere, I would not be telling this now. You would know.

Carol Zoref is a fiction writer and essayist. She teaches at Sarah Lawrence College and New York University. She lives in New York City.